By C. E. Murphy

The Queen's Bastard
The Pretender's Crown

THE WALKER PAPERS
Urban Shaman
Thunderbird Falls
Coyote Dreams

THE NEGOTIATOR TRILOGY
Heart of Stone
House of Cards
Hands of Flame

WITH MERCEDES LACKEY AND TANITH LEE
Winter Moon

The Pretender's Crown

The Pretender's Crown

C. E. MURPHY

 BALLANTINE BOOKS • NEW YORK

A Del Rey Trade Paperback Original

Copyright © 2009 by C. E. Murphy

All rights reserved.

Published in the United States by Del Rey,
an imprint of The Random House Publishing Group,
a division of Random House, Inc., New York.

DEL REY is a registered trademark and the Del Rey
colophon is a trademark of Random House, Inc.

LIBRARY OF CONGRESS CATALOGING-IN-PUBLICATION DATA
Murphy, C. E. (Catie E.)
The pretender's crown / C.E. Murphy.
    p. cm.
ISBN 978-0-345-49465-8 (pbk.)
1. Queens—Fiction.   I. Title.
PS3613.U726P74 2009
813'.6—dc22   2009005703

Printed in the United States of America

www.delreybooks.com

9 8 7 6 5 4 3 2 1

Book design by Mary A. Wirth

For Duane Wilkins

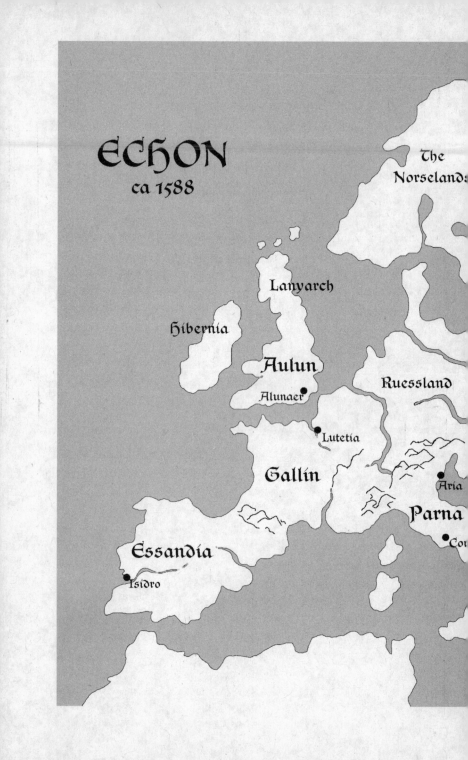

ECHON
ca 1588

The
Norselands

Lanyarch

Hibernia

Aulun
Alunaer

Ruessland

Lutetia

Gallin

Aria

Parna
Cor

Essandia
Isidro

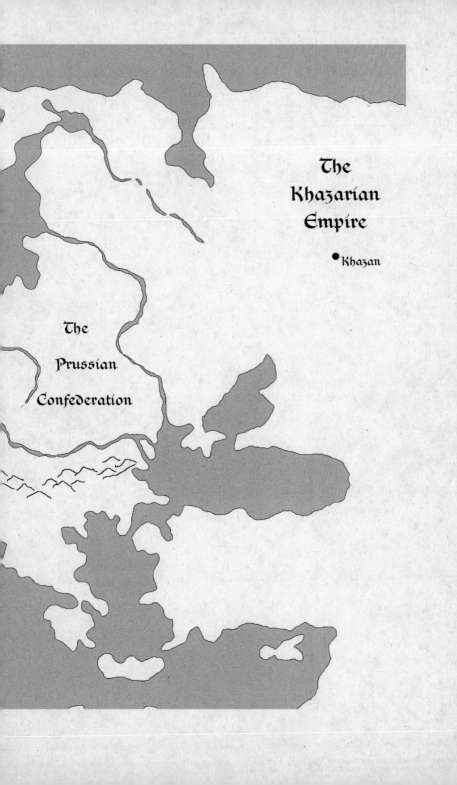

The Pretender's Crown

Prologue

Years and names are useless; they tie him to a calendar that means nothing to him or his kind. Still, if they must be put in place, he is—or will be—Robert, Lord Drake, and the date, by the reckoning of the people he'll have the most contact with, is the mid-fifteenth century. But that name, those dates, lie ahead of him: for now, he stands on a starship far above the surface of the small blue planet whose future he'll shape.

They call themselves Heseth, his people; the people of the sun, as the people of the world below him might someday call themselves Terran, for people of the earth. Every race the Heseth have encountered across the span of aeons and galaxies has been quite literal in their naming of themselves. Not even the Heseth themselves are immune to it; they're called the people of the sun for the never-darkening sky at the heart of a galaxy where they began. Even now, light burns at the back of his mind, reminding him where they came from and what it is they seek.

That, of course, is simple: they seek to survive, as do all living organisms. Their world has long since burned away, making their home the stars. They might once have searched for a new place to live, but every race learns a certain reality: there are no habitable planets so remote that they cannot be found and stripped to their core. Hydrogen to power starships is easily found, but the ships must still be built of something. All people with an eye toward exploration search out asteroids and planets from which to mine and shape their starships, and so any world that might suit settlement is also ripe for ruin.

They are a people of tremendous psychic power, the Heseth, their talent an extension of will born of large bodies meant largely to withstand dry hot places under myriad suns. Graced with less physical dexterity than other races, they found different ways to take their sentience beyond its rudimentary development. Their communication is largely silent, but shared by all; only the deepest intimacies are spoken aloud, made private between one person and another.

That gift has given them the easiest method of draining a populated planet of its resources: infiltration. They hide amongst its peoples, shaping them as they develop and raising them up to be unknowing slaves.

They cannot do this in their natural forms; the point is subtlety and intrigue, making a game out of conquering. There's little enough by way of entertainment between the stars, and so their plots are as much a way to provide a show as they are to develop resources. The creature who will become Robert Drake wasn't yet born the last time the Heseth queens conquered a world, but he has the memory of it, as do all his brethren. It's a time-consuming pursuit, taking generations, but it's more interesting than brutality, and safer for a people whose strengths don't lie in warfare. Besides, their enemies are far behind them, and interstellar distances are great: there's very little risk in taking a slow path toward victory. They've lost a world or two in the past, when their enemy has come on more quickly than expected, but that, too, is part of the game; there'd be no purpose if there was no challenge.

Challenge, though, is one thing; terrorising a young race of people is something else, and anathema to their ends. His natural form would cause horror amongst peoples unable to keep peace between themselves, much less understand a creature birthed on another world. The truth is, any young life-form fears that which is different, even strangers of its own race.

And so to conquer, a plan was devised to take away the fear.

It takes generations to splice the genes just *so;* to make a creature who is human in form and figure but retains a handful of Heseth markers. Loyalty, bred in the bone; psychic talent, vastly diminished by the new body but present; ambition to see his queen's race survive and prosper above all else.

He-who-will-be Robert leaves his viewpost, the blue planet long since memorised, and takes himself to the laboratories where scientists work to create that new life. There are already vats filled with mistakes, kept to study; they've been working at this for almost a human century, and it may be that long again before they succeed. It's time in which the chosen study the world they'll be entering, though by now they know most of what they need to: it's brutish, cold, and ripe for direction. The earth's wise men look to the stars and search for answers in science, and it's that ingenuity the Heseth intend to fan.

One of the geneticists becomes aware of his presence and turns to greet him. They have no need to face each other to make the other welcome, but making eye contact connotates particular honour. Within a moment everyone has turned to make that same greeting, and for an instant he feels he's already left them; that he's already become alien to his people. In so feeling, he sees them through human eyes.

They're delicate monsters, light catching silver scales and turning them to a host of shimmering colours that negates uniformity. They're sinuous beings, able to move with or without the help of many legs that are used as grasping appendages as well as for locomotion. They're creatures of cartilage and chitin, narrow chests coming to a rigid point from whence a long neck curves back and up into a slim, slit-eyed head. The queens have great and wonderful horns curling above their eyes, and the oldest amongst the males have similar, but smaller, protrusions.

Humans might call them dragons.

They're not, of course, not at all; they have neither wings nor breath of fire, but there's a certain pleasant grandiosity to the name. Robert-to-be likes the idea that a human legend will be birthed into mortal form to walk amongst them. He acknowledges his family's greeting, then takes himself away again: being watched over by one who is meant to change is distracting, and he has no wish to agitate them as they work. He'll come back in time; they, and his queen, will be the last thing in this life he'll ever see.

It will be worth the pain, when the moment comes; worth the long slow years of growing up in a human body, which is one of the necessities of this plot. They've never been certain if these created infants have personalities of their own, and rather than risk it, the chosen leave their first bodies behind when the geneticists are satisfied with their creations. They're guided by their queen's gentle touch into a new form, and there is no reversal: the journey is honor and death sentence both.

But Robert-to-be embraces it gladly, because if he succeeds in shaping this world—and the Heseth have rarely failed—then he will become a father to the next generations of his people. His genetic legacy will live on, a true prize indeed for a ship-bound race that must breed selectively and rarely in order for the whole to survive. It's a chance worth any risk: he'll die locked in human form, but his memory will live on, and his children will know his name.

There is, in the end, little else that drives a man, and Robert Drake is satisfied with his fate.

1

It had not taken long to escape Gallin.

It had not taken long, and yet it seemed she had never left there at all. A day to cross the channel, another to wait and meet the Aulunian spymaster Cortes in secret, and on the third morning that man's expression had remained impassionate as he told her of how an Aulunian spy had been uncovered in the Gallic court. "Beatrice Irvine," he'd said. "They also called her Belinda Primrose, and she is dead."

Astonishment and ice coursed through Belinda, though wisdom had warned her there could be no other way for her story to end. The woman she had been lay dead, her head no doubt on a pike for all to see, and the woman who had returned to Alunaer would become someone else entirely. In a lifetime of doing murder, Belinda had never lost a role she'd played to death's dark hand. To do so now unmoored her.

She had drawn a soft breath, steadying her outward countenance: it would never do to show the spymaster how her hands wanted to shake or how the pulse in her throat threatened to choke her with its urgency. There were other matters to attend to; there always were. Matters more important than herself: matters such as Robert, Lord Drake, whose name she voiced quietly, hoping against an answer of a fate as black as the one Cortes had named for Beatrice Irvine.

"Ransomed," Cortes replied unexpectedly. "Ransomed, but not yet returned to her majesty's court." There was a question in his voice, and Belinda, constrained with relief, answered it.

"Ransomed because he escaped before he could be put to death. Sandalia would have preferred to start a war by returning his head in a basket, but her majesty would know if it was other than Robert himself. Ransoming him instead was clever," Belinda had acknowledged, more to herself than the spymaster.

Cortes had nodded, then lifted insubstantial eyebrows. "There's something more you should know. Rumour, fed by Lord Drake's precipitous departure from Aulun and his abrupt arrival in the Gallic court, claims the woman who died was Drake's adopted daughter whom he'd gone to rescue. It's a story without purport as those close to Lord Drake know his adopted daughter joined a convent a decade since."

Bemusement had darted through Belinda, chasing the shock of her own death away. It would return, but she was grateful for a brief respite. "The girl was wise enough to accept God's embrace rather than risk her majesty's well-known jealousies?"

"Indeed." Cortes had dismissed her with a promise that all the news she bore would be brought to Lorraine's ear.

Barely a day later stories of Sandalia de Costa's death swept Alunaer. In the week since, Belinda had waited to be called on, and in waiting found herself turning again and again toward Gallin, where she had died. Gallin, where she had found in Javier de Castille a soul as lost as her own, and betrayed him.

Dignity, it seemed, was no longer hers to court. Belinda permitted herself a snort of disgust and turned away from memories of Gallin and Javier alike. Turned toward what she had awaited since leaving Gallin; toward what she had awaited, in any meaningful way, every day since she had been eleven years of age and had realised she was the natural-born daughter of Lorraine Walter, unwed and so-called virgin queen of Aulun.

When Belinda permitted herself to dwell on that thought, she enjoyed the blunt unforgiving words: *the queen's bastard*. They meted out her place in the world with raw boundaries, admitted she was a secret and a shame in one breath and conceived of daring and drama in the next. There was no better way to describe the unknown child who had grown up to be her mother's best-hidden and loyal assassin.

Boldness had driven her to an indulgence: rather than the formal, straitlaced gowns of Aulunian fashion, she wore a Gallic gown, one of the impetuous, flirtatious designs by Javier's friend Eliza Beaulieu. It had no waist or skirt in the manner of dresses worn in Lorraine's court, but fell away from high-shelved breasts and a waistband just below them in layer upon layer of delicate thin fabric entirely unsuited for the January weather. In deference to winter, the tiny puffed caps at her shoulders had been laced through with ruched sleeves that came to a point over the backs of her hands. Belinda refused to rub at those tips, denying the reminder they offered of a gown made to fit her so tightly it had become a gaol. Instead she folded into a deep curtsey, skirts floating and settling around her as she lowered her gaze and waited a little longer.

There had been no concession to the cold in the gown's neckline. It curved very low and wide, a gentle scoop that displayed an astonishing amount of flesh. That, in the end, was why she had chosen to wear this particular dress.

It was a dangerous choice for myriad reasons, least subtle being that it suggested her loyalty no longer belonged to her royal mother. More subtle, but not much more, it was a youthful fashion, and that was a challenge to a queen who struggled against age and therefore came to it without grace. Moreover, it was pink, a colour the red-headed queen couldn't wear easily even if it wasn't considered too strong a shade for women. Good reasons all not to dare Eliza's design in Lorraine's court.

A breath of warmth stirred the air, the only indication that a door had opened. Fabric rustled, footsteps fell, and the hint of heat faded again as familiar scents brought excitement and fear in equal parts: thinned-out white lead makeup; a hint of perfume she didn't know the name of, but which was etched indelibly in her mind as belonging to the queen. Only Lorraine would wear that perfume, so its name was of no import, if it even had one. A faint sharpness beneath those two: ordinary mortal sweat, such as a monarch shouldn't suffer from. Belinda hadn't known she would be able to find Lorraine Walter in a darkened room, more than ten years after the only time they'd met.

"We are unobserved?" The words were a matter of ritual, given to her by Robert. Speaking them was entirely new to Belinda, but she was comfortable with ritual; it had shaped much of her life. Most of it, perhaps, even before she knew she was being shaped.

"We are," came Lorraine's response, tart with impatience. "We do not have a rash any longer, girl. We thought we told you, eleven years ago, to dispose of modest coverings in the spring, not in the dead of winter a lifetime later."

Triumph rose in Belinda's breast, flowing so brightly she loosened a smile of delight at the floor. Ah, she had changed, she had fallen: the woman she had once been would never have allowed such a transparent change of expression. But the woman she had played over the past six-months had laughed too easily, smiled too readily; Beatrice Irvine was easy to cling to. A joyous smile was an indulgence she ought to have excised, and yet she was glad of it.

"I beg forgiveness, your majesty," she murmured, and did nothing to still the wide smile directed at the floor. This was no way at all to present herself to her monarch, her mother, but the threads that held them together were dark and deep and buried. To play the single one that lay in the light, and to have it recognised and struck back as a matching note, was a risk and a gift beyond revelation. "I was not at court that spring, and loathed the thought of disappointing your majesty in any small way at all."

Lorraine Walter, queen of all Aulun, gave a snort that sounded very much like the one Belinda had indulged in earlier. "Stand up, for pity's sake. You look like a rose ready for the plucking, down there in all that pink. Whoever heard of a woman wearing such a colour?"

Belinda stood slowly, leaving her gaze on the floor until she was certain her expression could be schooled, though it was still with merriment in her eyes that she met Lorraine's pretence at irritation. Oh, but Beatrice Irvine had been bad for her. Only a handful of months earlier she would never have allowed herself so much emotion, much less the boldness of assuming that the queen's annoyance was perhaps not entirely genuine. The ability to control her own humour was still there. The stillness she had learnt as a child, and shored up with golden *witchpower* in the past months, would never truly desert her.

But witchpower and the stillness had their price. The latter left her untouchable, as she had taught herself to be, and the former left her greedy for power and blind with ambition. Even a lifetime's training in constraint was barely enough to master it. She would no more dare release witchpower in Lorraine's presence than she might set a wild boar free upon the unarmed queen. She was her mother's daughter, and a creature of her father's making. Loyalty defined her; duty made the boundaries of her life. It had, for nearly twenty-three years, been enough. If she could now reach back to a solitary meeting with Lorraine, more than ten years earlier, and make a small jape of it, then perhaps that was diplomacy, and its success worthy of a smile.

"Do you laugh at us, girl?" Lorraine was cool as winter winds, drawing herself up. She was tall for a woman, taller than Belinda herself, and beneath full square skirts, boxy shoes added to that imposing height. Illusion, but effective: Belinda ducked another curtsey in a show of contriteness, and when she lifted her eyes it was with no hint of merriment.

Nor did she feel it any longer, its spirit quenched beneath necessity. Beatrice Irvine might laugh too easily, but Beatrice was a construct, and as such could even yet be put away when needs be. "No, majesty. I beg forgiveness," she said again, and this time meant it.

Lorraine stared down a long nose at her, weighing the sincerity of that plea. Proper deference would have Belinda drop her gaze and wait on the queen's clemency; proper as a subject, a daughter, and a secret. Proper, too, if she fully embraced the learned ability to not offend, to hardly be there even when she was obviously present. She had spent her life honing that talent, and could make herself small and meek and unthreatening, everything in her stance and stature hinting of her place beneath notice—or, if noticed, beneath the lord of the manor. It would work on Lorraine; it worked on everyone, except perhaps Belinda's own father, and on Dmitri, the other witchlord man of Robert's acquaintance.

Belinda did not do what was proper, and saw in Lorraine's eyes that she marked it. She met the queen's gaze and looked her fill: it had been more than ten years since she had seen the woman who'd birthed her, and might well be ten years before she saw her again. There was little enough chance for making such memories as these, and she judged it worth risking Lorraine's wrath to burn the monarch's image into her own flawless memory.

Ten years earlier, Lorraine had still held the last edge of youth that gave her beauty. Then, as now, as always in Belinda's memories, titian curls fell loose, bloody against translucent skin, but now the translucency was born of far heavier white paint than Lorraine had worn a decade ago. She had been in her forties then, a woman of unprecedented power; indeed, she had set the precedent of a queen ruling without a king. Sandalia in Gallin had held her own throne partly in ironic thanks to her bitter rival across the straits: if Lorraine could manage alone, so, too, could the onetime Essandian princess. And much farther to the east and north, Irina Durova reigned as imperatrix of the enormous Khazarian empire, unchallenged on her throne since her unlamented husband's death. They were a sisterhood, these queens, a sisterhood of loathing and distrust and tension, bound together by a determination to hold power in the face of innumerable men certain they were incapable of doing so.

Those things were etched around Lorraine Walter when Belinda looked at her; as much fixtures of who she was as the signs of aging: the wattling neck; the length of nose brought out by flesh falling away; the long lines of a face that had once been striking and now fought age in an inevitably losing battle beneath the white lead face paint. Belinda saw that it had been years, perhaps decades, since Lorraine's hair had been naturally red, and knew that even at the height of youth it had never been that especial shade. But those were trappings, a prison to the spirit housed within, and that spirit burned bright. Her eyes showed it, thin grey gaze expecting and receiving adoration. Even, perhaps especially, from the secret daughter, adoration.

"You are not afraid," Lorraine said in time. She sounded a mix of pleased and perturbed, and her mouth pursed as though she'd encountered an unexpected flavour. "You are unafraid of us. We wonder if you realise how rare that is."

Belinda folded a deep curtsey, eyes lowered. "No, majesty."

"You were not afraid when first we met, either. Rise," Lorraine said sharply. "Rise, for I would see your face when you give me answers. Why are you not afraid?"

Belinda did not rise, but lifted her face so she could look at Lorraine. The position put a crick in her neck, but she held it, exhaling a quiet sigh of satisfaction. Small discomforts were how she had begun training herself in stillness. To have one upon which she could now fall back helped her to remain steady as she watched her queen. "My life has not taught me to fear, majesty, but to be bold. I would dishonour myself and you by pretending otherwise when in your presence."

"So much so that you are willing to disobey my direct command." Lorraine snapped her fingers and Belinda finally straightened, hairs on her arms dancing with awareness. Twice Lorraine had forgone the use of *we* and spoken of herself as an individual. A monarch did not do that lightly. Belinda remembered all too clearly, and with blistering shame, how Sandalia had used that apparent intimacy to draw Beatrice's eager, foolish plots to light, even when Belinda had known better. Such a slip could easily prove fatal, and Belinda dared not trust that being her mother's daughter would save her from perfidy now. She held her tongue, and Lorraine breathed a sound of exasperation.

"I suppose you'd be of little enough use if you couldn't see what lines you might walk, and on what ropes you might balance. Where is he, girl? Robert left our side six weeks ago, and we have been obliged to pay a ransom for his return, which has not yet manifested. Tell us what we must needs know, Primrose."

Belinda's stomach clenched, cold running up her arms despite the sleeves she'd added to the dress. *Primrose* belonged to a woman now dead, and when it had been hers, only Robert Drake had used it. To hear her mother say it carried more strength than Belinda might have imagined, and to hide that she dropped her gaze, no longer permitting herself the daring of meeting Lorraine's eyes. The curtsey she dipped this time was punctuation, an acknowledgment of Lorraine's demand and a physical intent to respond. That action, like the words she'd spoken to begin their audience, was so familiar as to be ritual, and in the wake of hearing *Primrose* pass her mother's lips she became aware of how very precious ritual was. "I don't know where he is, majesty. He only said elsewhere, and that I must return to Aulun and take his place at your side for a time. I am here, and yours to command."

"We have heard stories of his capture. We wish to hear the truth of them." Lorraine's tones were wondrous to hear, such haughtiness in them that Belinda believed, for a moment, that she could see through them; that she could understand the depths of concern and worry, and perhaps even love, that the peremptory arrogance was meant to disguise.

She murmured, "They're more true than not, majesty," but refused any mark of emotion in her own voice. She was not high enough to offer one such as Lorraine a sympathetic shoulder, nor rude enough to burden a queen with her own anxiety over Robert Drake. "He was imprisoned for a time."

"How is it he was betrayed?" Still ice, still caring contained within fury, still every inch a queen. Belinda wanted to wrap herself around that flawless execution of enquiry, to sing admiration she had no right to voice.

Instead she shook her head. "A courtesan, majesty. One I knew briefly and who, it seems, knew my fath—"

Lorraine's grey gaze snapped to her as Belinda broke off the word, appalled at herself. Beatrice Irvine might have said such a blatant thing; Belinda Primrose ought never have let it pass her lips. But once upon a time, before she knew him to be her father in truth, she had called Robert *Papa,* though she was supposed to be his sister's child, and he her uncle. That, perhaps, could excuse her, and Belinda finished, "father," with as little hesitation as she could manage.

It was not enough. She knew, even without meeting Lorraine's eyes, that it wasn't enough. A vision of flagstones rose up in Belinda's memory, her own fingers raw and rough as she pulled herself across them in the name of duty, fighting her own desire to turn her back on it and flee toward passion. She had chosen duty. She would always choose duty: it was what she had been raised to do, to be.

She could not, therefore, permit herself a slip as blatant as the one she had just made. "My papa," she said lightly, "is a handsome man, majesty. I think this courtesan may have had dreams that outstripped her reach, and when they came to dust, found revenge in whatever manner she could."

"Your papa," Lorraine said after a long cool silence, "is properly your uncle, girl, and has the eye of a queen. Do not be so bold in naming him father to one whose jealousies can unmake him as easily as he has been made."

Belinda whispered, "Majesty," and sank deeper into a curtsey.

Lorraine held her silence another few eternal moments before moving, shaking off reprimand with a rustle of skirts. Belinda lifted her gaze, though she didn't stand again, and watched the queen pace a few steps before coming to a stop at one of the windowless walls. "We have seen the papers you removed from Lutetia," Lorraine said. "They give lie to treaties in negotiation between our royal self and the imperatrix of Khazar. They speak of our sister-queen Sandalia's ambitions toward our throne, and they are ratified in her own hand. We had thought our position with Khazar to be sacrosanct, if for no other reason than favours done by our assets at Irina's behest."

The room was not warm; her gown was not warm. Still, a second rush of bumps over Belinda's arms startled her. She was accustomed to more control than that over her own body, but then, Lorraine, queen of Aulun, wasn't supposed to know that murder had been done by her people for another regent's benefit.

Lorraine shot her a pointed glance. "We know what you are, girl. We know *why* you are. Do not for a moment imagine that we do not know what you do. You are very like Robert. He, too, thinks we are blind to what is done in our name, and that we cringe from a violent path because of feminine weakness."

"No, your majesty." Belinda bit her lower lip, cursing her impetuous tongue. Lorraine arched an eyebrow in challenging surprise, and Belinda fisted hands in her skirt before continuing. "I do not think, and I doubt Robert thinks, that you hesitate out of weakness. I think it to be wisdom. It is a dangerous game we speak of now, and a queen should not trouble herself with its details, most especially when the subject should be other heads of state. Once such a play is set in motion it is far too easy for thoughts to turn from one regent to another. It is not weakness that stays a hand like yours, majesty. Not at all."

A new leaden silence filled the room before Lorraine, drily, said, "We thought you were supposed to be meek and controlled, girl. We are surprised to discover you have so many opinions."

"Forgive me, majesty." Belinda fixed a gaze so expressionless it felt like a glower on the floor. Beatrice's impulsive words, Belinda's own struggle to choose duty over desire, inexplicable images stolen from her father's mind, hours of foolish gazing toward Gallin; she no longer knew herself, and wished briefly for a retreat to Robert's estates, where she might re-familiarise herself with the stillness that had sustained her through most of her life. Return to the beginning and start again; if nothing else could be done to reestablish the woman she'd once been, then that was what she would do. "I have been keeping peculiar company of late."

"With a prince and his peers. Have you got above yourself?"

"I do not think so, your majesty." Her response was soft, but golden witchpower flared with outrage. Jaw set, Belinda quelled it, holding back its petulance with a willpower that was beginning to slip. She was not *above herself* in mingling with a prince and his fellows; they were of no better blood than she, and only the necessity of preserving Lorraine's reputation kept Belinda from standing beside Javier as an equal. Even more, his witchbreed blood whispered that Javier was not the son of any man his mother had married. Only Sandalia's reputation kept him in line for the throne, and to face the truth that the prince of Gallin was as illegitimate as Belinda herself, yet held a place of respect, tasted bitter as almonds.

Her own witchpower cried that it was unfair, and that, at least, was so absurd as to allow Belinda to quash it without remorse. Nothing in the world was fair or unfair; those were expectations born of a belief that things should be easy, and nothing was, not even for a queen. Belinda thought of Robert, and thought, *perhaps most especially, not for a queen.* "I am trained for something else," she murmured. "My place is not on a throne, and I have never set my ambitions so high."

"Have you not?" Lorraine's question startled Belinda. Its asking gave substance to the truth of her birth, a topic about which she, by all rights, should know nothing. Lorraine couldn't possibly know that Belinda's memories stretched back so far, so clearly; that she remembered bloody curls and thin grey eyes, remembered a regal voice then worn with exhaustion, even remembered her mother's swollen belly rippling with afterbirth in the brief seconds before her father had taken her away.

They had shared a moment, mother and daughter, twelve years later, just before Belinda had murdered a man to protect Lorraine's safety. There had been endless things unspoken in that instant, a weighty nothingness, and in that nothingness Belinda had found everything. Her reason for existing, her strange aching pride in being an unrecognised secret; it had all been there, in what she did not see in Lorraine's grey gaze. She had imagined that Lorraine, too, had seen that admission of silence, and that it had bound them in a way that logic defied.

That the queen should ask such a question now gave credence to Belinda's childhood whimsy, though that light word belittled the strength of emotion that had overtaken her that day. Usually quick with an answer, Belinda stayed silent, gauging what she might and might not say, and at the end, settled on a truth sufficiently unpolished as to discomfit her. "No, your majesty. I have known what I am since I was a girl, and have taken a sort of pride in it. Playing this recent part . . ."

She pushed out of her curtsey without having been bade do so, and turned toward the small room's round walls. Stone of a lighter shade suggested a window had once broken the unrelenting solitude, and she spoke to that brighter spot rather than dare Lorraine's countenance. "Your majesty has looked through old glass, has she not? Thickened and wavering, distorting all that lies beyond it? So the part I have played has seemed to me: a thing lying on the wrong side of that glass, unrecogniseable and uncomfortable in all ways. I have never looked to stand beyond the glass. I have never needed to. I have loved my place on this side of it, and hoped for nothing more than to serve my country and my queen as best I could."

Truth in all ways but one, and for that one falsehood, Belinda forgave herself. Witchpower demanded recognition and a place on Lorraine's side of the glass, but that was an ambition never to be pursued. She wouldn't overthrow a lifetime's training and willingness to serve for a madness born of golden magic and the sensual touch of a prince's hand.

"And if the boy had married you?"

Belinda blinked over her shoulder at Lorraine, realised she'd turned her back on a monarch, and nearly allowed herself the luxury of throwing her hands up in exasperation. Perhaps it was the intimacy; perhaps it was witchpower daring to put herself on the same level as the queen in small but noticeable ways. Whichever, *what*ever, drove her to those tiny indiscretions, they would cost her her life if she didn't regain control and become once more what she had always been: meek, modest, unremarkable. "I can't imagine a world in which that would have been permitted. The engagement was a ploy to see if wedding a Lanyarchan noble to the prince of Gallin might frighten the Aulunian throne into foolish action; you must know that as clearly as I did. Sandalia would have had me killed before she would allow me to marry Javier, though I should think I might have escaped that fate through my own wits, if not Javier's—" For the second time she found herself verging on dangerous language, and ended with "fancy" rather than words with more emotional weight.

"And Javier? Would he have pursued the union?"

Might he yet? underlay the question, and Belinda permitted herself a rough chuckle. "He would have, but no longer. I should think myself his enemy from ten days ago until the end of time."

"Youth," Lorraine said, "is much given to dramatics. Enemies are a luxury we indulge in from time to time, and make bedfellows of when a new one comes along."

Belinda, daring, asked, "Sandalia?" and Lorraine gave her another steady look that turned to a soft answer Belinda knew she had no right to expect.

"We did not dislike her. We might once have been friends."

"If the world had been other than it is."

Lorraine nodded once. "But it is not, and we are pleased, girl, to know that you do not look for it to be."

"Never," Belinda whispered, and crushed the flare of witch-power in her mind.

LORRAINE WALTER, QUEEN OF AULUN

The girl is not what she expected.

She has been dismissed, has left the private chamber in a flurry of ridiculous pink skirts and soft feminine foolishness, and has left Lorraine more alone than usual in a room meant for secrets. More alone than usual: that, for a queen, is a thought of some weight. Were she to give in to it, it might be a thought of some despair.

Lorraine Walter, queen of all Aulun, is fifty-five years old, and that frothy child is the only heir she will ever have.

When Belinda is well and truly gone, not just from the window-less chamber but has left Lorraine's rooms through other secret passageways, Lorraine exits her cold tower room and enters her own apartments again. They're warm, which she's glad of, though she would no more admit to cold than she might admit to loneliness or fear. Those are things to be acknowledged only in the deepest and most private part of her: to the world, she must be untouchable, un-affected: the virgin queen.

Belinda, Lorraine fancies, has a hint of that same cool core to her. Women require it, if they are to succeed in a world shaped by men. Women must become masculine, and yet make eyes at their men, play both sides and hold a place in the middle. Lorraine has worked at that game for a lifetime. So, too, she thinks, has Belinda Primrose.

There is wine, set well away from the fire that it might retain its coolness. Lorraine, not wishing to be disturbed by servants, pours a glass herself, and takes a box of sweets to the fire with her. She believes chewing them improves her breath, but for the moment they're merely an indulgence. No more than two: even at fifty-five, she has her figure to maintain, especially if she intends to continue the endless rounds of marriage negotiations with Essandia's Rodrigo.

A brief smile curves her lips as she taps a marzipan treat against them. Neither she nor Rodrigo has any interest in marriage. How much easier it might have been for both of them if they could have set that absurd dance aside decades ago and instead turned their might and ambition toward other lands. But that is not, has never been, the way of Echonian countries, and it is not the way of the Ecumenic church. It is, and always has been, everything or nothing: Cordula will reclaim Aulun at any cost; Aulun will retain its Reformation church at any price. They cannot, it seems, find another path.

Faith, Lorraine thinks, is a dangerous business, and one that men should resist fiddling with. But not even her own father was immune to that particular folly. Indeed, had he been, the legacy he'd left might have played out very differently.

And that future, had it come to pass, might well have seen Lorraine married, or not queen, or both, and with heirs born to pomp and circumstance rather than silence and secrecy. That, as Belinda said, was a world seen through ancient glass, too warped and misshapen to truly consider.

The wine is warming in her hand. Lorraine sips at it and sets her second sweet aside, less hungry for delicacies than answers. Robert should be here; Robert has always been here, offering advice when it was sought and silence as full of commentary as his words when it was not. Of all her courtiers, of all her advisers, indeed, of all her lovers, Robert Drake has been the most faithful and least likely to pressure her. Men accept that she is queen and do her bidding because they can do nothing else. Robert does it because he believes in her, and if that's a caprice a queen ought not indulge in, well, on this one topic she permits herself to do so regardless.

If he ever betrays her, she will be destroyed. Oh, so, too, will he, more visibly and quickly than Lorraine, but the handsome bearded lord's devotion is the one thing she truly believes she cannot do without.

Then again, as lines work their way into her face and take heavier paint to fill, it begins to seem there may be one other thing she cannot do without, and that is a legitimate heir. Lorraine has always understood, in a way her half-sister Constance did not, that their father Henry's desperation for a son drove him to the extraordinary ends that begot half a dozen marriages and a new church in Aulun. It's easier, perhaps, for Lorraine to be forgiving, for she's the daughter of the second marriage, and Constance was born of the first. Of course, Constance's mother survived, and Lorraine's did not; maybe Lorraine should be less understanding than Constance was.

But this is an old cycle of thought, as useless now as it was when she was a girl. Then, she'd understood well enough; now, as an adult, as a woman, as a queen without an heir, Henry's concern is no longer a thing to be imagined. Lorraine lives it every day, hiding panic behind a regal aspect. It's easy enough to do when she is looked on as God's vessel on earth; she is not expected to have weaknesses, and so she simply does not allow them to show. An impassive face, white makeup, elaborate gowns, all go far in disguising a knot of sick worry that disturbs the heartbeat with its intensity. Without an heir Aulun faces the all-too-real possibility of civil war on Lorraine's death, and though she is so very loathe to admit it, Lorraine is not a young woman any longer. She is, in fact, *old,* and it's God's grace that has kept her in health and wits these many years. God, however, has not granted the miracle necessary for her to bear a child should she wed at this late hour, and Lorraine's own disposition does not incline her to do that anyway.

Even if she should, *who* she might wed is a difficulty. Rodrigo has no children of his own, which means marrying him does not solve the problem of an heir. Or rather, it does, in the most bitter way possible: it sets the crown toward Javier de Castille, Sandalia's redheaded son, and Lorraine will be damned before she hands her kingdom to that family. Sandalia held the Lanyarchan throne in Northern Aulun for two short years and thinks it makes her heir to Aulun's; Lorraine has no intention at all of making a pretender's crown legitimate.

That leaves, then, in any practical sense, Ruessland or the Prussian confederation, which is made up of principalities headed by young bucks whose ultimate allegiance slips between sprawling Prussia and smaller westerly Ruessland as quickly as the wind changes. In their favour, they've begun to embrace the Reformation church; that, at least, helps to reduce the chance of war within Aulun.

But it also means, should she wed a young man, that when she dies her young king will marry again and make children for his throne who have no tie at all to Aulun, which is hardly an appealing thought. No: the time to marry was twenty years ago, and she had no more desire to do so then than she does now.

And so she is brought back, again, to Belinda.

Twice. Twice in twenty-three years she's laid eyes on her daughter. Lorraine remembers the first time clearly: the child was pretty, self-contained, with wide hazel eyes bending toward green and thick brown hair. She looked nothing like Lorraine, a blessing to them all. She curtsied, then lifted her gaze, and even now, more than a decade later, Lorraine recalls the shock of meeting the girl's eyes, whose fathomless depths said, without apology or explanation, that Belinda Primrose *knew*.

How, Lorraine has no idea. Robert had not told her; of that, Lorraine was, and is, certain. It was as though the girl recognised her, and more, recognised that neither of them could ever admit the truth. There was acceptance so forthright it was challenge in the twelve-year-old's eyes, and Lorraine had been well-pleased, though she trusted herself not to have shown it.

Exactly the same expression had been in Belinda's eyes today. So bold, so calm, that Lorraine tread on topics she has rarely had occasion or desire to voice. Had thrown Belinda's brief engagement to Javier de Castille at the girl, and under that cover demanded to know if the daughter she had borne had any ambition toward the throne she has more than half a claim to.

Unless Lorraine is a fool, and she is not, Belinda meant it when she'd said her aspirations didn't reach so high. Unless Lorraine is drowning in sentiment and fear, Belinda spoke truth, and while Lorraine admits to herself—and only to herself—that fear exists, it does not rule her. No one can retain a throne for thirty years and by ruled by fear; no *woman* can retain a throne for thirty minutes if fear holds the upper hand. And sentiment is something the queen of Aulun excised from her life long ago, except, perhaps, in the matter of Robert Drake. But if he is her weakness, so be it: Lorraine may be God's vessel on earth, but only the Heavenly Father himself is without flaw, and Lorraine might have done far worse than to find her own vulnerability in Robert. He has, after all, held the most dangerous piece of knowledge about her close to his heart, utterly secret, for nearly a quarter of a century.

She recalls clearly what her thoughts were, when she realised her pregnancy. She had been thirty-two, queen for a handful of years and already determined never to marry. Wisdom dictated ending the pregnancy, and it was not sentiment that had stopped her. It was this far-off day that she'd known she must eventually face: a day when she was old, and her country in danger of being left without a sovereign. The risk had been tremendous, but she had been young, and already in the habit of taking a long holiday every year or two. For many months corsets and heavy gowns and the fact that it was a first child helped to keep her body to the slender tall lines she was known for. The maidservants who saw to her were allowed to on pain of death, and when they disappeared, one by one, Lorraine had allowed herself to look the other way and ask no questions.

The last few months of her pregnancy coincided with the fifteenth anniversary of her father's death. Lorraine, deeply affected by his memory, retreated from the public eye for a time, and when she emerged a little heavier, a little paler, her people loved her for it. They loved her even more dearly when she discovered Robert Drake had dallied with another woman while she had been in mourning, and blasted him for it. She sent him from her side for almost a year, and they loved her best of all when she relented and began to be seen with him again.

Politics, Lorraine thinks now as she thought then, is showmanship and misdirection, and a child born and bred under those two stars, a child whose ambitions are to serve loyally and whose heart is undisturbed by being unknown, is a child who might, at the end of it all, serve as a suitable heir.

For the first time since her courses stopped, giving lie to the story she might one day wed and bear children for Aulun, the knot in Lorraine Walter's stomach loosens a little, and, alone with her wine and sweets, she smiles at the fire.

2

JAVIER DE CASTILLE, PRINCE OF GALLIN
22 January 1588 ✝ Isidro, capital city of Essandia

Typically, an honour guard was just that: men sent to lend importance to a visitor's arrival. Oft-times that importance lay primarily
in the caller's mind, but not when it was the heir to the throne who
came to visit.

It was wrong, then, that Javier's escort bristled the way they did,
blocking his view of the city more thoroughly than he might have
expected. They were not ungentle with him; that would be too
much rudeness to show a prince, but neither were they deferent.
Their loyalty lay with another monarch, his uncle. It had been years
since Javier had visited Isidro, but it seemed that his younger self
had been made far more welcome. Perhaps it was the difference between being a man and a child: one might be expected to lunge for
a throne where the other would not. There was irony in that; Javier
had never demanded his mother's throne, much less succumbed to
the lunacy of pursuing his uncle's, hundreds of miles to the south.
He was heir to both already; time would bring both the Essandian
and Gallic crowns to his head without any impatient action on his
part.

His recollections of Isidro were of a vivacious city, warmer and
friendlier than his native Lutetia, but too much silence filled the
streets now. He ought to have demanded a horse that he might see
better; that he might ride as befitted a prince, rather than walk as

the lowly sailor whose part he'd played the last fortnight. A glance at his grim-faced guard, though, told him his demands would have gone unheeded, and that it was as well he'd not made them, for the cost would've been his own embarrassment at being refused. Chagrined at the realisation, he took a few light steps on his toes, peering beyond the tall helmed guardsmen surrounding him.

Black banners fluttered far ahead of them, dancing from windows where nobility and the wealthy made their homes near the palace. Rippling fabric slashed against creamy buildings—Isidro was built of pale stone, a city of brilliance against the day's blue sky—and danced out toward the sky so lightly it took long moments for their import to settle in Javier's thoughts.

Then, with witchlight clarity, he saw, silver-streaked horror lighting all the crevasses of his mind. It set him to running, shouldering past the guards with youthful strength and the advantage of surprise. A shout came after him and he ignored it, fear rabbiting his heart as he careened through the streets, slamming into passersby and sending up desperate prayers with each slap of his feet against cobblestones. He had not meant to come to Isidro to find a throne, but to seek advice; he could not fathom Rodrigo's death, or what it might mean. Rodrigo was aging, yes, in his fifties, but fit and strong, and Javier's world became an unrecogniseable place without the idea of his uncle on the Essandian throne.

New banners unfurled above his head as he ran, telling him the news of death was fresh, so fresh the people were still whispering it to one another. There were cries in the street now, voices lifted in sorrow, but power drove him forward and washed away any sense he might have made of their words. He had never run so fast, not even as a child unburdened by anything but a desire for speed; it was as though the magic within him hastened his feet, and shot out before him to clear a path. No longer did he smash into people on the street; instead they staggered aside as if rudely shoved, and all he could be was glad for it. Behind him, the honour guard gave chase, but they were encumbered by armour and swords, and Javier ran, if not for his own life, at least for word of a life dear to him.

Black-banded guards crossed spears at the closed palace gates, blocking his way. Fury rose up that he should be denied, and he neither knew nor cared whether it was boiling witchpower or the guard running to catch him that gave strength to his roared, "I am the prince of Gallin and you will *let me pass!*"

The guardsmen faltered, then scrambled to fling the gates open. He heard a curse from his escort, but he was already gone, racing through halls his feet recalled with more certainty than his mind did.

They brought him not to the throne room or council chambers, but instead to Rodrigo's private rooms, where surely his uncle's body would lie attended by doctors. Sandalia had seen Rodrigo only a few months earlier and had said nothing of illness; had said that the prince of Essandia seemed to be growing bold at last. Only now did Javier wonder if that had been a sign of Rodrigo's health faltering, an indication that he, like any man, wished to leave behind a legacy for the ages, and thought himself running short of time to do so.

Guards stood outside Rodrigo's doors. Impatient fear seized Javier and witchpower shot out, a concussion blast like the ones he and Belinda, oh, damn her, Belinda, had discovered together. His silver magic slammed into the men, knocking them against the wall so hard he doubted they'd rise again, and could not bring himself to care.

The doors to Rodrigo's rooms blew off with the same force that had downed the men. Shards exploded inward. Terror of disfiguring his uncle's body sent a shield of silver ahead of the blast, catching splinters and sending them to the floor in a rain of wood. Javier burst through behind them, and took in the incomprehensible.

Rodrigo the prince sat beside a low-banked fire, swathed in black, his dark head lifted from a curved hand as though surprise had taken him from grief. Very much as though: water, silver as Javier's power, shone on his cheeks and glinted in his beard, and astonishment made sorrow all the more haggard.

Bewilderment sparked under Javier's skin, the witchpower feeling as though it would burn through him. He and Rodrigo stared at each other, both speechless, until sense leapt through Javier's mind and reversed the story, giving him understanding where none had been before. The ship: he would have been seen, despite his ef-

THE PRETENDER'S CROWN · 27

forts, at the docks in Lutetia, and storms had brought his ship to port many days late. It was not Rodrigo the city mourned, but the only heir to its throne. Relief turned itself to a kind of tight laugh in Javier's throat, and he flew the last few steps across the room to bury his head against his uncle's thigh.

"I've come," he whispered. "I'm well. All is well, uncle. The ocean did not take the ship. My God, I thought it was you they flew the banners for, my lord. I feared the worst."

Rodrigo's hand stirred his hair, but it was another voice, one with a lifetime's familiarity, one that did not at all belong in Isidro, one that was laden with pain, that spoke. "I'm sorry, Jav," said Marius Poulin. "I'm so sorry."

The silver rage inside him went dull with incomprehension, so flat and wet it seemed to Javier a pool of molten fear, waiting to be poured into the shape that it would hold for the rest of his life. He raised his head, feeling Rodrigo's fingers fall away, and turned his gaze, by increments, toward the tousle-haired youth who had been his friend since childhood. Marius, who had all unknowing introduced a viper to their nest, but to whom the blame could not be given, for it was Javier who had accepted Belinda Primrose into their midst, and who had then stolen her from Marius. Stolen her and her golden witchpower, and gentle Marius had forgiven his prince for it, as he had forgiven all trespasses against him in all their years of friendship.

Marius, who could not be there but who stood in a corner some feet away from the door, well out of Javier's line of sight as he'd made his extravagant entrance. Another man stood beside him, a handsome one, but Marius's presence needed explanation beyond any questions Javier had about the stranger.

"It's the queen," Marius whispered miserably. "It's your mother, Jav. It's Sandalia. She's dead ten days since, poisoned from a cup she thought safe. I'm sorry, my king. I am so sorry."

TOMAS DEL'ABBATE, AN ECUMENICAL PRIEST

Tomas del'Abbate knows his God to be a kind one. God is kind, for He has offered Tomas, the bastard son of a Primo, a true calling in the church. God has also granted their father enough interest in his offspring to have kept their mother in a proud style; this is far more than other children of the church's princes have been given, and Tomas supposes that it is his father's dedication and piety that makes the Almighty Father wish to watch over his family in particular. Tomas, the only boy, has been educated in fine schools, taught doctrine and faith by his father, and has in truth never wanted for anything.

God is kind in that He has made fine matches for Tomas's three sisters, most especially Paola, the youngest and by far the most lovely. Her eyes are astonishing: the usual earthy brown seen in Parnan faces has been drained away, leaving gold in its place, so that her gaze is always bright with sunrise.

Tomas, like Paola, is a youth of what he is told is considerable beauty. He is torn on that flattery: false modesty is unbecoming, and vanity a sin. He's a child of wealth, and as such has been lent the opportunity to stand long hours before unblemished mirrors, not in womanly and weak self-admiration, but seeking truth in the lines of his face. Yes: he is handsome, or perhaps even more than handsome, but he takes pride only in his sister's comeliness, and not in his own. God has seen fit to touch him with it, and it is unseemly to revel or take advantage of a heavenly gift.

But it is in part because of that beauty that he has been sent to Isidro. Rodrigo, prince of Essandia, is not too old to father children, and the Pappas of the Ecumenic church hopes that a youth such as Tomas will remind the prince of his duty to the throne and to the church. Rodrigo must wed and father an heir to ensure Cordula will never lose its grip on the warm westerly country. The Pappas does not consider Javier de Castille, prince of Gallin and Rodrigo's nephew, a safe enough contender. One country is enough for any king to manage.

Unless, of course, that king is the King of Heaven, who speaks to His flock through the Pappas, who must therefore exert control over the Echonian continent in God's name, and in any way he can.

So Tomas, guided by the Pappas and by God's will, has left Cordula, his sisters, and his studies, and has come to Isidro to stand before a prince as both confessor and reminder of that prince's duties.

He has, these past few months, argued scripture and has heard royal confessions; has prostrated himself on marble floors and worshipped with a passion that burns through him so brightly that he wonders how he does not come alight with it, and set all the world on fire.

He has also, now that he is beyond Cordula, come to recognise that the admiring gazes that fall his way are not only for his knowledge. While he has no desire to pursue those gazes into satisfying carnal needs, he is shyly (if not secretly, for God knows all of his thoughts) delighted by them. His ambitions have ever only been to serve his church and his God. To be granted the chance to do so in such a wondrous and worldly way is a gift beyond his imagination. Yes, God is kind, and his beautiful son is humbled and grateful from the depths of his heart.

God, though, has not prepared him for the surging presence that is the young prince of Gallin.

There are terrible rumours afoot; rumours barely more than alluded to by Marius Poulin, friend to Javier de Castille and bearer of tragic tidings. Javier flees Gallin and his mother is dead within a day: the two things sit poorly beside each other, even to Tomas's unsophisticated eyes. Javier, after all, is young and meant to be a king, and Sandalia is—was—still in her prime, unlikely to abdicate. Unlikely in the extreme, for even schooled in church learnings and not in the ways of politics or queens, Tomas knows that there is an old and bitter rivalry between the female monarchs of Aulun and Gallin. All of Echon understands that, though the words are never spoken aloud or set down on paper, Sandalia has never intended to rest until Lorraine has lost her throne.

And yet Javier has come into this room—burst into it in a manner more literal and frightening than Tomas has ever seen—clearly expecting to see his royal uncle lying dead, which is against all sense if his hand guided Sandalia toward death. Perhaps the prince is a consummate actor, for his next thoughts, as played on the stage an astonished Tomas watches, are full of terrible apology for frightening others over the status of his own life. It might be play-acted, yes, but to embrace such reversal of emotion so desperately does not smack of lies to the quiet Cordulan priest.

There is something in the air around the prince, a presence more palpable than anything Tomas has felt from Rodrigo, and Rodrigo is not a man to be taken lightly. Javier takes up more space than his slender frame allows; more than Rodrigo; more, even, than the Pappas. The Pappas bears God with him at all times, and yet even without Javier's gaze on him, without Javier's awareness of him at all, Tomas is more awed by the young prince's strength than he has ever been by the Pappas.

It comes to him very clearly, the thought: either Javier has been touched by God Himself, or he is the devil's child.

And then Marius speaks, shares dreadful news, and Javier turns from his uncle with a tide of rage rising in his eyes. Silver rage, silver eyes, making the ginger-haired, pale-skinned prince Tomas's opposite in all ways.

Another clear thought comes to him in the instant before furious, inexplicable power blasts him. *I am lost,* he thinks, and everything he knows beyond that is pain and breathlessness and blackness.

JAVIER DE CASTILLE, UNCROWNED KING OF GALLIN

Beatrice had asked if using his gifts had awakened a desire within him to dominate. Javier, standing over Marius's still form, over the slumped shape of a beautiful priest, recalled the question and his mocking, dismissive response with cold anguish. *No,* he wanted to say to her now. *No, not domination, but destruction.* Destruction came of the unchartered use of his power: two men lay at his feet to prove it, and two more lay beyond the shattered door.

But Beatrice had been Belinda, and nothing at all of what he thought she was. Nor, indeed, was Javier what he believed himself to be: a prince in control, hiding his cursed magic, a creature alone in the world. Now he was a king, and moreover a king who had shown his hand to another monarch, and shown it against his childhood friend, whose life was as dear to him as his own. Marius could be trusted; Marius had spoken of Javier's weighty will naturally, as if it was to be expected of royalty, and now he lay unmoving under that will's lashing strength.

"The priest had better not be dead." Rodrigo's voice cut through Javier's thoughts, getting a flinch out of him.

"The priest. What about Marius?" Foolish words, pushing away the inevitable: refusing the admission of what he'd done. Javier's knees wouldn't bend, wouldn't lower him to check Marius for a pulse.

Rodrigo came to Javier's side, scowling, not an expression of anger or fear: it was too controlled for that, too examining. Javier read nothing in his uncle's gaze, and set his jaw against giving the Essandian prince anything to read in his own.

No: he searched for one thing, after all. He sent a whisper of witchpower, of profound will, to test Rodrigo's. The magic came from somewhere, and for Belinda, it had come from her father Robert. If there was a glimmer of such power within Rodrigo, all of Javier's fears and hopes would be answered. King and prince, for Essandia called its monarch a prince, met ferocious gazes a few long seconds, and it was Javier whose shoulders slumped as he looked away.

Strength of will reigned within Rodrigo, as it must. Strength of will and of vision, as any ruler who sat on the throne as many decades as Rodrigo had done must have. His word was law and none would stand against it, but they would bow and buckle because of his position and their awareness of it, not because witchpower fueled it and made his desire impossible to refuse. Rodrigo bore no magic; no gift tied him to his nephew in ways ordinary men could ever fathom. Javier might have rolled his uncle's will and taken his country in that moment, had it been his wish. It was not; it never would be.

Not, whispered a hateful voice of truth, not unless Rodrigo should try to cast him aside, or have him burned, or in any way threaten him. Javier had exposed his hand and now must play it. He had survived a lifetime of denying his own fears, and cool silver certainty told him that he would not now permit someone else's to damn him.

"You're not surprised," Rodrigo said softly. "You've destroyed our Aulunian oak doors and knocked two men senseless, and yet you are not surprised."

"Four men," Javier said dully. "The guards outside the door. I have never done this before, but no. I am not surprised." *We,* he thought; he was a king now, and should use *we* when he spoke of himself. "And you are not afraid."

Acknowledgment flickered in Rodrigo's eyes, notice that Javier had forgone any kind of honorific and called Rodrigo "you," as though they stood on equal ground. Whether it was daring or not caring, or perhaps simply an assumption of his rights, Javier felt uncertain. The idea of his mother's death was in most ways beyond him, only a few cold pieces of meaning slipping through still-boiling silver power allowing him to make choices and move onward.

"My sister is dead. I may have no room for fear left in me." Rodrigo's gaze shifted to the men on the floor and he muttered a curse. "Unless the priest is dead, in which case you will have far more to answer to than the simple *how* of what has happened." He knelt, unceremoniously pushing Marius off the priest. Marius's cheek slid onto the cold stone floor and he groaned.

Relief swept Javier and he, too, knelt, pulling his brother in all but blood into his arms and mumbling an apology over him. "What does the priest matter? He's pretty, but I didn't think your tastes ran that way." No sooner had he spoken than he regretted it, catching his tongue between his teeth.

Rodrigo gave him a look that said once, only once, and only because Sandalia was dead, would he be forgiven such crudity. "His name is Tomas del'Abbate, and he is the bastard son of Primo Abbate, who will in all likelihood be the next Pappas. Abbate is very fond of the boy, and we none of us want to make an enemy of the church's leadership."

"Jav." Marius turned his face against Javier's chest with a weary smile, then stiffened and pushed away, memory all too obviously coming back to him. Javier knotted his hands, trying not to reach out in supplication and a hope of forgiveness. The air in the room went still, not just with Marius's sudden wariness, but with Rodrigo's tense anticipation as he turned his attention from the priest to the two wakeful young men. Javier recognised the flavour of waiting: it tasted of the moments before a fencing bout was met; tasted, he thought, of what the seconds before war broke out must taste of. Danger lay all around them, a presence of its own. Shielding magic surged, briefly illuminating the room in witchpower, and for that moment, Javier understood.

Rodrigo *was* afraid. Afraid on more than one level: afraid of Javier's inexplicable magic, afraid of the priest's death, afraid of Marius's response. Afraid, at the end, of losing a nephew as well as a sister, and so each of those fears mounted the other until the last was all-consuming. There would be a price to pay later: the narrow hard lines around his uncle's mouth told Javier that much, but for now, the Essandian prince would neither show fear nor allow harm to come to the young Gallic king.

"Javier," Marius said again, but this time the name was a question, edged on desperate. He had pulled away, but his hand made a fist of itself in Javier's shirt. Rough loose wool, that shirt, not the fine stuff that befitted a prince, not at all. Witchlight twisted, giving him leave to step outside himself and see himself as clearly as he saw others. Narrow-cut black pants, the wide leather belt, the tall sturdy boots: they had suited him on the sea. He looked the part of a brigand, not a prince, and wondered that the guards had opened the gates to him, despite his raging command. Marius's hand, by comparison to the weathered fabric it gripped, seemed clean and soft and cultured.

Javier closed his own hand over Marius's, struggling to call on ordinary human strength and not the silver power that lit everything he saw. He had little doubt he could allay any fear Marius felt or frighten him further into pretending that nothing was wrong. The idea soured in his mind, liquid silver turning black and poisonous as mercury at the thought. They had spent a lifetime together, he and Marius and Eliza and Sacha, and ever since Javier had recognised that his friends didn't share his magic, he had reined in every impulse, stepped on every opportunity, to influence them with his will. He *could,* if he so desired; he had learned only lately that he *had,* whether he willed it or no, but he *would not* deliberately subsume Marius's impulses, even if the cost should be scored on his own skin. Rodrigo, yes: he would do whatever necessary to survive his uncle's fears, but not Marius. Never Marius.

"What is it?" The question was softer than the echo of his name had been, Marius's gaze and grip tight on Javier's. His voice shook as though exhaustion or pain had come to bed down with dread, leaving him nothing to control himself with. "Javier, what is it that you do to us?"

"I call it *witchpower*." Javier lowered his head over Marius's, more afraid to look away than to continue meeting the merchant lad's eyes. "When I was young I thought everyone had it. When I realised I was the only one . . . I've never meant to hurt you, Marius. I've tried so hard to not influence you with it. Any of you. My friends. My family."

"Witchpower." Marius and Rodrigo both echoed the word, and it was Marius who continued as Rodrigo fell silent. "Witchery is the devil's work, Jav."

"I know." Javier kept his gaze on Marius, trusting he would find censure in Rodrigo's face and hoping against all wisdom that there might be some hint of forgiveness in Marius's. "So perhaps I'm Hell-born, for neither my uncle nor my mother carried this power in their blood. Did my father?" He glanced up with a sharp look, and saw instantly from Rodrigo's expression that Louis of Gallin had been as ordinary a man as any. Resignation drooped his shoulders and brought regret to his voice. "I thought not."

"Beatrice had this power." Comprehension was worse than condemnation, Marius's whisper knifing through Javier with its weight of pity and absolution. "That first night when I brought her to meet you, something passed between you. She defied you, Jav. No one defies you." By the time he finished, bewilderment had replaced pity, and Marius's brown eyes were wide. "My God, Javier, why didn't you just tell me? I would have understood."

"Would you?" Savagery drove Javier to his feet, sent him pacing away from the three men on the floor. The priest hadn't roused yet, as much cause for relief as alarm: Javier's family of blood and friendship might yet forgive his damnable magic, but a man of the cloth would do no other than call for a green oak stake and thick chains to bind him with. "Would you have understood if I said I carry power within me that forbids men to deny my will? Would you have ever trusted your thoughts with me again? You have been my friend all my life, Marius. You, Liz, Sacha. I couldn't risk that. I'd have been alone."

Marius rubbed his shoulder as he sat up, then dropped his head, strong fingers lacing through his dark hair. "It's easy to say I would've understood, Jav. Maybe I wouldn't have, but I knew the boy you were and the man you are. You're a prince, my lord. A king, now." His voice shook with the recollection, but he freed his hands and looked up at Javier. "Even as children we all knew who we played with. It didn't matter that much, not to me, because I was still stronger than you, and you never cried mercy on your rank when we wrestled. It was only as we got older that I realised I should have let you win." A fragile smile skirted his mouth, then fell away again. "I thought no one stood in your path because you were heir to the throne, Jav. That was mystical enough for me. You've had a lifetime in which you could have used this *witchpower* to be cruel, and you've never done it." Hesitation followed the last words, highlighted by a blanch Marius failed to hide.

"Except to you," Javier said softly, putting voice to the thought he knew had burdened Marius's mind. "Except to you, in the matter of Beatrice."

"Aye, my prince. But I think I would have understood."

The fire left Javier as suddenly as it had come on, leaving him drained all over again. It was no longer witchpower, he thought, plying his emotions, but simple human fear and misery. His mother was dead, his friends scattered, his uncle wisely wary of him. Even a man accustomed to heavy burdens would buckle under such a weight, and for a bitter instant, Javier recognised that he was not at all accustomed to bearing difficulties on his princely shoulders. "You might have," he whispered. "Perhaps I've done even more badly by you than I knew, my friend, and I have known that I have done badly by you indeed. But without you I'm alone. You three, my only true friends. And then Beatrice . . . Belinda," he corrected himself wearily. "Belinda came to you, to me, to us all, with her own power, and I was no longer lonely in spirit or in body. I had thought to give up the throne."

He lifted his gaze beyond the palace walls, turning it north, toward Gallin; toward, in the end, Aulun, the country of Belinda's birth and heart. "I must have seemed very foolish to her," he said quietly. "So eager to give up so much, all so I would no longer be alone."

"It is not a choice we are given, Javier." Rodrigo rose from beside the fallen priest. "We who are born to these families are born to serve, not to choose selfishly. Your mother knew that, and married twice for God and peace and power, and it is your duty now to follow her."

"For God and peace and power?" Iron: the words were iron in his mouth, flat and hideous on his tongue.

"Oh, yes."

Javier had never heard his uncle sound so, and turned to see calculation on his handsome face. "Oh, yes, Javier. For God, for peace, and with this magic you bear, oh, most certainly for power. I think you've named your gift poorly, nephew. I know you to be a good and godly boy, and I will not believe that this talent has been granted by the fallen one." Calculation turned to avarice, driven by grief and anger. "I believe it is a gift from God. Call it so: call it God's power, not witchpower, and with it we might at last retrieve Aulun from its unholy church and return its people to Ecumenic arms and Cordula's wisdom. And if there is so much as a whisper that Aulun's hand guided Sandalia's to a poisoned cup, then we will raze its throne, its nobility, its very heart and soul to the earth, and when the new sun rises we will crown you king over the western islands and a bold new banner for our faith."

Power wrenched Javier's heart, brightening his eyes with tears. He dropped to one knee, head lowered and hands outraised to honour Rodrigo's passionate vision. "Aulun's hand will have tipped that cup, my lord prince. I have no doubt of it," he grated through a throat gone tight with emotion. "Belinda Primrose, called Beatrice Irvine, is the daughter of Robert Drake, the Red Queen's courtier. I saw the truth of it in the witchpower I shared with her, and that she shared with Drake. I had hoped I would see that same power in you, uncle, or you would tell me it had ridden my father Louis."

"No," Rodrigo whispered. "More proof that it's God's gift, nephew, our holy father preparing you to stand against a black and terrible magic born from the Reformation church's devilish ways. Trust in God, Javier. Trust in your gift. We will exact our vengeance together, in God's name.

"Do not kneel to me." Rodrigo drew Javier to his feet. "Do not kneel to me, for you are a king now, and bend knee to no man. Instead stand beside me and allow my age and wisdom to guide your youth and talent. Do this and our sister, your mother, will be avenged, and you will wear the crown she had long since sought for you. Some measure of vengeance has been taken already," he offered. "Marius tells me this Belinda Primrose is dead, and Robert Drake ransomed at a handsome price. These were Sandalia's final acts."

"No." Javier's voice cracked. "Not Belinda. Someone else in her place, perhaps, but I . . . took her from the oubliette. She was like me," he whispered again. "She bears the same gift I do, and so, too, does Robert Drake. I raised no hand to save him, but I couldn't let her die. I was a fool." Rage cold enough to turn grief to ice rose in him, closing his throat against more words. His weakness had brought his mother's death to pass, an unforgivable offence.

Rodrigo went silent for long and deadly seconds, absorbing that. "Any man can be bewitched," he finally breathed. "If she's free, it's a mistake we'll set to right, and if she has power, we can be certain it's a gift from a false and dark god. We will prevail, and she will burn as befits a witch."

Despite fury, despite loss, sickness lurched Javier's stomach as a childhood terror came real in Rodrigo's threat. Pale skin blackening, the stench of burning hair, screams of horror and pain: he had seen them come to pass in his dreams. For all Belinda deserved such a fate, it came too close to how his own life might end, even with Rodrigo's confidence and trust at his side. "I would have her made mine to deal with," he whispered, and wondered if it was sentiment or self-preservation. "I have, I think, been cut more deeply than any by her ways."

"So shall it be." Rodrigo drew Javier into a hard embrace, then loosened the grip, hands remaining on his shoulders. "We have a great deal to do, Javier. The armada will sail come spring, but before then we must learn the depths of your ability, and train." Rage and sorrow flitted across his face. "And even before that, we must put our beloved Sandalia to rest. It will call the Gallic people to arms, Javier, and where Gallin rides, so, too, does Essandia."

"And where our brother countries go, so, too, does Cordula," Javier whispered. "Cordula, and the might of all the Ecumenic armies it can call to bear."

"Aulun will be ours." Rodrigo tightened his hands on Javier's shoulders. "In time, if we are bold, all of Echon will be ours, brought safe into the fold of our church and its wise fathers." A dark smile creased his face. "You're young and unwed. Perhaps we might look farther than even Echon's borders."

The thought lifted a shudder on Javier's skin, even as he said the words Rodrigo didn't: "We might look as far as Khazar."

"In time," his uncle said with satisfaction. "In time."

"Your majesties, forgive me." Marius's voice broke through the rising tide of ambition. "Forgive me, but I think the priest is waking."

3

Tomas del'Abbate

"I'll see to him." It's the silver prince's voice, gentled by what a half-conscious mind hears as resignation. Tomas forces his eyes open to see Marius leaving his side; to watch the youth join Rodrigo and the pair of them move away, abandoning Tomas where he lies. He tries to push up and finds pain: something is wrong with his arm, his shoulder unable to support him. He hears a whimper, and realises, with shame, that it's his own. Surely God might expect him to show more bravery in the face of injury, even when that injury has been given in such a peculiar way.

For he remembers, and wishes he didn't. There's silence as Javier kneels at his side, and Tomas is terribly aware that whatever has transpired here, he's the only witness not bound by blood or life-long friendship, and that Marius and Rodrigo have chosen to turn their backs on what is about to happen. There's a great deal about the world he doesn't know, but only a fool wouldn't see the danger, and Tomas is an innocent, not a fool.

"Highness," he whispers, then remembers himself: "Majesty." A strange taste fills the back of his throat, uncomfortably familiar for all that he's sure he's never tasted it before. He swallows convulsively, learning it for what it is: blood. A wave of relief washes through him on that red flavour. It means he's broken inside, and that he will not much longer be witness to the terrible, wonderful events that he's been privy to. Since that's so, he swallows again and dares to ask, "Will you tell my father I died well, my lord?"

Silver rises in Javier's eyes again. They are grey to begin with, Tomas thinks, and the silver is brought on by his passion. That such passion should be turned to God's work, oh! There would be a wonder indeed. The young Gallic king's expression deepens into an uncomfortable mix of rage and compassion.

"I will not," Javier says. Tomas thinks to correct him in several ways: first, that with Sandalia dead, Javier should be *we*, not I, but then the priest thinks, *no, I am dying, I will enjoy a moment of equality with a king*. That might bring a smile to his lips if it were not for the other way in which he wishes to correct Javier. The new king has just refused a dying man his final wish, an unforgiveable offence. "I will not," Javier says again, "because no one is going to die here today. Your shoulder is out of joint, and I think you've half bitten off your tongue, but these are not harbingers of death."

"They must be," Tomas responds with a regretful clarity. "They must, my lord. I've seen what you can do, and you cannot trust a man of the church to hold a secret of witchcraft."

"No, not any man," Javier agrees. "Not any man, but I can trust you, can I not, Tomas?" Suddenly his voice seems both much farther away and much more intimate, as though he speaks into an echoing cave, but whispers promises of desire. His gaze is locked on Tomas's, and there is an expectation in his eyes.

Tomas has never seen anything like it, is not sure he wishes to now see it, but it brings a pulse up in his throat, high and fast as a butterfly's wings. He is damaged, his body a thing of betrayals, but those betrayals die beneath an exposure of new failings: it seems that every fibre of his being responds to Javier's eyes. There is blood in Tomas's mouth; with that taste so clear, it is wrong that his cock should jolt to erection, that a sting of want should turn his belly molten and his knees weak, for all that there's no weight on them. Hot silver in Javier's gaze demands everything and promises nothing, but for that promise, Tomas fears he would do anything.

Inexorable will is in the weight of that look. The command is all but spoken in Tomas's mind: *you will not speak of this. My secret is yours to keep and you shall not betray me.* It is as though God has offered a single searing touch, and Tomas trembles with it.

Then protest whispers in the back of his mind: God is a kind

God, and has given unto Man free will. It is not God's intention that one man should seize another's mind with his heated and hungry gaze and charge him hold his tongue on secrets of deviltry. Tomas catches his breath, tastes blood, pleads for God's strength, and rallies against the Gallic king's call.

Confidence fills him, soft and warm, soothing all the aches of his body. The taste of blood fades, and the jutting desire in his loins lessens. Such is the power of faith; such is the power of God. Javier falters, astonishment replacing expectation in his face. For a heady moment Tomas understands that he and this young king *are* equals, in God's eyes if not in man's, and that understanding fills him with joy.

Then new things come into Javier's expression, and with the first of those things, with the devastating hope that lights Javier's eyes, Tomas's heart catches. God is good and God is kind, but God is not kneeling at his side in all-too-mortal glory, looking at him as though he might be a saviour himself. He tries to sit up, but his arm fails him, denying an urge to capture the king in his arms and make a promise of his own, that somehow all will yet be well.

Before he rallies, hope sluices from Javier's face, and after it washes anger, fear, desperation, all the sentiments of a man who has been deluded by hope in the past. Tomas, lying so close, can feel the change in Javier's body, the staunch clenching of muscle that precedes an onslaught of will, as though domination of his physical aspect can lend strength to his desires.

And perhaps it can, for though Tomas whispers "Don't" it's too late. The gentle assurance of God's love fails beneath mortal demand. He reaches for it, scrabbles in the confines of his own mind and arches his body to remain close, but Javier's determination cascades into its place. Under that princely power, the arch of his body becomes something else entirely, a sensual act, and now, only now, does Javier catch Tomas in his arms after all. He is hot, his heart crashing through his shirt as his chest presses against Tomas's, and there is fire where they touch, wanton liquid flame.

Nothing should soften in Tomas, nothing should acquiesce, and yet his will bends beneath Javier's. He feels Javier's breath on his lips as the king whispers a benediction that is also a damnation: "I will not see you come to harm, priest, but I cannot let your tongue run loose, for my own sake, for my people's sake, for the sake of my sweet murdered mother. You must be mine, and may God have mercy on us both."

God, for the first time in Tomas's life, is very far away.

IVANOVA, THE IMPERATOR'S HEIR
25 January 1588 † *Khazan, capital of Khazar, north and east of Echon*

A pigeon arrived in the night.

Ivanova knows this almost before she's awake: there are sounds of bustle and hurry in the palace that only come when dire news has arrived. The last time was Gregori Kapnist's death, but only a coach had been sent then, not pigeons. Lying quietly amongst blankets, she wonders what it is that makes her certain of the birds. It's something in the rise and fall of voices, or perhaps she caught a word or two while still asleep.

The palace courtiers consider her too young to be regarded with much import. They're wrong, of course: Ivanova is fourteen, and heir to the vast Khazarian empire. Whatever news has come in the night, she'll be apprised of it, either by her mother, the beautiful imperatrix, or by the hawk-nosed priest who is her mother's closest advisor. Ivanova likes Dmitri: he is cool and cutting and spares her none of his wit, and he seems to look on her with expectation and respect. He appears tremendously aware that she'll hold the throne, and so regards each day and every decision as a test for her to pass or fail.

Ivanova is quite proud of the fact that she rarely fails. Her mother is even prouder. Dmitri, though, shows no pride, only a sort of innate satisfaction, as if she does precisely as he imagines she will, nothing more or less.

There are moments when she is so pleased by this that she considers sharing her secrets with the priest, but of course she never does. She is young, not stupid.

"My lady." The door opens with a rush of cooler air from the hall, and a fussed maid scurries in, throwing back covers and stoking the fire and laying Ivanova's clothes out all in a mad dash of en-

THE PRETENDER'S CROWN · 43

ergy that leaves Ivanova hiding her giggles behind the blanket. She's been told tales of whirlwinds, gusts of twisting air, some so powerful as to pick up beasts of burden and throw them elsewhere. Ivanova thinks this woman must be a whirlwind personified. Even when the day is calm and steady, she believes everything must be done *now,* or better yet, the half hour past. She's Ivanova's favourite maid, and someday this whirlwind of a woman will become one of her ladies-in-waiting, the circle of women who advise an imperatrix whether the men around them realise it or not.

So Ivanova is dressed and out the door with a piece of bread to tide her until the morning meal, having been told for certain that there was a pigeon, that the maid doesn't know its business for surely it's none of hers, and that the imperatrix would see her at the counsel chamber with all due haste.

Truthfully, Irina doesn't expect to see her at all. Bread fisted in her hand as if she were a child, Ivanova scoops up her skirts and goes flying pell-mell through the palace halls, skidding around corners and shooting breathless smiles toward those she nearly overruns. There's a reason they think her unworthy, but her appearance as a knowledgeable player within the court will come as that much more of a surprise, take that many more people off-guard, and will allow both herself and her mother to see who adapts, who resists, and who becomes sycophantic. Ivanova's fifteen birthday is six months away, and she expects to enter the court a woman that day. Until then, she will make full advantage of sliding down banisters and taking corners like a racing hound.

A few minutes later she nestles herself into the listening nook above the counsel chamber. Tapestries hide her from view, which is just as well: the cosy little space isn't supposed to be there, and is reachable only through Irina's own rooms. The imperatrix has long since given Ivanova a key, so she might learn the ways of court in a more subtle way than Irina herself did. *She* was married young to ferocious bearded Feodor, Ivanova's unlamented father; *she* learned the tricks and manners of politics in a public forum, finding herself holding the reins of the empire while Feodor raced off on horseback to expand it.

Ivanova knows his portraits, paintings of a big barrel-chested man with little fierce black eyes and wild black hair. She thinks she resembles him more than she does her stunning mother, though Irina's delicacy has blunted the worst of Feodor's roughness. Ivanova's eyes are larger, and green instead of black, but she has the same impossible hair, always out of control, and she imagines that, bearded, she would be her father's slighter ghost. She is grateful the thickness of Feodor's nose had been tempered by Irina's fine features, and is too aware that the tempering has left more hawkishness to her face than she might have liked.

On the other hand, she's seen portraits of herself, too, painted in anticipation of marriage negotiations, and if she grows into the girl the artists portrayed, she will count herself well-satisfied. It is not vanity, but practicality: her mother is beautiful, and Ivanova sees how men and women alike respond to that. Irina has held her throne for over a decade; a plain woman would have a harder time reigning unchallenged.

Ivanova, of course, will marry, whether she wishes to or not. Lorraine, on Aulun's throne far to the west, makes example of why a monarch must wed: the woman called the Titian Bitch is old now, without an heir, and ravens circle her throne, waiting for her death and a chance to pick away at her kingdom. Ivanova has no intention of allowing the same to happen in Khazar.

Voices lift in the room below, muffled by the tapestries that hide her, but Ivanova is accustomed to deciphering what's said through the heavy woven cloth. After a moment her mother cuts in, not so much loud as very firm, and male arguments fade away.

"There is no treaty," Irina says, calmly. Wonderfully calm: her unflappability, as much as her beauty, helps keep her court in rein. "It was negotiated with Sandalia, and Sandalia is dead. There will be new negotiations with Javier."

"If he'll listen," a man snaps. "The second pigeon says Akilina was found with Sandalia's body. He may well think her the murderer."

Ivanova's heart seizes and she realises she's crushing the unfortunate bread in her hand. She puts it aside and leans toward the chamber below, as though a few scant inches of closeness might fill in all the details she's missed so far.

Sandalia is dead, murdered in Lutetia. Ivanova knows that Irina has offered cautious treaties to Gallin and Aulun alike, and that she negotiates with Rodrigo in Essandia through slow-carried missives and hints of flirtatiousness. Neither Rodrigo nor Irina wishes to marry, but a nod toward conventionality must be made to keep the people happy and in gossip, if nothing else. It's a lesson Ivanova intends to take to heart.

If she's given the chance. Eyes closed, she listens to the discussion below; to Irina's dismissal of Akilina's potential hand in the Gallic queen's death; to the weight of what it means that there are papers missing, papers negotiated in Irina's name and signed by Sandalia and Irina's emissary Akilina Pankejeff. Those papers are a breath away from committing Khazarian troops to a war against Aulun, but that breath is what's important: Irina's hand has not signed them, and she is too astute a statesman to do other than express surprise should those papers come to light. It is well-known, after all, that Irina looks favourably on Aulun and its navy—

It is *not* well-known, someone protests; barely a six-month ago Irina dismissed Robert Drake with apologies for fearing Cordula's strength and a refusal to ally herself with Aulun and its heathen Reformation church.

A silence fills the chambers below, even Irina quieting at the reminder. Ivanova remembers the day; she discussed her mother's wardrobe with Irina that morning. Irina's words had said one thing to Robert, but her gown had been of Aulunian make and style, a gift from Lorraine on Ivanova's birth. On such subtleties were covert relationships built, details that hint of support without making it too obvious.

The problem, of course, is that subtleties are rather overshadowed by pieces of actual paper promising troops to a rival kingdom.

"Well," Irina eventually says, "if we lose the game with Aulun, so be it. All we can offer Lorraine is troops. We can do rather better for Javier de Castille."

Nerves flutter in Ivanova's belly, making her both aware of her hunger and grateful she hasn't eaten the bread, for fear it might come back up again. Her heartbeat feels light and fast, as though it might wing its way out of her chest. She can anticipate the next words; can anticipate that they're why she's been summoned to listen in on this conversation between her mother and her advisers.

"Your majesty—"

"We know your objection already, and understand it. Ivanova is our only heir, and we would not see her away from Khazar, sitting on another's throne while some regent or ambitious nobleman reached for imperial heights. Regardless of our intentions, however, she is a bargaining piece. She's young, pretty, and heir to an empire with inexhaustible resources. Javier would be a fool to refuse her, even if his own intentions go no further than the interim. What we have heard of him suggests he lacks ambition, not wit."

Ivanova hears every word clearly, but she is fourteen and cannot help herself: her imagination leaps forward to her wedding day. Khazarian wedding garb is splendid, so encrusted with gold and pearls as to be almost too heavy to stand in. Javier would wear a fashion of his own country, but perhaps they would find a way to make the two meet, some subtlety woven into the wear of two cultures. He is handsome, at least from his portraits, though very pale. In wedding white he might look a ghost at her side, but then, as Irina has pointed out, he's known to lack ambition.

That is not a failure Ivanova shares. Even at fourteen, even chasing down fanciful futures, she does not object to the idea of a prince, a king, a husband, who can be shaped to her will. Indeed, it is best if he can be, because Ivanova intends to rule as her mother has done; as the great queens of Echon have done for far longer than the span of her own years.

Breath held with anticipation, Ivanova settles back down against the tapestry to listen and dream while her mother sends envoys to Gallin, to Essandia, and to Aulun.

RODRIGO, PRINCE OF ESSANDIA
28 January 1588 † *Isidro*

For nearly a week, Rodrigo has avoided his nephew.

Not entirely, of course not; they have mourning in common, and grim futures to face, and they have spoken together as men and

THE PRETENDER'S CROWN · 47

heads of state. They have looked toward war and glorious battle, ideals Rodrigo has attempted to forsake in his years on the throne, and which he now accepts must be pursued. Yes, they have been men together.

But they have not been family. There have been no evenings sitting together over a glass of Essandian wine, bickering over whether it or Gallin's make is superior. No agreements that Parnan wine, at least, is clearly the inferior, and another glass poured to toast that. No teasing about women, no sorrow drowned in cups, no dreams spun across a dark January night.

Instead, Rodrigo has sent Marius Poulin running back and forth as a messenger boy when he must speak with Javier outside the halls and chambers of business. Marius, either wiser than Rodrigo knows, or a fool indeed, does not fear Javier, and the Essandian prince, though he will never admit it aloud, is terrified. The devil has taken his nephew, and Rodrigo sees no way to take him back.

In his life, in more than half a century of memories, he cannot recall the same witless white panic that shattered through him when his chamber doors erupted to expose Javier. Man is incapable of such power, but Javier's eyes had blazed with it as he entered. Rodrigo had believed, for a gut-wrenching moment, that his own life was at an end, only days apart from his beloved sister's. Never, not even when he had ridden to war as a youth, had he seen mortality so clearly; never had he been so grateful for his faith in God, and never had he realised how much he wished to continue living.

Even now his heart is a fist in his chest, refusing breath for his body. His hands are cold, most particularly the fingertips, and when he looks to them they're bloodless, whorls standing out in dreadful relief, as though all the wet beneath his skin has been sucked away. Every part of him clinches with fear at the thought of the boy who is his heir.

He has felt God's power, has Rodrigo de Costa. He has stood in church and chapel and courtyard and felt God's grace, His warmth and generosity, and seen the wonders of the world He has created and granted life. God has guided Rodrigo, to the best of his frail human ability to follow, through all the years of his princedom. He has tried to act with wisdom, with grace, with compassion; it is why he has avoided war as best he can, when other kings and queens of Echon have made or agitated for it.

It's not that Rodrigo believes infidels and heathens will be spared Hell; it's that he doubts God would approve of murdering unlettered peasants and unwise children as a means of spreading His word and changing their minds. There are better ways; if there were not, men would not have been granted reason or free will, but would have been born to follow blindly. To Rodrigo, it is far more a triumph to bring one thinking man to God's path than to slaughter thousands of innocents who have been led astray. The dead, after all, cannot convert.

Faced with Javier, Rodrigo wonders if it may be better, this once, to condemn a soul to Hell so that many more might live.

Because Javier is not touched with God's power. What Rodrigo saw in his nephew was selfish hurt, lashing out. God has more mercy and more wisdom than that: His chosen few are not of a temperament to redress personal wrongs with the power He grants. Of this, Rodrigo is confident.

And yet; and yet; and yet. There is the matter of Sandalia's death; there is the matter, perhaps even more pressing, of Sandalia's heir. Of his *own* heir. Yes, Rodrigo is afraid of the boy, but far worse than Javier's selfish use of power might lie ahead if neither Essandia nor Gallin has an heir to take their thrones. Aulun will sweep in and roll over the Ecumenic countries with its armies and its heretical faith, and while Lorraine has no heir of her blood to put on the throne, she has lackeys and hangers-on a-plenty, and no small willingness to back a pretender to the Gallic and Essandian thrones.

Humour ghosts through him. It's only fair; he and Sandalia are happy enough to put their prince on Lorraine's throne.

Were, he reminds himself. He and Sandalia *were* happy enough, and now that duty lies with him.

Mouth thinned with determination, Rodrigo leaves the fire he's been contemplating and rings a bell. In moments a servant enters, and Rodrigo orders his nephew brought to him. Fears must be faced, and weapons must be forged.

When Javier enters, Rodrigo's before the fire again, fingers steepled against his mouth, eyebrows drawn into a headache-causing crease. He has been thinking—thinking of the instinct that made him seize on Javier's devil's power as a gift in the first moments he saw it manifested. That's the pragmatic streak in him, stronger than the fear; it's to that which he must now turn. Ambition can be shaped, is what Rodrigo is thinking, and when Javier hesitates at the corner of his vision, the Essandian prince drops his hands and gestures to the other chair settled before the fire. He says "Nephew" gravely, and Javier sits with the wide-eyed expression of a child uncertain if he has been caught at some illicit activity.

"Uncle." Javier hesitates again, then makes a feeble smile. "You've had the door fixed."

Rodrigo's smile is much better than Javier's, but then, he has many years more practise at dissembling. "I thought you might be more comfortable returning to my chambers if everything appeared normal."

"I'd be more comfortable, or you would be?"

"Some of both." There's no sense in lying; he needs Javier's utter trust in order to guide him. He needs Javier to believe what Rodrigo does not: that his power is God's, and that God intends him to make war on Aulun.

For the briefest moment Rodrigo looks at himself as though from the outside, as though he is another man listening to his own thoughts. They are contradictory and complicated, pulled one way and another, and yet from within they feel a steady course. He is not one who likes war, and yet when it must be made—and it must, because Sandalia is dead and there seems little doubt Aulun's throne struck the blow—he will use whatever weapon is at hand. If that weapon should be his nephew, bedamned with a power that no man should carry, then he will use it even without trusting it. He, who believes so strongly in God and faith that he has set aside certain earthly expectations of a king and has chosen not to wed, not to father children, will lie and corrupt in order to achieve the ends he must have.

God, he thinks irreverently and unusually, might have done Man no favours in giving him free will.

"Some of both," he says again, hoping it will sound like a ruefully considered admission, and that it will warm Javier's heart to him a little. "I stand in awe, Jav, you know that."

"You sit, uncle," Javier says, deadpan.

"My legs are too weak with wonder to hold me," Rodrigo says promptly, and Javier grins. He's a handsome lad when he smiles, brightness of expression bringing life to a pale, long-featured face. Javier has nothing of Sandalia in him, unless her nut-brown hair and Louis's washed-out blond somehow mixed to give Javier his ginger head. "I have questions, Javier. This godspower of yours, do you practise with it?"

"No." Javier's voice has gone as pale as his skin, all a-shudder and revulsion. "I did, but no longer."

"You must. Javier—" Rodrigo leans forward, but it's Javier who lifts a cutting hand this time, and bounds to his feet with the unconstrained energy of youth.

"What would you have me do, uncle? I made the priest's will my own, took from him what God granted Man. I *cannot* continue that way. It makes me—"

"Desperate," Rodrigo interrupts, strongly. "Desperate, perhaps, and also perhaps guided by the hand of our Lord after all. The priest is pious, yes, but he's not the one granted this talent. You and I and Marius know that Tomas would see it as his duty to condemn you to the church, and we all know that you are not the devil's instrument. What *cannot* be permitted is Tomas's declamation, not when God has laid a clear path for us from here to Alunaer. It is a necessary measure, Javier." Wisdom, compassion, age, passion: Rodrigo would believe himself, if only he were not obliged to live with his own contrasting thoughts.

"I don't sleep for fear of it." Javier sinks into his seat again. "For fear of what I might become."

"A king?" Rodrigo asks, arch as a woman. "Your crown is not meant to help you sleep more easily, Jav. It carries responsibilities, often hard ones. More often hard than not."

"Have I no responsibility to Tomas?"

"You have served that. He lives. Beyond that, to permit him leave to betray your gift to Cordula fails to serve your own people, or your dead mother's memory. God forgives us our sins if we truly repent, Javier, you know that. I have no doubt you repent, but sometimes we must sin to answer the greater call. What aspects does your talent have?"

THE PRETENDER'S CROWN · 51
Javier looks blank, as though he's forgotten where this began,
then scrubs his hands across his face. "Shielding. Manifestations of
light. Wanton destruction, and the ability to take a man's will from
him and make it my own. God would not give one unwise youth
such power, uncle. I cannot fathom it."

"You presume to know what God might or might not do?" Rodrigo puts rich humour in his voice and Javier shoots him a scowl.
"Unwise, perhaps. Untried, indeed. Is it of use on the battlefield,
Jav? These shields, this wanton destruction? We must explore it," he
insists, even as sympathy slices through his soul. For his own sake,
Javier would be better served by a monastery cell, where he might
stay on his knees through the length of days and long nights, begging mercy for succumbing to the temptations offered by his devil-
born *witchpower*.

For Gallin's sake, for Essandia's, for Cordula's, and for Sandalia's,
he must be made to believe God has graced him, and be made to
train until his dark gift can reach forth and destroy that which has
harmed his family and would ruin his people.

"Explore it how? Would you have me march out to a hayfield
and see if I can murder straw men, like a youth new to the bow or
sword? Men *understand* the blade, uncle. They would not understand this."

"But that's precisely what we must do. In secret, yes, I'll grant
you that. There are unused halls in the palace—"

"And what if I bring them down around my ears?"

"Then you'd best hope your shielding is strong." Rodrigo's
voice is wry, but he means what he says. Then curiosity seizes him
and he takes up his wineglass. Drains it, because it *is* a fine vintage,
and then without further warning flings it toward the young king
of Gallin.

Silver flares and glass shatters, both so sudden that Javier flinches.
Then outrage darkens his cheeks and he springs to his feet again.
"What—?!"

"A test," Rodrigo says, mildly. "Have you always reacted thus
when an object flew your way, Javier? That must have been inconvenient, playing games in the gardens."

"No." Javier is sullen now, not at all a nice aspect for a king. He sinks into his chair like a kicked dog, lip thrust in a pout. "I only learned it in playing witchpower games with Beatrice. I didn't know it had become instinct."

Beatrice, Rodrigo notes: the boy has corrected himself in the past, but this time lets it slip. The Aulunian witchbreed girl he saved is still "Beatrice" in Javier's mind, and that could prove dangerous. It will be worth watching, as well worth watching as his unholy magic. "You're born to power, Javier. Wielding it, even if it comes in this strange form, should be natural to you. Did you and she play at explosives, as well?"

Javier slides him a look that suggests he thinks he's being mocked, but he finds no teasing in Rodrigo's face, and relaxes. "Only once. It's noisy, but I learnt I could do it."

"As can she?" At the second hard look from his nephew, Rodrigo raises an eyebrow and a hand. "I'm not looking to raise uncomfortable memories or to ridicule you. Belinda Primrose is alive and our enemy, and we must know what we can about her." He hesitates, facing a question he doesn't want to ask, but makes himself do so on a long exhalation. "Might she have managed Sandalia's death through her power?"

Javier pinches the bridge of his nose, a gesture that makes him look older than he is. "Belinda," and now, reminded, he emphasises the name, "is different than I. She has extraordinary willpower, enough to stand a while against me, but she falls beneath an onslaught. She calls it 'stillness,' an internal gift," he mutters, bitterness in the words, "as benefits a woman."

Silence reigns a few long moments as Javier stares into his own palm, before he breathes a curse and continues. "She said she used the stillness to hide in shadows once, so she went entirely unseen, but that she had forgotten how. That was before she and I woke the witchpower in her, though, and so I would say she might have managed Mother's death by witchpower, yes, but not in the way you mean. Marius says Mother was poisoned." The words came raw from his throat, as though in voicing them he finally made the terrible and impossible real. A quaver, barely steadied, accompanied what he said next: "If Belinda used the kind of power I've shown, lashing out . . . it wouldn't look like poison. She has the ability to do

what I've done, but she's a snake, uncle. Slithering into our friendships, into my bed, into the palace. Poison suits her better than blast-
ing. She might have slithered into Mother's chambers and set the
trap, perhaps by hiding within her stillness."

Rodrigo swallows the implications and refuses himself the luxury of expressing his thoughts. But Javier makes it unnecessary,
looking up with grey eyes turned orange by the firelight. "I woke
the power in her. I gave her the ability to murder my own mother.
I *am* damned. I cannot do this, uncle. I can't follow this path."

"What will you do, then?" Inexorable tone to his voice, the one
that his advisers and the men of his court know not to argue with.
Javier has literal power behind his voice, but Rodrigo has a half-
century's practise, and most of those years he's been a king. "Will
you slink to a monastery and shave a tonsure, spend your days on
your knees and castigating yourself?" For all that it's what he'd have
Javier do if he could, it's not what must be done. If it takes heartless
derision to push Javier to the path he has to take, then Rodrigo will
be cruel. Life is made of difficult choices, and as he told his nephew,
being a king makes none of them easier. "Will you abandon your
throne as you threatened to do? Show yourself a coward in God's
eyes?"

"I am not!" Javier's cry is as plaintive as a child's. "This isn't God's
gift I own. How could God do other than approve if I walk away
from it?"

"Because you are His chosen son for the Gallic throne, aye, and
for mine. Who would you pass it to, if you walked away, Javier? You
have no sons, nor do I. Would you let Gallin be swept away by
Aulun or Ruessland, left as nothing more than a memory of a place
that once was?"

"No." The answer is dull now, no longer plaintive, no longer
sullen. "I have no other answer."

"Then accept it." Rodrigo comes to crouch before his nephew,
putting his hands on the youth's shoulders; making himself small
before the king of Gallin. His stomach churns as he does it, all the
warrior in him cringing from the weakness of his stance, but he is
not on a battlefield now; at least, not one of swords and archers.
"Come with me. We'll go to one of the lower halls, and we'll see

what can be done with this talent of yours. I'll guide you when I can, Javier. I have faith you'll stay on God's path and make use of this gift as He intends. Do not be afraid."

Javier nods slowly and both men come to their feet together, Rodrigo making a playful light gesture that Javier should precede him. Javier echoes it in response, and smiling, they walk shoulder to shoulder from Rodrigo's chambers.

Shoulder to shoulder, both pretending not to be afraid.

4

BELINDA PRIMROSE
14 February 1588 † *Alunaer, capital city of Aulun*

She had no last name, not properly. Robert had always called her
Primrose, for his imaginary sister who was supposedly Belinda's
mother. But if she had taken her adopted father's name, she might
have been Belinda Drake, who had been sent to a convent at age
twelve, and who had never returned from it.

Belinda Primrose wore those shackles now. For nearly a month
she'd slept in a dull grey cell and said her devotions five times or
more a day; had worn a scratchy woollen shift and knelt on cold
stone, and had heard achingly little of the world beyond sturdy
convent walls.

The nuns were kind to their new ward, whom they'd been told
had come from another convent. Belinda, when she spoke of her
past, murmured obediently of a poor but pious abbey in the Aulunian west. She knew the names of her wimpled sisters, details of her
mother superior's life, and could sketch a fair layout of the buildings
if asked. Belinda had no doubt at all that such an abbey and such a
woman and such sisters existed: she had no doubt, in fact, that a
hazel-eyed, brown-eyed girl had played her role for ten years and
more at that quiet western convent, and she had very little doubt as
to what fate had greeted that woman when Belinda entered the
convent in Alunaer.

She tossed restlessly, sleep evading her more thoroughly tonight than it had in weeks past. If she were not obliged by Lorraine's orders to remain hidden, she would climb over the walls and explore Alunaer, seeking out whatever trifle it was that disturbed her dreams.

A month ought to have been more than enough time to reestablish control over her actions and behaviour, but instead curiosity plagued her, a wondering to what purpose Lorraine had had her ensconced amongst religious women; to what purpose she was wearing the mantle that had been created for Robert Drake's adopted daughter over a decade earlier. It had been a lifetime since Belinda had been required to wait, and in that time she had become accustomed to performing one duty or another. For eleven years, since the day she had watched Rodney du Roz fall to his death and lie twitching on snow-covered stone, she had had purpose, and had known the purpose even of waiting. As a child, not knowing why she was put aside, ignored and hidden, had chafed; now she had come full circle, and once more suffered the frustration of being uninformed.

Eleven years. Her eyes opened and she sat up, blind gaze across the darkened cell. The sisters had spoken of it, but she'd paid no heed, assigning no meaning to the preparations for the feast of Saint Valentine that so occupied the others.

Du Roz had died this day, eleven years ago.

There would be no more rest found this night. Belinda flung her blanket back and slipped her feet into unpadded slippers, hurrying to pull her novice's robe on over the shift she slept in. More mundane clothes might be found in the laundry: there were often visitors to the abbey, rich or widowed women in need of time away from families or troubles, and from time to time they left behind gifts. Anything other than a robe would do, and she could escape the convent walls to—

To go to the palace, and look down from the steps at the place where du Roz had died. Belinda stopped in the middle of her room, motionless, wondering at the thought; wondering what good it might do, or what doors in her mind it might open.

That, then, was how the abbess found her moments later: standing frozen in a dark room, dressed to face the day, her face turned up toward the ceiling and sky as though God might offer an answer to some unknown question.

Impulse had left Belinda by then, had left her cold and appalled. There were no answers in du Roz's death, not even if she knew what questions to ask. She knew why he had died: he, and all those who had crossed her path whose graves were now filled with rotting memories. He had presented a danger to Aulun and its queen, and there was nothing else to be taken from his short life or her hand in ending it.

"Forgive me, mother," she said in the quiet, cultured voice Belinda Drake had been given. "My dreams have disturbed me, and I thought to visit the chapel and find comfort in God's presence. Did I cry out in my sleep?"

"You did not," the woman said crisply. Everything about her was crisp, from her soprano to the parchment-fine lines around her eyes. Had Belinda not been so hideously bored, she might have liked her. "I came to wake you," the abbess said. "Your father is here."

The abbess here—perhaps even the one in western Aulun—would not know Robert, Lord Drake, the queen's favourite courtier, for her ward's father. Drake was an uncommon enough name, though more expected in the western counties where she was meant to be from, but last names were rarely used in the convent. It was a mark of worldliness that Belinda used her given name at all; she would have been better suited by a saint's name, and that she was not might mean there was a fate for her beyond the convent walls.

And there was: that, at least, Belinda was certain of. Her heart sang, thrill of joy entangled with wholly genuine befuddlement. Robert had no place coming to the abbey, nor had there been any word of his return to Alunaer. Sequestered as Belinda was from Cortes's spies, she might not have heard, but for a good and godly group of nuns, the sisters knew and shared a fair bit of gossip about the world beyond. Robert Drake's return might have warranted discussion.

Belinda spoke over the rush of her own thoughts, asking, "My father, my lady?" with shy confusion.

The abbess came forward and took Belinda by the upper arms, an offer of strength. "I suppose you must be used to thinking of yourself as alone in this world, child. Your mother in the west wrote to say you've heard nothing from your family since becoming a novice, but he is still your father."

"Yes, I-I suppose." A high soft voice, trembling with uncertainty and a hint of hurt to come. Belinda admired her own performance, though astonishment still whirled in her mind. Even if Robert had returned, visiting her here seemed unlikely in the extreme. There would be some desperate task for her to accomplish, if he was willing to breach Lorraine's orders to see her. Excitement fluttered up, though it remained tightly bound within her, coming nowhere near her face.

The abbess drew Belinda into an unexpected hug, all her crispness melting away into the gentleness of the embrace. "It must be shocking to choose this life so young, and to only now discover the outside world may still want a part of you, too." She stepped back an arm's length, still holding Belinda. No one, Belinda thought, had shown her such unstinting compassion since she'd been a child; since before the queen had come to Robert's estates, and the life she'd known made her wonder at the cost of such generosity. There was nothing of price in the abbess's quick reassuring words, though: "You need not see him tonight, child, or any night, if you wish me to send him away."

"No!" Belinda's voice broke as she tried to modify the command in it. The abbess's eyes widened, then wrinkled again with sympathy as she squeezed Belinda's shoulders. "Forgive me," Belinda whispered. "I didn't mean to be brash, mother. I only—I think I must see him."

"Yes." Sympathy deepened in the abbess's eyes. "You may be right, child. Come." She took Belinda by the hand as though she were a much younger girl, and guided her from the cell and through the dark quiet abbey halls. Belinda kept her breathing smooth and even, forbidding the rushed beat her heart wanted to seek out, and allowed herself to cling to the abbess's hand, a child indeed. It didn't matter how or why: Robert was alive, safe back in Aulun, and once more the waiting was over.

The abbess stopped outside the visitor's hall. The cessation of footsteps let silence leap up all around them, a creature with its own presence. "Were he any other man I would insist on joining you, child, but because he is your father the choice is yours. Would you like me to be there?"

"No." Belinda cleared her throat to put more strength into the word, and offered a tentative smile as she shook her head. "I think I can be bold. But you'll be nearby if I need you?"

Pride bloomed in the old woman's face. "I will. Only pull the bell and I'll be there in a moment."

"Thank you, my lady." Belinda caught the abbess's hand and pressed her lips to the ring the woman wore. Then with a quick flash of a nervous smile, she pushed open the hall door and stepped inside.

A rug lay over the stone floor, rare luxury in the abbey, and meant only to help welcome guests. Cushioned chairs and a sturdy table sat beside a well-built fire, and tapestries hung on the walls, holding in heat and making the hall the only truly warm place within the abbey. That, Belinda told herself, accounted for the sudden flush in her cheeks, the excitement that suffused her. She kept her gaze downcast, hands folded in front of her, a picture of modesty while the door swung shut and closed away the abbess from hearing their conversation. Only when she heard it latch did Belinda whisper a single word, the double-edged blade she always permitted herself once each time she remet Robert Drake: "Father."

"Hardly." Dry word, familiar voice, not at all expected in this place or time. Belinda jerked her gaze from the floor, surprise too great to hold in check with the stillness. Better that way, perhaps: he would expect her to be surprised, and with a man like this it was safer to play to his expectations.

Like Robert, he'd changed little in the years since Belinda had first seen him. Thick black hair was fashionably cropped, and a sharply trimmed beard enhanced his hawkish features and thin sensual mouth. Deep-set eyes were dark enough to reflect firelight, and his figure was as slim and well-dressed as any courtier in Lorraine's court.

But he was not of Lorraine's court, no more than Sandalia herself might have been. He had been in Khazar at Irina's side; had fathered a child on the imperatrix if Belinda did not miss her guess. He had the *witchpower* that Belinda shared with Javier de Castille, the new king of Gallin, and with her own father, Robert Drake. They were alike, all of them, and nothing at all of things she understood.

"Dmitri."

His pupils contracted, surprise bleeding darkness from his eyes and turning them hazel. Only then did Belinda remember she wasn't supposed to know this man, certainly not by name. He had not given it the once she'd seen him in adulthood, nor had Robert offered it up when Belinda had mentioned the man who'd come to her in Khazar and set her on the road to kill a queen. It was childhood memory that gave her his name, and that memory was one she had not been intended to possess. Even now, thinking back, she could feel the waterwheel rush of power draining into her mind, trying to lock Dmitri's presence into an unreachable place within her; even now she could recall the sting of certainty upon waking; the knowledge that Robert had tried to alter her memory and had failed. She'd kept that secret, as she'd kept many others, well-hidden until now, when a careless slip told the black-haired Khazarian consort that she knew him better than she was meant to.

But there were ways she might know him besides her own faultless memory. Robert might have told her his name; studies of the Khazarian court would have mentioned this man, with his intense eyes and sensual hands. She could know him without betraying herself, and at the heart of it, she no longer cared too dearly if she had given herself away. Dmitri belonged to the secret circle of witchpowered folk her father seemed to head, and as such would have answers.

More than answers; sudden recognition spilled through her. Her unusual restlessness harkened back to the summer night in Khazar when she had awakened, prickling with awareness that some unknowable game was afoot. Then, as now, it had seemed that Dmitri had drawn her from sleep, his very presence sparking things in her that had never before existed.

As suddenly, a third point made a line. The night Dmitri visited Robert at his Aulunian estates had been the first and only time in her youth that Belinda had called the witchpower to life. With his nearness, she had awakened to the ability to draw shadows around herself, and had stood boldly before two grown men, eavesdropping and unseen.

Witchpower ambition flared, kindled desire, and spilled through her as golden fire. Abandoning caution, Belinda stalked forward, pressing herself close to Dmitri and lacing her fingers in his hair. "You."

The low command in her own voice was unfamiliar. Wantonness, subservience, yes; those things she could call on at any moment, and use them to manipulate and guide the men around her. She *could* command; she had proven that to herself with sweet biddable Marius and with the less tractable Viktor, but even so, she didn't expect to hear demand in her words, particularly when she spoke to a man of Dmitri's easy, arrogant self-confidence.

Even less did she expect the way his eyes widened and his chin lifted, giving her a show of throat that seemed as against his grain as issuing orders lay against hers. Incongruity struck him as obviously as it did her, and he froze, expression caught between consternation and acquiescence. She had won: certainty thrilled within her, tightening her belly and nipples and making a pool of heat between her thighs. He might struggle with it, fight against her, offering up delicious challenge, but she had already won, by being nothing more than what she was. That knowledge settled over her like a cloak, foreign and strange and unexpectedly comfortable.

"Dark prince." Belinda spoke against his throat, her lips finding his pulse. "I know you, Dmitri. I have known you since I was a girl, and I am weary of playing the part of the unschooled child. You will teach me what my father has not. You must. Your presence awakens power in me, dark prince. I have been waiting for you."

Ambition flared in him, not the clarity of language she'd learned to steal from Javier and Marius, but profoundly recogniseable regardless. Emotion wasn't bound to weak words: it ran deeper than that, and whatever witchpower talents Dmitri had, they were not enough to mask his thirst for conquest. She was a dichotomy to him, a creature caught between being worthy of veneration, and simply being desired as any woman might be. Not for the first time, with his body pressed against hers, she thought that a man's own weapons were the best to use against him, and so when she spoke again it was with more sexual hunger, and less burning command.

"You wanted me, in Khazar. Had you time, you said. I was almost naked then, ready for taking. Do you like that more, Dmitri, or do you like me as I am, trussed in a sister's robes, innocent and unworldly? I like this, I think." She touched her tongue to his earlobe, then bit hard, and knotted her hand at his nape when he jerked violently.

"I like this," she murmured again. "Then, I might have welcomed you, spread my legs and cried in pleasure, but here my abbess stands just beyond the door, waiting to see if her daughter needs her strength or guidance to face a man. Perhaps I'll scramble, naked, for that door, full of silent sobs for my shame and fear, and you'll pull me back and have me like a dog. You will put your hand over my mouth to keep me from crying out, and I, struggling for breath, will fold and bend to your will . . . ah!" She caught his wrist as he brought his hand up, denying him the leverage to tear her novice's robes. "I'll play at your game, but we must not give the abbess cause to think me abused at your hands, *Father*. And if that's a game you like we'll play it, too, darling papa, but the part of me that is not your innocent sister knows men, and I will have my pleasure before you are given yours."

He was taller than she, much taller, but went to his knees with surprising willingness when her fingertips on his shoulders directed him there. She stepped back, aware of an edge of cruelty at leaving him to follow, but the witchpower that rode her both exulted at the freedom of making a man come to her, and whispered that it was no more than his due: God knew she'd crawled to enough men in her life. And besides, when she found the table's edge to lean against, and dropped her robes around her ankles, follow he did, and ended with his tongue and fingers in her cleft and little hint, even with her witchpower-laced awareness, of resentment. Too aware of the ancient nun outside the door, Belinda bit her hand to keep silent as deft skill and willingness brought her to come with more speed than she had often known. Power broke in her with climax, silent golden tide overwhelming her senses for long seconds. It had been mere weeks, and still too long, with hungry magic in her veins. When she shivered herself to full consciousness again Dmitri still knelt, watching her now; it was not the action she might have expected from the man. He might have thought their bargain met, and flipped her on her belly to have her on the table before she made thoughts or words again.

"Stay." Her fingers were still in his hair, as though she would put him where she wanted him, but even she heard the plea in the throaty word, no more command or witchpower riding it. "My dark prince, stay a while and be tender and give me more. My need is not yet met." Trembles shook her from the core, a cry for pleasure to continue unabated.

"I have more to teach you than to squirm and cry out beneath my tongue." He had not, she realised, spoken since she'd recognised him, and the sardonic quality of his voice was not at all lessened by the cup he'd drunk from. "I think perhaps you'll be more eager for lessons if I leave you now, *daughter,* and do not return until I've secured safe quarters for you beyond these cold grey walls."

Shock coursed over her, tightening her belly and breasts all over again. "You can't."

"Can't what?" Dmitri stood, gaze suddenly bright with amusement and the awareness that such humour was callous. "Can't take you beyond the abbey? I can by daylight, most certainly, though perhaps I'll have to return you to this prison at night, as your red-haired queen has seen fit to ensconce you here, and she may have worthy reasons. No matter. Cold nights alone in your little cell should make you glad enough for morning to bring me to your side." Challenge crept into his eyes, darkening them again, and his voice dropped lower, more sensual and more dangerous. "Or do you mean I cannot walk away from your desires? Perhaps I can't. Would you like to wield your power and see? Do you believe you can roll my will as easily as you did a foppish boy's, or a lustful guard's?"

Memory cascaded over Belinda, the inexorable line of her father's will, and the way Javier's had broken against it, sand castles dashed against glass. And she herself had fallen beneath Javier's power, that externally focused desire, so different from the stillness she'd developed. Dmitri would be more like Robert, and she too fragile to stand against either.

Aware, very aware, that she still stood exposed, and finding a kind of strength in it, Belinda took a slow breath, and on it warned, "Someday I will be able to, dark prince."

Dmitri's gaze slid down her body, taking in the changes made as she breathed in, then came back to her eyes with no more hint of laughter. "Aye, so you will, and on that day I'll kneel before you and be your vehicle for delight until needs you've never known you had are sated." His eyebrows quirked upward. "Until then, I suggest you dress yourself so we might face your abbess with our happy reunion and make arrangements to spend time together outside the convent walls."

Chagrined, Belinda did as she was told.

ROBERT, LORD DRAKE
14 February 1588 † *A village of Alania, in northeastern Essandia*

Seolfor, inexplicably, is not there.

It is unquestionably the right village, though its name is of little enough importance that Robert has never learned it. He recognises faces who were children when last he visited, faces that now have children of their own. He recognises a handful of remaining elders, and one of them, a man who must be in his nineties by now, ancient indeed by human standards, recognises Robert in return. They do not speak; they never have spoken, but this is a small village and strangers are remembered. That the old man nods a greeting is enough; even if Robert thought his own memory faulty, oddly, he trusts the elder's.

He passed through last night, in hours small enough to not yet be morning, even if the clock had struck twelve and begun anew. No farmers were up, save one he heard from a distance, tending to a cow bellowing with pain. Dawn had been a long way off, and Seolfor lived on the southern edge of the little town, far enough away that he only belonged to it by proxy, and because there was no other village farther on to claim him. Robert had taken no time to examine the township; it was only after discovering his third to be missing that he retraced his steps to make certain the village was the right one. Now, too surprised to be angry, he stands arms akimbo and looks around the village square as though an answer, or better still, Seolfor, might appear.

"You're looking for the white one," says the old man.

Robert turns to blink at him, hesitating in answering because he's uncertain he understood the words. They speak a different dialect in this part of the world, almost a different language, and while Robert's Essandian is flawless, he's had far less encounter with Alanian. "I am," he says after a moment. "Do you know where he is?"

"Forty years." The old man swings his head from side to side, almost a scold. "It has been forty years, or nearly, since you've come, and you think oh, the old man, he'll know where the white one's gone. Forty years is a long time, queen's man. In forty years your friend might be dead."

Robert says "No," because the other thing he might say is too tongue-tangled, too astonished. It's only a moment before he does say it, of course, because Robert Drake is unaccustomed to being genuinely surprised, and toothless nonagenarian village peasants are among the last he would think could surprise him. "Queen's man?"

The old man does that head-swing again, and for the second time Robert feels scolded. Robert can't remember the last time he was scolded, even by Lorraine. She has a knack for putting him in his place, yes, but that has a different aura to it. He finds a smile fighting for exposure at the corner of his mouth, perversely pleased by the old man's audacity.

"They're rheumy, you think, the old man's eyes are rheumy, filmed with blue and thick with age, but eyes aren't the only way to see. I saw it when you came here the first time, and the second, and the mark is stronger on you now. You serve no king."

"It's true." Intrigued now, Robert comes to crouch before the old fellow. He's sitting on a stump in the morning light, his village spread around him as though he's a king himself. A staff weights one hand, and his knuckles are gnarled and heavy around it. He was a big man once, near to Robert's size, and though the years have taken as much breadth as hair from him, there's still a hint of muscle in arms lined with flab. "Does it matter who I serve?"

"Pah." The old man turns his head and spits. "We in the mountains bow our heads to no one. What do I care if you choose a king or a queen, when what matters is you honour a crown." His gaze, rheumy indeed, narrows. "But a queen's man here means war's on the way."

"Does it?" Robert is accustomed to the people of this world unfolding their thoughts to him all unknowing. A few do not: royalty, largely; people who have learned to protect themselves in every aspect, for betrayal is so easy to invite. Children hurt very young: he has met a handful of those who are walled up and whose thoughts are not his to sip. They have perfect counterparts, others hurt in just the same ways, who bleed all their thoughts and hopes and fears over everything, emotionally exhausting. Most, though, most humans, are easy to steal a thought from here and there. Even Belinda, unexpectedly, has learned that trick.

This village elder is one who cannot be easily read. It's age that's done it in him, age and practise and guile, Robert would say; this is an old man who has learned charm and cleverness and can still flirt with the young girls without making them cringe, for what he's after is a bit of cheese or some fresh cream, and he's willing to barter it with a story or a pretty word. He's the sort of man Robert thinks he'd like, if he were given to the luxury of liking people. Mostly, though, he doesn't allow himself that indulgence, because human lives are brief, and his purpose much longer and greater than any of their transient appearances on this world.

And when he fails, when he learns to like and to love, it is almost always a woman who is his weakness. The titian queen of Aulun is one such, but in this moment it's Ana di Meo's dark eyes and rich colouring that comes to mind. There was a too-dear price paid for that fondness, too dear for all involved. Robert is not a man made for regrets, but a deep cut lies across his heart in that matter.

He puts the thought away deliberately, bringing his full attention back to the elder, whose head is now bobbling as he produces a toothless grin and waits on Robert's mindfulness. "It does," he says when he's sure he's got it. "You carry war on your wide shoulders and in your heart." He leans forward and taps Robert on the chest, confirming Robert's thought that there's strength in him yet. "I can *see* it," the old man proclaims, then cants a suspicious eye. "Do you think I'm mad?"

"I think when the eyes cloud the mind learns other ways to see," Robert says with utter honesty. When the eyes cloud, or when the body is weak, needs must, and while the people of this world rarely have such need, Robert believes in those few who have the second sight and avoids them. He places a hand on the old man's shoulder, a comrade's touch, then straightens so that his shadow falls and blocks sunlight from the man's eyes. "You're too old for war, grandfather. It'll be your grandson's children who go to fight. Let its thought pass you by."

Acerbically, the old man says, "Said like a man with no grandchildren. Leave our village, and take your war with you. Your white friend left before the winter. Went west and south, he said, to go north and east. Follow him, and leave us be."

Half-bidden by the old man's words, Robert turns west and south, looking beyond mountains and plains toward a river he cannot see, and further still toward the ocean that river leads to. "West and south to go north and east. Did he say where in the north and east?"

"The city of canals," the old man says, and now there's irritation in his sharp old voice. "There, and Cordula, to see the prince of God. You're in my sunshine." He's become querulous, age and temper making him a child. "Get out of my sunshine, boy."

Robert does so with a quiet smile. "Forgive me, old father, and thank you for your guiding words. I hope you have many more days of sunshine, and that war never reaches your doorstep."

"Pah!" The old man, sulky and sullen, waves his staff and hunches back against the wall, arms folded and eyes defiantly closed, denying any stranger in his village's midst.

Not until he's halfway to Aria Magli does Robert realise the old man was Seolfor.

5

JAVIER, KING OF GALLIN
22 February 1588 † *Isidro, capital of Essandia*

Wind caught Javier's hair and blew it into his mouth, warning that it had grown far too long. Rodrigo had given him a dour look or two; another such and Javier would make an outrageous claim, insist no blade would touch his head until Sandalia was avenged, Aulun's Reformation yoke was broken, and Belinda Primrose was dead. Might, less dramatically, claim that he intended to set a new fashion, as was his right and even his people's expectation, as their new king. Besides, he thought it suited him: his face was long and narrow, and he imagined the fullness of longer hair gave him more presence.

Black banners still fluttered in Isidro's streets, blocking out the city's clean white lines. Javier tried not to see them: they might have been painted with his mother's face, so clearly did their presence bring it to mind. Emptiness tore his chest apart, breath too little to fill it when he thought that she was gone. He was a man grown, but he'd stood in her shadow without complaint or ambition, and to know he would never again see her was a fist squeezed around his heart. Tears blurring his vision, he tried to look beyond the banners, all the way to Lutetia, so many hundreds of miles to the north. He should be there; he should have long since left his uncle's palace and returned home, a king in mourning, to guide his country toward inexorable war. Sandalia had been loved, and the Gallic people would rise under Javier's banner. Still, he lingered, more afraid—despite the priest—to go than to stay. Lutetia was not home, not with his mother dead, and in Essandia at least he could make believe that all was as it should be in the country of his birth.

"Jav?" Marius, speaking quietly, as though he knew he would be unwelcome. Javier bit down on a cutting reply, miserably aware that of all people, Marius should be most welcome at his side now. They were all but brothers, and Javier had no one else so close to him in this foreign land, not even Rodrigo. Marius had not turned away when his witchpower had been exposed, had not condemned him as did the priest, nor encouraged use of that power as a weapon, as did his uncle. He remained what he had always been, steady, loving, gentle; a pillar whose strength could not be whittled away. Javier should be grateful, and turn his confidences to Marius's ears, and no others.

Instead he saw promises broken and hopes shattered in Marius's face, and could hardly bear to look on him. The very ability to forgive which made a man like Marius so vital to a man like himself seemed a cruelty, for Javier couldn't absolve himself. Not for taking Belinda from Marius; not for loving Belinda himself; not for allowing that love to make him so blind as to cost his mother's life. There were terrible moments when Javier thought he must hate his old friend, and if he could hate Marius, surely there was no place or person in the world whom he might love, not even himself.

Not until he was certain all of those thoughts were schooled out of his expression did Javier turn, smiling, toward Marius. "You look out of place here, Marius. Isidro's architecture swoops and soars, and you're so very solid."

"Grace has cast me amongst the stars, my lord. I should look out of place. I came only to bear news of your mother's death, and should have returned to Lutetia long since." So, too, came the unspoken conclusion, should Javier have, and his lingering presence in Isidro was all that kept Marius there. Guilt twisted Javier's belly and he faced the city again, unwilling to meet Marius's eyes.

"I'll go home soon." The promise sounded sullen and childish. Javier heard Marius's footsteps, then felt the weight of his friend's hand on his shoulder. Unusual, that; Marius, of his three lifelong friends, had always been the most formal. Sacha was nearer in rank to Javier, so less concerned about niceties, and Eliza had never given a damn, not from the moment she'd tumbled from the palace garden's walls and broken both her fall and Javier's arm by landing on her prince.

"You hear nagging in my words, my lord, but I mean none. Javier, so much has changed this past six-month, and not the least of it you."

"I've only been exposed, not changed."

"No, my lord," Marius said with unexpected firmness. Javier, surprised enough to glance Marius's way after all, found resolution in his brown eyes. Resolution and worse, compassion. "Beatri—Belinda—changed us all, in ways for better and worse."

"Better?" Javier demanded. "What did she make better? We're scattered to the winds, the four of us, and my mother is dead, and Gallin's treaties with Khazar are laid bare. In what manner did she improve any of our lots?"

"Eliza unbent far enough to accept a hand in turning her dressmaking skills to a profitable business," Marius replied without hesitation.

"Out of jealous rivalry."

Marius ignored him, admitting, "I can see no especial good she did Sacha, but no matter how it ended, she gave you joy for a little while, my prince. She gave you joy and she gave you a confidence that none of us had ever seen in you before. You've always been easy with power," he said more swiftly, when Javier would have spoken. "It's a prince's right and his domain. But with Belinda at your side you shifted toward action. With all the years we've known each other I think it's safe to say you had not often shown an impulse to act. I hadn't understood why, but I do now. I can't imagine the weight of your *witchpower* burden, nor the relief you must have felt at finding you were no longer alone. It would have given me strength as well."

"And you, Marius? What good did she do you?"

Marius gave a little sigh and let his hand slip from Javier's shoulder. "I suppose she stole some of my innocence. My belief in happy endings. Perhaps that's not a gift, but then again, it may well be. I've always been the young one amongst us," he said without heat. "In experience if not in years. Sacha's more cynical and Eliza was born poor, and you've had the weight of a kingdom on your shoulders all your life. I've been the frivolous one, but all children must grow up one day."

"And what if I need that innocence at my side?"

A beat or two passed, Marius catching his breath and holding silence, so clearly an indication of searching for words that Javier smiled. "Go on, Marius. We've been friends long enough that whatever you have to say won't break the bridges. You've been rude to me a time or two before."

"It's not rudeness that stays my tongue, my lord, but fear."

A cold blade sliced deep into Javier's chest, the contraction of his heart lurching and faltering around it. His breath cut short, knife slicing his lungs into pieces and leaving black spots dancing in his vision. He reached for power instinctively, wanting the soothing silver moonlight to make things right, wanting Marius to buckle under its weight and say only the things Javier wanted to hear.

Shame gurgled in his belly as he recognised the impulse. A lifetime of trying so hard not to influence his friends, and yet when they spoke words that sparked alarm, he acted, without thought, to dominate.

He ought not have scoffed at Belinda for her terrors.

Only when he was certain the witchpower was controlled, no longer desiring Marius's acquiescence, did Javier dare speak. "Fear? Of me?"

"Fear that you have found that necessary innocence in another." Marius's voice was soft, so soft it could betray nothing of envy, of doubt; not even of fear: so soft it revealed all of those things in its attempts to keep them hidden.

"Tomas," Javier said, and in the saying knew he should have said "the priest." A quirk ran over Marius's mouth, commentary enough, and Javier pressed his eyes shut, reveling for a moment in denying the world.

But doing so brought Tomas's golden gaze to his mind's eye. Forthright, honest, faithful, full of challenge and confidence that only became murky when Javier exerted his will and bent the priest's thoughts away from the thing they both held to be true: that Javier was devilspawn, and his gifts a danger that ought to be turned away from, not embraced.

"He's my confessor, Marius, nothing more." Javier had no strength to put behind the assurance, his answer as soft as Marius's own voiced fears.

"What he is," Marius said unexpectedly, "is beautiful. And he bends beneath your power, Javier, but he doesn't break. I saw it in that first moment in your uncle's chambers. He doesn't have Beatr—Belinda's strength to stand before you and hold her own, but he has some of that, and it draws you. I suppose if I was certain everyone would bow to my whim I, too, would hunger for those few who didn't."

"He cannot replace what you are to me."

"Nor can I be what he is to you," Marius murmured all too in-sightfully. "Will you take him with you when you go, Jav?"

"Yes." The answer came too easily, and with it came regrets for how his certainty would make Marius feel. "When I go, it will be to call an army. I'll need Cordula's support, and I can find little bet-ter assurance of that than Primo Abbate's son, a priest of the church, riding at my side. I'll still need you," Javier added more qui-etly. "If Sacha has always tried to be my impetus, you, Marius, have always been my steady right hand."

"And Eliza your heart?" Marius wondered aloud. A note in his voice said he knew he treaded dangerous ground, and said as surely that he'd cast caution to the wind for these few moments of time stolen with his prince.

"Eliza is Gallin, Marius. She is of the people, and if she is my heart, if I am hers, then I have the people behind me and we can-not fail in Aulun." Sudden clarity rang in the words, making a path through torpor and reluctance. "I have to find her."

"My lord?"

"I have to find Eliza." Understanding came in bursts, clarion calls that brought the first vestiges of joy and enthusiasm back to his life. "With her at my side, Gallin will support me and we'll take Aulun before winter. It hinges on her, Marius. I'm a fool for not seeing it before." Javier turned to his friend, seizing the merchant's broad shoulders. "I let Belinda turn me from pursuing Liz as fast and far as I needed. She'll be my angel, my icon. I cannot do this without her."

Something dark filled Marius's eyes, so rare as to be unrecogniseable. "Your angel and your icon, standing at your side. That's a queen's role, Javier, not a friend's. Will you marry her?"

Javier swayed, regret taking the strength from his body. "I can't, Marius. I can't, even if I would. She's barren. A king must have heirs."

Darkness deepened in Marius's eyes, finally making a name for itself: bitterness—and that was not an emotion Javier's friend was given to. Incongruously, Tomas's golden gaze leapt to Javier's mind, washing over Marius's familiar features and wiping away disillusion. Repelled, Javier released Marius and stepped back, struggling to understand whether his revulsion was born from putting Tomas in Marius's place, or from the acid look in his friend's face. "Do not look at me so, Marius. I cannot help being what I am."

"A king, or cruel?" Discontent marked Marius's features a few more long seconds. "She deserves better, Jav. If you'll make her an icon, make her a queen as well. Get a bastard child on some serving wench and give him the throne, if you must, but let Eliza have her due."

"You would make me Henry of Aulun?" Javier snapped.

Exasperation flickered over Marius's face. "Yes, my lord. I would have you bed and wed half a dozen women, get girl children or sickly boys on all of them, and give up Cordula and Ecumenic faith for the Reformation. I would have your only strong heir be a woman as redheaded as yourself, and I would watch her rule Gallin and Essandia both for thirty years with her iron fist. Javier, forgive me. I love you, but I wonder if this *witchpower* isn't addling your mind. Henry had one strong son out of marriage, and would have made that son king had the lad not died a-hunting. Eliza would understand that decision. I don't know that she'd be willing to play the part of your angel of battle without a taste of something sweeter to carry her along. You know they already call her the prince's whore."

A fist flashed out and knocked Marius aside, so fast his cry was as much astonished as pained. He fell back with his hand against a bleeding lip and stared at Javier, who stared at his own betraying hand in turn. "Marius, I . . ."

"It is of no matter, majesty. I spoke too boldly, and beg your pardon." With grace powered by infinite hurt, Marius knelt.

"Don't. Please, Mar, don't." Javier reached out to draw Marius upward, but the merchant man offered no extended hand, no gesture of peace. Nor did Javier deserve one, but Marius's refusal sparked infantile pique. Grinding his teeth against doing further damage, he muttered, "I didn't know, and had never dreamt of hearing such vile words come from your lips, even in the form of reporting them. My hand flew quicker than my thoughts. It doesn't matter anyway," he added desperately. "Liz has been gone for weeks, and no one knows where she is."

"I know." Marius spoke to the flagstones, a wonderful precision in his words. Cutting precision, Javier thought: damning precision. That was the price, then, of Javier's thoughtless action: he would be mocked with knowledge he didn't share, mocked with the end of innocence, for once upon a time Marius knew nothing of keeping secrets.

Anger flared again, this time with less physical intent, but far greater heat. "How can you know? Did she tell you where she was going? Why have you not said so?"

Marius, still with exquisite precision, said, "No one asked me, my king."

"I shouldn't have had to ask!"

Marius looked up, careful picture of mild surprise. "One friend's confidences ought not be broken at the unspoken whim of another's, my king."

Javier, through his teeth, said, "Stop calling me that."

"Yes, your majesty."

He had learned, Javier thought through a hazy tide of silver fury. Marius had, in the last weeks or months, learned to play a game of politics that had been beyond him. Had learned to use words as weapons, and not the blunt heavy ones that Javier might have expected, but subtle as a blade slipping between the ribs. And if his once-sweet Marius could make such a play on words now . . . suspicion snagged him, bursting forth in a demand: "Did you bed Belinda?"

That same black bitterness slid over Marius's face. "Never."

"You're lying!"

"There's no purpose in lying to a man with your talents, majesty. Any truths you want of me you'll have." Resignation and regret were in Marius's voice, creating a weariness that alluded the death of something Javier didn't want to see die, and felt powerless to save. Marius should be kinder than that: Marius should be the rock he had always been, and make an allowance for Javier's loss, his fear, his unwelcome gifts.

All of Javier's hurt and anger rolled together into the same question, demanded again: *"Did you sleep with Belinda?"* It was necessary that he know, more necessary than abiding by the rules of friendship he'd imposed on himself a lifetime ago. He let his silver-stained willpower roll toward Marius, certain that it, at least, could pull truth from his friend's lips, if all the years of friendship could not.

And, as with everyone save two—three, including the priest's knack for brief resistance—he felt Marius's will sunder to his own. It was not a breaking, but a softening; an agreement, willing or not, to do Javier's bidding. He was unaccustomed to using his gifts to draw answers out; usually it was enough, more than enough, to have agreement from those around him, so his own path might be clear. But the one was merely an extension of the other, an expectation of verbal response rather than a simple shift of intentions.

Marius met his gaze forthrightly. "My lord king, I did not." There was too little acquiescence in his voice for Javier's liking, too much awareness of what the king was doing, and no forgiveness for it. Until that moment Javier had imagined that Marius, more than Sacha or Eliza, understood the need for his friends to be truthful with him. But an understanding friend wouldn't be so resentful at sharing the truth, or so insulted that Javier sought it through whatever means he must.

And though perhaps under duress, Marius had given his answer in bold flat words, no room for equivocation in them. Relieved, and with fresh hope for their friendship, Javier asked, "And what about Eliza, Marius? Where is she?" Witchpower still danced, expecting truth, though its significance faded in Javier's mind. Marius would tell him anyway; Eliza was too important to them both, and to

Javier's cause, for Marius to keep such secrets. When they spoke of Eliza, the witchbreed magic spun between friends could be ignored.

"I would look to Aria Magli, your majesty."

Delight sparked in Javier's breast. "I shall. I'll go myself, through Cordula, and there will ask the Pappas for his blessings in our crusade against Aulun. Thank you, Marius." Javier offered his hands again, friendship re-sealed with the gesture.

Marius, with more delicacy than Javier was accustomed to seeing, touched his palms against Javier's, putting no weight on them. He climbed to his feet wholly on his own, not accepting any help from Javier, even when Javier grasped his wrists and made as if to pull him to his feet. "My honour, your majesty."

Released from Javier's astonished grip, Marius took a step back, bowed more deeply than he had ever done before, then crossed the rooftop and trotted down the stairs, leaving Javier alone with his witchpower.

"I am becoming what I've most feared." Javier spoke from the shadow, the words his only herald. At the chapel's other end, Tomas straightened from prayer, crossed himself, and turned toward Javier. Setting sunlight broke through rich stained glass from the rose window above Javier's head, spilled down the simple chapel aisle, and by chance a swath of lemon light fell across Tomas's face, lighting his impossible eyes to golden fire. In that light he was everything a priest should be: holy, rapturous, serene. A sob rose up in Javier's chest, fighting to break free. Rather than give it voice he knelt, far too aware that as king he should kneel to no one save God, and then only if the Almighty seemed worthy.

Moments later Tomas's fingertips touched Javier's forehead, a cooler touch than Javier expected, as though his enflamed colours took the very heat from him. The dead felt like that, though there was more give in the priest's hand than there would be in waxy cold death.

Tomas moved away, footsteps quiet against the empty floor, and a door opened, then closed again. Javier got to his feet, following Tomas to the confessional still with the weight of sobs burdening his breath.

Sheer creamy silk woven with gold thread in the mark of the cross hung between priest and confessor. There was no anonymity to it, but there was never meant to be. Rodrigo and his priests knew each other by name, by touch, by breath; so, too, did Javier and his own confessors. The pretence at privacy, though, made dark secrets and sins easier to whisper, and so the gauzy fabric did its duty. Tomas moved on its other side, crossing himself; Javier did the same, then gripped the window's edge.

Tomas's cool fingers slipped over his, reassuring, confident, his touch everything Marius's should have been. Javier whispered, "I barely know the name of my sin" to their entwined fingers. "Pride? Pride, yes, because I can't bring myself to apologise to a man when I've done him wrong."

"Royalty rarely needs to, though God looks kindly on the humble, even when they are kings. Perhaps especially when they're kings," Tomas murmured. "You speak of Marius."

Javier flinched. Thin silk kept him from seeing any expression, but he felt his own must be stained with guilt so clear Tomas would feel it pushing through the barrier. "Yes."

"And you wish for me to relieve you of choice, and order you to make amends. If you are directed to do so by God, you are absolved of your own weaknesses. That would satisfy your ego, would it not?"

Shame burned Javier's cheeks until the air around him felt chilled. He said nothing, answer enough, and Tomas's response was mild. "I will not do it. I will not for two reasons, one being that it is not our Lord's duty to make your days easier or your pride less puffed."

Javier locked his gaze on the window's edge again, hating the truth in the priest's calm voice more, even, than he had loathed watching Marius walk away a stranger. "And the other?"

"If you fear what you're becoming, it tells me you're growing more reliant on your devil's power, Javier. Marius does not condemn your use of it, and I cannot in good conscience direct you to his side. I would keep you from those who encourage its use, that you might yet find your way back to the light."

"You would keep me from my uncle, then."

"If I must." Implacable sorrow edged Tomas's voice.

Javier choked on the sob that had taken up residence in his chest, twisting it into a raw miserable laugh. "What if I have no choice? What if this is the path I'm meant to walk?"

"Did the Son have a choice in the gardens the night of his betrayal?" Quiet confidence imbued Tomas's question, cadence of a lecture spoken from the heart, lowering Javier's eyelids as he rocked with the words, trying to embrace them. "Knowing that his friend went to betray him, might he not have walked away and lived? But he did not, and that was an act of free will, God's greatest gift to us, his weak mortal children. No matter how dark the path may look, no matter how easily it leads to Hell, we may step off it at any time, and find ourselves in God's grace and bosom. I believe you wish to reject this power you carry within yourself. God will welcome you when you do. God does welcome you, Javier. He forgives us all our sins. You've told me you've spent a lifetime struggling against this power. Perhaps God's grace has allowed you to succeed for so long."

"And now?" Javier's voice shot up with despair. "Now has He abandoned me?"

"The world around you has grown harsh, my son. Your mother's death, the new crown you'll soon wear, your friends scattered and a lover, traitorous as she may have proven, lost. These are none of them easy things to face, and to confront so many so quickly . . . we all stumble, Javier. We stumble so we may rise again and trust God with each of our days."

Javier gave another laugh, as broken as the first. "I want to believe you. I want you to be right. Who made you so wise, priest? You're no older than I, but you speak my fears and offer answers with more clarity than I can imagine."

"You've been given a heavy burden, one that has perhaps clouded your sight. The weight I carry is lighter," Tomas murmured. "Do not fault yourself, but rejoice that God has put us together so I might ease your way."

Javier blurted, "Will you come with me?" and cringed at the childish hope in the question. He was a king; he ought to command, not plead. He was a king, and that was something he shouldn't have to remind himself of with every breath.

"Come with you," Tomas echoed, clearly surprised. "To Lutetia?"

"To Aria Magli, to seek a friend. To Cordula, to seek the Pappas's blessing. To Gallin, to seek an army, and finally to Aulun, to seek—" Audacity caught his breath, but he finished with all the confidence he could muster: "To seek a throne."

"You would return Aulun to the Ecumenic fold," Tomas breathed.

"I would." Saying such things to Marius or Rodrigo carried less import than whispering them to a priest. Rodrigo had Aulunian plans of his own, and Marius would never betray him.

Uncertainty sharpened that thought, making it stand out. The Marius he'd known would never betray him, but that man seemed gone now, reforged by bitterness. Javier shook away the idea, denying it. Marius would forgive him; Marius always did. He would find a way to make friends again. A few months of strain, a disagreement or two, did not undo a lifetime's brotherhood. Satisfied with his promise to himself, Javier tightened his hand on the window and waited on Tomas's answer.

Only when the priest's silence lingered too long did Javier become aware of the sick fast beat of his own heart, of the way each breath was cold and heavy in his chest. His fingers, too, had chilled, and wanted to tremble, though they were denied that pleasure by his grip on the windowsill. Always pale, they were bloodless now, and a growing certainty rose in him. If Tomas demurred, he would have to make the beautiful young Cordulan see that Javier required his presence, and could not accept a refusal. He had only to meet Tomas's eyes and hold them long enough, and the priest would buckle under his desire.

"Persuade your uncle to wed," Tomas said abruptly. "Persuade him, and I will join you."

DMITRI LEONTYEV, THE KHAZARIAN AMBASSADOR
22 February 1588 † *Alunaer, the queen's court*

Dmitri Leontyev hasn't seen Lorraine of Aulun in nearly a quarter century. He's been in Aulun, even in Alunaer, many times in those intervening years, but he's never crossed paths with the Titian queen, and would not now do so except he's under orders from his imperatrix, Irina of Khazar.

Twenty-five years ago, or near enough to count, Dmitri played the part of priest to more than one Echonian queen. Lorraine had a fortitude Sandalia did not, or perhaps she simply already had a lover; she'd certainly been sharing her bed with Robert Drake even then. That was as well with Dmitri; he'd preferred Sandalia's curves to Lorraine's narrower form, and had been in no hurry to hitch up his cassock and use the Aulunian queen.

Still, she is a queen, and has reason to remember the events and people of twenty-five years past. Consequently, Dmitri has taken some trouble to disguise himself. His beard, the easiest way a man might change his appearance, has grown out, and it itches ferociously; he has never, and never will, become accustomed to that. But it's the least of his changes, and the rest are *witchpower*-born. He is thicker and shorter and altogether less elegant than his priestly shape; than the tall narrow form that's his more or less naturally. He moves differently, with less grace, and everything about him is a little coarser, for all that he's meant to be Irina's so-civilised ambassador. That's the price of being Khazarian, he thinks, though Khazarians are no more brutish or loutish than any other race of men on this planet. Still, their cold northern country and their tendency toward heavy beards and heavy bodies hidden under thick coats and enormous furry hats makes it easy to think of them as more animalistic.

He has, at least, forgone the hat; Alunaer is warmer, and the black of his coat with its brightly-coloured epaulettes is enough to mark him as the ambassador. Lorraine's court is crowded, and the curious are giving Dmitri and his contingent enough berth that they've become an island of their own in the busy hall. No one wishes to be seen fraternising with them until Lorraine's actions make it clear how they're to be treated, and so instead they're made a spectacle of.

That's all right; he'll do his duty here, and then return to his warm house and Belinda Primrose, who is far more interesting to him than the intrigues of Lorraine's court.

Lorraine makes her entrance before he can pursue that happy

consideration much further, and for a brief while the court is in chaos, everyone milling and moving to situate themselves as rank and need demand. It's not hard to move through them: they make way for fear that either taking offence or lingering will associate them with him, and no one wants to risk seeming either ally or enemy to the Khazarian ambassador. Within a few minutes, Dmitri is at the base of the throne dais, on one knee as he murmurs, "Dmitri Leontyev, majesty, ambassador from the imperatrix Irina—"

"Yes." Lorraine interrupts, looking him up and down. Dmitri, who cannot allow himself the luxury of a smile, finds one struggling to crack his beard. Irina is beautiful, but Lorraine has all the disdain in the world at her command, and with that single word, with the flat cutting glance that accompanies it, she tells her court precisely how Dmitri and the other Khazarians are to be treated. "Yes," she says again, and it's as cold as a Khazarian night. "So we see. We are sure we shall have time to discuss your concerns in the near future, sir." She looks away, and it's as if Dmitri and all the men with him have simply disappeared, not just from her interest, but the entire court's. He could command their attention with the witchpower, no doubt, but even the most ostentatious display might fail to garner a reaction from Lorraine: she is, he thinks, that good, and besides, if she did react it would be to have him burned.

Still refusing himself a grin, Dmitri bows very low and backs out of the queen's presence before turning and leaving the court, all the better to pursue Belinda Primrose.

BELINDA PRIMROSE
22 February 1588 † *Alunaer, capital of Aulun*

It was said change came slowly, but that, Belinda thought, was only at the highest levels of the world. Revolution came slowly; the killing of a queen came slowly. Those were vast changes, needing preparation and forethought, but in the moment, death was quick; in the moment, revolution became inevitable.

All the changes in Belinda's life were changes of the moment. Robert's impetuous midnight arrival at his estates, setting her on the path to assassination; her world had changed with the swing of a carriage lantern. Recognising Lorraine and her own status as the queen's bastard; du Roz's death; denying Javier's will and drawing his attention; the name Belinda Primrose being called in Sandalia's audience hall, where she should only have been known as Beatrice Irvine—all the work of a moment.

Dmitri's presence, and what it awakened in her, what it made her feel, both in sensuality and power—those, too, were moments, and each of them sparked with change, taking her from what she had been and thrusting her toward what she might be.

He had come for her five days out of seven, with only a single day's delay between their late-night assignation and his securing her exit from the convent during the day. They had gone not to public places, nor grand manors, but to a humble warm home an hour's walk from the abbey. An hour there, and an hour back again: in late February, that gave her eight hours of day-lit freedom in which to study.

The first day had been full of questions: *where is Robert Drake, how did you know to come for me, what am I, what is happening,* and of those, Dmitri had ignored the last two and not known or cared the answer to the first. *He will come,* he'd said, *he'll come when he's done with whatever task he's set himself.*

The second, though, the second he looked down at her, took her chin in his fingers in a touch too possessive for Belinda's liking—and that was a thought she'd have never afforded herself less than a year earlier—and said, "I knew. I've been waiting to come to you all of your life."

When he released her the memory of his touch lingered on her skin, soft and warm and laden with either threat or promise; even with her witchpower senses stretched to their fullest, Belinda couldn't decide which intent was the greater.

He had not touched her again the first day, had only tested what skills she had and, if he mocked them, did so without words. Accustomed to reading men well, his internalised reactions unnerved Belinda until she recognised in them her own stillness. Then she drew her own centre of untouchability around her, and for the first time, Dmitri smiled.

Robert had smiled in just such a way once, the Yuletide after she had begun her game of stillness, a few months before Dmitri's presence had awakened the witchpower enough to hide her in plain sight. There was approval in that expression, appraisal and perhaps surprise, but most of all approval. For her nine-year-old self, Robert's approval had meant the world; now, at nearly twenty-three, Dmitri's suggested that she could yet learn to hold her own amongst the strangely powered men around her.

She returned to the convent that night flushed with excitement and nagging desire. Not uncontrolled: she had learned in Lutetia the extraordinary price of allowing her magic to rule her, and had not yet let it undo her again. Witchpower was hers to command, not the other way around. Anger could fuel it as well as passion, and that passion was so difficult to control angered her: the cycle worked for a few days, at least.

The third night, a bold young sister came to her, drawn, her captured thoughts whispered, by what she saw as the light of faith burning in Belinda. Belinda, thinking of Nina, sent her away, but when she returned two nights later, had no will left to deny her. Witchpower blocked the door against the nosy abbess, and a hand over the young sister's mouth quieted her gasps. The girl gave back as good as she was given, and if Belinda whitewashed her thoughts so the night seemed nothing untoward, at least she had not terrorised her, nor taken the raw, ruthless advantage she had of Nina. Perhaps it was only a modicum of control, but it *was* control.

The next morning Dmitri laughed at her. "You think sex is power," he said while she gaped, caught between insult and astonishment. "I suppose for what you are, what's been made of you, and what this place expects, you're right. But it doesn't feed your witchpower, Belinda. It doesn't revitalise it."

"Don't," she said, startling herself with the word. His eyebrows flashed up and she curled a lip, already cursing herself for giving something away. "No one calls me Belinda. Not since I was a child."

"You haven't been Belinda since you were a child," he replied mildly. "You've been Robert's Primrose, his thorned and lovely assassin, and you've been every name she's taken to make herself a success. But there's a core of you that owns the name, and who are you if you don't claim it?"

She had not slept at all, after that. Oh, Dmitri had worn her down, training her in the witchmagic in ways she'd never dreamt. She had taught herself not to flinch at pain: he taught her to draw heat away from a burn or blood from a cut, and how to make damaged flesh heal. Her power stuttered and stumbled, injuries filling with rough-seeming witchlight, as though it was nothing more than unpolished amber. It would do, Dmitri finally said in disgust, so long as she had only herself to treat.

When he tired of her faltering ability to heal, he turned her toward the alteration of wind and clouds, and that came more easily: witchpower and wind alike billowed, pushing at the world, searching for places it had never been. Clouds only marked its passage, making the invisible possible to see. Dmitri made a sound of approval, but his acid comment from the morning lingered, following Belinda back to the convent and settling around her with a weight of its own. When the young sister came to her cell again, Belinda sent her away, too caught up in thought to indulge in base desires.

She knew herself; she knew her place. Witchpower fought with that knowledge, pushed her beyond the space she had been carved for. That had been a discomfort, one she'd struggled against, citing loyalty and duty. Not just citing it, but feeling it so deeply that denying it was physically revolting, even when her heart might have guided her elsewhere.

In the cold dark of her convent cell, she allowed herself one low laugh. Her heart had never been a guide; until Javier she wouldn't have imagined it could be.

But with a few biting words Dmitri had thrown a lifetime's focus into question, far more sharply than Belinda would have ever permitted herself to do. It was almost intriguing when voiced by someone else, as though hearing her own uncertain thoughts spoken aloud by another gave them a legitimacy she wouldn't have dared assign them.

The hawk-faced witchlord was right: Belinda Primrose was almost no more than a creation, an idea that barely existed, and yet it was all she had. Robert called her Primrose in honour of a memory that had never been: Rosemary, his sister, Belinda's supposed mother. If she were to give herself a proper name, it might be Belinda Drake, or if she dared reach all the way, even Belinda Walter, for Lorraine held the higher rank in that assignation, and should it ever be legitimised, it would be Robert whose name would be subsumed.

She had always known what she was. That *who* she was might not be the same question had never struck her. She rose after a sleepless night, offered devotions that meant nothing to her, and clad herself in modest clothing so that she might go, for the seventh morning in a row, into Alunaer with the man who played the part of her father.

"How can who I am and what I am be different?" she asked when they reached his house. Other mornings they'd spoken quietly, but these were the only words she'd said beyond the show of pleasant greetings that they had, without discussion, settled on as the right show of emotion for the abbess.

Curiosity lifted Dmitri's eyebrows and he took her wrappings like a gentleman's servant might, hanging them so the spread fabric might dry in the heat while they studied. Belinda nodded her thanks and took herself to a padded chair by the fire, sitting to frown into the flames. Frowning: she had, it seemed, given up on all pretence of stillness. Instead emotion rode her raw, after nearly fifteen years of bending to her exacting control. Perhaps that was how, who, and what she was could differ: they had once been flawlessly intertwined, but that bond was crumbling.

She kept her gaze on the fire, finding it safer than Dmitri's slim body and hazel eyes. Aware that she broke a week's ritual in studies, but more interested in the discussion of who she might be than what she could do, she said, "Belinda Primrose is the only name that has ever belonged to me, and I don't care for you using it because it *is* mine. I have little that is."

"Ah." Dmitri came to crouch beside her chair, fire lighting his eyes and making craggy shadows of his face. "Shall I call you Primrose, then, or Rosa, or Beatrice, or any of the other masks you've worn?"

"How can they be masks if they're all I've ever known? There's nothing below them, only duty, only loyalty."

"And the witchpower." Dmitri rested his hand on her knee, then straightened again. "When I saw you in Khazar there were only the first two, but the third is born in you now, Belinda. Does it not change who you are? Does it not change what you desire, and what you find yourself willing to risk to have it?"

"But I have no . . ." Words failed her, turning her hands to a strangling gesture. "I do not exist, Dmitri. I'm not my mother's child, my father's daughter. I'm not a prince's bride. Whether I have *desires* or not, there's no path upon which I can follow them. I'm a servant, and—"

"You are a queen," Dmitri interrupted, voice sonorous. "A queen in the making, even if you must do the making yourself."

Witchpower awakened in her, a warm wash of light that spilled through her mind, heightened her heartbeat, tingled her fingers. Gentle warmth, not the compulsive hunger that it so often manifested as, and that seduction was more erotic than the burn. It stung, but sweetly, an ache of promise in her breasts and between her thighs. She had never in her life stoked ambition. To hear it offered heated the centre of her, deepened her voice to throatiness that no man could mistake for anything other than an appetite for pleasure. "Dangerous words, dark prince."

Her hand crept toward his; touched it, then passed it to touch his hip as she turned her gaze up toward him. "Dangerous words," she whispered again, and then let truth damn her, damn it all: "I would hear more."

6

Dmitri knelt, which Belinda did not expect. Knelt, and made himself subservient to her, gave her the position of power. Men had done that with startling frequency this past year, from rough lustful Viktor to the prince of Gallin, and now this dark-haired, hazel-eyed witchlord whose powers and ambitions reached far beyond Belinda's own. The impulse to open her legs and command pleasure boiled up. She squelched it, crushed her thighs together instead, and swallowed a sound of sweet anguish at the spike of half-answered need it drove through her.

"Tell me more, Dmitri." Belinda turned her hands palm up, encouraging. Dmitri gathered them in his own and lowered his face to their touch, almost reverent. Soft witchpower, ebbing and flowing within Belinda, gave her tastes of his emotions: not words, not the way she could steal clear thoughts from others, but an abiding sense of the peaks and valleys of what he felt.

The show of reverence was built on truth. It was not, perhaps, so profound as he pretended, but respect underlay the gesture with no cynicism, no ploys. Familiarity jolted Belinda; she had felt that same respect inherent in her father, bound up in an inexplicable combination of Lorraine Walter and a monstrous creature of silver scales and sinuous shape. The one made sense, though its depth had shocked her: men, in Belinda's experience, paid lip service to high regard and remained smug with confidence of their own superiority. To find her father's heart as true as his words had lain outside of imagination.

As did the other bewildering images she'd stolen from him, so far outside imagination Belinda had chosen not to dwell on them. Had chosen not to try to understand what Robert had told her she would not, and had instead grasped what she could: that Robert was incapable of surviving without that fathomless streak of esteem, and that she now felt a similar channel in Dmitri. It ran less deeply in Dmitri than in Robert, tempered with a different ambition, but it still lay within him, as much a part of him as his breath or bone.

"My father says I have a purpose." Belinda bent over Dmitri's bowed head, her lips almost against his thick black hair. Witchpower sluiced through her, contained within something like the stillness. Shaped by Belinda's will, rather than shaping it. Left to itself it would rage, but bound, it rolled slow and deliberately tantalising. Her heart pushed golden light with every beat, until she thought her fingertips would shine and illuminate Dmitri's hair. Force was unnecessary, when her ends could be achieved through subtlety. It felt right, and that rightness brought a flashing smile to her face. Lorraine, too, avoided force, instead teasing compromise and change out of delicate negotiations. It seemed a fresh and fragile link between mother and daughter, and Belinda took delight in it.

"Robert says someday I'll understand my purpose, but that for now it's enough to know I have one. I think your plans for me are different from his, dark prince. He has kept me all unknowing, stunting my power and then leaving me to learn its extent myself when it could no longer be held behind the wall in my mind. Will you do the same, or will you do me more honour? You call me a queen, Dmitri. You and I both know that it is your soul's duty to serve your queen in all ways, and as best as you can. You've already begun to teach me, begun nurturing my witchpower where Robert let me founder. Will you tell me his purpose, and yours, and where mine meets in the centre?"

Ambition and guilt wove together as she spoke, one part of her eager for Dmitri's lessons, the other still bound to the life she'd known. But then, Robert trusted Dmitri, and if the Khazarian witchlord had plans of his own, learning them was only part and parcel of what she had always been. The argument seemed a slender thread, yet enough to hang herself with. Hang herself, or balance upon, depending on how the wind blew.

Turmoil bubbled within Dmitri's mind, heavy in presence but unclear in detail. Belinda caught her breath and held it a long moment, waiting on Dmitri, waiting on her own curiosity, waiting to see how far he might go unprompted, and when he did not speak, gambled what little she had with all the gentle confidence at her disposal. "You come to conquer in your queen's name," she whispered. "You come to make this land yours, and not for Irina of Khazar. I know your secrets, Dmitri; I know the things I should not, so you need not bite your tongue and wonder at what you dare say."

Astonishment flooded all other expression from his eyes as he lifted them to meet hers. "How can you know?"

"From Robert, of course." Surprise lightened her voice, perfect artifice; there was no need to tell him she'd stolen near-incomprehensible images of invasion and conquest from her father's mind. Better to let him think Robert had confided in her, and to draw him out through illicit confidences.

Witchpower danced through her, unusually subtle, and with it came a daring thought: what she'd taken from Robert's unwilling mind might be improved upon by a glimpse of Dmitri's startled thoughts. She had failed to take words from him, but even pictures were a thing to work with, and so she let witchpower flow, searching for any unguarded idea in the witchlord's mind.

Nightmares came to her, fire pouring through the sky and a world so scarred by mining and ugly buildings it could hardly be her home. More half-caught ideas flooded with it, but she drew her fingers back from Dmitri's hair, trying not to flinch as her heart made a sick place in her chest. Too much truth went into the words "I don't pretend to understand," and she meant it, not only for what she'd gleaned from Robert, but for the too-dark and deadly pictures now swimming through her thoughts.

"I don't pretend to understand," she whispered again, and thought that at least there was purpose telling this truth: a lie twinned with honesty was a stronger one. "I understand very little beyond the idea you are harbingers of invasion, and that Robert refused to tell me of my part in this war."

"There will be no war, not with my queen, not with my people. Belinda—" Dmitri got to his feet suddenly, leaving her open to the fire and flushing with its heat. "You're familiar with brutish conquest, with all manner of violence. Imagine instead that you could take Gallin by slipping across the straits and offering work to its people. Imagine you could offer them salt and butter for prices far below what they might otherwise pay, and that what you asked in return was to be thanked in Aulunian rather than Gallic." He paced as he spoke, Belinda turning to follow him with her gaze, hungry to take her mind off the pictures she'd stolen. "Imagine you had a better way to harvest wheat, and that you would teach it to the Gallic people, school them in the improvements, but your schoolings were done in Aulunian. And then after that perhaps you have a better way to weave cloth for clothing, or you have better insulation to offer them for their homes, and you would teach them each of these things and in doing so make them a little more Aulunian with each new measure."

"Sandalia—well, Javier—would never allow it," Belinda said pragmatically. "He would see his country being stolen from him in bits and pieces, and retaliate with war."

"Yes." Dmitri turned, smiling. "But perhaps not if you had slow decades or centuries in which you might encroach upon Gallin and make these changes. Perhaps not if you only send one or two into a vast area, little more than missionaries, tolerable because they're so outnumbered."

"No one has that kind of time. Robert is aging well, as are you, but it would take generations to—" Belinda came to her feet with understanding. "You've fathered new generations."

"To guide and become the heads of state," Dmitri confirmed. "To shape our progression. Aulun is the heart of the Reformation church; Gallin and Essandia and Cordula all bond together to make the Ecumenic stronghold in Echon. Think, Belinda, if you had no reason to make war over religion, if you turned all those resources toward new ideas and technological development. Think of how the world might change."

"But Sandalia is dead. War will come." Belinda sank back into her seat, fingertips pressed to her temples.

"War will come." Dmitri crossed back to her, knelt again, this time with less subservience and more passion in his changeable gaze. "And from it we must make peace at any cost."

"Robert sent me to Gallin to sniff out a plot for Aulun's throne, to find an excuse to depose Sandalia. Why would he do that if he wanted the Echonian states to work together, to make peace and prosperity?"

"Because war is a time of innovation. It begins a creative process, and for Echon to move forward, it must make certain leaps that peace will not bring. It's only with those changes that gentler sub-version can begin to take place."

"And what is the end?" Belinda dropped her hands, frowning. "You serve a . . ." The alien images stolen from witchlord minds rose up again, bewildering, and she set her mouth, choosing words with cautious precision. "A queen from a foreign land."

Humour glinted in Dmitri's eyes, telling Belinda her careful choice of words betrayed how little she understood. But he nodded, and she took a steadying breath before continuing. "The purpose of ruling a land is to gather taxes and tribute, to mine its salt and gold and iron, and to call on its men for armies when the need arises. Is this your queen's purpose?"

Dmitri made a moue, a small throwaway gesture. "It's what I would offer you. My queen will never come here, no more than Lorraine might go to the Columbias to look on the red savages."

Each of Belinda's heartbeats became a knife's blade, cutting fascination and fear into separate things. Witchpower pooled in the silence separating beats, warming her blood, urging her to seize what was offered. Duty lay in the contractions and releases: duty to Lorraine, duty to Robert, and a never-imagined question of what her duties to herself were danced between them. "Then you would make me a queen and a vassal both, paying tithe to a monarch I would never see."

The words descended around her like snowflakes, each light and thoughtful, barely there and yet building to a white cloud that could break wagons and roofs with its weight. She looked within, searching out how ambitious witchpower reacted to the idea: how it responded to putting herself on high, but not quite at the pinnacle of power.

To her surprise, it lay satisfied, whispering *this will serve; you will serve,* in contentment. Belinda absorbed that, looked for meaning in it, and found what she sought.

It was not enough.

Oh, it was *more* than enough, had she been one raised to expect a throne, had she been born to the privilege that Javier de Castille knew. She might have accepted becoming queen and vassal both, had she been born to that kind of duty. But she had not been, and there was sudden secret delight in expecting more of herself, of Dmitri, of the world itself. There was a game afoot, and she had yet to see how the board was laid out. With careful clarity, Belinda murmured, "No."

Shock rose off Dmitri in a wave, so quick and hard Belinda was glad she'd returned to her seat. Within her, matching Dmitri's shock with its own, witchpower surged and turned the world yellow. Belinda denied every outward example of what it took to rein that power back in: she did not allow herself to clench her jaw or tighten her fingers on her chair's arms; didn't permit her spine to straighten or her stomach to clench. She remained in repose, relaxed and calm in the face of twin witchpower storms.

Unlike Javier, though, Dmitri didn't batter her magic with his, didn't pound on it until she failed. It danced and sparked around him, black magic where hers was gold, where Javier's was silver; the colours, she thought, meant nothing, no more than an individual fondness for wearing a particular shade. One hue was not more powerful than another, or more dangerous, except in the skill its wielder had.

And now, for now, she was certain Dmitri still had the greater skill. It was only that streak of respect that kept him from dominating her the way Javier had, and it was that streak which made him more difficult and more fascinating to play.

"No," Belinda said again, and this time she let a tremble come into her voice. This would be easier with Javier, with Marius, with Viktor; with any man who was not Dmitri, her father's friend, subordinate, and partner. It would be easier with a man who believed women inferior, as Dmitri and Robert seemed not to do. A man such as that, one like those she knew, would assume her fear and uncertainty to be natural, and his place as her guide and teacher to be obvious. Dmitri *did,* she thought, believe his position as her teacher to be obvious, but only because she was untutored, not because she was incapable.

And it would be easier with a man she'd lain with, because despite what the witchlord thought, sex *was* power. It deepened the link between Belinda and her lover, made stealing thoughts and guiding behaviours easier to accomplish. Perhaps she could unlearn that, but in the now, it was the weapon she had at her disposal. "I cannot, my lord. I am not bold or skilled enough, and I am far too alone. What you suggest, should it fail, rips away what little structure I've known. I have Robert, now. I have my duty to the queen. Perhaps it seems like nothing to you, but they are all I have. I will not risk it."

Furious witchpower boiled through her body, searching for a crack in her armour: searching for a way to burst free and assure Dmitri that every word she said was a lie, that she would be driven, will she or not, toward the ends he suggested. But she was diamond, or better yet granite, too hard to be broken, too solid to be seen through. She lowered her eyes, not because she was afraid her gaze might give her away, but because youth and fear and penance and apology could all be read into that minute piece of body language. She lowered her eyes, so she only heard, did not see, Dmitri's approach, and when he touched her it was gentle, as though she had become fragile. His fingers stirred her hair, nothing more, before he murmured, "You are not alone, Belinda."

"You are different, my lord." Belinda put a crack into her voice, kept her eyes lowered, waited on the weight of his hand changing; waited on his inevitable question: "Different?"

"You were rough with me in Khazar. Impatient, almost angry. Here, you have been . . . different." Now she glanced up, one brief look. He stood at her shoulder, almost behind her, so his glimpse of her was all eyes and appeal; she could, when she wished, be appealing, even innocent. Then she spoke to the floor again, gaze locked downward and words soft with a deliberation she didn't intend him to hear. "Because of my witchpower waking, I think. Because of what I asked of you at the abbey."

"Asked," Dmitri said, amused.

Belinda ducked her head. "Demanded," she admitted in a whisper. "But you didn't give me all I asked for, so I know you acted of your own will, not mine. Perhaps that's a man's talent," she added with a bitterness she didn't feel. Javier, Marius, Viktor, had all done as she'd forced or connived them into doing, from speaking lies to toppling a maid to freeing Belinda from a prison she would never have left alive on her own. She had no fears for her own talents; her purpose was to offer Dmitri the upper hand, the guiding touch.

"It could be your talent," Dmitri said. She could feel caution shifting in him, examining her stance; examining, she hoped, his own. He had treated her with deference in teaching her, even when exasperation was clear in his voice and words. Belinda wished she could taste his thoughts, to see if they followed the path she hoped they might. "I was eager to awaken your power, in Khazar," he said carefully. "Now, with it aroused, I had imagined . . ."

He had imagined, Belinda expected, that she would become as she *had* become, testy and angered by men showing dominance over her, over the innate assumptions that she was weak and incapable, and that she should naturally subsume her desires to fit what was expected of her. She couldn't allow herself the luxury of holding her breath. It would give too much away, hint too strongly that she waited on a progression of thoughts and dared not move again until they'd been worked out.

She felt his conclusion in the way his hand rested in her hair. The touch had been light, asking permission; it changed, taking possession. Listening to stolen thoughts became unnecessary with that subtle change: it said that he had followed through to realisations that would be anathema if he had not watched how men and women acted together for so many years. Belinda allowed her head to tilt back a little under that new weight, acquiescing to it. Making herself the creature men expected her to be, as she'd always done: making herself, in the here and now, seem weaker and more biddable than Dmitri presumed she would be. Making her fear larger than her ambition, and her need for guidance greater than it was.

Anyone could reach, greedily, for power, snatching and grasping at it like the edges of a dream. But Belinda had been raised as a secret, a weapon hidden behind thrones and courtrooms and lies, and to retain that, to build on it, to hold in her grasp not only her magic but the ambitions of the witchlord men around her . . .

That was power.

She had time enough to learn under Dmitri's tutelage. He was of a nature to accept her word as law, but the weight of his hand in her hair said he was ready enough to be the master. The better she knew his talent, knew his mind, knew his ways, the better she could judge whether his goals were ones she might support. Her own witch-power wanted more of him, wanted more of her, but she was its master, whether it spiked or throbbed with interest when appealing favours were laid at her feet. She had learned more of Robert's purposes in the last few minutes than she had in an entire lifetime previously, and that gave her a better sense of the game that her father had never intended her to be a player in, but only a pawn.

He ought, she thought with razor-edged surety, to have thought better of her than that. For all his passion for his queen, both mortal and . . . not, for all his reverence of Lorraine and females, it seemed he thought of Belinda as a tool, something to be manipulated and used. There would be more satisfaction by far in coming into her own than there could be in anything given to her by Dmitri or by Robert, be it the crown Dmitri made noises of or Robert's more ambiguous goals. They could all be manipulated and taken into hand. She had only to show patience, and patience was something she was very good at.

It was only the shell of a plan, but shells could be filled. If nothing else, Sandalia's death proved that, but indeed, all of Belinda's life had proven it. Du Roz's startled gaze in the moment before he fell to his death flashed through her mind; Gregori Kapnist's burgeoning illness, so much more rapid than arsenic could account for, and the death that had come on so suddenly it had earned Belinda an accusation of witchery.

Someday she would have to learn whether it had indeed been her will that had destroyed the Khazarian count's health, or if it had been a bad summer sickness and Belinda's good fortune in bedding him to exhaustion that had bound together to reach the same ends. Dmitri, who roused power in her, who had taught her rudimentary healing skills, would know the answer. Either way would do, but if it had been her new-birthed witchpower, then no man or woman in Echon could be safe from the queen's bastard.

Troublesome thoughts tucked aside, she allowed the tiniest catch of her breath as Dmitri's hand weighted itself in her hair. Submissive, fearful, excited, relieved: she could be all of those things without need of consideration, could use them to give herself into Dmitri's hands and see how he would mould her, without ever losing the core that was Belinda Primrose and belonged, at the end of it all, to no one but herself.

JAVIER, KING OF GALLIN
25 February 1588 † *Isidro*

Tomas's terms had laid heavily on Javier the past three nights. He'd held his tongue in meetings with Rodrigo, had held his tongue because with each breath he took he could not believe that Tomas's ambiguous phrasing—"persuade your uncle to wed"—meant what it seemed it must. Tomas knew more clearly than most just how persuasive Javier could be, and the young king of Gallin could not imagine the priest was suggesting he bend Rodrigo's will to match the church's.

Couldn't imagine, and yet could see no other possible way he might accomplish what Cordula and a dozen Echonian heads of state had failed to manage in Rodrigo's more than thirty years on the throne. The only wedding bed Rodrigo had ever seriously entertained had been Lorraine's, and that for the sole purpose of bringing Aulun back into the Ecumenic church. The Essandian prince's faith was all to him; for nothing less, not even for the certainty of his country's future, would he marry.

And Tomas had said, if not blithely at least with no apparent care for the impossibility of it, *persuade your uncle to wed.*

There was no witchpower practise tonight, as there had been every night for the month past. Javier had fought with Rodrigo over that, had finally thrown himself on God's own mercy: surely He could not want Javier squandering his gifts on unsuspecting forests and undeserving cattle. Better to accept what they now knew he could do, and save his strength for the coming war.

THE PRETENDER'S CROWN · 97

His uncle had eventually relented, and tonight Javier came to his chambers with a bottle of fine wine and the need to pick another kind of battle. He would not, he told himself, *would not* use the witchpower on Rodrigo de Costa, not for any reason, and even that adamant refusal sent a thin line of seething silver through him, as if the magic raged against denial.

Guards opened the door for him, ushered him into a warm room where an aging prince sat before an unbanked fire. Rodrigo twisted toward the doors, then chuckled and waved a hand toward a nearby seat. "You've a sour look about you, nephew. What's brought that on? We could burn off your temper with another bout of practise. Perhaps you've become accustomed to using your talents, and denying them sets the blood on fire?"

Bumps chilled Javier's skin, discomfort of fearing Rodrigo'd come close to the mark. Witchpower bubbled in offence and flattened under his grim denial as he scooped up cups to pour generous glasses of wine. "It's marriage on my mind, not power."

Rodrigo gave him an amused look and got to his feet when it became clear Javier would not sit. "You say that as though they're two different things. You're not yet crowned, boy. A wedding bed can wait a year or two."

"I'm Gallin's only heir, and yours," Javier said shortly. "If we're looking for delay, better to put off war, not weddings."

Rodrigo's eyebrows rose and he sipped his wine, trying poorly to hide amusement behind the glass. "Have you someone in mind, then? The Kaiser has daughters, if you've an eye for blondes, though the Parnan Caesar's girls follow the faith."

Silver-tinged exasperation flooded Javier. He tightened his fingers around the glass stem, obscurely certain that if he could keep himself from shattering fragile crystal, he could surely convince Rodrigo of what needed doing without witchpower coercion. "I'm not the only one who needs a wife, uncle."

Rodrigo went still, amusement draining away, then sipped again at his wine. "Don't tell me you've joined that harping chorus. I'm in my sixth decade, too old for such nonsense."

"You're in your sixth decade, and I'm your only heir, and you would have us all go to war." Javier's voice fluted high and broke, a humiliating reminder of his comparative youth. A sip of wine fortified him and cleared his head, and for a clarion moment he realised that, witchpower or no, Tomas's demand or no, he, too, believed that a marriage for the prince of Essandia was necessary. Neither Essandia nor Gallin, nor the Ecumenic church, could afford to lose their monarchs, and he was too fragile a thread to hang all hopes on.

Power flared, fueled by his sudden certainty. Javier grasped at it this time, not to roll Rodrigo's will, but to fill his own voice with passionate conviction. "I've never understood you or Lorraine in this matter, though in this one instance I grasp her motivations more clearly than yours. Marrying means putting a king above her, and losing control of what is now hers. You have no such excuse. No woman could wrest Essandia from you, and with this one exception, your piety has never made you foolish." Anger, more than humour, creased his mouth. "You're even willing to set aside any question of whether my own gifts are God-granted or devil-born because they're useful to you and to the ends you desire. So is a wife, Rodrigo."

His uncle's gaze sharpened on him again, marking clearly that Javier had used his name with no honourifics at all. "Think you my equal now, lad?"

"I think myself a crowned head of Echon. I have neither your wisdom nor your battlefield experiences, but I do have profound interest and concern over the Essandian succession."

"Do you not wish that throne yourself?"

Stupefaction rose up in Javier, blinding him with silver. "Do you think one throne is not enough for most kings? Oh, aye, an empire's an appealing thought, but I would be stable on my own throne before looking to yours. Nevermind *me:* you are about to go to war, and you will leave behind a people very nervous about their kingdom if there is no hint that you intend to do well by them. A marriage, even, God forbid, an unconsummated one, gives them hope. Do you not like women?"

Whether it was audacity or exasperation that drove the last question, Rodrigo's expression was worth any price Javier might pay for it. He might have been a cow, round-eyed and dull with witlessness, and despite his pique Javier laughed.

A backhand blow, much the same as he'd dealt Marius a few days earlier, exploded white light behind his eyes, littering it moments later with the red throb of pain. Head turned to the side, though he had not staggered, Javier touched fingertips to his cheek and found it split open, a divot of flesh marked by Rodrigo's ring of state. Dumb-foundedness had left the prince's eyes, replaced by rage and insult.

Javier found a thin smile and emphasised it with a mocking bow. "Forgive me, your majesty, my tongue has grown too bold." Then, with no more regret than he'd felt in speaking in the first place, he added, "It's a common enough question, uncle. You've had no faith-ful male companions any more than women, but a man, a king, of your age, without a wife or children? It's what people wonder."

There had been less of the knife twist in Marius's telling of what people whispered about Eliza. Shame shot through him, leaving a channel for anger: he had no reason or need to apologise to one of his own subjects, and kings did not belittle themselves with such talk betwixt each other.

"Are you through?" Rodrigo's voice was made of ice, colder and more distant than Javier had ever heard it. More ashamed than be-fore, and angrier still, Javier bit his tongue, wondering how he'd be-come the wrongdoer when he had held back witchpower temptation and used only words to make his arguments. Rodrigo, exuding calm and confidence, with nothing of a sulk in his stride, walked past Javier to open the door.

"What will you do?" Javier threw the words after Rodrigo in a shout, hearing a plaintive note where there ought to have been challenge. Rodrigo turned a disinterested gaze on him, then lifted his eyebrows at the open door.

Javier, witchpower rage boiling in his mind, stalked out.

RODRIGO, PRINCE OF ESSANDIA
26 February 1588 † *Isidro; the small hours of the morning*

The thought that rides Rodrigo as he closes the door on his nephew is a simple one: it appears he's made a mistake.

The admission's not a comfortable one for anybody, much less a prince of the realm. A king, in anyone else's terms, but old history keeps the Essandian royal line from naming themselves kings, though their women are queens. It's one part honouring ancient and pagan gods, and another part acknowledgment of the Maure peoples who conquered Essandia once upon a time. They have gone, for the most part, but they've left behind a racial memory of their ease in taking the westerly Primorismare country, and a recollection that, as rulers, they called themselves princes, not kings. Why solidarity with a conquering people seems important to Essandians, not even Rodrigo is certain, but he rather likes being the sole prince among the kings of this continent. No one doubts his equality, and in the end, that's all that matters.

Javier, though, might discount tradition and name himself king when the Essandian crown passes to him. The boy is unexpectedly arrogant, an aspect Rodrigo doesn't remember from his childhood. It may be his damnable *witchpower,* or it could simply be youthful fear, but it will not earn him any followers, and a young king intending on a war needs his people to love him. A young king who may become a young emperor needs far more: he needs blind passion from most and clearheaded, dogged loyalty from a handful. Arrogance will not earn him either.

And now, because the boy is arrogant, because he bears a cursed power, because his vision seems to end at the tip of his nose, because of all these things, for the first time in the thirty and more years he's reigned, Rodrigo finds himself genuinely considering the unpalatable possibility of marriage. There has always been Lorraine, yes; he would have married her out of duty to the church, but neither of them ever had any intention of stepping out that far. She has, in many ways, provided him with the perfect foil, for he couldn't seriously consider other offers while the endless negotiations with Aulun dragged on. But he'll no more marry the aging queen than he might marry beautiful young Tomas; neither could give him heirs, and if Javier has grown up a fool, Rodrigo may need an heir more than he believed.

The truth is that of the two—Tomas and Lorraine—Rodrigo would prefer to bed the former. He's known since childhood that a man's clean lines are more appealing to his eye than a woman's curves, but he's known as well that to lie with men is a shocking sin. He knows a few men who have struggled with this, and others who have embraced their doom, but for himself it has never been an especial difficulty. He sleeps with neither, not for purity's sake, but to keep his lineage uncluttered on the one side and to avoid castigation and guilt on the other. Whether God has given him this bent to test him or to tempt him makes no difference: Rodrigo does not succumb.

He is, for a moment, sharply aware of the parallel between his desires and Javier's magic. It stings him, stiletto pricks on his skin, and then fades. Such is the price for wielding power of any sort: it makes hypocrites of men, and Rodrigo prefers results over a consistency that cannot be maintained.

That, in fact, is one of his beloved church's weaknesses. It's slow to change, unsurprising given its size and age, but it demands its followers cling to consistencies that fly in the face of fresher knowledge. God's power and mystery are not lessened by science, to Rodrigo's mind, but are instead deepened by it. Still, it's Cordula's faith he walks in step with, not university radicals.

Irritable and temperamental, Rodrigo sends for Tomas del'Abbate. When the sleepy golden-eyed boy appears, it occurs to the Essandian prince that he might have waited until morning, but then, one of the benefits of being a monarch is arranging the world to his whim. Tonight he wants to talk to Cordula's young priest, and the only apology he'll make is pouring and offering the young man a glass of wine.

Tomas has brought a narrow satchel, the sort that quill and paper might be kept in: he is prepared for whatever Rodrigo might want, but he sets that parcel aside to accept the wine and a seat by the fire, and to huddle over both drink and flames. Rodrigo gives him a few moments to wake up, though he himself strides around his rooms like a man twenty years younger than he is. When he judges Tomas has had time to gather himself, he says, "What do you think of Javier?"

Whatever Tomas might have expected of a three o'clock rousal from bed, it's clear that question was not it. He straightens, momentarily agape, then visibly regains his centre, growing pensive. "He is troubled, your majesty, and if I may be bold . . ."

"You may," Rodrigo says, amused, because anyone who asks permission to be bold usually intends to be whether permission is granted or not. He rarely denies it, but once in a while there's entirely too much pleasure from an airy "You may not" and the chagrin on the applicant's face. Tomas, however, is Rodrigo's confessor, and a priest of the church, and might very well speak regardless of whether Rodrigo gave him leave.

"He's troubled, and you're not helping. His talent frightens him, as it ought, and you well know he should turn his back on it. Instead you have him explore its boundaries with intent."

"We have a war to attend to, Tomas." Rodrigo brushes off his own words and sets aside the royal persona for the singular; it is, after all, three of the morning, and these his own chambers, and this his confessor. Surely he may be himself now and here, if nowhere else. "I need what weapons I have. No, I meant what manner of man is he, to your mind? Will he make a good king?"

"He would make a better one if he were not tormented by this demon power. Each time he uses it he succumbs a little more. By the time your war is finished, there may be nothing left of your nephew to repair."

"I see." Rodrigo retires to his own chair by the fire, hands templed in front of his mouth and long legs spread out so his feet are close to the low flames. "And so we come to the matter of succession yet again."

Tomas doesn't move, but he seems to sharpen, as though only now coming fully awake. "Javier's indisposal puts two thrones at risk, majesty. Unless he weds now and fathers quickly, there's nothing to be done for Gallin, but you can still change Essandia's path."

Rodrigo's toe taps in the air, irritable twitch that ends when he asks, "And who does Cordula have in mind for me?"

He knows the answer, has seen the lists, has turned a deaf ear to many pleas, including Tomas's, that he consider them seriously. But this is their plot, not his, and he's put no mind to remembering names or faces. Nor is he surprised when Tomas is prepared, drawing a parchment scroll from his satchel and offering it over without commentary. Rodrigo takes it and snaps his fingers; the same servant who fetched Tomas comes out of shadows and lights candles, so Rodrigo can read.

An overwhelming number of the names are Parnan. Rodrigo lowers the parchment to eye Tomas over its top. "Could you find no Essandian noblewomen to litter my choices with?"

"Your faith has always been such that the Pappas thought you would be honoured by closer ties to our church," Tomas murmurs with a surprising lack of pomposity. In another that statement would have been ludicrous; from Tomas it sounds sincere.

Rodrigo says, "Mmf," and raises the parchment again, skimming the names. There are likenesses drawn next to many of them, all lovely, dark-eyed women with a sameness to their faces that says more about the artist than about his subjects. "And what would Cordula say if I found myself a round peasant girl from an Isidrian field and made her Essandia's queen?"

"Cordula would rejoice with the birth of your sons," Tomas replies evenly, and Rodrigo grins at the parchment.

"Beautiful *and* diplomatic. Your father must be proud, Tomas." He sees a shadow of action as Tomas crosses himself and murmurs, "I hope so."

"I'll consider them," Rodrigo finally says, once the list is memorised. He'll consider one or two, at least; the rest he's already discarded for family reasons, and he's not happy that there are so few Essandian women on the list. He can do better, he believes; he's spent a lifetime in negotiations, and while he'd marry Lorraine for his church, he's less enamoured of marrying some slip of a girl for the same reason. If he must wed, then there will be something brilliant made of it; that, at least, he can give himself.

"Send for my scribe," he says, a dismissal, and Tomas rises, bows, and leaves to do as he is bidden, while Rodrigo sits alone with a parchment full of women who are meaningless to him.

7

Nothing, not one thing in the past eight weeks, has gone as Akilina Pankejeff intended it to, not in its entirety. For others this is a matter of course, simply the way of the world, but she is dvoryanin, a grand duchess of Khazar, and she is accustomed to having things her own way. She has the men she wants, when she wants, at least, until untimely death takes them. That's happened often enough in her thirty-three years of life that behind her back the servants and even some of the courtiers call her Baba Yaga, the black witch.

There are worse fates than being a witch, as Akilina sees it.

There is, for example, boredom. She is too high-ranking to be thrown in a dungeon cell, and so instead she sits in a tower with a single window, thirty feet above the ground, her only chance of escape. She has been six weeks in this room, and looks on the long drop with more favour every day, but not that much. Never that much.

Six weeks since she shared a cup with Sandalia, queen of Gallin, both women grimly determined to drown the tensions of a stolen treaty in the aroma and flavour of an old and fine vintage. Sandalia sipped first, then asked a question; Akilina waited on drinking to reply, and before her words were finished, the petite Gallic queen lay writhing and dying on the floor.

Akilina, naturally, screamed. Flung the betraying cup away and dropped to her knees, uselessly grabbing at Sandalia's shoulders, trying to hold the woman down, trying to comfort her. That was how the guards had found her, and since then she has been locked in a tower room, pacing its small area and, she is certain, slowly losing her mind.

She has money and power enough—and perhaps beauty enough, though hers is a sharp beauty, challenging, and not all men are eager to face it—to have bribed guards to let her send carrier pigeons back to Khazar bearing news of Sandalia's death and, by proxy, news of the treaty's failure. Whether she'll be rescued from her tower by a missive from the Khazarian imperatrix or whether she'll be left to rot, an apology in body if not in words, she does not yet know, and so Akilina is trying to earn enough favours that she might obtain release on her own.

Favours, she is finding, are in short supply these days.

The worst of it—worse even than the boredom—is how clearly she can see the fall she's taken. She was very nearly outplayed on Sandalia's courtroom floor, in the matter of Belinda Primrose. Bitchy little Ilyana paid for Belinda's secrets with her life; rough-hewn handsome Viktor had faltered in the face of his onetime lover's pleas. Akilina had counted on neither of those things happening, and yet had held a secret back, waiting for the right moment to expose him.

Capturing Robert Drake, Lorraine's longtime lover and once Akilina's, had been a triumph. It had, indeed, been the very last thing that had gone right, and so Akilina savoured it more fulsomely than she might have otherwise.

She had seized him through a woman, of course. A striking courtesan whose dramatic colouring let her wear outrageous hues to great effect. Akilina's tracker had learned the courtesan's name, and had found a trail bringing her to Lutetia; it had not, after that, been difficult to locate the woman calling herself Ana Marot, who was known to Robert Drake as Ana di Meo, and who was his spy and his whore.

Like anyone, Ana di Meo had a price, and hers was finery: an easy life, a duchy from a grateful crown, enough cash to see her to the end of her days. For these things she was willing to write a letter to Robert Drake, calling him to Gallin and into Akilina's grasp. For that, and not her occupation, Akilina thought Ana di Meo a whore, and the whore had betrayed him in court. She had named Robert Drake her lover and named "Beatrice Irvine," whom she knew as Belinda Primrose, his daughter. That, *that,* at least, had gone as it was meant to.

Ana di Meo was not supposed to die two nights later, in all likelihood at Robert Drake's hands. No, the courtesan was meant to live, and Robert had been meant to rescue copies of the Khazarian-Gallic treaty before Sandalia moved so hastily as to destroy them. Akilina wanted that leverage, wanted it most particularly because Sandalia had offered hospitality that amounted to arrest. Until all matters international were settled, Akilina would be Sandalia's guest. The queen insisted, and such insistence could not be refused.

Nothing, Akilina thinks for the ten thousandth time, has gone right, and she has nothing but her own thoughts going in circles around it to keep her company. She is therefore both startled and grateful when the heavy locks on her door are undone, hours away from any meal time. Like any woman would, she rushes to her window seat, snatches up the mindless embroidery that's all she has to occupy her time with aside from her thoughts—and the latter are preferable, in her opinion—and looks the picture of a settled and calm woman when the door opens to reveal the prince's confidant and lifelong friend Sacha Asselin.

Somehow, he is not who she expected. Akilina lowers the embroidery into her lap and looks across her prison at the stocky young lord, and wonders not so much what he is doing there, as how his presence can be turned to her advantage.

Then she's on her feet, curtseying, and sees through her eyelashes that he sweeps a bow deeper in proportion than her curtsey. She's pleased, as he is by far the inferior in rank, and indeed she need not make knee to him in any fashion. But she is the prisoner here, and will accord him any slight honour that might help her to walk through the door behind him as a free woman. In fact, she'll gladly accord him a great deal more than that, and regrets she had no warning of his arrival so she might have enhanced her charms.

"My lord Asselin," she murmurs from her curtsey. "You give a poor woman gladness by visiting her lonely cell."

Sacha snaps his fingers at the guard, who closes the door without interest, leaving them alone together. Akilina straightens, not bothering to play at demurity any longer; Asselin likes women who bite, that he may bite back all the harder. She says, lightly, "I thought you had abandoned me," and he barks laughter, as rough a sound as his bite is hard.

"I've been waiting for word from Javier. For anything," he says, and there's bitterness there. Bitterness is a tool Akilina can use, and she makes note of it, though there's only interest and a hint of sympathy in her gaze. "Anything that might be worth bringing to you."

"And waiting long enough that no one wonders at why you come running to my poor prison door." That he's waited shows more wisdom than she might have assigned him, even if it's meant week upon week of drudgery for her. She retreats to her window seat and pats it, inviting. "Come. Our plans have gone awry and I have faith you've found a way in which to fix them."

"Our plans. *Your* plans." But Sacha comes to sit beside her, and Akilina clucks her tongue.

"I'm only a woman, Sacha. A woman with ambitions, perhaps, but you're Javier's right hand, not I. All I am is Irina's ambassador to Gallin." That had not been her plan, not after Gregori Kapnist's death. She'd intended on retreating a while to Aria Magli, taking herself away from Khazarian politics until whispers of her witchcraft had faded a little, but instead a host of riders had come after her, and she had found herself an emissary where she'd never looked for such a duty at all. It is Irina's way of controlling her, but Akilina has no objections. It has offered the opportunity to approach Javier's closest friend, and through him begin a scheme to wed a throne. It's a little thing, truly, the desire for safety. That's a wish she made early in life, with her father's death and her mother's remarriage. Those lessons and others have long since taught Akilina that the safest position is one of power.

And Sacha Asselin's ambitions make him an easy mark. She puts her hand on his thigh and leans in, trying for a winsomeness that isn't natural to her. If he were wise he would move from under her touch; instead strong muscles relax, invitation for her hand to go where it will. "All. All, and yet you're one of the few, man or woman, whom I've seen move boldly. For years I've watched Echonian politics creep and crawl along, a chessboard full of mild players afraid to take a risk."

"But I'm Khazarian," Akilina murmurs. She's guessed some of this, but this is the first time the ambitious young lord has spoken so freely. It's the venue: locked in the tower there can be no spies, no one who might overhear his intentions and report them back to a wary king. Only the guard is beyond her door, and that door is made of heavy oak: words will not pass through it.

"Khazar borders Echon's eastern states, and is an empire to be reckoned with. Gregori Kapnist had an eye for the empty throne that sits beside Irina Durova." Sacha gets out from under Akilina's touch after all and strides a few steps away before turning on a heel to stare down at her.

She tips her head, invitation for him to continue, and something not unlike a snarl pulls his features out of line. He's not handsome, his features a little too puggish and his hair too sandy with curls. Nor is he ugly, not by any means: indeed, he's appealing to look on, somewhere between cherubic and impish. Now, though, he's got the devil in him, and his easy charm lies hidden.

"Kapnist had his eye on the throne, and you had your eye on him. More than your eye. Had he lived, you'd be the voice breathing in his ear when he sat beneath the imperator's crown."

Akilina lifts a shoulder, lets it fall. "Perhaps. Or perhaps you give me too much credit, my lord." He doesn't: he gives her precisely the right amount, or possibly not enough. Irina kept Akilina close out of caution, not friendship, but in doing so was obliged to make at least an appearance of taking the dvoryanin's advice. With her ear and Gregori's both, Akilina would have held tremendous power in her homeland. Gregori's death put paid to that plot.

In that light, she realises things go her way less often than she likes to think. She considers that, then puts it away again; it doesn't matter. What matters is the attempt, and her own confidence that she'll win herself a throne or the power behind one as she advances through Echon and Khazar's societies.

"The Khazarian alliance is a good one for Gallin," Sacha says aggrievedly, as though it's Akilina he must convince. "With Gallin on Echon's western border and Khazar on the east, the combined armies and navies could crush the land between until an empire is made of it all. If Beatrice hadn't been in the way—"

"Belinda," Akilina murmurs, but it's of no import. "His mother never intended for Javier to marry her anyway. The treaty you had such high hopes for bedded him down with young Ivanova. Hardly the throne I hoped for, my lord."

Sacha waves a dismissive hand. "She's a child, and treaties can be altered. You would have no trouble replacing her in his affections and gaining yourself that coveted crown."

"And you, my lord, from all of this you get nothing more than the satisfaction of seeing your prince elevated to emperor? Is that your dream?" Here, Akilina is genuinely curious. The motivations of others rarely concern her, but with nothing much to think on in the past weeks, it's a question that's danced through her mind. "Or are you like me, willing to be kingmaker if you cannot be king?"

"I want power, not a crown. I've been Javier's friend our whole lives. I can see the constraints on him. Give me a seat at the head of his council table and I'm more than happy. Give me that and a bonny lass or two for pleasure and I'm happier than a king might ever be. Besides, Jav's got no ambition of his own. Someone's got to have it for him, or he'd sit quietly waiting for the world to take notice."

He falls quiet, still standing in the middle of her cell, and Akilina waits in silence until curiosity wins over a second time. "You didn't come to share stymied plans with me, my lord."

"Ah." Asselin regards her a long moment. "What price would you pay to leave this place? Whose cock would you suck, dvoryanin? Whose prick would you lift your skirts for, if it meant leaving your prison?"

"You are here" is her reply, a hint of humour in it. If he means to shock her with crudity, he will have to try harder than that: sex is a game she rarely loses at, and she is in most ways surprised that she has not taken Asselin to bed yet.

It's only later, when he's used her thoroughly, and the heat of his seed is still throbbing in her womb, that he leans over her and breathes, "I have a letter from Rodrigo of Essandia asking to take you to wife," and Akilina Pankejeff realises that this game, she has lost.

JAVIER DE CASTILLE, KING OF GALLIN
23 March 1588 † *Cordula, capital of Parna and heart of
the Ecumenical faith*

Two weeks had passed since he had last used the witchpower. Two weeks of travel, of prayer, and of friendship rebuilt with Marius. Javier smiled, a fragile expression, at his own reflection in a glass mirror. It hadn't been so hard, after all, to knock his shoulder against Marius's and admit his own fault in the distance that had grown between them. Reconciliation was made easier still by a point of gossip neither could bear to leave alone: the cow-eyed, sheep-brained Essandrian woman Rodrigo had chosen as his bride.

He had, so far as Javier and Marius could tell, taken utter leave of his senses. The girl had no political allies, no wealth, nothing at all to make her worth the marriage bed. Nothing save broad hips and large breasts, at least, but even so, Javier shuddered at the thought of bedding a woman so dull in wits. He had accepted his uncle's charge to sail for Cordula and beg the Pappas's blessing on the marriage as much to be on his way to Aria Magli as to avoid having to stand at Rodrigo's side and watch him exchange vows with a woman not bright enough to remember what words were hers to say during the ceremony. With Marius and Tomas at his side, Javier had taken sail a full two weeks earlier, and now stood fidgeting his finest garments into place mere hours before meeting the Pappas, the father of his holy faith.

For all that time, he had abstained from the witchpower. Surely that was enough time for its mark to leave him, as the mark of too much drink might leave a man who has renounced it. No one had ever seemed to see the power that rode beneath his skin, but he had never before faced God's right hand in human flesh. If anyone could, the Pappas would be able to see Javier's magic without it manifesting.

And if he saw that Javier bore the mark of the devil, then he would rightfully cast him out of Cordula and the church and from his throne, and so he could not be allowed, in any way, to see the damnable gift that was Javier's burden to bear.

Two weeks was enough. It had to be enough. Javier clenched his fists, relieved that he had stood strong against his power and had not used it to try to shore himself up, that he had not flexed it against Tomas or any of the crew as they'd sailed from Isidro to Cordula. The only moment of folly had been in playing with Marius, and even that he had tamped down upon, denying it. It was enough. It had to be.

So long as Tomas held his tongue, did not force Javier's hand by condemning him to the Pappas, to the church, then the quietude in which Javier had held his magic would hide all sins, and the Pappas would grant blessings on each and every point that Javier asked for.

"Are you ready?"

The question startled Javier; he had not noticed the manservant's departure, nor the silence of the room as he'd sat alone in it. Tomas stood in the doorway, black-cassocked and solemn, and when Javier gestured, he entered, coming to stand before the uncrowned king. He looked holy, with soft black curls around his face, and impossible eyes shining with goodness. Javier got to his feet, hoping to throw off some of Tomas's effect, and asked, "Shouldn't you wear your hair in a tonsure?" Nothing could take the beauty from the square strong lines of Tomas's face, but the religious haircut might help distract, and that, Javier thought, would be welcome.

Tomas grinned. "I'm a priest, my lord, not a monk, and I hope God will forgive me for the little sin of vanity which is grateful for that distinction." His smile faded. "Javier, there is something we must speak on before you see the Pappas."

The wings of panic that he'd soothed leapt to flight again within Javier's belly. "I have done everything I can to deny it, Tomas. I've not used it, not acknowledged it these past two weeks, not since I've left my uncle's side. You know they'll put me to the stake if you tell what you've seen."

"I do know." Tomas's eyes darkened, turning almost brown. "And you know my duty as a son of the church."

"Tomas." Javier heard desperation in his own low voice. "Please, I beg you to support me as I struggle on this path, not to thwart me. I am a king without an heir, and heir to another throne. I cannot allow myself to be branded a witch and burned. I need your strength, priest. I need your belief in me. Do not make me stop you."

"Make you," Tomas whispered, eyes darker still and proving him equally troubled. "I will not make you do anything, but I know you must accept God's light in any way that it's offered to you. Better to burn on earth than in Hell."

"Easy words for a man not facing the pyre." Javier rolled his jaw and stepped back from Tomas, knocking askew the chair he'd risen from. "I beg that you do not betray my weakness," he repeated tightly. "I am desperate and frightened, but I will not go to the Pappas with witchpower dancing on my skin. My fate is yours, priest. My life is yours."

He stumbled over the chair as he rushed from the room, sending it tumbling, but there was no sound of a fall. Tomas had caught it, Javier supposed, and hoped that single gesture gave shape to the priest's intentions toward Javier, too.

TOMAS DEL'ABBATE
23 March 1588 † *Cordula, capital city of Parna; the Lateran palace*

Tomas has had audiences with the Pappas before, granted largely because his father is Primo Abbate, whom everyone expects to take the white when this Pappas leaves his earthly prison and ascends to Heaven. He has also met the Pappas on many occasions, bowed to kiss his ring and receive benediction without specific purpose; this, too, is because of his father, and Tomas is in all ways grateful for these gifts. They are more signs that God is kind, which, until Isidro and Javier, he never doubted.

This, though, is the first time Tomas has been part of an envoy, not visiting the Pappas for his own purposes, but to support another. It is in all ways less alarming to play this part rather than to stand in the Pappas's presence on his own behalf—in all ways save one. Tomas is young, and should not carry a man's fate in his hands, most particularly a man who he is ostensibly there to support. And support him he would, without hesitation or fail, if that man were not beleaguered with the *witchpower* that Javier de Castille commands.

Javier did not steal Tomas's will this morning before coming to the Lateran palace. He could have, could very easily have done, and as they walk through marble halls lit with exquisite stained-glass windows, as prisms of colour fall down upon them and change mere humans into creatures of fae with their blues and reds and greens, Tomas wonders if it would not have been much wiser of Javier to have done so.

But it's trust that Javier is showing—trust, and his own determination to set the devil's magic aside. Tomas understands, and yet as they enter the Pappas's presence, is still uncertain of what path he will choose.

The Pappas's audience hall is more dramatic than any throne room Tomas has ever seen. It's easily ten times the height of a man, like a great cathedral, and all the tremendous arches and lines bring the eye to the solitary throne at the far end, where sits a man resplendent in white. He is, indeed, the only thing in the room of so little colour: everything else is brilliant to the point of bedazzlement, but it is appropriate that God's voice on earth should wear simple robes in unadorned white. The Pappas in his hall is an awesome sight, and Tomas notes that Javier does not hesitate or falter, though his breath catches. Lesser men have fallen on their faces and wept at simply crossing this threshold; Javier is made of sterner stuff, and for an unworthy moment Tomas wonders if it is the witchpower that sustains him.

The Pappas rises, which he does not always do, and greets Javier first with the ring to be kissed, and then with an embrace and kisses for the young king's cheeks. Javier turns ruddy with pleasure, unattractively: blushes do not sit well on his ginger-born skin tones. He is given a backless chair, one step below the Pappas's, and they speak for a few minutes of comparative inconsequentialities: Rodrigo's health, the Pappas's sorrow over Sandalia's death. Javier smiles on discussing the one and becomes grave over the other; that, then, is the Pappas's cue to murmur, "And you are here, I think, for blessings, my son. What might I ask God to grant you this day?"

To Tomas's surprise, the often-arrogant prince slips from his chair to kneel before the Pappas, and hope bursts in Tomas's heart. If Javier is willing to bend knee to the father of the church, perhaps his desire to put the witchpower behind him is genuine, and Tomas might dare hold his tongue on the dangerous topic. He doesn't want to see Javier burn; he has seen men sent to that fate before. It may be better than allowing their souls to be condemned to Hell, but it is not a good death.

"I would ask so many blessings you will think me bold, Father," Javier whispers. His Parnan is flawless, as though he was born to the tongue; so, too, is his Essandian, and Tomas is sure the prince has many other strings to his language bow. "I would beg for your prayers for my mother's soul."

The Pappas puts an age-spotted hand on Javier's head. "Do not beg for this, my son. Such prayers are gladly made, even without the asking."

Of course they are; Tomas knows that Javier knows this, and knows, too, that the uncrowned king is playing a game of proportions. It's well-handled, and Tomas wonders briefly if that would relieve Rodrigo, or only irritate him. Very likely irritate him, as it will be only a matter of hours before Rodrigo has taken the cowlike Essandian girl as his bride, and for him to learn now that for all his faults, Javier *can* be a diplomat . . . well, it would not make the situation any easier.

Discomfort trickles down Tomas's spine as he considers these things. Rodrigo has, perhaps, caved too easily, after a lifetime of refusing to consider a marriage bed. It's a thought that should have come to Tomas earlier, but until now, he's been full of youthful triumph at the prince's decision. He bites the inside of his cheek and casts a glance upward, seeking guidance or reassurance: anything that puts quiet to the question suddenly in his mind.

Javier's voice does the job, asking his next boon. "I bear glad tidings for all of us, holiness. My uncle Rodrigo has finally chosen to be wed—"

It is only then that Tomas becomes fully aware that there are others in the hall, the Pappas's Primi, those bishops who select and ordain and guide him in matters more mundane than God. A clamour rises up, delight and astonishment, and Tomas glances to his left and right, discovering more than a dozen crimson-clad men have appeared just out of his line of vision, standing back to make a half-circle around the petitioners. Now that he knows they're there, he half-recalls hearing quiet footsteps after their own, but overall their presence is a surprise, and his heart's gait leaps with it.

Javier, it seems, either knew they were there or has most wonderful control. He waits just long enough to speak again, waits for their questions and comments to begin to fade before his voice rises to command attention. An odd surge of pride fills Tomas's chest, confusing him; he has no reason at all to be proud, or not, of this young king.

"Rodrigo has chosen to marry on this very day, finally moving in haste to answer the topic of succession that is such a concern to all of us. He has chosen his own bride, a woman of remarkable aspect," and there is not a hint of irony in Javier's voice as he says that. Tomas wonders how long it took him to settle on a phrase that suggested one thing without ever saying it at all, "and of unquestionable faith. It is his sorrow that he cannot beg your blessing himself, Holy Father, but I would ask it for him, that his union be one of contentment and of many strong children. Will you bless them from afar?"

Because Tomas has met the Pappas more than once, he sees in the Holy Father's eyes something that he perhaps should not. A smile of benediction graces the old man's mouth, and his hands rise and make the sign of the cross with grace and deliberation as he speaks words of blessings on a marriage taking place far away. But in his eyes there is the slightest thread of irritation, and Tomas believes he knows why.

The greater number of names on the list of Rodrigo's possible brides were Parnan, many from Cordula herself, and yet the Essandian prince has broken rank and is marrying a woman of his own selecting. It is difficult to be infuriated, because he has at last agreed to a wedding bed at all, but it is easy to be less than pleased, when Cordula believed this gesture would make its hold on Rodrigo absolute. Tomas ought not be torn between loyalties, but he sees a little humour in Rodrigo's tricks, and has a touch of sympathy for the Pappas whose control is not without cracks. Still, he's wise enough to keep that from his face while the Pappas completes his commendation. For a moment silence reigns in the hall, and Tomas wonders if they are done.

"I would beg one last boon, Holy Father." Javier lifts his eyes to the Pappas's, and caution trickles anew through Tomas's belly. He doesn't know what Javier will ask, but he feels that it will set something in motion, something that can perhaps never be stopped.

Briefly, very briefly, he gives thanks to God that he is permitted to be here to see such things, and only after the fact does he remember that he has also been made to keep secrets through someone else's will, and wonders at the price of inclusion.

"I go from Cordula to seek a bride of my own," Javier says, and his voice is strong now, liquid silver with passion. "To seek a bride, to claim my throne, and then, Holy Father, to make war in my dead mother's name to reclaim Aulun from the Reformation church. My plea to you is that you would bless the marriage I will make, bless my sword so it might carry God's freedom to the heathens, and for your hands to place a crown on my head that all might know I am chosen by you and by Heaven for this duty that I fear is mine to bear."

There is no crown in the Pappas's hands, and yet they come down on Javier's head as though they hold one. It is benediction, it is honour, it is confirmation, and it is as though God Himself has touched Javier's brow, for a bolt of silver so bright it bleaches all the colour from the room explodes outward.

Voices cry out, but Javier surges to his feet, shining, yes, *shining* with what must seem to all to be God's light. He seizes the Pappas's hands and kisses his ring again and again, while cheers, first of astonishment and then of excitement, begin to ring in the massive audience hall.

Beside Tomas, Marius kneels, slow action weighted with respect and, to see his face, sorrowful resignation. Javier is lost to him, Tomas thinks, but his gaze returns to the king of Gallin, and he knows that much worse is true.

Javier is lost to them all.

ROBERT, LORD DRAKE
23 March 1588 † Aria Magli, in northern Parna

In Aria Magli, many miles to the north, hairs lift on Robert Drake's arms and he turns southward, frowning across a distance too great for eyes to see. After long moments, discomfort fades and he lowers his gaze, lips pursed as he finds himself wondering, wondering, wondering.

8

Rodrigo, prince of Essandia
23 March 1588 ✝ Isidro; Rodrigo's private chapel

Every crowned head in Echon will be furious with him, but it's the young woman's mother Rodrigo is concerned about. The girl has not an ounce of cruelty—or sense—in her, and she will spend her life pampered and treated like a queen. Indeed, if Rodrigo were of Maurish faith, he might marry the girl as well, just to distract her mother from the insult she'll perceive.

He regrets that there was no other way, but diversion is an excellent tactic, whether in war, politics, or religion, and this matter combines all three. Cordula, nevermind the Kaiser in Ruessland or the warring kings of the Prussian confederation, would not have allowed him to do what he intends to do, and Rodrigo de Costa is not a man to be dictated to. If he must marry, he will by God do it on his own terms, and he will make a match worth mentioning of it.

He takes a moment, because he's in the chapel, to be somewhat apologetic for taking God's name in vain, but then footsteps echo on the floor behind him and there are more important things to attend to than the unlikelihood of an offended Lord.

To his relief, he's never seen the woman who stands backlit by morning sunlight streaming in the open doors. Amusement follows that thought; to his relief, but she's the woman he intends to marry. Still, he expected the girl's mother, and he'd rather face a political opponent than an insulted parent.

For that's what Akilina Pankejeff is: a political opponent, not an ally. Not yet, perhaps not ever, though wedding himself to her makes a bed their two countries will share, and that, in theory, means an alliance between lovers.

It's a long and interesting moment before Akilina curtsies, and he wonders what she's thinking as she does so. When she straightens he offers a bow in return: unnecessary by rank, but crucial in that it will smooth waters that are by their very definition troubled.

That, he suspects, was more or less what she was thinking, too, although as dvoryanin, a grand duchess of Khazar rather than royalty, she should, in fact, bend knee to a prince whether she likes it or not.

Because she stands in the light, she can see him, but he cannot see her clearly. He knows the picture he makes: aging, but well, with silver at his temples and brightening the small sharp beard he's taken to wearing. Long-legged and fit, he has taken some care in maintaining his shape, both from vanity and practicality. A man burdened with extra weight cannot go to war so easily, nor, should the need arise, fight off an assassin. Rodrigo likes to think he's a practical man.

And because he's practical, he won't make the Khazarian duchess come to him. Instead, he steps down from the altar and into her shadow, amused at the implications imagining Akilina is seizing on them, hoping she might also seize the upper hand in the marriage that is about to take place.

When he steps out of the light and shadows that she casts, what he sees first of all is that she wears a sheepskin around her shoulders for warmth, and what he says, all unintentionally, is, "Oh, well done, my lady. Well done indeed. Those who remember will remember well, thanks to you."

She curtseys again, and her smile is, he thinks, meant to be demure, but to his eyes it only hides her teeth. Her eyes, though lowered, slide to follow him as he circles her, one shark waiting on another. There will be blood soon, of that Rodrigo is sure, and he intends the greater part of it will be hers.

She is, at a glance, all the things he has heard she is: beautiful in the way an obsidian dagger might be, black and dangerous and sharp. It is not her nature to stand and be circled, even when she wears, as she does now, a gown encrusted with gold and pearls; a gown intended for little more than to be looked at, for it weighs a woman down. No one travels with this kind of dress at hand, not without long preparation for an anticipated wedding. That she wears it means she has found strings to pull and favours to call in, not an easy thing to do with only two weeks' notice for impending nuptials, and with a long journey made in that time besides. She's clever, then, and drives a hard bargain, both of which are commonly believed.

But the sheepskin tells him that she's more than clever. She binds herself to Sandalia with that skin, intimates friendship with a dead woman, and tells him clearly that she understands politics and marriage beds and all the reasons for putting them together. It verges on brilliance, and he admires her for it.

When he's made a full circle he stops and says what he intended to say as his first words to her, before she surprised him into speaking unrehearsed: "I think we shall look well at the altar together, don't you?"

"*Da,* my lord." Her voice, like her cleverness, pleases him. It's warmer than he expected, richer: a woman with her sharp beauty might easily have had a piercing voice. Curious to hear it again, he asks a question he knows the answer to, but then, hearing her response will tell him things, too.

"Irina is informed?"

Her eyes are black; this Khazarian raven's eyes are black, glittering, and intense. "*Da,*" she repeats, then gives over from any pretence at her native tongue to speak very good Essandian. "She's informed, and a bird should come to Isidro to tell you of her pleasure. This is an alliance that will free her from the necessity of marrying Ivanova to your nephew, and ends all risk of your pursuit of her hand." There's a moment's hesitation in which it seems Akilina will say something else, but it passes and she simply concludes, "She will, I think, approve."

Indeed, Irina has approved; the bird arrived two days ago, before Akilina herself did. But Rodrigo's interest is piqued again, and his eyebrows lift. "What did you not say, dvoryanin?" This time he speaks her language, a meeting of minds, or, at least, an affectation of it. Akilina quirks an eyebrow, too, and for an instant he thinks he sees humour in her gaze. That would bode well, though in the end it matters not at all whether they like each other in the least.

"I didn't say that I'm young enough to bear children, which Irina is not, or that the imperatrix will have considered that in this dance of alliances. She wouldn't give up her own reign to allow an imperator to sit over her again, or risk Ivanova's inheritance of the throne. A child of noble Khazarian blood in Essandia's royal family is the best outcome she could hope for."

"And yet she did not bargain you away to this throne, or any other," Rodrigo says thoughtfully, and Akilina, whose posture is already perfect, draws herself up further, insult and disdain written on her features. Able to see what she's about to say, Rodrigo makes a soft sound, hoping to dissuade her, and when she draws breath anyway, speaks before she does.

"Do not, Akilina. Don't make your protests, don't trade on the high road of your own pride. We are all of us slaves to our thrones, whether we serve by sitting on them or by bowing to them. Had Irina chosen to trade you away you would have gone, because that is the duty you owe your queen. I haven't chosen you because I need an obedient wife. I require a woman of wit and intelligence and boldness, and one who brings political alliances powerful enough to permit me to wage the battles that must be fought. We both know what is expected of us and we will both fulfill those roles."

Colour mounts in Akilina's cheeks, reminding Rodrigo that although she's a woman grown, she is also half his age. A reprimand from him is very likely in the same vein as a scolding from her father, though if memory serves him, that man died when Akilina was only a child, not yet ten years old. Regardless, she's furious, and she's furious because he's right. It's not an ideal way to begin a marriage, but then marriage isn't an ideal Rodrigo holds to. Still, because he has no wish to enter a battlefield in the marriage bed, he does soften his voice and add, "The sheepskin truly is well done, my lady. You will be loved for it."

Akilina nods, then wets her lips and glances the other way, more of a submissive act than Rodrigo expected of her. "By your leave, my lord, my women will want to finish preparing me for the wedding." She sounds soft and compliant, and her game comes into focus for Rodrigo: it *is* an act, and she is playing the part of the chastened wife.

"Of course." Rodrigo waits until she is nearly at the chapel door, framed by it, framed by sunlight that brings out the red and gold in her black hair, and then he says, "Akilina."

She stops at the sound of his voice: that is good. He waits until she's turned back toward him, and that she does is also good. "Do not think me weak because I admire your wit, lady. You will be queen, but I am and will remain your prince. Do not forget that."

Akilina goes still before dropping a tiny and very precise curtsey. Then—clearly dismissed by her own reckoning, if not by Rodrigo's explicit permission—she turns on her heel and stomps off in an obvious fury to prepare for her wedding vows.

BELINDA PRIMROSE
23 March 1588 † Alunaer; the spymaster's office

"What news of Echon?" Impatience ill-suited Belinda: after weeks of tutelage and convent life, she ought to have been grateful that Cortes had called her to his offices. *Was* grateful, in most ways: being cut off from the spying and intrigue that had been her lifeblood for ten years and more made her feel displaced from the world. Still, impatience held her: impatience that she didn't already know the details of what she'd come to learn; impatience that whatever she might hear, it was unlikely that she'd be sent across the channel to once more involve herself in the machinations of continental politics.

Impatience, too, that she was kept in a cold grey box while Cortes sat in the comfort of his office with a healthy fire in the hearth and a cup of good wine at his elbow. The latter, at least, he offered some of, and Belinda took it with a wretched attempt at gratitude. Only after she'd sipped did he lean back in his chair and speak with unusual satisfaction. "Akilina Pankejeff has been ransomed from her Lutetian prison and has fled to Isidro under Rodrigo de Costa's banner. What think you of that?"

Belinda's poor temper fell away, and so, too—nearly—did the glass she held in her fingertips. She clutched the cup, sloshing wine over her hand, and for long seconds indulged in simply staring at Lorraine's erstwhile spymaster. He was second to Robert Drake in the network, but first in the eyes of the court: Belinda's father was merely meant to be a courtier, not a master of lies. "He means to marry her."

Conflicted astonishment bubbled in her chest, wanting to turn both to laughter and horror. The idea of Rodrigo, so wedded to his faith that he'd never taken a wife, finally allying himself with any-one was too unexpected to be anything but laughable, but his choice was cold and calculated. Akilina was not, perhaps, a queen, but as a Khazarian dvoryanin was powerful enough to be sent as an ambassador, which meant she was important enough to be bar-gained in marriage. Her hand meant an alliance between the Ecu-menic and Khazarian armies, and that was bitter dredges indeed for Aulun. Belinda murmured, "I should have killed her," and was un-surprised at Cortes's nod. "What more?" she asked after a moment. "What else must I know?"

"That Javier de Castille has gone to Cordula," Cortes said. "That in all likelihood he seeks the Pappas's blessing in a matter of war. You are here to tell me if he's an able leader, if we should fear his army on our border."

"Not his army," Belinda said without hesitation, "but his armada, or more rightfully, his uncle's. The Essandian navy is new and strong."

"But Rodrigo's old, and it'll be to the pup that the people look. Is he a threat?"

Belinda rose, setting her wineglass aside as she went to stand be-fore the fire. "He's been sore tested of late," she eventually said. "His mother dead and his friends scattered. He's a king, Cortes, and he has a matter of vengeance to address. Of course he's a threat. But he fears himself and his own power, and that may cut the legs from under him." She turned her head, giving her profile to the spymas-ter. "Do not tell her majesty that he's unworthy of attention; he is not. But neither is he of a nature to press forward when standing still might do. My counsel would be caution: give him no reason to feel Aulun is moving toward war, and perhaps he'll talk himself out of it."

All true enough, though if Javier had gone to Cordula, it was perhaps too late to stem a tide of battle. Not unless he betrayed his witchpower to the father of his church: they might burn him, then, and all of Echon would fall into chaos as Gallin became a prize for plucking. Belinda caught her breath, about to warn Cortes of the Gallic king's extraordinary magic, and let the impulse go again: he would not believe her unless she showed him her own hand, and that she'd never do.

Akilina Pankejeff, queen of Essandia. Belinda turned her gaze back to the fire and indulged in the luxury of baring her teeth. Javier and his witchpower fears travelling to Cordula and seeking godly sanction was to be expected, next to Akilina's sudden rise. That Belinda was confined in a convent while the woman who had nearly destroyed her wed a king—she clenched a fist, then made herself relax, calling stillness to the fore. Lorraine would have a purpose in ensconcing her in the convent—that much she had to trust. In time whatever need drove her incarceration would pass, and she would be free to join the world again.

Until then, the meat of these matters would give her grist to chew on, and a queen's downfall would be a sweet plan to set in motion. Belinda, certain Cortes was done with her, dropped a curtsey and slipped back to her prison, the better to consider her rival's fate.

JAVIER, KING OF GALLIN
23 March 1588 † *Cordula; the Lateran palace*

Tumultuous cries rose in the palace, roaring sound that Javier could barely distinguish from the magic surging through him. His vision was silver, witchpower throbbing in his veins. He had not looked for or controlled the terrible burst of power that had shattered through him at the Pappas's blessing. Now, as though it had scooped up the responses around him and dragged them back to settle within his bones, he could feel the awe and shock of the Primes.

He raised a hand to his eyes, pushing his thumb and middle fingers over their lids. Silver squelched away, leaving ordinary mortal red and black spots swimming under the pressure he exerted. Some of the rushing left his ears as well, turning a din into distinguishable voices, all of them excited beyond what seemed appropriate for aged fathers of the church.

His hand fell away from his eyes of its own will, slow and graceful, as though he'd been granted some special gift of beauty for this brief moment in time. Uncertain of what he would see, he looked up at the Pappas, and found in that man's eyes wonder equal to that of a child. As Javier watched, the Pappas crossed himself, then lifted his hands, lifted his gaze, and with that dramatic gesture quieted the hall.

"Javier de Castille has come to us a humble petitioner, seeking solace for his mother's soul, seeking blessings for his uncle's wedding, seeking, at last, God's ordinance in the wearing of his crown and in the duty of the church to win back those who have been led astray! I have anointed him king, but it is truly God's miracle that we, all unknowing, have gathered here to see. These old hands have crowned many heads, but never in my memory has God marked his chosen monarch so clearly. Witness he who is God's warrior and leader of our crusades!"

He drew Javier to his feet, turned him to face the Primes and many, many more: word of God's blessing had spread already, and people flooded into the Lateran hall, eyes alight with joy and hope and reverence. Astonished, a smile crept over Javier's face—small, he had the presence of mind to keep it small, and to lower his eyes in modest acceptance as the people began to chant his name. Over the din the Pappas shouted, "Cordula's armies are yours to command! We will win back our brothers and sisters in Aulun, and we shall turn God's chosen son and his warriors to all of Echon and beyond!"

Breathless, Javier took up the Pappas's hand and raised it high, then turned to the old man and knelt, receiving a new blessing in front of hundreds of believers. Power beat at his skin from the inside, shouting that he might reach out with his will and have all of these people as his own, to do with as he pleased. He quelled the impulse as he'd quelled it that morning facing Tomas. These masses needed no coercion; they were his already, won over by what the Pappas, the *Pappas himself,* called a miracle. Surely, surely this man of God could not be wrong. Surely the witchpower was God's power, not deviltry, if it had been triggered by the Pappas's touch and if that holy man himself had not recognised and recoiled at it.

Tears scalded his face, and he brushed his fingers over them not with shame, but astonishment. Even with the relief of finding Belinda, whose magic and soul were like his own, he had not been moved to tears of joyful release. A lifetime's fears washed away as salt water slipped down his cheeks. The Pappas, standing above him, offered Javier an avuncular smile, perhaps mistaking his tears for awe at God's gift, almost certainly seeing them as a mark of unpretentious piety. Afraid the truth was visible in his eyes, Javier glanced down, then turned his head to search out Marius's gaze, and Tomas's, hoping for their faces to be as elated and accepting as he felt.

Marius, who had once been the merriest of their foursome, was solemn, but with the grave pleasure that often marked men of means. He inclined his head when Javier caught his eyes, a small gesture that seemed to Javier to hold all the promise of friendship in the world within it. Smiling, and no longer trying to hide it or seem demure, Javier turned his gaze to Tomas.

There was no pleasure at all in the priest's face, but instead, despair. Javier saw it in how he looked from Javier to the Pappas to the Primes; in how he glanced back at the throng of cheering faithful, and in how his eyes finally came back to Javier. He had lost his will to the young king of Gallin once, said his gaze; he has lost his will once, and did not at all trust that the same thing had not just happened now, in a flash of brilliance that stole men's wits from them all unknowing. *You are damned,* his golden eyes warned. *Javier, king of Gallin, is damned, and I will see this abomination ended.*

Matters of state and religion separated Javier from those he called friends long before he might have stolen a moment to speak with them. Marius waved a wry good-bye as Javier was swept by him, but Tomas's lingering glance was grim. There would be time, Javier judged; there had to be time for him to seek out the priest and speak with him before Tomas was granted an audience with the Pappas or with one of the other high princes of the church; before he sought out his own father. He could be made to see sense, if Javier swore on holy things that he had not acted with deliberation; Javier was sure of it. Had to be sure of it, for the alternative bore no consideration: Tomas could not be right, and his magic could not be devil-born. The priest was young and as fearful of evil as Javier himself, but Rodrigo was older and wiser and had seen God's will in Javier's talent, and the Pappas himself had named it a miracle. Tomas would see it, even if Javier had to bend knee and beg his forgiveness for the terrible things Javier had done to him. The idea stung, but not as badly as did the fear of losing what he'd been given, or the still-greater terror of burning.

Only later did he realise how well-suited he'd been, that day, for what transpired. He had been dressed in greys, shades that suited his pale skin and red hair; a cloak thrown over his shoulders turned him to a king in white, God's very banner thrown to the sky. He was carried, literally, lifted on shoulders and made high so all might see him clearly, and he called out thanks and blessings until his throat was sore from it, and someone thrust a glass of fine red wine into his hand. He gave the last sip to an old woman, and if she did not quite shed her skin and rise up a beauty in the flush of youth, she at least seemed to throw off the worst of her age in a flush of excitement, and voices around her cried out that she had been healed of cataracts and aching bones. Hands reached to touch his cloak, to brush his thigh or catch hold of his fingers as he was borne through the crowds, and with each caress an increasing benediction grew in him, filling him as full as the witchpower ever had. He thought he might burst with pride, as though light might rush from his body and scatter over all the Cordulan people, and for the first time he felt no fear at the thought.

They carried him, Primes and merchants and paupers, through the streets, up Cordula's revered hills and down again, away from the Lateran palace to the Caesar's palace, and there set him on his feet, and fell back, waiting for his praise. Delight so strong it felt of idiocy bloomed in him and he lifted his hands, lifted his voice, and if the witchpower gave it strength to carry to all the corners of the palace square, today he did not shrink back in horror at the thought.

"No king could ask for a more generous welcome to his crown than that which you have given me. You, a people who are not my own, but who share a faith with me, have carried me on your shoulders and backs to a place of honour, and I think no monarch could ask more of any people. It is my pride to have been touched by you. I will do all in my power, and in God's name, to take the love and belief I have felt in your hands and bring it to our oppressed brothers and sisters in Aulun. I go now to beg your king for his support, and when I leave this place I pray that you good men and women will be at my back, an army of God armed and ready to fight a battle for the souls of our lost brethren!"

Caught up in the exuberance of youth and his own drama, Javier spun around, cloak caught in one hand so it made a tremendous whirl, and on the screams of thousands, entered another king's home.

The slightest modicum of good sense penetrated the thunderous noise that followed him, and he made a knee to the Caesar of Parna, giving that man all honour due to him. Anything else was dangerous in the extreme: Cordula's streets were filled with the faithful shouting Javier's name, and only a foolish king would not fear for his crown when a young and handsome monarch was so beloved in his city. Eyes lowered, voice soft and carefully emptied of amusement, Javier said, "Forgive me, my lord Caesar. A little madness has overtaken us all, and I have gone and made speeches on your doorstep without your leave."

Doors boomed shut behind him, cutting off the last of the sound from the streets: Javier had travelled through three halls to reach the Caesar's private audience chambers, and the noise had followed him all that way. Now silence rang in his ears, not just the choked-off shouts from beyond, but the profound silence of one king considering whether another had gone too far.

In time, though, the Caesar sighed. "You had best be relieved that we are accustomed to sharing this city with the Pappas and his princes, and therefore accustomed to fervourous riots held in a name not our own. The Kaiser in Reussland would have your head as a warning to any with an eye on his crown."

"Then I am profoundly grateful to be in Parna, my lord Caesar." Javier kept all trace of humour from his words: he had trespassed, and a man of lesser confidence or compassion could easily have taken offence. As much joy as Javier'd found in spilling through the streets and speaking fine words to eager ears, his apology was sincere. He would not have liked another king to do what he had done, and this once preferred to eat crow over risking argument.

"As you should be. Well, rise, then, my lord king. We hear that you are crowned by the Pappas's hands, yet another audacity in our city."

Javier did rise, truly looking on the Caesar for the first time. Even seated, he was clearly not a tall man, and was given to both roundness and baldness, but his eyes were sharp and knowing. As all the kings of Parna had done for time immemorial, he wore a wreath of shining gold-leafed laurels on his head. He wore modern fashion, but garbed in robes he might easily have sat on his throne a thousand years earlier and looked at home there; such was the impression he left.

Now on his feet, effectively the Caesar's equal, Javier spread his hands and turned to the same style of speech shared by royalty across Echon. "We hoped that the Lateran palace's unique position as the seat of Ecumenic power within the heart of Cordula might allow your majesty to overlook our boldness in asking that boon."

"You've all the answers, haven't you." The Caesar eyed Javier a long moment, then pushed up from his throne and stumped down its stairs with all the grace of an old sailor left on land. He offered a hand that Javier grasped gladly, and slapped Javier's other shoulder with enough force that he was obliged to brace himself against being knocked aside. "Come," he said with no further preamble, "you might as well see my daughters. There are eight of them, so you'll have your pick, and I shall call you Javier, and I shall be Gaspero to you forevermore."

Bemused, Javier said, "Gaspero. My honour," and fell into step beside the older man, thence to meet his daughters.

The boldest, if not the oldest, was a creature of seventeen with a wicked demure glance that made Javier glad he wasn't housed in the palace, else he feared he'd find himself bedded and then wedded with no say in the matter. He murmured politenesses over each of the girls, even the toothless five-year-old, and upon leaving their boudoir said with honesty, "They're beautiful, my lord Caesar. We heard of their mother's passing, of course. My deepest sympathies."

Creases appeared around the Caesar's mouth, aging him more than first glance gave truth to. "Thank you. And ours to you, of course. It is not easy. So which of them will you have?"

Flustered, Javier let a few steps pass in what he hoped seemed thoughtful silence, then risked an aspect of truth in his answer. "The third daughter has a fire to her that struck me. But I am in an awkward position, Caesar, and I hope you will hear it through." He waited on Gaspero's grunt, then went on, hoping he treaded carefully enough. "I can think of no alliance that would make me happier than to wed Gallin's house to yours. It would strengthen our church and our ties to one another—"

"So the wedding will be tomorrow."

Javier coughed. "My lord, we have these things in common already; they are things upon which alliances can be built and armies forged. I fear I cannot yet bind myself to your house in marriage, not until I've assured myself and my people of Khazar's support in the war that comes against Aulun."

"Khazar." Gaspero stopped in the middle of a marble hall, framed, as though he had chosen his stopping place deliberately, by tall butter-yellow columns that reflected warmth and light against the walls. It made him timeless once again, an emperor of any era. "Khazar shares neither religion nor a hint of family ties with Gallin."

"But it has an army of terrible and tremendous might," Javier replied. "The Pappas supports me in asking Parna for troops, and Essandia and Gallin both will bring their armies and navies to bear. But Aulun will make treaties with Reussland and perhaps Prussia, and if the Norselands can be shaken from their icy ways, perhaps them as well. They have all turned from the Ecumenic church, and follow Reformation paths. Together, those armies are greater than the ones Cordula commands, my lord. We all of us need Khazar, and loathe though I may be to admit it, I am our best bargaining piece there. Irina has a daughter."

"She's fourteen."

"As was my mother when she was first wed," Javier whispered, remembering too clearly playing the Caesar's role in the same conversation with Sandalia. He shook himself, putting away sorrow for politics, and passed a hand over his eyes in a moment of genuine weariness. "If we are swift with our divine mercy upon Aulun, I will never need marry the girl at all, and might turn my eyes to where my heart more closely lies. But until then, I must view myself as a game piece to be bartered, and for all our sakes, look to Khazan and the imperator's heir." *Agree,* he whispered silently, and felt witch-power flex before he reined it back in a spurt of panic. Surely the Caesar would see sense; surely Javier had no need to coerce a fellow king, not with war on the horizon and a plain need for troops. *Agree,* he thought again, and wondered how many times unvoiced desire on his part had shaped the actions of his friends and others around him.

Gaspero regarded him a long moment, then fell to walking again. "You are either very clever or very foolish, Javier of Gallin. I think all of Echon waits with interest to see which it is. I will give you my support and my troops for a single season without a marriage contract to bind it, and that because the Pappas and his Primes will hound me without mercy if I don't. Win the summer season and prove to me your alliances with Khazar are solid, and I'll give you a second year, but I'll have the contract in hand by your twenty-fifth birthday or Parna will leave you to your holy war, and return to its wine and women. Do we have a bargain?"

"A very fair one, I think," Javier said softly. Two years was time enough; in two years everything could change. Silver washed through him, too subtle for him to know if it had set the Caesar on the path Javier needed him to walk. But if it had, it was with God's blessing: Javier clung to that thought, trying to believe. The witch-power was a gift, welcomed by the Pappas and the church; if it influenced Gaspero, then that, too, was God's will. A hand knotted against his own uncertainty, Javier ducked his head and whispered, "You're generous, my lord."

"I am. Don't forget it, boy, or the cost will come out of your royal hide."

Welcome or not, witchpower flared more sharply, giving shape to an offence Javier was just wise enough not to voice. Instead he bowed, taking his leave and his temper from the Parnan Caesar before low-boiling witchpower tempted him too far.

He might have spent the night—might have spent weeks, for all of that—in Cordula's streets, admired by the people, drowning himself in drink and burying himself in women. It was a pretty thought, seductive, but harsh reality scratched at the insides of his mind, pulling him away from revelry and back toward the expensive inn he and his men were housed at. Once Tomas was convinced that Javier's magic was God-given, not the devil's tool, they would travel to Aria Magli and find Eliza.

Guilt slid through Javier's belly, looking for a place to stick, but found nowhere and slipped out again, leaving nothing more than a cool space where it had been. Eliza, even more than Ivanova of Khazar, would bring him the people. Marius was right: she deserved better than to be a symbol, when she could be a queen. The marriage would have to take place quietly, to allow Javier room to negotiate with Khazar, but Parna had given him two years, and that was enough time to change the world. Before those long months were over, he would hold Aulun in his palm, would hold his wife's hand in the open, and would, with Rodrigo, turn his eyes to Reussland and Prussia and the far Khazarian empire. God was with him; Javier knew that now, and all his doubts were faded.

Three times: three times now he had denied the witchpower in coercing a man. First Rodrigo, then Tomas this morning, and now Gaspero. He was the master of his magic, and needed only to convince Tomas to hold his tongue.

Marius was in the common room, gambling; he, unlike the others at his table, rose when Javier came in, his eye more for the door than the game. He dug for coins to pay off his bet, but Javier waved a hand, stopping him, and hurried up to their room.

It stood empty. Javier turned a curious eyebrow to the guard at the door, who shrugged: he was paid to watch over the prince, not the priest. Annoyed, Javier returned to the common room and slipped up to Marius's side. "Tomas?"

Marius shrugged as well, but more helpfully. "I think he's gone to pray. Here, lend me a bit of coin, Jav, I'm losing."

"All the more reason why I shouldn't," Javier said, but dropped a handful of coppers into Marius's palm before slapping his shoulder and turning for the door.

There were churches a-plenty in Cordula, the nearest a surprisingly modest thing at the foot of their street. The kind of place the poor went, Javier imagined, and took himself in on the thought that Tomas might well wish for simple surroundings in which to wrestle with his conscience.

Indeed, he was there, knelt at the altar with others, some of whom recognised Javier and sent a whisper stirring about the church. He spread his fingers, palms down, to silence them, and made some show of crossing himself so that they might see he was as they were, devout and in search of answers. Unlike the worshippers, though, his answers could come from mortal lips, and he knelt at Tomas's side, whispering, "Have you in your heart condemned me, then?"

Tomas shot him a glance full of daggers and turned his attention back to the bleeding Son before them all. Javier counselled himself with patience and lowered his gaze to the mosaic floor, tracing its patterns and idly impressed at the artwork in even this poor church. Then again, so close to the palace, perhaps it was only modest, and not so poor at all.

His knees were bruised and the witchpower rolling with impatience when Tomas finally rose from his devotions. Javier scrambled to his feet as well, more than half certain if he hadn't joined him, that the priest would have been on his knees all night, seeking guidance. When Tomas turned toward the doors, Javier caught his arm, full of hope. "Come, let us whisper amongst ourselves here, my friend. Surely I cannot foreswear myself in God's house. Please, Tomas," he added at the other man's surly expression. "Can we not discuss this?"

"There is nothing to discuss. The devil may quote scripture to his own ends, Javier. How am I to know you haven't bent the Pappas's mind as you did mine?" Despite the refusal, Tomas went with Javier as he tugged him toward a side chapel.

Determined to speak in privacy, Javier willed the smaller room empty, and was caught between delight and alarm when two older men and a beautiful girl exited it as they approached. Subtle influence: that much, he could live with, though a dagger of guilt found a home in him and lanced back to a night in Lutetia. His curiosity about Beatrice Irvine had driven his friends to make excuses and stay away from what had been meant as a night at the opera for them all. He could shape the world, and so must learn to take care to do it only with intent, and for the best of reasons.

Tomas watched the three leave and turned an accusing gaze on Javier, who lifted his hands in admission and apology. "I am trying, Tomas. I truly am. It's a part of me, and I rarely mean to push people into doing my bidding with it." He gestured after the trio, then caught Tomas's hands, surprised at how cool they were. His own felt hot, as though the magic within him had turned his blood molten. "I need guidance on this path, that I do not overstep my boundaries."

"As you already have done with me." Tomas kept his voice to a murmur, but the words were sharp. "I must go to the Pappas with this. He's wiser than I, and will lay my concerns to rest."

"Or take up your banner," Javier said with low intensity. The back of his skull began to throb, every heartbeat pulsing incandescent light through it, molten blood turning to silver fire. He clenched his jaw, struggling to use reason over power. "Tomas, you trusted me this morning. I beg that you do so now."

"You've become easier with begging, when it's your soul you fear for. Had you pled in Isidro instead of commanded, we might not be here now. I am sorry," the priest said firmly. "I will visit with the Pappas in the morning."

Javier whispered, "I can't let you."

"If you stop me, then we'll both know that I'm right. That this power is the devil's, and that you're on a path to Hell." Challenge lit Tomas's golden gaze. "Are you God's creature, king of Gallin, or are you the devil's spawn?"

Javier seized Tomas's arms, a grip hard enough to make his own hands hurt; harder, it felt, than any mortal should be able to hold something. There would be bruises left at the least, warning to the bold priest that he should not stand in the face of a king's will, much less the witchpower tide that surged within Javier. He twisted Tomas toward the small chapel's altar, forcing him over to it; the priest bent like a reed, awkwardly arched beneath Javier's weight. His expression, though, was calm as he gazed upward, beyond Javier. Incensed, Javier glanced up as well, searching for whatever gave Tomas such serenity.

The Madonna rose above them, babe in arms, her smile sweet and soft as she looked on her child and the light of all humanity's hope.

A strangled noise erupted from Javier's throat all unbidden, cutting off his witchpower will. He staggered back and Tomas straightened easily, smoothed his robes, and then lifted his gaze to Javier's, unspoken sorrows written in it.

Javier gasped, "Forgive me," even knowing he deserved no forgiveness, and Tomas made the sign of the cross before leaving Javier to fall before the Madonna in prayer for his own soul.

TOMAS DEL'ABBATE

24 March 1588 † *Cordula; the Lateran palace*

He has put this meeting off too long, has Tomas; has done so out of misplaced loyalty to the witchbreed prince. He ought to have come to the Pappas's palace the day they arrived in Cordula, rather than steal long days of relaxation with Javier. With Javier and Marius, but it's the fiery-haired prince—now king—whose company Tomas has coveted, as though the willpower Javier wreaked on his mind has left a channel of weakness, like some men have for wine. No longer: even if he might have, Javier's struggles with his devil's gift are growing too uncontrolled; it is twice now that he has barely stopped himself from rolling Tomas's will, and the second time was quite truthfully through the grace of God alone.

An earnest-faced boy, younger by some years than Tomas, hurries toward him, and gestures eagerly when he sees he's gained the priest's attention. "The Pappas will see you. Please, come this way."

THE PRETENDER'S CROWN · 135

Tomas is brought not to the audience hall, but to more private chambers, still grandiose and awe-inspiring, but less inclined to echo and carry voices. Tomas kisses the holy ring and is invited to sit, but worried energy keeps him on his feet. The Pappas himself does sit, and watches with beneficent amusement. When he's judged Tomas's fussing has gone on long enough, he says, "You have done well, in Essandia, my son. If this is your concern . . ."

"No." The abruptness of the word brings Tomas to a stop, and he kneels in horrified apology. "I mean, yes, of course it's to my shame that I was unable to convince Rodrigo to wed one of the Pappas's choices, but that isn't what has brought me here. It's Javier, holy father. The king of Gallin," he corrects himself. "It is the— It is what we saw yesterday, that brilliant light."

"God's blessing," the Pappas says with genial reverence. "We are fortunate to have a king so well loved by the Lord."

"I fear it was not God's blessing, your holiness." The words scrape Tomas's throat and it takes all his nerve to peek up at the Pappas to see how the holy man takes to being corrected.

He appears to take it with all the astonishment Tomas might expect, and not yet, at least, any of the offence. Tomas's explanation tumbles out, from Javier's impetuous arrival in Essandia to the overruling of Tomas's intention to bring the deadly power to the church's eyes; from the destruction Javier learned to wreak under Rodrigo's tutelage to what Tomas fears is the truth about Rodrigo's decision to marry: that Javier has stolen his will, too.

Here, the Pappas raises a hand and leans forward, a question on his lips: "This compulsion you say Javier placed on you has faded, though. Would it not have done the same with Rodrigo before he set foot in church to be wed?"

Miserable with uncertainty, Tomas replies, "I think my faith has protected me, Holy Father. I believe I may have been more difficult to convince to keep silent than he is accustomed to. I fear Rodrigo, who is his blood and bone, may not be as strong in his faith when it comes to family."

The Pappas nods thoughtfully and gestures for Tomas to continue. The remaining story pours from his lips, his decision to trust Javier until that terrible burst of silver dominated the room; his fear that weaker minds, never implying that the Pappas himself might be so affected, for such an idea is anathema, but weaker minds may have been led to believe a thing that was not true. He ends with the night before, with his free will saved only through the grace of God, and when he falls silent, so, too, does the Pappas for a long while.

"I am glad that you have told me of this," the Pappas finally says, heavily. "It seems the road I thought lit by sunshine has darker shadows hanging on it. You say that the symbol of the Madonna broke his will, though?" He nods when Tomas does and goes on, more thoughtful now than weighty. "And it seems that he trusts you. I am loathe to put you in the devil's sight, my son, but I think Cordula needs you at Javier's side."

"He has asked for me to accompany him," Tomas whispers. He cannot, it seems, speak above a whisper: these are matters too large for his slender shoulders, too important for a youth of his years. "I have agreed already, if I have your leave."

"My leave and my blessing. Do not worry, my son." The Pappas leans forward and puts his fingertips against Tomas's forehead, soothing for all that his hands tremble with age. "God has shown us a path to reclaim our lost brothers and sisters in Aulun, and we must trust Him. Javier's power, if it is as extraordinary as you say, will stand us well in the war to come."

Then, casually, as if intending to reassure, the Pappas smiles and adds, "We can always burn him later."

9

JAVIER, KING OF GALLIN
1 April 1588 † Aria Magli, in Parna

Javier, king of all Gallin, heir to the Essandian throne, child of the last Lanyarchan queen, and pretender to the Aulunian crown, leaned across a gondola seat, arms crossed to support himself, and, in utmost confidence, murmured, "I am looking for a woman," to the gondola boy.

The boy, who was perhaps twelve and more probably ten, leaned on his pole, edging the boat along its busy canal, and offered a heartfelt sigh of sympathy. "Sì, signor, so are we all. A beautiful woman, no? A woman with eyes like diamonds and hair like spun gold, with skin softer than silk and arms warm as the fire. Her touch may burn," he said mournfully, "but for such a woman the pain is worth everything."

Javier blinked, first at the boy, then over his shoulder at Tomas and Marius, neither of whom made even an attempt to control their laughter. Javier cleared his throat and turned back to the boy, whose expression had been wiped entirely clear of theatrics in the moment Javier'd looked away, and who now looked cheerful and expectant. "This is the woman you seek, no? I will bring you to her. I know many fine ladies, and you are a man of wealth, I can see that in your clothes. You will be pleased with me, and I shall bring home a fat chicken to my father and my brothers and sisters with the payment you give me."

"Ah," Javier said, still half outwitted. "I'm looking for a specific woman, I'm afraid."

"And you start by asking me because I am the finest gondola boy on the canals," the boy said without hesitation, "which is wise, for I know many people, but there are many more people I do not know. But perhaps my people will know people who know your lady. She is a courtesan, sì?" he added in a tone that suggested they were the only women worth seeking out.

"Sì," Marius said from behind them, though Javier'd shaken his head in disagreement. He looked back a second time to find the laughter gone from Marius's face. "A courtesan, a foreign woman, from Gallin, with black hair and brown eyes, and she wears an alabaster ring on this finger." He lifted his left hand, touched his middle finger. "She would wear dresses of her own fashion, not the usual that you would see."

"A courtesan, Marius?" Javier asked through his teeth, and in Gallic.

The look Marius turned on him was almost pitying. "That or a widow, Jav. She's got some money, but she'll need more, and in Aria Magli the easiest way to be a woman of means is to be one of them." He jerked his head toward a high window, where a woman much like the one the gondola boy had described leaned out, breasts on display as she waved and blew kisses at the passersby. "Eliza has the beauty, the wit, and, thanks to you, the education for it. Why not?"

"I thought you thought her better than the prince's whore."

"Here, she would be her own whore, and I would mark that higher, aye, my lord."

"What kind of dresses does she wear, signor?" The gondola boy's voice broke over their argument in a clarion call, pure and utterly without awareness of growing tension. Javier, irritated, looked back at the child and found determination in his eyes, much older than his years. He wasn't unaware after all, but deliberately pulling them away from feuds, no doubt in concern over his payment. Anger faded beneath an appreciation for the boy's business sense, and Javier traced the shape of one of Eliza's flowing, high-waisted gowns in the air.

"Like this, with a band beneath the breasts that makes a false high waist, and the necks are scooped low."

"Like her," the boy said with a nod up the canal. Javier twisted to see a woman in just such a gown, who wore extravagantly coiffed black curls tumbling around her shoulders, accept a gypsy man's hand in helping her into a gondola, and leapt to his feet.

"Eliza! *Eliza!*"

The gondola boy squawked "Signor!" in alarm, while Tomas and Marius both grabbed for Javier's hips, trying to pull him back to sitting. Men and women—women, particularly—passing on bridges and looking out windows paused to look first at Javier, then for the woman he called for, titters of romance and teasing floating over the brackish waters. The woman herself didn't look back, and Marius, tilting to examine her once Javier was seated again, said, "Not unless she's put on two stone since we saw her last. You're not going to endear yourself to her if she hears you're mistaking a barge for a sailing ship."

"Catch up to them," Javier snapped. "I need to know where she got the gown."

"Oh, but it is dangerous, signor, to push and shove on the canals. If my boat capsizes my father will beat me—" His complaints stopped as he snatched the coin Javier threw to him. There was almost no break in his poling as he secreted the money away, and then his voice rang out in a song of emergency, unrequited love, and thwarted passion. That the details clashed and muddled, making no sense at all, bothered no one, and laughing gondoliers made way for the boy and his boatful of hopeful young men.

"You," the child said to Javier as they approached the woman's gondola, "you hold your tongue, signor. I will talk."

"He's got no faith in your romancing talents, Jav." Marius, grinning, reached out to thump Javier's shoulder. "Perhaps he knows you better than we think."

Javier scowled and the boy aimed a kick at him, unknowing and uncaring of his passenger's rank. "Look winsome, signor, or the lady will not care about your tale of woe."

"My tale of what?" It was too late: the boy had leapt from his own boat to the neighbouring, causing a shriek of dismay and then of laughter as he knelt beseechingly at the woman's feet. Javier, hoping to look lovelorn, unwisely thought of Beatrice, and felt his expression turn to rage. He dropped his face into his hands, and listened to the story of how he was a cloth merchant's son, wealthy enough to dress well but beggared when his father's silk shipment had been drowned in the Primorismare. Now all his hopes of love and happiness rested on wooing a beautiful girl who did not yet know of his misfortunes.

He had, according to the boy, promised her a gown of extraordinary beauty, of rare and subtle cut, and his heart was inspired by this woman's dress, though in truth even his beloved could never fill it so generously or well as this woman herself did. It was his fate to be unable to look so high as to this woman herself, but perhaps she might share the name of her dressmaker, and where to find her, so that the poor cloth merchant's son might take the last bolt of good fabric he had to his name and have a wedding gown made to change his destiny.

Through all of this Marius and Tomas held fast to the other boat's side, so the boy could return, and through all of it they kept straight faces while Javier's flush of anger faded into amazement. The woman gave a name and an address, and the boy leapt back with an air of unmistakable triumph. "You will pay me *very* well," he told Javier, and then, thoughtfully, said, "and perhaps introduce me to your lady friend, for I am a better talker than you, and you might need help."

Too astounded to be offended, Javier asked, "How can you tell? You haven't given me a chance to say anything."

The boy sniffed and leaned his weight into poling. "A man who talks as good as me would have put his words in."

Eliza Beaulieu

There has been a rumour that the prince—the king—of Gallin is come to Aria Magli. The courtesans have talked about it with great interest, gathered in Eliza's receiving quarters to examine material and finery and to stand for fittings and argue over trimmings. They've asked her, because she is Gallic, if she knows the king, and have laughed merrily when she has said yes, she does. They have asked for stories of him, and she's told them, from the story of the pauper girl who fell on him and broke his arm while trying to steal

pears from the royal gardens to the story of a minor Lanyarchan
noble who wore Eliza's fashions to court and caught the prince's
eye. She does not speak of her rage at Javier's engagement, nor of
the knuckle she broke in bruising Beatrice Irvine's jaw. The others
are stories everyone knows a little of, and that she is Lutetian-born,
and speaks with quiet confidence, delights the courtesans and sets
them to laughing and teasing, which is enough.

They are her best customers, these beautiful and intelligent
women. Well, mostly beautiful: there are those whose wit outstrips
their looks, but Eliza, who is beautiful herself, is coming to learn
that beauty can be made up of imperfect parts, if there is enough
cleverness and kindness in their making. There's one woman, a true
blonde of icy perfection, who is possibly the most flawless woman
Eliza has ever seen, and who is so haughty it steals her beauty. There
are moments when Eliza wonders if her own pride has turned her
into that kind of woman, and in those moments she thinks of
Javier's oft-made offer to take her away from her cheapside beginnings. It may be that the courtesans of Aria Magli have taught her
something about both pride and regret that may do her good in
later years.

She has surprised all of her customers with her language skills: a
woman from Gallin is not expected to have the Parnan tongue so
thoroughly in her mouth. The courtesans love it, and laugh uproar-
iously when she tells them that the prince taught her the languages
she knows. Eliza's not accustomed to having fun, and it's taken her
several weeks to realise that she's enjoying the small life she's built
here. She's stolen enough from Javier over the years to have started
her business, but because she is young and lovely and has coin, she's
widely assumed to be a courtesan herself.

This, to her surprise, bothers her not at all. There's a certain
amusement in letting the men wonder which of them she's bedding and for what price, and when they all protest that it's not *they*
who are lucky enough to find pleasure in her arms, they all believe
each other to be lying in order to maintain discretion and keep
competition at bay.

There are even one or two she might consider taking into her
bed, when she feels ready to become that committed to this vibrant
community. It is not at all like Lutetia, this city: it seems to grab and

give more, both at once, with a madcap fascination for other people's business that is familiar, but more heightened here. Perhaps it's that she's never been quite so included; in Lutetia she was always aware that she was the pauper, and the wealthy folk around her were even more aware than she was. Here, she is merely who she says she is: Eliza Beaulieu, a Gallic woman with a talent for dressmaking.

She is not a woman who expects a king to turn up on her doorstep, staggering from a gondola to the stairs with a leap as clumsy as anything she's ever seen from him. It's only because the gondola boy, a handsome lad with a broad bright grin, is bellowing her name, that she comes to the window at all, another dark-headed flower amid a bouquet of curious courtesans.

The women around her call out cheers and raspberries at Javier's awkwardness, while Eliza simply gapes. A girl at her side elbows her and offers a wicked grin. "No wonder you've stayed away from Parnan men, if it's gingers you like. Do his cuffs match his collar, lovey?"

"They do," Eliza says absently, though she knows this from young adulthood, when they were all still free enough with their bodies to dive into the Sacaruna bare as babes, and not from any more intimate experience.

She cannot actually believe he's here; it's a little as though one of Parna's ancient sun gods has come down from the sky to alight in her courtyard. She knows of Sandalia's death, of course, and knows that Beatrice Irvine proved a spy and an assassin and worse, because neither winter nor Echon's breadth keeps stories from spreading, but regardless, it's quite impossible that Javier should have travelled all this distance, most particularly to find her.

Which is clearly his intent, because while the boy has stopped bellowing her name, Javier has lifted his eyes to the window, and for the first time in their lives, his gaze is only for her. There's a smile in his grey eyes, and relief, and joy, and love, though not the depth of that last that she might wish. At least, that's what her head tells her, while her heart bumps and crashes and makes sick places of wild excitement inside her.

It's impetuosity that makes her call, "Have you a pear, my lord?" though at ten she'd had nothing like the wit to have asked such a question.

Javier, though, responds perfectly, patting his pockets with increasing alarm in the gestures and brightening laughter in his eyes. When he comes up empty, the boy in the gondola sighs with terrible exasperation and jumps to the steps with all the grace Javier lacked. He, somehow, has strawberries, if not pears, and he presses them into Javier's hand, then gives Eliza a look that suggests she'd be better off with his young self. Amused and full of roguish hope, Javier lifts the berries toward the window. Half a dozen women squeal and reach for them, but Eliza is not among them. She watches, not quite letting herself smile, and says, "If I fall I'll break your head, and there was trouble enough when I broke your arm. And you were a lesser man, then."

"I was the same man I've always been," Javier says, and lowers the berries. The women all coo disappointment, but their giggling and delight fade into the background until Eliza is barely more aware of them than she is of the light breeze that cools her. Something must cool her, at least, because the warmth within her seems to be growing, and if there's no breeze she may well light into fire, burning up the skies out of not-so-secret hope and joy.

"I was the same man I've always been," Javier repeats, more softly, "only younger and more foolish. Much more foolish, Liz. I didn't know until you were gone how badly I needed you."

There's murmuring in the background, and Eliza takes her eyes from the young king of Gallin to look at the gondola, where Marius appears to be translating Javier's words for the benefit of the gondola boy. The boy's mouth is pushed out, ducklike, and he wobbles his head dubiously, then finally turns his palms up in reluctant approval. Marius grins and ruffles the boy's hair, then turns his attention back to Javier and Eliza, offering a bow from the waist when he sees she's looking at him. Javier twists, offended, to see what's taken her attention from him, then turns a plaintive look back toward her window.

"The boy thinks I'm poor with words, and shouldn't be allowed to speak for myself. He may be right, as I've had a lifetime to say the things I should, without realising how badly I wanted to. We've been so careful of our balance, the four of us," he whispers. "I should have seen long ago that you were worth upsetting it for. I have been rescued from my own folly and have brought these," he says wryly, and offers up the berries. "Hardly a fitting gift for wooing, but pears are not yet in season, and I find myself on the edge of desperation. Will you have me, Liz? I go to war, and need you at my side."

The women all around her are silent now, clutching one another, clutching her, holding their breath to hear her young lover's words more clearly, turning to her with wide eyes to see how she might respond. Oh, whores all of them, perhaps, but born to a culture that admires the ideal of romantic love and plays to it, even if they don't believe in it themselves.

And there is the grain of truth at the centre of it, the few rare moments when love does conquer, and makes glad fools of all. There's a stillness in those moments, a greatness waiting to happen, and not even the most jaded courtesan wishes to let those grains escape when hands might clasp to catch them.

"Damn you, Javier de Castille," Eliza finally whispers, and her throat is tight with the curse, and her eyes bright with tears. "Damn you, for there's nothing I can deny you, least of all my heart."

JAVIER, KING OF GALLIN

The courtesans, not one of them believing Javier was in truth the king of Gallin, left in a drove, scattering to the canals to tell tales of how the king of Gallin had come to make love to an impoverished but beautiful woman under their watch. Truth hardly mattered; it was the delight of the story they wanted to share.

When they were gone Eliza came into her courtyard and caught first Javier, then Marius, and then both men together, into a hug with strength enough to belie the softness of her gown and long shining hair. None of them spoke for long minutes, until Eliza finally took back a few steps and pulled her wig off to rake her fingers through short matted locks.

Her hair had grown out in the months since he'd seen her last; had grown out considerably since she'd begun her business under Beatrice's tutelage, but it was still too short to be anything but a man's cut. Even that couldn't take away from the delicacy of her face and the largeness of her eyes. Given a crown, she could stir men's hearts to wonders, and it was a wonder to Javier that he had never seen it. Unaware of Javier's thoughts, though, she gestured to her gown, muttered, "I feel ridiculous in this," and fled upstairs to change.

Bemused, Javier watched her go; watched her leave behind the vestiges of softness that had shaped her moments ago. He thought it strange, that she could be soft and feminine more easily when surrounded by strangers, but when her family of friends arrived she fell back into more masculine ways, making herself hard and practical. If that was what their friendship cost, then the three men who were her near-brothers had done her a disservice.

She returned in clothes that were familiar to him, lightweight pants and a loose linen shirt, cinched at the waist with a belt of leather and metal. There was a dagger at her hip, a new addition; she had not needed one in Lutetia, even dressing as she did, not with all the city knowing she was under Javier's protection. With it, she looked the part of a pirate, soft boots and all, though no pirate had such curves, and his straining memory couldn't remember seeing the shadow of her breasts so clearly before.

Tomas, at his side, made a sound of dismay. Eliza's eyes flashed to him, then darkened and came back to Javier. "Don't tell me you've brought a priest to mend my wicked ways."

"Not unless he'll mend them by marrying you to me," Javier replied, and felt ice slide down his spine at the weight of both Tomas and Eliza's gazes.

Tomas recovered first, if barely, hissing, "She wears *men's clothes,* my lord, and shows her body without—"

Javier snapped a hand up, cutting off his words. "She always has, and always may, so far as the king of Gallin cares. Do not condemn her, not in my hearing nor out."

Tomas's jaw tensed, but Eliza curled a smile and glanced from Javier to Marius, then beyond the priest. "Sacha?"

"In Gallin still, searching for you, the last I knew." Javier came up a few steps toward her and offered his hand.

Eliza's faint smile stayed in place as she put her hand in Javier's, though her gaze went to Marius again. "So you're the one who betrayed me, are you?"

"Sacha didn't know where you'd gone." Marius arched an eyebrow at Eliza's hand in Javier's. "And I think you're not as betrayed as you might pretend, Liz. Tell me you didn't want us to come after you."

Eliza shrugged, a small tight motion that said even more than her words did. "I didn't believe you would."

Javier tugged her closer, pulling her off-balance on the steps and catching her weight when she might otherwise have fallen. "I will always come for you, and I beg forgiveness that it's taken this long. I was a fool, Liz. I've always been one."

Eliza put her hands on his chest and pushed herself back, one eyebrow cocked dubiously. "Marius, who is this man? He looks and sounds like Javier de Castille, but my prince only apologises when he's drunk."

"There have been some dramatic changes these past months," Marius said drily, then glanced at Javier and made a face. "Let him explain, and when you think you're as mad as he is, come have a flask of wine with us and be told that we all are."

"My curiosity is piqued," Eliza said, and laughed as Javier turned her around with his hands at her waist. "I can turn myself about, my prince. You need only ask." But she went upstairs with her hips swaying, a more provocative sight than Javier had ever noticed. He looked back, dropping a wink at Marius, whose expression was a mix of pleasure and melancholy, but who nodded them off with a gentle smile.

Eliza led him into what had to be her own bedroom, open and airy, windows flung wide to let in sounds of the canal, but with gauzy curtains that forbade anyone from glancing inside with too much casual ease. Only the neighbours might, but the neighbours unquestionably would. He caught her waist and tried to pull her to the bed, but she smacked his hand as if he were an unruly child, and went to close first the shutters, then the door, against sound and light alike.

Quietude settled over the room with the shadows, taking some of Javier's good mood with it. Eliza stood in front of the door, arms folded under her breasts, and glowered at him: not at all the expression he wanted to see on a woman he intended to marry. Befuddled, hopeful, feeling more than a little foolish, he asked, "What's wrong?"

Eliza snorted. "Where to start? Four months ago you'd all but broken with all of us over Beatrice Irvine, and today you're here pleading love and marriage, which are words I've waited my whole life to hear and which make no sense to my ears now that I do hear them."

Javier clenched his teeth. "Beatrice—Belinda—was a mistake. I'm sorry, Liz. I was a fool."

"And he apologises again." There was no pleasure in Eliza at his modesty. "I could start there, too. What's come over you?"

"God's light." That was not what he'd intended to say, not at all how he'd meant for this conversation to go, but Eliza's anger was greater than he'd imagined it would be.

Her glower hardened further. "Is that a curse or an answer, Javier? Has the priest addled your brains? He's pretty enough."

"Eliza, you need not speak to me so." Too much tension leaked into the words, his jaw aching with it, but a note of recognition and satisfaction leapt into Eliza's eyes.

"There's my king," she said, though a note of mockery seemed to hang in the word. "My sullen prince."

"If all you want is to rail at me," Javier said tightly, "why do you still wear that ring?"

Caught out, she glanced down, then covered her left hand with her right, as though the pale stone might disappear if it couldn't be seen. A long time passed before she whispered, "Because a boy I loved gave it to me, Jav. All right. All right, you have my ears, I am listening."

"God has given me a gift. Please don't scream."

"Scream? I've yet to see a gift God's given a man that made me want to scream. Laugh, perhaps—"

The dimness in the room was a gift now, too, as Javier cupped his hands and called the witchlight. Silver spilled through his fingers and down to the floor, crawling over itself, pushing motes of sunlit dust out of its path as it swirled toward Eliza. She caught her breath, then scrambled away, jumping onto the bed and staring first at the dancing witchlight, then at Javier, and back again. He remained where he was, letting the magic flow, watching it, watching her; most especially, watching her.

"All my life I've feared it was the devil's power, Liz. It's what's kept me remote from everything. From you. But I knelt before the Pappas to be crowned and the power leapt at his touch, and he welcomed it. A holy man would know if I were the devil's get, and has told me instead that I'm blessed."

"I don't understand." The intensity of Eliza's voice pushed the witchpower back, almost frightening Javier. "What is it? How— Javier, it's—"

"It's just light," Javier whispered. Didn't dare lift his voice louder, as though soft tones might keep her from bolting. "This part of it, it's just light. Perhaps a little warmth. Touch it, you'll see."

"*Touch* it?" Their eyes met, and a memory rose in Javier's mind, a day not very long after they'd met. His arm was still broken, and a toad of preposterous ugliness had made its way into the garden pond. He wanted it, and Eliza's hands were the only ones he could rely on to catch the monster. She had said the same thing then, in much the same tone, and after a few seconds of horrified staring at him, she broke into laughter.

"Dammit, now I'm ten years old and you're a toad, Jav. This will never do." Cautiously—more cautiously than she'd approached the toad some fifteen years earlier—she leaned forward, watching the dancing witchpower warily. Javier reined in the impulse to let it wash over her, afraid he'd send her skittering again, and eventually she put a hand toward the light and it rose from the floor to greet her. Barely audible, she muttered, "How like a man," then twisted her hand to see if she could swirl it, too.

Light wrapped around her wrist; fathomless caress that brought unexpected heat to Javier's loins. Belinda had never stroked his power so, and he had no expectation of its response or how it brought sensation back to him. "It's warm," Eliza murmured. "Alive."

"It is my will," Javier said. "I have . . . done things with it that I'm not proud of, Liz. It's why the priest travels with us, to help guide me. But I need you even more. You are honest and blunt and beautiful, and you are the Gallic people. You've stood beside me all my life and I've never seen that. I can only hope I haven't come to it too late."

Eliza lifted her hands, wreathed in silver power. It trickled down her arms, shaping her sleeves beneath the weight of careful intent. There was no colour in her hair to bring out; silver simply reflected there, reflected in her eyes, and made her skin moon-pale. "You were too late years ago, Jav, when the fever took me. I've told you I can't bear children, and you can't have a barren queen. I would make a fine rich man's mistress," she said for the second time that Javier knew of, but this time, curled in light, there was no bitterness or false levity in her voice. It was merely a fact, spoken as gently as she could.

"These last few months I've learned that this power doesn't begin and end with the witchlight, Liz. I can shield. I can fight. I can bend men to my will, if I must, though I believe it's wrong and I am trying so hard not to fall on that path. Perhaps I can do more." Tendrils crept up her arms to follow the exposed line of her throat, to push her shirt's collar open and trace her collarbones: the things he wished to do, made manifest with the witchlight.

Eliza's eyes were smoky in the magical light, humour and desire and curiosity roughening her voice. "Are you bending my will now, my prince?"

Javier whispered, "Never," and she smiled, then tilted her head under the witchlight's caress. The laces were open at her collar, showing him a spill of breast; with witchpower alone he found a nipple and played it, moving closer himself as Eliza gasped and arched under the power's touch. Then she laughed, trembling sound, and breathed, "This is, yes, more, Javier."

"But not what I was thinking. If I can destroy with this gift, perhaps I can heal as well." He was close enough to reach for the heavy belt that cinched her waist, to unfasten its buckles and let it fall away. Her breathing deepened, eyes unfocused as she put a hand out toward him, but he moved back, smiling, to loosen her boots and put them aside. She watched, amused, and pointed her toes daintily as he exposed her feet, then reached toward him again. Javier shook his head and stepped back again, as enamoured of exploration with his magic as he was of the woman reclining on the bed.

Once it was loosened from the belt, it was easy to edge her shirt out of the way with power; easy to strip her trousers and discover she wore nothing under them. She became shy then, closing her thighs, twisting away from him and tossing a coquettish glance over her shoulder. Bathed in witchlight, glowing with it, even her short hair looked feminine, soft and touchable. Magic tousled it, then ran down her spine, sending her into another arch that exposed more of her body to him.

He knew that she was beautifully formed, had always known it, but knowing and seeing, knowing and *feeling*, with the intimacy of his magic, were different things entirely. He clung to the bedpost, dizzy with his own want and delighted with Eliza's: witchpower teased her nipples and parted her lips like a lover's tongue might, spilled down her belly and nestled in the dark curls between her thighs, then secreted itself in hidden places closed too tightly for fingers to go. Witchpower gave him the shape of her, as clear to his mind as if he could see her, and guided by his own excitement and her growing need he stroked and circled increasingly desperate flesh until desire overcame shyness and her legs parted again, wanton and hungry.

Javier's low rough laugh was for himself, was for the strength of will it took to keep from diving forward into offered sweetness. He ached, cock swollen as though he'd stroked and teased himself, not Eliza, but one thought clawed its way to coherency and remained with him: he could do damage so easily with his powers; to give pleasure with them, and them alone, surely made a weight against the horror of what he could too easily become.

And if there was another gift to himself in giving Eliza all she could desire without ever touching her, it was in seeing her body so clearly as she gasped and shuddered under his magic's touch. Her knees were spread wide, hips rising to meet magic and falling again when he eased off, unwilling to bring her to a final climax so soon. Her stomach clenched and trembled with little deaths, and her hands fisted in the covers as she flung her head back, making her throat long and beautiful. Witchpower traced the delicate hollow there, plucked at her nipples and found the tender spots behind her ears. Kissed her thighs and licked her mound, and spread her with finger's-width touches, all at once. There was beauty in that, in the overwhelming sensation he could offer with the touch of his witchpower, and the high flushed colour in Eliza's cheeks, the unexpected whimpers and soft keens that she kept clenched behind her teeth, told him that there was wonder in being so inundated.

When he finally took her it was with magic still, her body softening and accepting him as though he lay above her. Heat washed back to him, surrounded him as it rode the witchpower, and filled him with the same base pleasure that drew a groan from between Eliza's teeth. She drove herself toward the power he filled her with, and gave over to an incredulous cry as, heaving for concentration, he turned the magic to all the same sweet points of bliss he'd learned on her already.

The wave that swept her took him along with her, no surprise but for his inability, in its wake, to retain any grip at all on the witchpower. Eliza let go a tiny sound of dismay while Javier fell at the bed's foot, silent laughter of chagrin shaking his body. "Forgive me, Liz," he finally mumbled from his lowly place. "I had no idea it would all fall apart at the end."

She appeared above him, flushed and bright-eyed, and put out a hand to him for the third time. Finally, he accepted it, and let her draw him into the bed, the better to explore possibility and passion as one.

ROBERT, LORD DRAKE
2 April 1588 † *Aria Magli*

Power has burned through Aria Magli since the afternoon, so strong, so flavoured, that Robert Drake could follow it to its source with his eyes closed. He has chosen not to, for two reasons. One, he has tasted this particular talent before, and knows, even if rumour were not aswirl in the island-built city, that it belongs to Javier de Castille, young king of Gallin and unexpected heir to a skill not of this world.

Two, to follow it would be to show himself, and there are better things to do than give his hand away. Javier plays his own hand loudly, all unknowing: if he can pour magic into the air the way he has done today, then he is fully grown in confidence, and there is only one end to be expected now.

Aria Magli is rarely a silent city, with traffic on its canals at all hours, voices lifted in song and praise and anger echoing off the water and the homes that line it. Rather than hunt down Javier de Castille, Robert has sought and paid for a room with no windows overlooking the canals, paid a dear price, for tonight he has need of what quietude he can get.

There are so many things that can be done with what Belinda calls the *witchpower*. It's as good a name as any; his people would call it no more than language or physicality, its presence so integral a part of them that words failed it. But here, bound by humanity, it's an unnatural thing, separate and apart from what ordinary people might do. So it is the witchpower, and there are so many things that can be done with it that he almost no longer remembers them all. It has been a mortal lifetime and more since he's given up the boundless power and ease of use that came with his other form. Then, he might have reached halfway around a world with no more effort than the thought; might have touched his queen's mind and sought her direction. But that was long ago, and the body into which he has been born anew is so much weaker in its capabilities. To do what once would have been of no import he now needs silence and hours of preparation.

The room is warm, a fire built higher than most people would find comfortable. That, too, is expensive in this city: there is little enough to burn here, and what there is must be brought in from Parna's mainland. But heat helps to remind him of what he was, and to loosen his muscles, loosen his mind, so that he can gather his focus over the long hours.

He imagines it as a stream of sunlight punching through the clouds, one brilliant streak of gold against grey and black and white. The clouds are the distance of minds on this blue planet, murky and thick and roiling with solitude even as each one brushes up against another in physical form; sunlight is the power that can separate them and illuminate the relevant, if only briefly. It's a pretty picture in his mind, and he wonders if once upon a time he would have been so poetic, or if that's the human nature that's become so fundamental to him.

In time, that thought, like all others, drifts away. Robert Drake is not like the daughter he fathered: calling witchlight is not especially natural to him, or indeed of any importance at all, but in the silence he's created in this room, in his mind, the sunlight he imagines manifests in his hands, a warm glow that steadily builds in strength. His eyes are closed and he does not see it, and fortunately for him, very few people are awake at this hour to study the brightness that leaks from beneath his door, or to note how its brilliance becomes too much to look upon.

To Robert, it is a weight in his mind, gathering the critical mass to slam through clouds. It's closer to dawn than he might like when it has finally grown strong enough, and to his way of thinking it becomes an arrow, shooting across a continent in search of the rare mind capable of receiving it.

To the handful who are awake in Aria Magli, it is a falling star that flies in reverse, one brilliant streak that races away to the west and fades so quickly it might never have been there at all. They will speak of it, and wonder at it, but as for Robert Drake, weary from his efforts and unaware of the spectacle he has created, he will sleep where he sits, in front of a fire finally ebbing with the dawn.

BELINDA PRIMROSE
2 April 1588 † *Alunaer*

Her father's voice awakened her, so loud and unexpectedly clear that she jolted to her elbows, staring around her cell in heart-racing anticipation.

It was empty, as it had to be, nothing more than herself and a sliver of moonlight to occupy it. But Robert's voice lingered, reverberating from the walls. She could smell chypre, the cologne he always wore, and slowly she realised that the scent lit flares of witchpower in her mind. Chypre had haunted her when Javier had helped to waken her witchpower, too, its familiar scent part of the barrier that had been erected to keep her magic caged.

She whispered "Robert," but by then she knew he wasn't there, and that his voice had only spoken within her mind.

Prepare, the echoes said again. *Prepare, my Primrose. Prepare for war.*

10

It wasn't done for a bastard daughter to demand to see her mother. The audacity would have driven Belinda from comfortable thoughts, had her thoughts not already been so badly disrupted by Robert's missive. She had left the convent with Dmitri, meek and pious as always, and between a corner and a straight place had called the stillness to her, wrapping herself in it more swiftly than she'd ever done before. Shadows had flooded from sunlit places, drawn to her, and though Dmitri, attuned to her use of power, had whirled, it had been too late.

She had run full speed through Alunaer, had stolen quill and paper from a scribe within the palace, and, too frantic to waste time trying to explain to Cortes how she'd come by her information, had left an imperious note on his desk: there was word from *dearest Jayne,* and it must be imparted to the queen at once. Her majesty would know the meeting place.

And now she waited, heartbeat high but chin held higher yet, for Lorraine's arrival in the secret chamber. Illogical certainties surged through Belinda's mind, upsetting the calm she could normally call at a whim. Lorraine would know what to do in the face of war; Lorraine *had* to know, for she was the queen. She must be warned, as early as possible, and then she would take Belinda from her hours of study and give her a task of toothy import. Belinda longed for that, longed for the action she had been raised to. Weeks of studying had broadened and deepened her skills, yes, but weeks of Dmitri's guidance had taught her little more of his plans. Like

Robert, he wanted a pawn most of all, intending to play her and sacrifice her when need be. But Belinda was the daughter of a queen, and if she played the pawn, it was now only a part, a learning place until she was ready to remake the board.

With war on the horizon, that time might well be soon.

The silent door opened, bringing the same warmth it had last time. Belinda whirled on her mother, ignoring all protocol to blurt, "There will be war."

Lorraine lifted a finely painted eyebrow and said, drily, "We are unobserved, yes, and we are honoured by your obsequience."

Teeth grinding, Belinda sank into a curtsey that scratched plain grey wool over her skin, and remained there until Lorraine said, "You are meant to be in a convent, girl, not running about Alunaer wearing garb that places you as missing from one."

Belinda muttered, "No one saw me, your majesty."

Lorraine sniffed. "Not even Cortes, who claims a note appeared on his desk from nowhere, though he was looking at it at the time. We are curious as to how you arranged that."

"A lady never tells, majesty." The ground-out words brought her back to Aria Magli, where Robert had teased her with that very phrase; to her surprise, Lorraine echoed it now.

"A lady never does, girl. A gentleman never tells."

Edgy to the point of daring, Belinda lifted her eyes to meet Lorraine's. "As a lady who's never done, loved by a gentleman who never tells, will you tell me, majesty, if it is never done nor told, what matters how it might be done?"

Astonishment too fresh to be offence flooded Lorraine's face. For the briefest of moments Belinda allowed herself a feeling of solidarity with the queen: perhaps it was only with each other they might both strip away certain masks and allow true emotion to come through, for she doubted Lorraine would have permitted herself such an expression in a courtroom.

Then again, rare indeed was the courtier who would dare the rudeness Belinda had just put to a reigning queen. She set those thoughts aside, making her words into knives. "There is war coming. I have it from Robert's voice. Aulun must prepare."

She knew as soon as she spoke that she had chosen her words

poorly, and yet she'd picked them with as much deliberation as she could. Still, anticipation lit Lorraine's aging features. "Robert has returned?"

"No, majesty. It was—" Belinda clenched her hand in the shapeless convent robe. "His voice came to me as if in a dream, majesty, but I was awake. It sounds a fool's lark, and I know it, but this is not a thing to make light of."

"We will decide what is and what is not to be made light of." Lorraine's voice was ice, pure and hard. "What else did he say?"

"Only to prepare. Majesty, I know I am rude and uncouth and young and not supposed to be here—"

Lorraine humphed, but Belinda bowled on, as much determined as she was any of the other things she named herself. "—but I am also your majesty's—"

There was no break in Belinda's speech, no silence she could hear, and yet words unspoken fell after that phrase, words so clearly unspoken that Lorraine stiffened even as Belinda continued what she had never broken in saying: "—loyal servant, and have been all my life. You do not know me well, but you know Robert. He would not have sent me here with things to say to you if I were flighty or unreliable, and he would not have given me this warning, no matter how esoteric the manner, if it was not something that Aulun should act on."

"And if we do," Lorraine said, still wonderfully cool, "what will your role be, girl?"

Startled out of her passion, Belinda opened one hand. "As it has always been, majesty. Whatever you command it to be."

"Remember that," Lorraine said. "Remember that, in the days to come." She turned and stalked from the round chamber, leaving Belinda bent in a curtsey and bewildered to her core.

She stole a pastie from a street merchant on her way back to Dmitri's home, savouring the hot gravy that dripped over her fingers and the fatty, tough meat that required long and careful chewing. The convent's food was plainer, and Dmitri's much finer; this simple fare harkened to the innumerable roles she'd played as a ser-

vant girl, and gave her comfort. Grease ran to her elbows and
stained her clothes, and she cared not at all, licking her fingers clean
as she pushed Dmitri's front door open and, content, breathed in
warm scented air.

Blinding pain shattered across her face, white at first and then
fading to throbbing red. She staggered, catching herself on the wall,
and lifted a tear-blurred gaze to see Dmitri's hand coming down
toward her again. Choler flowered in him, spilling over without
words; always without words, from the dark witchlord, but vivid
and clear none the less: she had given herself to him as a student, a
vassal, and to break away as she had done, to call her power and hide
from him so she might pursue an errand of her own, was a slight
that must be answered.

Her own witchpower flared and a golden shield caught the blow
with the reverberating force of a blade smashing into armour.
Dmitri's wrist cracked, getting a yell from him, and without
thought Belinda struck back. Not physically: he was the larger and
had the advantage, and besides, outraged magic had her in its grip
and intended its own methods of subdual.

The surge of power came from her core, gut-deep and roaring
through her. It took Dmitri in the chest, slamming him across the
room with more force than she'd imagined having to command.
She felt from him a response, a quick cloud of darkness that sprang
to cushion him as he smashed into the far wall. Saving his life, she
supposed, but in her rage she saw it as providing her with a chance
to play with her catch a while longer. Her head swam with pain
still, flashes of white that disrupted the golden haze she saw him
through.

He got one hand under him—the left, the one he had not hit
her with—and began to shove upward, fury blackening his eyes.
Belinda barely knew the sound she made, derision so harsh it hurt
her throat. She knocked his hand from beneath him with the satisfaction of a kick, realising distantly that he had shielded against her
this time, and that it had been as though she'd had no more than
empty air to push against.

"How dare you." Her voice was as distorted as her scoff had
been. "Have you forgotten what you are? What I am?" She stalked

158 · C. E. MURPHY

toward him, crouched over him with a clawed hand at his throat. "I have asked for guidance and wisdom and teaching, none of which, *none of which,* give you leave to make so bold with my person. How *dare* you."

His pulse throbbed quick and hard beneath her fingers, his breath coming shallow under the pressure she exerted. With skin touching skin, she could feel him gather power, preparing another strike, though his thoughts were still his own. She reached for the memory of what Robert had done to her, the chypre-scented wall he'd placed in her mind, and a waterwheel of sensation built within her. She pushed that toward Dmitri, a cascade of power that shut away the gift he called his own. Shock lit his eyes and she leaned closer, aching with power. "I can neuter you with a thought, witchlord. Your magic is mine to control. Name me."

His answer came raggedly, almost a defiance: "Belinda."

Belinda's fingers tightened at his throat, nails digging in. She did not, in that moment, much care if he lived or died; his audacity in hitting her outweighed any skills she might learn from him. *"Name me."*

"Belinda," he grated again. "Belinda Primrose."

A spark of appreciation for his willpower glittered through her anger, but the anger was greater. She didn't speak a third time, only brought all the golden fire within her to bear, power rushing toward him. Teeth clenched, Dmitri resisted a few seconds longer, then, in so much as he could, threw his head back, a cry tearing from his throat: "My queen!"

Triumph spattered through Belinda. She swayed above Dmitri, riding the waves of his raw, forced submission. *This,* the witch-power whispered, this was what she was made for: for placing herself above others, for veneration, for brooking no weakness in herself or haughtiness in others. A path of domination lay before her, so bright and clear it seemed to burn through her mind, through the walls, all the way to the horizon and to the distant stars.

That thought twisted, dredging up the memories stolen from Robert, the explanations offered by the man who sprawled beneath her. To the horizon, to the stars, and to a queen and a war she understood too little of. For an instant she saw that impossible monarch as a rival. Ambition blazed before the greater part of her pulled back, turning away from worlds beyond in order to deal with the one she belonged to. Whatever esoteric fate might lie tangled with Robert's plans, there was a war coming to her country, and if its first battle was here, in Dmitri's fine warm home, then she would win, and worry about the next as it came.

Dmitri struggled to reach his power again; Belinda could feel his indignity and astonishment that she'd cut him off from it. Part of her took pleasure in it, though part of her was filled with offence that he should think his magic was not hers to command. If Robert could shape her ability to touch the witchpower when she was a child, she should be able to control Dmitri's, or any man's. She caught his undamaged wrist and brought his hand to her face. Even in the midst of her anger and power, she felt the sting of his touch against the bruise he'd left there, though despite all the ways she'd forgone the stillness, she could not let herself wince in time with the pain. She whispered, "Heal this," instead, and released the slightest trickle of Dmitri's own power.

Everything that he had surged toward that break point, a black wall of magic determined to overwhelm her own. Belinda steeled her core, meeting that onslaught with confidence that turned to a deep thrill as Dmitri's power splashed against hers and rolled back again. Warmth spilled through her, nestling in her belly, her breasts, between her thighs, and her pulse heightened as she acknowledged desire that had been forcibly put away in the last weeks of study. Dmitri was right: the witchpower was not sex, nor was sex power, but he was wrong as well, and all the things that helped her live in her flesh were things that fed the magic.

"Heal this," she said again, and this time all the power that came to bear turned toward the talent she had no knack for. She could almost hear Dmitri's thoughts, could almost, in holding his magic, understand the science he said lay behind the healing. Blood and bone; those were things she knew, vessels and veins, but from his power's touch she caught glimpses of other things, too small to be seen, which healed and regenerated under his magic. They were the stuff of life, but then the healing retreated, taking with it any chance of comprehending and leaving her hungry for the intimacy of that touch again. Belinda reached for it, her power surrounding Dmitri's, and in doing so she brushed old intent and aspiration within him.

She'd not had the skill in Khazar to sense that focus, not in the way she could do so now. She had known then that he wanted her; now she could taste the ambition in that want, as though she were a means with which to obtain an end.

Staggering clarity told her that he, too, could be a method by which she might create her own purpose, rather than simply following the path laid out before her by Robert and Lorraine, or even Dmitri. Witchpower heat scalded her skin from within, coaxing that thought to fruition. Once, not long ago, she had been unable to turn her back on duty. Now she grasped eagerly at new possibilities flowering in her mind, then let them go again before they became whole concepts, for fear Dmitri might share her talent of stealing thoughts, and not wanting to share these.

The loose novice's robes were easy enough to shed, even holding Dmitri's throat; she rucked them over her head and flung them to the side, shaking them off her wrist as she changed hands to keep the witchlord pinned. His gaze went black as he looked on her, simple human desire unladen with complications. Belinda wet her lips and released a thread of his power as she nodded toward his injured wrist. "Heal that."

She felt the surge a second time, felt tantalisingly close to comprehension as he mended cracked bone. Muscle flexed in his shoulders as he brought his attention back to her, minute warning that, healed, he might attempt to seize the upper hand. She hissed a warning, soft primal sound, and he stiffened, earning her quick grin. Stiff was how she wanted him, but not so much that he thought himself the master in their tête-à-tête. She leaned forward to put her mouth by his ear, shifting some of her weight on his collarbones, but leaving enough on his throat to remain a reminder that he would pay for foolishness. "Your power is mine to command, dark prince, and I am tired of teasing. I would have you please me now."

His lashes tangled over dark eyes, a thin smile curving his mouth. "I am still clothed, my queen."

Belinda bit his earlobe. "That should hardly stop you."

Chagrined amusement ghosted through her on the trickle of power she allowed him access to. Then, behind the chagrin came new purpose, flavoured with the intention to overwhelm her. That near-awareness of knowledge flooded her again, though its focus seemed changed. No longer healing, but still exciting the blood, triggering changes—once again, she almost grasped the thought and the science behind what he did, and then sensation became something to ride on, making her heady and uncaring of how, so long as it was done. Heat swelled between her thighs without a touch, without caresses or soft words or hard hands, without any of those things she'd been trained to. Desire came on like a dream, intense, half-imagined, drumming an incessant beat that had no physical component and yet aroused her as thoroughly as any man's hand might.

She didn't know when clawed fingers left his throat in search of tugging open his breeches. It was witchpower, it seemed, which held him down: even freed from her grasp he stayed where he was, gaze heavy on hers even when she tilted her head back and rolled with pleasure. He remained still as she settled on him, more strength of will in that lack of motion than most men had, and it was her own sound of liquid delight that echoed in her ears as he filled her. His length curving inside her brought the finish to what magic had begun, sending spasms through her and the slightest sense of smugness through the witchpower link she shared with her lover. Had it been Javier, she might have laughed; with Dmitri it only stoked challenge and a need for further control.

It was only later, much later, as she dragged herself back to her convent cell, that she wondered if that, too, had been a lesson in her magic, or if it even mattered.

AKILINA DE COSTA, QUEEN OF ESSANDIA
7 April 1588 † *Isidro, Essandia*

Akilina Pankejeff, for that is how she still thinks of herself, and always will, hates vomiting.

Not that she is under the illusion that there are those who enjoy it, but the roiling of her belly, the beaded sweat on lip and forehead that turns to bitter chills, the anticipation of sickness, the terrible retching sound torn from her throat when bile surges upward; these are things she loathes. Even as a child she preferred standing in the frozen outdoors, sipping tiny breaths of icy air, to curling up and letting illness take its course. Her father, in the years before he died, called her a soldier when she would do this, and she'd taken pride in that, used it to shore herself up against a twisting belly.

Her father has been dead for more than twenty years, and no tall tales of soldiers prevent sourness from poisoning her stomach and coating her teeth as they have done every morning for the past three weeks.

For some reason she has always assumed that the sickness of pregnancy was something that affected other women, and would not dare to bother her. But it began literally the morning after she was wed, a hideous rising that sent her running for a chamber pot without a chance to defeat it. Rodrigo had pushed up on an elbow and watched her shudder and gag over the pot, his handsome features arranged with a degree of surprise. When, shuddering, she fell away and wiped her mouth, he rang a bell for a servant, then, with the same mild amusement he'd shown before their wedding, asked, "Am I as bad as all that, lady?"

Akilina raised a look full of daggers to the prince lounging in her bed, and his amusement turned to a full-out laugh. He rose, damnably lithe and well-formed for a man twice her age, and pulled on a robe that gave him a bit of decency as the maids came running. "My queen is indisposed," he said with due formality. "Attend her."

Admiration for his virility had spread through the capital city by noon, and, Akilina imagines now, as she did then, had reached the coast and the northern mountains alike by sunfall. *She* has spent weeks feeble with sickness while *he* has accepted congratulations and hearty smiles; it is not at all how she imagined her first month as a monarch. Still, she staggers to her window and looks out over Isidro, a hand over her still-flat stomach, and she smiles. Events have spun out more rapidly than she might have expected, but not badly. Pigeons have winged back and forth between herself and Irina, and the imperatrix is satisfied with Akilina's new position. More than satisfied: Ivanova is no longer a necessary bargaining chip, but the alliances with Essandia and therefore Gallin are now solid.

There is the matter of what is to be done about Aulun, from a Khazarian standpoint, but that is not Akilina's trouble. That's for Irina, whose backstabbing and double-crossing treaties and alliances have become difficulties, to deal with. Essandia has its own plans for Aulun, and Akilina is more concerned with them than with Khazar's. Essandia, after all, has made her a queen, and that is a title she could never have aspired to at home.

The women come to dress her and she manages that without another bout of illness; it is, for her, the worst immediately after awakening, and only triggered again by overpowering scents. Things she once enjoyed now make her nauseous, and cautious ladies-in-waiting have learned already to offer treats slowly, so Akilina might thrust them away should they unexpectedly offend. It's a delicate dance, all done in Essandian, though Akilina hopes a few of them are learning Khazarian. Once summer comes she'll send for servants of her own household to join her here in Isidro, but until then a little talk would be a welcoming gesture for the new queen.

And they are welcoming of her indeed, with pregnancy coming so soon after marriage. Akilina lets the women go and stands on her own, still fighting sickness, but one stops at the doorway to offer a shy curtsey. "Forgive me, your majesty—"

Akilina almost doesn't hear what the girl says after that; she is still too taken with hearing those words, "your majesty," spoken to her. It's an indulgence, but one she has no intention of letting go of soon: there's nothing more worth savouring. Her thoughts catch up to the servant's question, and she nods agreement, then shoos the woman out.

Not much later, Sacha Asselin enters. Akilina is arranged at the window, much as she was when he took her from the Gallic prison, but she's forgone any pretence of embroidery and only looks out over Isidro. This, after all, is her city now, and she its queen. Sacha bows deeply and without irony; she likes that in him, that he can hide all signs of mockery as he comes to sit near her, once she's granted leave with a wave of her fingers. "How do you find Isidro, my lord Asselin?"

"The wine is sweet, the women are willing, and I have my queen to command me," Sacha says lightly, as he has said every day when she's put that question to him. "Though I fear I'll need to return to Lutetia soon, my lady. Javier intends war."

"And you intend to guide him in it."

"I'm of more use there than here," Sacha says, which doesn't answer the implied question. "I've done my duty by you and Rod— the prince."

There's a self-satisfied smugness in his voice, the cockiness of youth. Akilina supposes she, too, would be smug were she in his shoes, having cuckolded the prince of Essandia. Only for a few nights; what might have become a dalliance over the length of the journey to Essandia ended early, in part because Akilina is cautious. True caution would have refused Sacha her bed at all, but true caution would never have offered her the chance of a child close enough in conception to be Rodrigo's, but no part of him. Perhaps it's a woman's thought: that a child begat by a man not her husband is somehow a thing entirely of her own, but it's a thought Akilina holds to. She'll have the shaping of the babe in her womb, with its true father unacknowledged and the man who claims it not bound by blood. Women have only what they take in this world, and Akilina intends on taking all she can.

Sacha shifts, her silence going on too long, and she brings her attention back to him. The other reason she sent him from her bed is one she will never admit to: boredom. He can be creative, but he's more often coarse and hurrying for his own pleasure. Rodrigo is the better lover, for all that Akilina doubts very much that the prince bedded any women before herself. There were those he'd kept company with, and whom he'd assiduously set aside and watched over to make certain there were no by-blows. Those few women are all wealthy now, well-kept in glorious homes. Royal castoffs often do well in society, but not all of them; not each and every one with the degree of success Rodrigo's former paramours have seen. They're too talented, too witty, too wise; Akilina has met them, and they are all, to a woman, perfect consorts. No man can choose so wisely each time his heart leads him, and so Akilina is certain Rodrigo's has never led him. These women are contrivances, selected to create a discreet reputation.

She approves, actually, not that her approval makes the slightest difference. Still, it tells her things about his cleverness, and tells her, too, that if they should find themselves on the same side, they could be a devastating force.

Akilina Pankejeff does not, for one moment, believe she and Rodrigo de Costa are on the same side.

"More than your duty" is what she murmurs aloud. Sacha suspects, but does not know, that the child she carries is his; they were not lovers long enough for him to know the march of her red army. But the chance that it might be will keep Sacha on a long string, ready to dance for her when she whistles. She'll let him wonder as long as he's useful, and will dispose of him when he ceases to be. For now, he's her nearest man to Javier de Castille's ear, and that's worth keeping him alive for.

Avarice and interest flash in his eyes at her words as he takes them to be a hint of her child's father. Akilina indulges in a dismissive thought: *Men. So easily manipulated.* That, of course, is entirely unfair: women are just as easy to shape and lead. "You have brought Khazar and Essandia together," she says, more than a little sanctimoniously, and rather enjoying it. "You've helped forge a great alliance between the east and west, and have strengthened your faith's military arm considerably. I should think your name will be written in history books, Lord Asselin, as harbinger of a new era."

Colour burns Sacha's cheeks, making him look younger than he is. Akilina thinks of him as a boy even without such reminders, though he's less than a decade her junior. "Word from Cordula says Javier returns to Lutetia by sea. Will he stop here?"

Still ruddy with imagined pride, Sacha shakes his head. "He spent too much time in Isidro already, and spring is all but on us. He'll need to rally an army and move on Alunaer by June, so he's got no more time to lose. He'll go straight to Lutetia."

"There to meet his oldest friend." Akilina lifts her fingers, a welcoming soft gesture toward the young lord, and he catches them with a light gallantry that would stand him well if he'd learn to use it at all times. "Guide him well, Sacha," and this she says with all seriousness, because an empty Gallic throne is not to Khazar's advantage, not with her new marriage to a Cordulan king. Rodrigo and Javier are tied by blood, and present a unified front that no other contender for Lutetia's crown could offer her. Or Khazar, she reminds herself fastidiously. After all, she does what she does for Khazar, not herself.

Irina wouldn't believe that, either, and that may well be part of why the imperatrix has permitted this marriage. Akilina sniffs, making a mockery of insult in her thoughts. She aimed for a power behind the throne by choosing a lover in Gregori Kapnist, not the throne itself. Of course, had the handsome count managed to wed Irina, then as his lover Akilina might have seen herself just one step from the imperial crown. A pity Belinda Primrose had thwarted that chain of events by murdering poor Gregori. That he most likely would have met the same end should he have taken the throne and taken Akilina to wife is utterly beside the point.

Akilina's sniff turns to a smile full of unexpected and genuine good nature. The web is a tangled one, and rarely spins in any predictable manner. Machinations for one throne have gotten her another, and when all is said and done, Akilina intends on being mistress to an empire that will rival Irina's. She turns her thoughts from conquering and her smile to Sacha, and finishes her plea to him: "Guide Javier wisely, and we'll all of us profit from Alunaer's fall."

JAVIER DE CASTILLE, KING OF GALLIN
7 April 1588 † The Western Ocean, off the coast of Gallin

Javier suspected Eliza's complicity in the matter of the gondola boy. The child had been hauled from belowdecks on the fourth day from Aria Magli looking suspiciously well-fed and not even slightly repentant.

A tremendous argument followed his discovery, the captain offended that anyone should stow away on his ship and determined to put the boy off on the coast. Eliza refused, and since then tensions had been high. Bad enough that she was a woman on board, but far worse that she dared cross the captain, and insult doubled when Javier indicated she should have her own way. Marius cracked a smile and elbowed Javier in approval of his errant wisdom. The king of Gallin could afford to anger a sea captain or two, but not the woman he intended to wed.

Tomas had refused, thus far, to perform the ceremony. Not for the first time Javier eyed the captain, and not for the first time, put the thought away. First, the man was irritated with him, and second, a shipboard wedding presided over by a merchant sailor lacked both pomp and circumstance, both of which should attend a royal wedding.

Third, the disconcerting realisation that Eliza had agreed to bed him, but hadn't as yet said she'd *wed* him, had crept up through Javier's haze of lusty good cheer. She could refuse him nothing, but somehow had thus far refused him this, or avoided him in it. Twice he'd approached her; twice the gondola boy had deflected him, standing arms akimbo and boisterously proclaiming his own worthiness as the light of Eliza's heart. Twice the child had nearly gone over the boat's edge by Javier's hand, but Eliza's mirth had stayed him both times, and left him evermore impotent. Thwarted ambition bubbled under his skin, silver warm beneath the grey April skies, but words and wits seemed to leave him at night when he might have spoken privately to the dark-eyed beauty he meant to make his queen.

During the increasingly long days he found ways to convince himself that that was for the better: it meant the impulse to command her with his witchpower was under his control. But with Gallin's coast growing steadily darker by the hour, he wondered—

"What did you promise the Caesar, my lord?" Tomas's murmur interrupted Javier's thoughts, earning a flinch, then a frown.

"How do you know I promised anything?"

"Because we saw the Parnan navy gathering when we sailed back around the peninsula, and because the Caesar will only bend so far for the Pappas." Tomas put his hands on the rail, a light balancing touch that made him look as though he belonged on a ship. "I grew up in Cordula, Javier. I grew up watching the interplay between the Pappas and the Caesar. The Caesar is a devout man, but

unlike your uncle he's always in a power struggle, back and forth
with the Pappas and the Primes. He'll rise to the church's call because his faithful heart demands it, but he'll not commit full resources without a certainty of stability from outside Parna. He
needs his army and his navy to hold his own country. So if the navy
is gathering, you've made a promise he believes you'll keep. What
was it?"

"Marriage. In a year if the war goes badly, in two if it goes well,
but no longer than that or he'll withdraw his support."

"And yet you've romanced that woman."

A near-silent bark burst in the roof of Javier's mouth. "Ah. This
is what you really wanted to talk about."

"Am I wrong, your majesty? You have an alliance built on a
promise you seem to have no intention of keeping, and you would
throw it away for a guttersnipe?"

"Watch yourself, priest," Javier said mildly. "That guttersnipe is as
well-educated as you are, and dear to a king."

"I understand that," Tomas grated, "but I also understand that we
are near to Lutetia and that the king must not be allowed to make
a foolish public statement that could shatter his alliances before his
war has begun."

Javier pushed away from the rail, eyebrows lifted. "The priest has
grown teeth."

"The priest was asked to join you as a moral compass, majesty,
and finds himself—" Tomas broke off, gold eyes flashing irritation,
and began again. "I find myself unable to hold my tongue on political matters, either, Javier, because your imperative is greater by far
than pleasing your libido."

"I need Eliza. She's of the Gallic people. They'll love me for loving her."

"You're their king. They'll love you anyway. You need Parna, and
Khazar if you can get it."

Javier sucked his cheeks in, gaze gone to the shore again. "So you
would have me make her nothing more than a symbol to be set
aside. I have no way out, Tomas. Marius will have nowhere left in
his heart for me if I use her so."

"Marius has always been too gentle." Eliza's voice came from behind them, rising and falling on the ocean wind. Javier turned to find her gaze hard as agates, and cursed that he'd not noticed her scent on the air. "They'll love you for loving me, Javier? Surely even a guttersnipe might aim higher than being a tool to funnel emotion through. All you had to do was ask. The game of love was unnecessary. Go away, priest. The king and I have things to discuss."

Tomas's eyes flickered to Javier's. Javier waved him away and the priest's nostrils flared before he bowed, sharply, and strode across the ship's deck to disappear below. Eliza watched him go, and Javier watched her: long body, rich curves, clothes dampened by seawater pressed against her skin, and he said, "It's not only a matter of politics, Liz."

"Isn't it?" She came to his side, a finger-length of hair tucked behind her ear where the wind couldn't snatch it away. "Then your timing is convenient, my lord."

Javier's voice dropped. "Please don't call me that."

"What other weapons do I have against you? My king, my brother, my love, my life. I would have played the part you need me to, Javier. You must know that."

"Yes." The word came slowly, torn away by rising winds. Unless their direction changed, they'd not be putting in at Lutetia tonight; the coast would be too dangerous to navigate, open seas less likely to shatter a fragile hull. "And yet when Marius said you deserved better than that, I thought him right."

"You thought him right, but do you love me?"

Heaviness pulled Javier's heartbeats into slow measures. "Belinda answered something in me that I thought couldn't be answered. She has witchpower, and showed me I wasn't alone. I would have thrown my crown away for her." His eyebrows pinched, words coming hard. "That was passion. It was desperation. Perhaps it was love. But none of it was as terrifying as standing on your doorstep, with that idiot child spinning sonnets to charm you, while I struggled for the boldness to *keep* my crown for you. Belinda was right. I'd grown inured to true beauty, because you were always at my side. I think perhaps I've always loved you, and have never been wise enough to see it."

"You've always loved Sacha and Marius, too."

Javier gave her a sharp look that twisted into humour. "Aye, but never enough to bed them. The balance between the four of us was fragile, wasn't it? It would have been easy to tip into something that would have changed us all, and I never wanted to risk it. Easier to see you as a sister, until Belinda came and upset it all. Now I find myself here with you, and . . . Liz, do you not *want* to be queen?"

"I want to be a mother, Javier, and neither dream is within my grasp. Turn your magic to my womb and give me my blood back, and aye, I'll want to be your queen, but I will not watch you father a bastard on some serving girl of no higher birth but greater fertility. You have what you need in all of us, Jav. The poor and guttersnipes in me, the merchants in Marius, and the young lordlings eager for war in Sacha. You're our king," she said softly. "Use us as you must. Perhaps we all deserve better, but this is the price of befriending a prince.

"Come, now," she added into his pained silence. "Belowdecks, to tell your priest he'll have his way, and then you've a speech to practise for, king of Gallin. Lutetia awaits."

11

TOMAS DEL'ABBATE
10 April 1588 † Lutetia, capital of Gallin

Tomas is beginning to think God has a cruel sense of humour.

A storm came over the sea yesterday, but this morning dawned clear and bright over a sailing ship washed clean of all visible signs of sin. The captain might have painted it white to make it gleam more, but he could have done nothing else. God might have commanded the sun to rise in the west so the light would be behind the new king of Gallin, but not even He could have done much else to trumpet Javier's return so beautifully.

It is on calm waters with a westerly wind that the ship sails into Lutetia, and Tomas the priest has no idea how the city knows to turn out for this particular ship at this particular time, but they do, and they have.

They're gathered by their thousands, lining the docks, lining the riverbanks, their voices raised in a cheer so solid that it seems a wonder that the wind is enough to push the ship forward against it. Javier's hair, which has grown long, is fire in the morning light, red and gold, and he stands at the ship's prow a pale aesthete thing of power. He is not clad in royal finery, but wears the simple rough shirt of a sailor, breeches buckled with a broad belt, and long boots that make a fine line of his slender legs. A naked sword hangs at his hip and catches sunlight, making silver streaks bounce in the crew's eyes and sending bolts of light into the shore-bound crowd.

He is, in these clothes, of the people, and is, by the wearing of a sword unsheathed, an open declaration of war. He's a thing of beauty, and this without even a hint of the magic Tomas knows he can command. Tomas has learned to feel that power, a weight in the air and a thickness in his own chest, and it is not yet present in the young king. This is pure humanity graced by divine right, and if Javier can command orgasmic screams with nothing more than his arrival, then if God has granted him the witchpower as well, it must be out of a perverse, inhuman sense of satisfaction at Tomas's discomfort.

It's a sign of how far he's fallen that Tomas doesn't even chide himself for the arrogance of that thought. Instead, like everyone else, his full attention is for Javier, and then for the two whom he gestures to join him.

Tomas has become accustomed to seeing Eliza Beaulieu in men's clothes, though his eyes twist away from the shadows of her body within that inappropriate garb. But this morning she is playing a different part, and even Tomas, who neither likes nor approves of the cheapside woman, finds it hard to look away from her.

She has taken the fine black wig of her own hair from safekeeping, and shining locks are bound up with a handful of curls to cascade free. It doesn't lend her the height that so many hairstyles offer women, but Eliza is tall, and perhaps the added extravagance of a dramatic hairstyle would detract from Javier. Her gown already does, to some degree: it is one of the loose floating things of her own creation, shelving her breasts high against a low scooped neck, and the layers upon layers of fabric are so light as to be easily caught in the wind; it billows and presses against her body, as provocative in its way as the men's clothes she likes to wear.

Eliza is beautiful in repose, almost icy, unapproachable. But when she smiles something happens to nearly perfect features, and she becomes, if not ordinary, at least mortal. She is smiling now, and with that smile and her soft hair and softer dress, she's captivating. The city knows this woman, and from Tomas's understanding, many of them despise her, but not now. Now she is the king's left hand, a creature of unearthly beauty and delicacy, and that she comes from the streets and has risen so high is, in this moment, a triumph. Javier is right, in his way: marrying her would be a coup. But Tomas is also right, and it's a step the young king can't afford to take.

At Javier's right hand is Marius, who looks terribly earth-born beside the other two. Tomas has not known the merchant man without Javier, not in any meaningful way; Marius arrived to tell Rodrigo of Sandalia's death literally within a few hours of Javier's impetuous Isidrian entrance. Marius had been sombre, as might be expected, and then their lives had all been shattered with the advent of Javier's witchpower. Of all of them, Marius had accepted that power the most easily, his heart still given unquestioningly to Javier. Now, in his darker clothes and with his feet spread wide as he stands at Javier's side, the look of him is trustworthy and solid. He looks like a man to be depended upon for practical matters, and as such helps to ground the fiery-haired king and the astonishing woman at his side.

All of this in their presentation of themselves, and not a word yet spoken. Thronged viewers along the shores call out and applaud. With their will to embrace Javier already so strong, Tomas cannot imagine that they will refuse him his war, or that they could grow more fervoured in their enthusiasm for him.

A drawbridge pulls up in front of them, shuddering ropes straining with water and weight as men kick oxen to a higher speed. A young man dangles himself from the bridge as it rises, waving like a fool, and Javier's unexpected laugh breaks over the sounds of the crowd. Eliza shouts with delight and runs forward, but Javier waves her back, then lifts his hand higher and calls out a halt to the astonished bridge-keepers, who haul their beasts of burden to a standstill.

Marius turns on a heel, snapping, "Drop anchor, *drop anchor!*" to the captain as Javier, lithe and light as a boy, swings himself over the ship's prow and runs the length of the figurehead. He should fall: the maiden who breaks the seas is soaking and slippery with seaweed, but watching him, Tomas never doubts he will succeed.

Frantic, the captain bellows orders to drop anchor, and chains rattle and scream, water splashing as iron weight slams into it. The bridge is drawn barely far enough to allow the ship's body to scrape through; the sails catch and twist, eliciting a gasp of horrified expectation from the watching crowds, and a heartfelt curse from the captain.

Javier, with the confidence of a young goat, flings himself from the figurehead and toward the youth dangling on the bridge.

There is an instant where this is not going to work. There is too much distance, too much movement from the ship, too much give in the bridge. Tomas's bowels clench in sympathy for a king about to be half-drowned and entirely humiliated.

But the man on the bridge finds an extra inch or two of reach, and seizes Javier's wrist with surety, as though they've practised this a hundred times. Javier bellows with delight and swings upward, the man's arms bulging with muscle and his neck straining with effort. Then Javier is on the bridge and the two of them are howling like fools, pounding each other on the back and shouting nonsense that is lost to the greater screams from the viewers. Eliza and Marius do a madcap dance on the deck, swinging each other around and shrieking with laughter, and Tomas can hear none of it over the uproarious joy roaring from the throats of the Gallic people.

The man on the bridge with Javier is sandy-haired, stocky, dressed more beautifully than his king, and must, therefore, be Sacha Asselin, the last in Javier's family of friends. Javier looks slight beside the other man, though he's taller; with both Sacha and Marius at his side, he will be flanked by muscle that most would think twice before rushing. It could not have been deliberate; all the world knows that these four have been friends since childhood, and there is no way Javier could have selected two strong men and one beautiful woman deliberately.

Javier could not have; God, perhaps, might have. Uncertainty blooms in Tomas's chest, making his breath come shallow. His faith is shaken; this, he knows. The Pappas didn't experience what Tomas has, didn't suffer the loss of will, and it does not disturb that great man to use a king and discard him.

Tomas realises he is glad he will never be the Pappas himself, and this is a revelation: he had supposed it might be a dream of his. Now he knows he isn't made for such pragmatic and hard decisions as the Pappas faces. And the Pappas, perhaps, cannot risk a crisis of faith, which Tomas struggles with even now. He believes a man who stole his will must be a man guided by the devil's hand, but looking at the formidable gathering of friends capering with joy, he wonders if God has put them together for a reason, and if his own arrogance and fear is blinding him to a truth that the Pappas can see.

"People of Gallin!" Javier's voice, a roar of sound, cuts through Tomas's thoughts. No man can quiet a gathering such as this one, not with his voice alone, but all along the shore a quietude ripples out. Not silence, not with so many people, but the quality of the noise gentles, becoming a hiss rather than thunder. And it stretches *far*, much farther than a man's voice can carry, and that, Tomas knows, is the witchpower at work.

Javier has released Sacha; the stocky lord, in fact, has reversed the king's show of bravado, and has leapt to the figurehead, and runs down it to crash gladly into Marius and Eliza's arms. If ordinary mortals might call up power through nothing more than their own will and emotion, then these three are, in this moment, a source for Javier to draw from. He glances down at them, a smile splitting his face wide, then flings his free hand up and shouts out again to the throngs.

"People of Gallin, I am Javier, son of Louis de Castille and Sandalia de Costa, and I come before you to beg you cry me king!"

Never, never in his life has Tomas heard voices rise with so much certainty, so much passion; never in his life has he thought he might find his own voice lifted in a shout so loud it tears at his throat. Thousands kneel on the shores; so, too, do those on deck, from the trio at the prow all the way to the stern, and the captain puts a fist over his heart.

Javier's voice drops, almost to a whisper: Tomas should not be able to hear him, much less the straining masses on land. But he can, and they can, and for all that Tomas is afraid of the power that lets Javier share his words up and down a riverbank, he is also filled with an aching admiration, a desire to serve that he has only ever felt within the walls of a church. This man before him, this king, could be great, and he, humble priest that he is, could walk his path and be remembered, too. Tomas does not think of himself as wishing a place in history, but watching the fire-haired king leaning rakishly from the bridge above, he knows that he will struggle to stay at Javier's side, not just for Javier's soul, but for his own.

"I come on the wings of sorrow," Javier whispers, and then there's his own silence filled by the roar of his people, because the ship on whose deck he rode is called *Cordoglio,* "sorrow," and he could not have chosen better had he meant to.

"I come on the wings of sorrow," the king calls again. "I come in the wake of our beloved queen, my darling mother, Sandalia's, death. I mourn with all of you, my people, but in Cordula the Pappas himself placed a crown on my head, and today, and for many days to come, I will not turn my eyes, blind with tears, to Sandalia's grave and weep and honour her as she deserves. I cannot bring myself to face her, even in death, while she lies unavenged, and *Gallin will have its vengeance!*"

The faceless mass that had been on its knees is suddenly on its feet, hands flung into the air, screams of approval shaking the very boards of the *Cordoglio.* The gondola boy creeps to Tomas's side, eyes wide as he watches the dramatics that Javier commands. So softly as to be audible beneath the thundering noise, he whispers, "I was so wrong, Padre Tomas. He is good with words after all."

The crowd will never cease its cheering on its own. Javier lifts a hand and brings them down with his palm, acknowledging and grateful, but in command. "I come before you with my friends, these men and this woman whom I have known since childhood, who have taught me so much of the Gallic people. They are my heart and soul, these three, my Sacha, my Marius, my Eliza, and they are *you.*"

Without bidding, the three have come forward, making themselves seen, making themselves a strong steady base upon which Javier stands. Dangling as he does from the bridge, not so very far above their heads, there is an obvious action to take, and Eliza, who Tomas may be forced to admit is clever, takes it: she raises her hands. Within a moment the other two have done so as well, and now Javier all but *does* stand on their support, the pauper and the merchant and the lord.

By now the watching people are insensible, the noise they make so profound Tomas begins to wonder if it is simply the sound of the world itself, and this no more than a rare occasion in which he notices it. And still Javier's voice carries, not smooth, for there's too much emotion for ease of words, but strong and certain, up and down the banks of the River Sacrauna.

"I must go to war, my people. I go on these shoulders, those of my friends, and I go with Cordula's blessing." Javier's gaze falls to Tomas, sees the gondola boy at his side, and seizes the opportunity. Tomas propels the boy forward without thinking: responding to what's in Javier's eyes, and in a moment priest and child are standing with Eliza and the men. The air here is scalding, too hot to breathe, and its weight is terrible, laden with Javier's power as it rolls over the *Cordoglio,* over the river, over the thousands gathered to welcome their king home.

As Tomas comes to the prow, Javier shouts, "Look you to my ship, my wings of sorrow, and see here my priest and confidant Tomas del'Abbate, who brought me to the Pappas to earn his favour. See the child who stands with him, who has come from the canals of Aria Magli to join in our holy war!"

Marius, as clever as Eliza, or as caught up in breathless fervour as is Tomas, scoops the gondola boy up and sets him on his shoulders, putting a child in the eye of the world. Javier leans precariously far and catches the lad's hand, lifting it high as he calls, "This boy is the banner of Cordula, and he rides at my side! *Will you join him?*"

Here, at the heart of it, standing within the circle of Javier's power and at the centre of Lutetia's attention, tears spill down Tomas's cheeks as Gallin answers its king's call. He is on his knees somehow, reaching toward Javier as though he bears God's light within him, and it is a terribly long time before Javier leaps back to the ship's deck and into the arms of his brothers and sister. A terribly long time before he comes to Tomas, and takes his face in his hands, rubbing tears away with his thumbs. The thunder of voices still crashes around them, but there's nothing in Tomas's world but Javier's warm hands, and the whisper of hope in the young king's voice: "Is this forgiveness, then, my priest? I have done you wrong, but I would have your love if you will give it."

Oh, God's sense of humour has grown perverse indeed, for Tomas del'Abbate turns his face against Javier's palm and lays a kiss there, benediction and absolution, and knows himself for a fool, for he would do anything for Javier of Gallin.

JAVIER, KING OF GALLIN
11 April 1588 ✝ Lutetia, capital of Gallin

Javier de Castille, son of Louis, son of Sandalia, new king of Gallin, lied to his people.

Not out of maliciousness; that, at least, is something he can console himself with. Not in any way that will harm them, either, and the larger part of him knew that words spoken in the heat of political rhetoric were hardly to be relied upon. But guilt sparked in another part, scolding him for weakness.

The reality was that should word of this weakness leak out, his people would probably love him for it all the more. Might: after the day that had passed, Javier was uncertain if he could command the fire of their ardour any higher. The morning's performance on the river had blurred into an afternoon of meeting with advisors, generals, counselors, priests, and two enterprising mothers who had laid out propositions of marriage with the same warlike determination the others had shown.

It was almost impossible that any further pageantry could be staged after the river speech—that was they were calling it, *le discours de la Sacrauna*—and yet a little before sunset tailors had descended upon him, and carriages had taken him and a host of retainers to the cathedral, where he was crowned a second time under the greedy watchful eyes of the Lutetian people.

When he exited the cathedral, cautious beneath the weight of his crown and his robes, it was to discover the entirety of the broad avenue before him had been turned into a feast table. Lutetia's wealthiest were closest to him, of course, there at the head of it all, on the cathedral steps. But burning torches by their hundreds lit the long street, showing him that the wealthy turned poorer as the feast went on, until it seemed every soul in the city must be there to eat at his crowning feast and to cry his name with a thunder that rattled his bones.

Twelve hours had passed since his arrival in the city. Javier, thinking of the long list of accomplishments necessary to have brought him to that place with such grace and honour, wondered that one such as himself might need to be born, when ordinary humans with no witchpower magic could make so much out of so little, so quickly. He had climbed onto the feast table and spoken to his people again, the words disappearing from his mind like quicksilver, but he knew he'd spoken of their skill, their ability, their proud hearts; and then he'd taken up a handful of meat and walked the length of the avenue on the tables, crouching every few feet to stop and talk. When tables became street, he walked among the poor, making certain the harried guards who followed him handed food out to those who had come to see and celebrate their new king.

It was after midnight now, long after midnight, if his weary bones told him right. He hadn't seen his friends since the *Cordoglio* had put into dock; he'd been swept one way, and they another, though he was certain they would have been at the recrowning. Sacha would have seen to it, if nothing else, and no one would have refused the king's closest friends, not today. Javier would have welcomed them with him now, but even if they guessed where he'd gone, even if they might have made their way through crowds and guards, they might still have left him alone, out of respect, out of privacy, out of concern.

Javier de Castille knelt before the effigy that sealed his mother's tomb, and did what he had sworn to his people he would not do: turned eyes blind with tears to her grave, and wept.

Time passed; time enough that the cathedral bells far overhead rang away the small hours of the morning in favour of the large, and in that time Javier railed, and sobbed, and bargained, and threatened, begged forgiveness and warned of vengeance, and at the end of it all came to be sitting against the marble casket carved with a pale lifeless rendition of his mother. Exhaustion held him in its grip, and he was grateful for it: it washed away thought and feeling, leaving him staring across a little distance to the tomb that matched Sandalia's. Louis, his father, who had died six months before Javier's birth. He had never missed the man, had never been given the impression that Sandalia missed him. Louis was only a beautiful still carving to the two who might have been his family.

Tears, which Javier had thought himself emptied of, burned his eyes and slid away from their corners as he leaned his head back against Sandalia's tomb. Family was inexplicable stuff: blood and bone, but more than that, heart and home. Rodrigo was family, aye, and so were Eliza and Marius and Sacha, but none of them had been Sandalia, centre of all Javier's youth. The world ought not go on without her; the world, it seemed, intended to.

Footsteps finally sounded in the vault, light and long-expected. Javier left his eyes closed, his head back, too weary to care whether it was priest or assassin who came to find the king in mourning. With his eyes closed the world beyond them might not exist; he might go undisturbed if he refused to acknowledge another's presence.

Fingers brushed his hair, an intimacy Eliza and no other would use, but the touch was not Eliza's. Javier opened his eyes, wishing their tearful itch away, and found Tomas standing above him, terrible gentleness in his gaze.

"I've brought cool water, cloth to wash your face with, and new clothes to greet the morning in," Tomas murmured when Javier remained silent. "They are waiting for you, king of Gallin."

"Who?" Javier's voice broke more hoarsely than he expected, still tight from sobs and too dry for words.

"Your people." Tomas knelt, slipping a satchel from his shoulder and withdrawing soft cloth and a wineskin. "Drink a little, my lord. Loosen your throat." He put the wineskin down at Javier's side and took out a second skin, spilling water onto the cloth with it. Javier closed his eyes again, letting the priest press the damp cloth against his face; felt Tomas take one of his hands and clean it, too.

"Would you wash my feet as well, priest? And nail me to a cross when this is done?"

"Drink," Tomas said again, steadily. "Wash away some bitterness with the wine, and if it rises again spill it on me if you must, but not your people. They gather in the street, Javier. All of Gallin knows you entered these halls last night to bid Sandalia farewell. They wait to see if you will exit a king or a broken man. You must be a king."

Javier made a broken sound, pretence at a laugh, and took up the wine to drain a long draught. "I thought I had my privacy."

"Royalty never does. A new shirt, Javier."

"No." Javier knocked the offering away, not hard. "Let them see me as I am, if they must see me."

Tomas echoed, "No," more firmly, and put his hand to Javier's collar. "In mourning, yes; in despair, no. I'll not let them see that. You made a fine figure on the ship yesterday, king of Gallin, as a pirate and a prince. In the evening you showed them the king. Today you will be the warrior, whether you wish to or not. Strip off the doublet and wear the tunic and your unsheathed blade." He unfurled the former with a snap, drawing Javier's unwilling eyes to it.

The Gallic fleur-de-lis coat of arms shone in gold thread against a background of blue. "For another man black might have suited," Tomas muttered, "but you're too pale. This will make the most of your eyes without washing out your skin. I didn't bring chain mail. I wonder now if I ought to have done."

"Why are you here, Tomas?" Javier knotted a fist over Tomas's hand, wrinkling the tunic. "Why are you not Sacha, or Marius, or even Eliza? Did your kiss offer forgiveness? I need the words, priest. For all my power I know not what's in your heart."

Tomas went still, but not with the wariness Javier'd grown accustomed to seeing in him. He looked at Javier's hand on his own, then gently shook it off, smoothing the tunic. "You're in the bowels of the church, majesty. The bishop preferred a man of the cloth to come after you than one of your vagabond friends." He made a small impatient gesture and Javier, resigned, sat up to strip his doublet off and take the tunic. "And because they're your lay support, and as such belong in the public's eye, even now. I'm the church at your right hand, and to remind all of Echon of that, should always walk there. A sword on one side, Javier, and God on the other."

"So now you're God." Javier found a faint smile and reached out, clapping his hand at Tomas's jaw and neck. "No wonder you have such a beautiful face." He pulled Tomas closer, butting foreheads with him, and held the priest there for a few long moments. "I am stronger than the witchpower, Tomas. Your faith, if not in me, at least in God, helps me remember that. I am glad you stand at my side. I haven't fallen yet. Don't let me."

"My faith is in you, my lord king." Tomas sounded strained. "I beg God's mercy on my soul, but my faith is in you. Keep me at your side always and I will not let you fall."

Javier tightened his hand, then released Tomas and took up the tunic, the wineskin, and, at the end, his sword. The wine he drained and set aside, then let Tomas tug the tunic over his head and belt his sword into place. "I will be king of Aulun if we win this war," Javier said quietly. "Our coat of arms for that crown will be the sword and the cross over a penitent man, Tomas. Our coat of arms will be for what you have given us."

"My lord." Tomas bowed deeply and fell into place beside Javier as they left the catacombs for a cathedral brilliant with colour, sunlight saturating stained-glass windows. Javier knelt at the altar and made the sign of God across his chest, then strode out massive doors into a dazzling spring morning.

Into a roar of welcome that belittled the fracas from the day before; into a city of men rattling their swords, firing pistols, smashing together shield and blade, all to make greeting to their warrior king. Eliza and the two men, his best friends, stood at the front edges of the cathedral steps, their presence and Tomas's all the support he needed; their presence seeming to hold back the gathering through their will alone. Javier walked forward to join them, agog at the mass of humanity and refusing to let his awe show on his face.

Yesterday on shore they were a mob; last night in the boulevards, a crowd. Now, as he stands on the cathedral steps and looks out at the faces awaiting his command, Javier de Castille knows them for what they are.

They are an army, and war is coming to Echon.

IVANOVA, THE IMPERATOR'S HEIR
16 April 1588 † *Khazan, capital of Khazar*

War is coming to Echon.

It is coming in the form of the Khazarian army, seventy thousand strong and guided by big-bearded generals who, in her youth, bounced Ivanova on their knee and gave her model horses and soldiers from their campaign tables as toys.

She was seven, and playing at a game of cannons with those toys and a bread roll, when a General Chekov took note of her. He sat down on the floor as though she was one of his own grandchildren, and a boy at that, and with plates and boards and other foodstuff, taught her how to best use height and landscape to a cannon's advantage. Taught her, too, how a small group of soldiers, disguised to blend in, might successfully ambush a whole supply train. He told her then what she had already heard repeated in Irina's war chambers, and what she hears still today: *an army marches on its stomach. Destroy its food source and you weaken, perhaps cripple, your soldiers.*

It made an impression on Ivanova, always hungry as a child. Chekov, sitting on the floor, taught her the danger and the necessity of pillaging the land her armies marched through in order to feed its ravenous stomach, and taught her the wisdom of keeping her men under control. There were two choices, he said: kill everyone in the army's path, or control the men, take only what they need, and do what can be done to make reparations to those whose lands have been sacked.

Ivanova, arrogant with youth, tossed her black hair and said, "But I will be imperatrix. I can take what I like."

When she returned to her room that afternoon, everything but a thin straw mattress was missing. Incensed, she flew to her mother, who looked bemused and told her to solve it herself. It took two days to realise Chekov had stolen her things, and when, insulted and haughty, she demanded them back, he said no.

It took another full day to recover from the shock, and to think to demand why not.

"Because I'm the commanding officer of the Khazarian army," Chekov said. "I can take what I like."

Ivanova still remembers with uncomfortable clarity the rage she flew into. She also remembers the moment in which she understood Chekov's point, and the general's indulgent chuckle when he saw she'd learned the lesson.

He never did return her things, and Irina, most unreasonably, refused to countermand his orders and have them returned. Half the summer passed while Ivanova plotted his downfall and stole back what bits of her belongings she could find, but she was seven and eventually lost interest in both recovery and revenge. That, too, was a lesson, because as she's aged, she's realised that she has lived a life of luxury, and could afford to forget about the dolls and pillows that were taken from her. Had it been her food, her fields, her only livelihood, she could not have forgiven or forgotten so easily, and this is what Chekov wanted her to understand. An army is a dangerous thing, but so, too, are the people it passes by. She has learned that when she is imperatrix her duty will be to be generous when it seems she can least afford it, for the price of stinginess is high.

Chekov endured the ridicule of his fellow officers to sit on the floor with her, and when she was a little older, to lean over war tables with her, teaching battlefield manoeuvres and troop movements. She learned quickly, fascinated by the abstract while Chekov repeated the adage that no battle plan survives the first encounter with the enemy. Under his tutelage she learned recovery tactics, sneak attacks, direct strikes, and from his comrades understood that, as a woman, she would never be in a position to command men in the strategies she was taught. They indulged her studies only because she was still a girl, too young to be of any concern or danger.

Irina and she decided, when she turned twelve, that she would lose all interest in battles and war preparations, and a sigh of relief went through the officers' ranks. But Chekov continued to teach her in private, and today he finds her leaning over a map of Khazar and Echon, studying mountain ranges and rivers as she amasses her army of toy soldiers outside Khazan's gates.

"How many will we lose in the march?" She is a girl, she is not supposed to care, but she does care, intensely. She will marry someday, and the generals believe her husband will control all matters warlike, but Ivanova has no intention of marrying a man with that much ambition. Javier de Castille would have done, but that plan has been set askew by Akilina Pankejeff's recent good fortune. Ivanova is content with that; she would like to find someone with wits in his head so he might be a worthy companion, but if she must she'll marry a handsome fool and let him imagine he rules both imperatrix and empire.

"Perhaps as many as six or ten thousand. It's a hard time of year to make a journey of fifteen hundred miles."

"There's no good time of year. High summer, maybe, but the war will be met by then. Winter gives the advantage of frozen rivers to travel on, but the mountain passes are too snowy. And spring means rotten snow, rotten ice, avalanches, no young crops to replenish supplies with . . ."

"But it's in spring we'll travel." There's approval in Chekov's voice; Ivanova has listened and learned, and he is rightfully proud. "The army marches within the week."

"If I were a boy, I would ride with them." This is almost a question: Ivanova knows it's true, or that it would be, at least, if they did not march across western Khazar and the entirety of Echon to meet their war. Even a son might be kept in reserve on such a long tour of duty, and sent to skirmishes within Khazar for his blooding.

"The imperatrix has never ridden to war. Don't count yourself a failure for not doing so yourself. You have as fine a grasp of battle-field tactics as any I've ever taught, and will be the better ruler for it," Chekov says with such conviction she can't doubt him, but she does make one argument.

"As any you've ever taught who hasn't seen battle."

Chekov tips his head, acknowledgment that her point is a valid one. Ivanova touches a fingertip to the head of one of her toy soldiers, and asks a serious question: "Do I need to?"

The old general's silence is answer enough, though he fills it with words after a moment. "Not in this war. There will be enough battles closer to home for you to fight."

"And will you let me fight them?" Neither of them mean *fight* in the way of expecting the imperator's female heir to be on the battlefield with a sword and shield. Ivanova knows which end of a sword to hold, and has been taught the rudimentaries of defending herself with a knife, but she isn't a warrior and doesn't fancy herself to be.

Chekov's silence once more says what words needn't, but again he does her the honour of honesty. "I would. My fellow officers will be more reluctant." A smile ghosts over his grey-bearded face, and he adds, "But you'll be imperatrix someday, and they won't be able to refuse you."

"Because I'll be able to do as I like." Ivanova grins back, then impulsively steps around the war table to give the old man a hug. "Live for me, General. You've guided me through childhood better than my father might have. I'll need your guidance when I'm grown, too."

Chekov folds a hand at her head and presses his mouth to her hair, the small gesture all she needs of a promise from him. And she, safe and warm in his arms, hopes that what she plans to do will not break the old general's heart.

12

LORRAINE, QUEEN OF AULUN
1 June 1588 † *Alunaer, capital of Aulun*

"You will go with the army, because we cannot." There is an un-truth in Lorraine's phrasing: "cannot" is a word she rarely applies to herself. But it's rather worth it for the expression on Belinda Primrose's pretty face: the girl looks as though she's been poleaxed, stupefied by a sentence.

The expression vanishes so quickly that Lorraine might doubt she'd seen it, if she were other than who she is. Lorraine Walter does not often doubt herself; a monarch cannot, and there's a time when that word is well-suited.

Primrose is good: Lorraine admires that, after the first moment of astonishment, she is unable to read Belinda's thoughts. There's no hint of greed, no hint of cunning, no hint of relief—and that, the queen thinks, is the most likely thing for her illegitimate daughter to feel. She's been cooped up in a convent for four months, and Lorraine doubts there's been a time in her entire life when she's been so constrained.

For a breathtaking moment, envy sears the queen of Aulun so hotly that a blush burns her throat, her face, her ears. Her heart lurches with a sickness more suited to a woman a third her age, and a tremble comes into her hands. It is only a lifetime's worth of control that keeps those hands from clawing, that keeps her from a sudden surge of hatred toward the curtseying girl.

Belinda gives no sign at all of seeing that flush of emotion, and perhaps she doesn't: the white paint that Lorraine wears as an affectation of youth is heavy, and may hide her colour. More likely wisdom stays both Belinda's tongue and her gaze, just as it has largely stayed her reaction to being sent with the army.

Begrudgment still prickles, but Lorraine puts it aside as she always must. She has been a queen since she was twenty-six, and she has not known any real sort of freedom since she was seventeen and her sister Constance took the throne. The freedom of being a queen is far greater than the freedom of being an unwanted heir: Lorraine spent nine years imprisoned before Constance's death and her own subsequent crowning. Now she takes her long holidays and rides her horses, and in the end, those small freedoms in the name of holding a throne are worth the price extracted. Because of that, blood-heating jealousy has no place in her life.

Besides, there's truth in the thought that she doesn't wish to face the battle that is coming to her. She cannot make herself a showpiece on the front lines as she might have done when she was a youth: she has too much sense of her own mortality, now. Belinda is too young to carry that fatalism.

"We have a question for you, girl."

"Majesty?" Belinda's voice and form are perfect: the willing servant, interested but not curious, confident in her monarch's commands. Robert is like that, but for some reason Lorraine finds it more delightful in the father than in the daughter, and so she says, irritably, "Stand up, girl. Let us see you."

Belinda manages to bob another curtsey as she stands, and then, as though Lorraine has given permission—and Lorraine supposes she has—she tilts her head and watches Lorraine with more open curiosity.

"We have acted on your dream of Robert's warning and we have prepared for war. Cordula's army amasses across the straits, with ships ready to carry armed men to our shore. Essandia comes from the south in her armada, and those ships are newer than our own, faster and lighter in the water. Khazar marches across Echon to stand at the Cordulan army's back, and we, girl, have nothing more than our army and our aging navy to fight with."

This is a sore point with Lorraine. Reussland should have joined her; should, at the least, be making the Khazarian army's journey across the Kaiser's lands costly. But the Kaiser's two sons are dead within days of each other, the elder by drowning and the younger in a duel over a young woman whose presence as the centre of such dealings suggests her honour's not worth the fight. All that is left to the Kaiser are three daughters, the oldest a girl of seventeen. He, then, with even more haste and less grace than Lorraine's own father, has set aside his aging wife and has buried himself to the balls in young women, intending on wedding the one who first gives birth to a son.

When this war is done and Lorraine Walter is triumphant, she will send subtle support to the Kaiser's eldest daughter, and be the first among equals to offer both condolences at the old Kaiser's death, and congratulations on the crown by then settled on a pretty blonde head.

But that's a plot for another day, only to be played out when she's certain of her own crown's security. Which is why she now turns a grim gaze on Belinda, and asks a question that neither the girl nor Robert would expect her to: "Or have we more?"

BELINDA PRIMROSE

Lorraine should not have asked that question.

Not *should not* in the suggestion that she had no right, but should not in that she should not have been able to. Belinda was struck dumb by the queen's command that she join the army; now she felt a gape drop her jaw and couldn't gather her expression into anything less telling or more flattering. It took long seconds to croak so much as, "Majesty?"

"We are not a fool." Lorraine's voice, nearly inaudible, was also ruthlessly hard. "We have considered long and hard the warning Robert gave us through you, and we have considered its manner of arrival. We have also listened to the stories that have come out of Lutetia in the matter of Beatrice Irvine."

Silence filled the room, broken only by the shattering strength of Belinda's heartbeat. This was adversity, the very thing she had been raised to face, and when she needed them most all her wits had deserted her. There was a clever answer to give the queen, a quip or a droll comment that would dissuade her from the path her thoughts took. But witchpower roared in Belinda's mind, golden wall of noise, triumph, and anticipation screaming wordlessly in her skull. She thought she might burst from it, or that she might be tipped over and have it spill out as though she were nothing more than an emptying vessel.

"And then," Lorraine said, so, so softly, "and then there is the matter of you and me, Belinda Primrose."

Belinda fell to her knees, graceless, uncontained, unconstrained, with an image brilliant against the golden light in her mind: a woman with thin grey eyes, a high forehead, a proud chin. A woman with titian hair worn loose, bloody curls against translucent skin. The image, the single image, that Belinda had borne with her all her life, since the day she was birthed, and with it a handful of words that had defined her as long as she could remember: it cannot be found out. It *cannot be found out.*

But Lorraine continued inexorably, giving lie to the boundary that had made up the edges of Belinda's life. "You knew me," the queen whispered. "It is not in the least possible, and yet you knew me in court on the day we first met. Robert did not tell you." The certainty and dismissal in Lorraine's voice would be laughable if she were not so terribly right. Robert Drake had not told his daughter the secret of her heritage; he had only come lately to learning she knew, and unlike Lorraine, he had been shocked that she did.

Belinda stared at the floor, eyes wide and dry, and thought that if tears should fall they would be made of fire, gold splashes against the floor, and wondered why she thought they might. She, who had a damnably flawless memory, could not remember crying since she had been a child, not since she had begun the game of stillness. There was no reason to weep now.

"I have put these things together, all of them," Lorraine went on. "I have put them together, and I have come to wonder, Primrose, if the rumours out of Gallin are fact. If the daughter I bore is, in truth, a witch."

Belinda jerked her gaze up, magic in her mind suddenly flat and silent, as though the queen's words had stripped away all her power. Ambition had fled; for the first time since Javier had helped awaken her to the magic she held, Belinda felt no hint of underlying expectation, no whisper of curious exploration. Her insides were hollowed and plumbed with lead, an iron casing around her heart, crushing it each time it tried to beat. The distorted window that allowed her to look at a life that might have been went black, not clear in the way she might have imagined it would, had she ever gone so far as to dream Lorraine might use those words aloud: *the daughter I bore.* They had danced around this acknowledgment; putting it between them in open words stripped Belinda bare, and left her ready for shaping, as though she were once more a child.

Lorraine breathed, "Such control," and touched a fingertip to Belinda's chin, turning her head this way and that. "I see astonishment in your eyes, child. Fear, horror, disbelief. These are all the things I should see, but unless I miss my guess the word that has torn you asunder is not 'witch.' So I am right, and this is how it shall go, Primrose. Heed me well."

Belinda nodded, barely a movement under Lorraine's touch. Nodded, because the words the queen used were the same ones that Robert has always used in setting her a task, and because that small familiarity was a line to which she could tie herself and find her way back to the world she knew. A distant part of her wondered if Robert had learned the phrase from Lorraine, but she couldn't voice the curiosity, not now.

"I do not care," Lorraine said with gentle precision, "how this came to be, how it has shaped your life, whether it is a damnable talent or a heavenly one. I have no wish to see demonstrations nor any worry for explanations. *I do not care.* What I care for is its use. I have an army that is badly outnumbered, a navy that is smaller and weaker than its opponent. I intend on sending you into war, Primrose, because I think you are a thing that will tip the balances. Am I right?"

"Yes." Witchpower bloomed again, a kernel of confidence so steady and bright that Belinda's own voice seemed that of a stranger. She drew breath to speak again and Lorraine cut it off with a commanding gesture.

"I do not care," she repeated. "I will not know the details, for my sake as well as yours. I will promise you this: you will not burn, not so long as a Walter sits on the Aulunian throne. Be discreet if you can, but if needs must, then discretion be damned and I will make an answer for my people. They say Javier of Gallin is blessed by God. So, too, will you be, if anyone dares ask. But you are a secret warrior still, as you've always been. You won't ride with the generals and admirals, though neither can you be a camp follower. Be clever, girl. Be wise."

"Majesty." Belinda's voice sounded more her own, demure and willing as she cast her gaze downward. For all that she'd cast it away in these past months, the stillness wrapped around her now, habit protecting her from emotional blows. She had a task, and such things were how she lived her life: even shaping those thoughts gave her a flare of purposefulness, of relief and pleasure at understanding that she had a duty to perform. Time to think it through would come later, well away from the dangerous territory that was Lorraine Walter. Knowing herself to be dismissed, Belinda rose and for once permitted herself less than a proper obsequience; she only nodded to Lorraine as she passed her by.

"Primrose." Lorraine's voice followed her to the door and Belinda stopped, not looking back, but waiting.

"Rid yourself of the babe. It's a complication I will not have."

Ice slid into Belinda's chest, sharp and cold as a dagger. She bobbed a curtsey, then left Lorraine in the secret chamber.

No one, Lorraine least of all, should have seen what Belinda carried beneath her novice's habit. Even she, lying in her cot at night with her fingers pressed against her belly, was only certain of it because she had twice now missed her courses, rather than any broadly visible change in her form. This was a thing that would not have happened had she been outside the convent walls, where it was easy to find the herbs that would unroot a child from the womb.

But until these past few weeks she'd left the convent daily, and might well have broken from Dmitri and found what she needed to loosen the unquickened babe from her body, and she had not done it. She met resistance from the witchpower when she considered it, a wall of determination that turned her thoughts from convenience to possibility. She was half of Robert's blood; the child within her was half of hers, and all of Dmitri's. There was more potential witchpower growing within her than she could command herself, and that was enough to stay her hand against steeping an abortifacient tea.

Dmitri did not yet know, unless her swelling bustline had informed him. She'd kept the knowledge wrapped close in her mind, walled it off with golden power as her own magic had once been tucked away. He would leap on a child as a way to bind himself closer to Belinda and pull her further from Robert, making the babe a wedge between them with plans to guide it toward his own ends.

Belinda intended that shaping for herself.

She paused where she was, letting a blind gaze come into focus. She had climbed the guard stairs along the palace's outer edge, and Alunaer spread out before her in the fresh new green of early summer. It had been winter the last time she'd stood on these steps, with blue smoke rising in straight lines toward grey clouds, and with snow making white patches over black rooftops. Rodney du Roz had lain twitching, and then all too still, on the flagstones many feet beneath her while she'd admired the view, and now she glanced toward the distant ground, half wondering if some other unfortunate might lie there in homage to the first man whose life she'd taken.

There was not, but a hand of guards trotted across the courtyard and turned sharply to come up the stairs. Not until they were almost upon her did Belinda realise that they hadn't seen her, that her own desire to remain hidden from Lorraine's too-sharp gaze had drawn the witchpower stillness in all its strength around her. She gathered her skirts and ran up the stairs, pressing herself against parapet walls with a gasp that bordered on laughter, though not of joy. Her power *was* growing, if she could gather near-invisibility without a conscious thought. Dmitri's teachings had stood her well.

The guards trotted by, leaving behind the sour rich scent of men, far more noticeable with pregnancy changing her body.

Drops of witchlight fell around that thought, golden and bright and illuminating. Belinda spread her hand across her belly, gaze gone sightless again as she stared over the city. Her sense of smell was more sensitive, her awareness of touch more exquisite, her witch magic more powerful.

Two were tales she'd heard spoken of pregnant women; the third was not an experience others might share. But if the two and the one were born of the same changes in her body, then the serenely confident answer she'd given Lorraine might depend on the strength lent to her in having fallen pregnant.

A bark of laughter gave away her presence to anyone near enough to hear it. It was a triumphant excuse, one Lorraine would accept; an inconvenient grandchild paled in comparison to a country lost. Besides, she was queen, and Belinda had no doubt she could and would find a doctor willing to say Belinda's child hadn't quickened, and could be ridden of in much later months without endangering anyone's immortal soul. It might, in fact, do very well to find a way to let Lorraine think the babe lost; then Belinda would have free rein in raising it.

It was a desperately large command to pit herself against, as the one she chose not to obey. Indeed, it shouldn't have taken Lorraine's orders; a lifetime's service should have sent Belinda to a wise woman weeks ago, removing complications before they were well begun. This, perhaps, was what the first sip of freedom was flavoured with: not defiance, but calm. Unrooting the babe had never been an option worth considering, and that, above all, was a thing in which Robert, and no doubt Lorraine, would find cause for alarm.

But a war was coming, one outside of Belinda's capability to grasp. Weapons for that war would be necessary, and if she had been bred to shape and guide her world, then the child she carried was also a weapon. No wise general facing battle threw away a potential weapon without first considering all the ways in which it might be used. Even the most dangerous—an unknown assassin, for example, in the form of an ordinary young woman—would rarely be discarded. Dismissed, perhaps; detained, yes, but not discarded; there was too much value in dangerous things, and the future always held a need for them.

The war season was only now beginning. Lorraine wouldn't expect to see Belinda again for weeks, even months if the weather held well into autumn. Seven months: if she could remain on the battlefields, a secret weapon herself, for that long, then the orders she'd been given could be disguised. If not, she could use witch-power to protect herself and the child. Belinda disliked the idea of tampering with Lorraine's memories; the woman was, after all, a queen, and not merely a parlour maid. But one brief thought to turn aside might not be too much to manage, in the name of protecting an unborn weapon.

Satisfied, Belinda crossed the parapets and left the view of Alunaer behind, going in search of an army and a choppy sea.

JAVIER DE CASTILLE, KING OF GALLIN
3 June 1588 † *Gallin's northern shore, some twelve miles from Aulun*

Sunset turned the sea crimson, turned sails to bloody slashes across the straits and men to red-skinned savages, the like of which Javier had heard tales of from the Columbias. The water was quiet tonight, letting soldiers rest instead of fighting for their sleep before they fought for their lives. Javier, for the thousandth time, turned away from watching ships and water, and stared bleakly at a map that told him the same thing it had always told him, ever since he was a child.

Alunaer rested some little distance away from the sea-mouth of Aulun's greatest river, the Taymes. It was a usual place for a capital city, near the ocean but not on it, a protected port. It might have been easy to sail up the Taymes and seize the town, but for one thing.

White cliffs made up Aulun's southern shores. Alunaer's centre was in truth no great distance from the straits, but the land sloped downward from those cliffs, until Alunaer's heart was at sea level, and its watery border was protected by high ground dangerous to send an armada through. With dawn they would have the tide with them, but the battle would not be met on the river, not until Aulun's navy had been ruined on the straits.

Twelve ocean miles separated Gallin from the island nation, and those waters were where Aulun's fate would be written. "Lorraine's ships are smaller and older. We have the advantage."

He spoke to himself, but wasn't surprised when someone answered: "We have all the advantages, nephew. Our navy is the greater, and our army vastly stronger. You," Rodrigo said with a hint of mock severity, "are meant to be walking among your men, giving them hope and cheer, not poring over maps that will tell you the same things they've always said, and wearing a line in your forehead with that frown."

"Uncle." Javier turned from his maps with a relieved smile, though the expression fell away in slow surprise as he took in the woman who walked at Rodrigo's side. "Akilina," he said after a moment. "Forgive me if I don't call you aunt, just yet. I have yet to accustom myself to our new relations."

It had been days now since he'd learned of Rodrigo's wedding coup, days in which he'd vacillated between astonishment and awe, and in which he'd wondered a dozen times what the Pappas in Cordula thought of the Essandian prince's daring. The Holy Father would be furious at losing control of Rodrigo, and yet almost had to admire the union that brought seventy thousand Khazarian troops marching under the Ecumenic banner. Not for the first time, Javier shook his head, and Akilina's brief smile said she suspected what he was thinking.

"We are all adjusting." Her Gallic was nearly flawless, marred by only the slightest hint of a Khazarian accent. That accent was the only thing that set her apart from a true Essandian beauty: she'd taken some colour in the few months she'd been Rodrigo's bride, and her hair was loose, as an Isidrian woman might wear it. Even her gown was of Essandian cut, as though she had put away all things born of her icy homeland and had embraced the life she'd married into. "Your expression says you think a woman doesn't belong on the battlefield, my lord king."

"I think I remember you from my mother's court," Javier said with honest diplomacy. "I think few men would conduct themselves as boldly, and so I think if you see your place as here, and my uncle doesn't dispute it, that I have no argument." His eyebrows darted up. "And I think Irina wants one of her own watching over the troops your alliance has provided us with. I grew up with a queen as the centre of my world, Lady Akilina, and when I find myself matched against an imperatrix and a dvoryanin, I am wise enough to hold my tongue in matters of where a woman does or does not belong."

"Besides," Eliza said drily, from a shadowed corner of the tent that had, Javier was certain, been empty only seconds ago, "if he can't keep me out of here, he's hardly going to try to keep you away. My lady queen," she added perfunctorily.

Javier spread his hands as he sent a look of wry despair toward Rodrigo. "Has it always been thus, uncle? Have women always come and gone on battlefields, despite what the men around them command?" Humour danced through him at the question, more comforting by far than scowling over maps and dwelling on the coming day's events. He had no more tried to keep Eliza away than he might have sent Marius or Sacha from his side; she, like them, was a symbol of confidence and support.

"Queens have ever ridden with their kings," Rodrigo said with a hint of more real dismay than Javier had voiced. "Or ridden without them, if their kings could not. I think it was your Gallic grandmother three centuries back who began this unfortunate habit. *She* rode to the crusades, and brought her favoured son a wife while doing so."

"Gabrielle," Javier murmured with rue. "We are besieged in history and in the present, uncle. Ambitious women surround us."

"And we make war in their honour." Rodrigo flickered his hand, dismissing the women of whom he had just spoken so highly. Akilina held herself still a few seconds, disdain and insult evident in her carriage, and then Eliza sauntered by and offered an elbow, one beautiful woman squiring another. Javier watched them go with uncertainty curdling his stomach: they were not, he thought, friends, and the prospect of them becoming so unsettled him. When they were gone Rodrigo exhaled a noisy sigh and flung himself into a chair; Javier's tent was well-appointed, even if its front flaps were flung back to show him the straits and the navy nudging its way around them.

"How are you, nephew? Well-crowned, I see, and with the Pappas's blessing shining along with the crown."

"My burden's become easier with his blessing." Javier sat as well, his eyes fastening on the map once more. "I imagine myself this magic's master, and if I'm wrong it has at least not yet managed to overwhelm me again. I'll be the weapon you need me to be, Rodrigo. Don't worry."

"Could I not worry for my nephew, instead of for his status as a tool of war?" Rodrigo's light voice betrayed strain.

Javier slid his gaze from the map to study the Essandian prince for a moment or two. "As well I might worry for you, who seem to have gotten a tool of war yourself. At least mine's not sharing my bed. Have you heard from the Pappas?"

Rodrigo's strain slipped away in a brief smile. "He wasn't pleased, but he can't undo this marriage without undoing the treaty that puts the Khazarian army at our back. Besides, now you're free of any possible marriage to Ivanova. You're a king, handsome, young—"

"Malleable," Javier said.

Rodrigo tipped his head, agreeing with the conclusion, but aloud said, "But less so than our Cordulan father might think. It's a shame, though, that you're not married, Javier. An heir would be useful." He glanced toward the open tent flaps, after Akilina and Eliza, then turned that look back on Javier, eyebrows elevated. "Unless . . . ?"

Silver warning seized Javier's throat, cutting off the dismissal he might have made. Eliza's lack of womanly blood would set any politician against Javier marrying her, and that was a road he would not yet sever himself from. Instead he curled a corner of his mouth up; tilted his head as Rodrigo had done, and let his body tell a story that his words would not. Then he returned to the map, putting away the topic of succession to repeat, "We have the advantages. But will we win?"

"A storm follows us up the straits. It's a day, perhaps a day and a half behind; it blackened the horizon before we made the easterly turn. It will fill our sails and drive the Aulunian navy back, unless I miss my guess. They'll crowd against their own cliffs, frantic to hold their one choke point, and when we break through we'll have them in a wedge." Rodrigo slapped his hands together, making Javier flinch. "They'll have soldiers on the cliffs to pour pitch and flaming arrows on us, and they'll drop stones to break our ships. We'll lose more in the mouth of the Taymes than in the twelve-mile of straits between us, but our navy is the larger. An arrowhead of our fastest and strongest ships will ride the tide into Alunaer's heart, and we'll take the fight to them."

"There will be garrisons upon garrisons in the capital." The worries were already familiar to Javier, as were the solutions: he echoed them in his thoughts as Rodrigo outlined them aloud, re-assurances to them both. The Parnan navy, not as strong or new as the Essandian, had ships barely off the Aulunian coast both north and south of Alunaer, soldiers already ferrying to land. Reports of skirmishes came by pigeon, but Lorraine was concentrating her army in the capital city. So, too, would Javier have done, in her po-sition: Alunaer represented Lorraine's beating heart, and should she let it fall her people would lose all faith. That was a price too dear to pay, and so the worst of the battle would be fought in the Aulun-ian capital.

And it would fall, crushed by a three-prong attack by an army far larger than what Lorraine could command.

On paper—on the map that continued to draw Javier's eye—it seemed as though they not only couldn't fail, but that devastation could be wrought within a day or two, that he might well stride through a burning city in a week's time and take the crown that his mother had intended for him.

He had never gone to war, but he knew the danger of dreaming it might be so terribly simple.

"Things will go wrong," Rodrigo murmured. "Lives you will not want to lose will be lost. Resistance will go on for months, even years, until we have routed out all of those faithful to the Reforma-tion and to the Walters. But we will prevail, Javier. We have the ar-mada, we have the troops, and we have you, guided by God and granted the unearthly power to strike at Lorraine in a way she can-not imagine."

"We've had no word of Belinda," Javier said softly. "Nothing from our spies, nothing that says she's warned Lorraine against my magic. But dare we trust Lorraine has no knowledge at all of what I can do?"

"Perhaps she's dead after all. She might never have made it out of Sandalia's palace. Even if she did, you've proven she can't stand before you, and nothing else can hope to defeat our numbers and your gift. Not in the longer game." Rodrigo pushed out of his chair, all long comfortable grace in a man whose age dictated he ought to be at home before a fire, waiting out the news of war while grandchildren bounced on his knee. "Sleep tonight, if you can, Javier. Take your woman to bed, and then sleep. You may not see another chance for days."

Javier nodded, and Rodrigo strode away, leaving the young king of Gallin to once more study his map, and wonder what unforeseen thing would go wrong.

13

BELINDA PRIMROSE
4 June 1588 † *The Aulunian Straits*

The sun rises red as blood over waters soon to be awash with it. Belinda Primrose is not a fool: she has not gone to battle on the sea. She could, if she must; her father taught her the sword, and her dancing master taught her the grace that stood her well in learning the blade. He would be horrified at the use his lessons had gone to. But she will not, today, make use of the rapier she wears; at least, she hopes not.

Because a storm is coming up the straits, black as hell on the horizon. It will fill the Essandian navy's sails and press them on to Aulun's shores; press them up the short cliff-lined distance between the straits and the palace at Alunaer's centre. Belinda has no doubt that this is what the generals and admirals of the encroaching army expect and hope for.

Any other day, they might be granted their desires. But this morning, Belinda Primrose is standing alone on a cliff-top, her hair bound so severely it looks short, and her breasts bound even more tightly: she is a man today, for the sake of making war. She wears pants, tall boots, a red coat; she might be any sentry, waiting for the first sign of conflict to be unleashed. A musket is held in one hand, loosely; Belinda does not like guns, though she understands their usefulness. A good general does not give up a weapon simply because he dislikes it.

The wind, always high on the cliffs, is coming up. It smells of seawater and gunpowder, and tastes of salt. Belinda quells the urge to fling herself into it: to trust its strength and hang above the cliff's edge, unfettered by the world's pull. She has seen soldiers try it, now and then, and has seen how the untrustworthy wind cuts out and sends men plummeting to their death. The impulse to fly is enticing, but the wish to live is stronger. There will be other ways to die today, and it is her purpose to make certain those ways are visited on her enemy.

The tide has changed in the minutes since she arrived on the crimson-lit cliffs. That will be the signal Javier's army is waiting for: water pulling toward Aulun's cliffs, not retreating from them. The first ships will be launching now, catching the storm's winds to drive themselves forward toward battle.

Aulun's small and aging fleet is already waiting in the straits. They're too distant to be seen, but the bindings that hold Belinda so tightly restrain only her body. Witchpower flows free in her mind, golden power strong enough to rival the bloody sunrise, and it is that magic which will tell her the ships are engaged, and that it's time to turn the storm.

JAVIER DE CASTILLE, KING OF GALLIN

Rodrigo told him not to risk himself on the sea, and Javier, cow-like, agreed. He lied, of course, but he agreed.

It is the *Cordoglio* whose wings he rides; the Maglian captain put a fist to his heart and offered the swift tidy vessel as the armada's flagship. Javier accepted out of symbolism and out of dramatics, and in no little part to remind his people that the army they make is Cordula's army: not just Gallin, not just Essandia, but those two countries and Parna as well, each equal in God's eyes and in the true faith.

The *Cordoglio* has been painted white, the better to be seen by the ships she leads and the better to catch the colour of the rising sun. The better, too, to be seen by her enemy: the colour is a calling-out, a bold statement that the armada is not afraid of Aulun's aging navy, that Javier de Castille mocks the Aulunian ability to harm him or his cause.

They left port before the tide turned, knowing Aulun would expect them to come with the tide, not ahead of it. The winds are high enough to make excellent time even against the tide; once it turns, the *Cordoglio* leaps forward with a speed that brings a jubilant yell from Javier's throat.

His shout is picked up among the sailors, and from them rolls through the navy at his back, until it feels as though he rides on the strength of their cry. Full of exuberance, he releases witchlight, a silver spray that turns the red waters around them to brilliance, then tears ahead with a will of its own, searching out their enemy. For a moment temptation is there, the impulse to see if he might simply smash through the Aulunian ships with his magic, but as he reaches for them, he feels a weakening of his strength: the distance is as yet too great, and there's no point in exhausting himself now when he knows in closer quarters he can deal devastating damage.

There's that, and there's another truth that has more to do with politics and morale: coming on the Aulunian navy already battered and broken, its ships nothing but empty hulls and weathered boards on the sea, will frighten his sailors, not encourage them. Javier may be Pappas-blessed, but his men expect a fight. A too-easy victory will leave them wary of what lies ahead; a navy of ghost ships will turn their bowels to liquid and sap their will. If they see Javier fight alongside them, see him call witchpower now and again, save their lives and take their enemies', they'll revere the gift, not fear it. No victory in the world is worth undermining his army's nerves.

Even now they're seeing the witchlight that guides them, awe and uncertainty turning to broad grins as Javier calls, "God's light guides us, my brothers. We cannot fail!"

It seems only moments later that they're on the Aulunian navy. It's not: battles at sea are not quick things, with tremendous time taken to close ships enough for combat, to turn and settle against the wind, to take the best advantage of weather and light. It is not fast, and yet it seems to Javier that one moment there is nothing but empty sea between himself and Aulun, and the next there is the uproar of battle, with cannon erupting from ship to ship; with terrible storm-born waves throwing them around when only seconds ago the water was their friend. But the sea is no one's friend, and the Aulunian navy, with everything to lose, is even less so.

Javier is on the prow, hands clutching the rail, throat raw from screaming orders not even he can hear. They're not yet close enough to the Aulunians for man-to-man battle; all Javier is good for here is shouting and watching as cannon-fire digs holes in ships and the sea both. He is wet to the bone and freezing: the storm has come on them and rain falls in sheets that he should stagger under.

Only with that realisation does the shield of power glimmering around him come into his notice, though from the way his crew have slowed in their madcap rush to battle, they have already noticed. A sense of foolishness descends on the Gallic king: he's good for more than standing and screaming after all, and indeed that was why he came into battle in the first place.

He gathers witchlight, gathers strength, gathers his willpower, and turns toward the closest Aulunian ship, his hands a-glow with devastating magic. He practised this under Rodrigo's tutelage, destroyed forests and fields and beasts, and he can forgive himself for losing his head a few minutes, and forgetting what he has at his disposal. God's light was guiding them; remembering to turn it into a weapon takes some doing.

Javier de Castille volleys witchpower toward the Aulunian ship with all his will behind it.

And encounters, to his astonishment, resistance.

MARIUS POULIN

Marius Poulin is not a soldier.

He is not a coward, either, which is why he is there, but he is not a soldier and has never wanted to be one. He has wanted to serve his king and brother, Javier de Castille, that is all.

That is why he is now meeting blades with a wicked-looking, scarred Aulunian soldier whose confident swordwork says he's killed before and has no compunction against doing so again.

The ship lurches, a trough found in the water, and Marius, almost by accident, gains the upper hand and shoves his sword into the Aulunian's chest. They're both astounded, but it's Marius's surprise that will last, because the Aulunian slides off the blade and into the ocean, never to rise again.

If he had time, Marius would be sick. Every part of his body feels in rebellion, his steps clumsy and his bladework ponderous. Men come at him with blinding speed and a few fall to his sword, many others to the soldiers around him. He thinks he lost his bladder when the Aulunian ship slammed into his, but he is so wet it makes no difference, not even in his opinion of himself. A braver man— Sacha, perhaps—would have held his water, would have died rather than humiliate himself in fear.

Sacha is a thought that helps keep Marius moving forward; Sacha and Eliza, and Javier. If he fights for them, he may do them proud, and that thought gives him some little heart. Not enough: he seems likely to die on this slippery ship deck, tripping over dead men and sliding in blood, and he would rather do them proud by living.

What Marius Poulin cannot see is himself from the outside. He was taught swordwork by the king's own swordmaster, and from the outside he's a whirlwind, leaping bodies and skewering men, using a blood-and-water-slick deck to slip behind enemy guard and come up again a savage-eyed beast standing over the dead.

He's flung to the side when something smashes into his ship. Through a daze of stars, he feels a wracking born from the bottom of the sea, and throws a panicked look around, afraid he'll see a kraken's tentacles capturing and crushing them.

Instead he sees another Gallic vessel has broadsided his. Eliza swings from the other ship's crow's nest, a knife held in her teeth and the gondola boy held in her arm. She is, for an instant, a wild thing, as unearthly as the kraken. Her eyes are bright with glee, and the gondola boy is laughing madly.

The mast comes crashing down behind them with a rip and shriek of wood, lying crosswise across Marius's deck. It barely misses their own mast, and for a moment everyone from both ships is arrested, staring, impressed, at the broad beam that has inter- rupted their fight.

Then the gondola boy screams and jumps on an Aulunian sailor, his slight weight enough to bring the man down on the wet decks.

Before the sailor can recover, before anyone else moves, the gondola boy slams two knives into the sailor's back: once, twice, thrice, before he leaps away, a demonic grin splashed over his young features.

Battle comes again. Eliza has Marius's back, and for a moment they're children again, fighting under Javier's disgruntled sword-master's tutelage. He had been willing to teach Sacha, and reluctantly agreeable to teaching the merchant son Marius, but Eliza he had taught only under high-handed and arrogant orders from a nine-year-old prince.

Eliza, of necessity, became the best of them.

Not in strength, no, though her lighter sword and lither body gave her an advantage in speed. It was her ruthlessness that set her apart, and their swordmaster had grown ever more bitter and ever more drawn-in as the little girl learnt, extrapolated, and defeated her playmates.

She stopped fighting when her family made her grow her hair again, and it became an encumbrance, long enough to grab. Marius has always supposed she gave up the blade for good at that time, an easy decade ago now.

With her at his back, with the flash of her blades in the rain, with the blood that sprays as they fight, he knows she has never stopped practising, and that until death claims her, she never will.

The gondola boy flings a dagger and it sticks in someone's eye. He shrieks delight and Eliza's approving shout echoes it.

The Gallic ship from whence Eliza and the boy came takes another cannonball, its shudder knocking their ship askew, and then it slides into the boiling sea, leaving them with a double-contingent of crew all thirsty for blood. The Aulunians retreat, slicing their grappling ropes as they go, and Marius hears an order bellowed from belowdecks. The Aulunian ship is barely thirty feet off their starboard when cannons send it to join Eliza's ship in sinking. The crew rush to the rail, drawing wet pistols to shoot the survivors and scream victory.

Marius, alone in blood and water, watches them, and knows he is not like these people.

RODRIGO DE COSTA, PRINCE OF ESSANDIA

Unlike his idiot nephew, Rodrigo doesn't find it necessary to be in the thick of battle. Perhaps because he's an old man and has seen his share of war; perhaps it's that a fight on land does not, at least, have the added danger of surviving a swordfight only to drown when the ship goes down.

Perhaps it's that he lacks Javier's witchpower, and the sense of immortality such a gift must carry. Or perhaps he lacks the sense of duty it might also bear, though Rodrigo would cut down anyone who dared suggest he lacks a dutiful nature.

"You can do nothing from here, Rodrigo. When the storm passes we'll learn what there is to know."

Rodrigo, who is standing over the maps and toy ships in the same way Javier did last night, allows himself a moment with his eyes closed, and a thought that he would never allow to pass his lips: perhaps he remains behind because the idea of leaving Essandia to his newly wedded wife is so appalling.

Then he speaks in the language she used, Khazarian; she often speaks to him in her native tongue, and he hasn't asked if that's so she doesn't forget it, or because she imagines his spies might not number it among their languages. "I know, and yet can't stop myself from studying them and wondering."

"Yours is not the hand of God. You can't direct the ships as you see fit. At best you can move them as they ought to move, and worry yourself sick over whether they do as you wish."

"Javier is on one of those ships." In the end, it's the only answer he has to give: Javier is his only living relative, and for all that the prince of Essandia can do nothing to protect him, nor can he sit and drink wine and eat sweetmeats waiting for an answer to come across storm-ridden waters. His nephew is an idiot, but he is something special as well, and Rodrigo wouldn't lose him for the world.

For the church, perhaps, and the world after, but not for this one.

Akilina sighs, nods, and comes forward to put a hand over Rodrigo's. It's a wifely gesture; it is, in his estimation, entirely calculated. Rodrigo almost enjoys that; it gives him a different game to think about, one he has a little more chance of controlling.

"You will return to Isidro, will you not?" His voice is conciliatory, all due concern from a husband to his gravid wife: hope and worry, not orders. Akilina Pankejeff does not respond well to orders. "If the winter is temperate and this war drags out toward Christmas, you'll return to warmer and safer climes to bear the child."

"We've yet to see a full day of battle, and you would already have me packed off to Isidro." Akilina is teasing, but her accusation is full of other emotions as well: exasperation, pleasure, anticipation. The pleasure is not for his concern, but for what she regards it as meaning: that he is weaker than she, and can be directed through his fear for her well-being and his need for an heir.

If circumstances were utterly other than what they are, Rodrigo de Costa and Akilina Pankejeff might have made a devastating team.

But they are not, so he gives her a rueful smile that will no doubt play into her idea of his weakness, and he shrugs. "I anticipate this battle," and he gestures between himself and her, "to be a protracted one, my lady. I thought I had best get my first volley in now, the better to begin wearing you down."

Coquettish is not a look Akilina does well: there's too much challenge in her sharp features, but Rodrigo can see her appeal, when she gives a sly look through black lashes. It stirs amusement in him more than any baser emotion, but he can see how men might fall before it, and so when she says, "There might be better ways to wear me down, my lord," he is obliged to take her hand and draw her toward a more private part of the tent.

Obliged to murmur, "We must be quick, then, and quiet, for the men will think poorly of their prince rutting in the shadows while they prepare to fight for their lives."

"And if I wish to be loud?"

Rodrigo releases her, and from the flash in her eyes that's not the answer she wanted to her challenge. "Then you'll get no wearing down until after our victory, my lady, when the men might forgive their prince his passion and dare to imagine themselves pulling those cries from their queen's lips."

Astonishment and perhaps offence parts those lips. "You would condone such crassness in them?"

"It's a rare man who listens to a woman in the heat of passion and doesn't put himself in her lover's place," Rodrigo says calmly. "Indulge in noisy desire in the heart of an army camp, and you'll become their fantasy. They'll undress you with their eyes where once they might have worshipped. Reverence is less dangerous than lust, lady. Choose your position wisely."

And she does, becoming a queen on her knees with her mouth hot on his cock, filling her throat and silencing any cries she might have made. It's a deliberate cruelty to leave her there when he's sated, but Rodrigo has a battle to worry over, and an interest in seeing to whom his lady goes if he leaves her with an itch unscratched.

BELINDA PRIMROSE

She doesn't have to be there to see the battle.

The glee that rises in Belinda Primrose banishes every other moment of delight in her life as if they were the stuff of dreams, wispy and unobtainable. It is as though the storm itself carries the shapes of ships and soldiers to her: the storm, and Javier de Castille's witchpower, which she can feel on the water as though it's a living thing. Javier is aware of where his ship is—in the lead, a place of arrogance and power—and aware of where the other ships of the armada are in relation to him. Silver spiderwebs between them, catching water drops and shimmering with life; Belinda only needs to touch it and it vibrates. She can imagine a quiet gasp birthing from that touch, a sound any man might make in the midst of intimacy.

Her own power searches out the other ships, the ones not latticed together by Javier's magic. Those ones are her own: they become golden with raindrops, not so much bound to each other as becoming bright spots in her mind, warm against the cold of the storm and against Javier's moonlight power. With these bits of magic, she draws an image in her mind.

The picture is a dire one.

The storm has driven the Aulunian navy back and the armada

forward, and the armada's greater numbers are allowing them to close on the Aulunian ships like a crab's pincers. They are not quite surrounded on all sides: the cliffs at the Aulunians' back are dangerous, and while they still may be miles from shore, the Cordulan captains are being cautious. The pincers are still open at their tips, leaving a narrow gauntlet that the Aulunians could try to run. Assuming they survived that run, it would leave them racing for the Taymes with the entire armada on their tails. Tall protective cliffs and men ready to drop boulders onto enemy ships would only slow the Ecumenic army a little, should it come to that.

Belinda, as though she reaches for a lover, opens one hand, then the other, and makes herself supplicant to the sky.

For weeks she has practised with the quieter weather in Alunaer. Has brought rain, has pushed clouds around the sky and has blown skirts and hats awry with wind. Once, walking back from Dmitri's home, she brought a patch of sunlight with her, no larger than a half step in front of her or a half step behind her. She imagined the sisters would see it as walking in God's light, graced by His presence, and had been obliged to let her little square of warmth go before entering the convent, for fear fits of giggles would overcome her. She'd scolded herself once more that Beatrice Irvine had been bad for her, but in the obliging tag-along sunlight, she'd felt no real remorse.

She has entertained herself with rainstorms and downpours, and they have only hinted at preparation for opening herself to the raw, uncaring weather of the straits.

There is no will behind the storm; that's her first thought. It truly is uncaring, a thing of neither malice nor goodwill; it simply *is,* just as the sun is, just as the ocean is. Nothing in it pushes back at her magic. Dmitri makes a warning in the back of her mind, things he's said in study: that a weather pattern changed *here* affects the weather *there;* that it is the sort of thing she must keep in mind.

She has, it seems, dutifully kept it in mind. Now she discards it, because like the storm, Belinda has no care for what happens *there,* only here, and *here,* she demands that the winds bend under her will, and break themselves on the silver net of Javier's power.

Astonishment lashes back at her.

Of a sudden, there are two games at play: there is the wheedling of the storm, calling on it to pitch and roll and fling silver-bound ships toward the sea bottom. She knows it's her own eagerness that she assigns to the waves; they themselves have no care for the destruction they wreak. But there's more satisfaction in imagining she's unleashed a fury hungry for purpose, and that she's given it that purpose through benediction of heart.

It needs to be kept tame, though, this storm, because without taming, its indifference to which ships it sends to the ocean floor counts in cost to the Aulunian navy. And there is the second game: Javier, in the midst of the straits, now tries to bend the storm to his own whim. He's in the heart of it, and she can feel his confidence, thrumming with the same power the bashing water holds. He has defeated her once, and now has rage to back his magic.

For an instant, deep inside her, a knife cuts, and lets stillness out.

Too much is lost in that moment. She's safe, protected from her own scattered and confusing heart, but the stillness is an internal thing, and has no use for magic vented on the outside world. Javier rips away her control as easily as he overwhelmed her in Sandalia's court. The tempest is his, and it turns, lashing at Aulun's navy: in her witchpower vision she can see ships shudder, can see men swept into the raging water, can see Lorraine's crown resting on Javier's brow.

Belinda Primrose has not known much fury in her life. It's a wasted emotion, difficult to hide and dangerous to show. She has trained herself so very carefully to take anger and feed it to her stillness, making herself untouchable. That training has slipped these past few months; slipped enough that she indulged in temper and commanded Dmitri against his will.

The insult and ambition from which that pique was born is a weak pale flame against the wrath that surges through her now.

She is on fire. Witchpower burns through her until her skin is lit with it, and it's her own sentiment that it helps put into words: she *will not* have her people destroyed, she *will not* have her mother's crown lost. She *will not have it,* and with her fury comes a backlash of power so extraordinary that a league away, Javier de Castille is knocked off his feet and smashes back against the *Cordoglio*'s mast.

DMITRI, IN ALUNAER; AND ROBERT, IN GALLIN

Two witchlords lift their gazes to the horizon, one looking south and the other north. They see power flaring: no, not flaring. Erupting, sustaining itself, boiling through storm clouds, announcing itself as a presence not to be contained, nor to be denied. Dmitri, in Alunaer, folds long fingers in front of his lips and wonders if the woman who bears such magic is his to persuade; Robert, twenty miles and a world away, smiles, certain that the woman who bears that magic is his to control.

JAVIER DE CASTILLE

Javier staggers to his feet among a white-faced crew and stares into the storm as though he can see a face in it; this is what the survivors will say, that the young king of Gallin's grey eyes were possessed, his face grim, and they will say that he, graced by God, looked on the fallen one himself . . .

. . . and then threw himself forward with a howl that cut above even the sound of rain and wind and lashing water. Threw himself into the eye of it and from the bow of the ship slammed his hands together and sent forth a terrible lance of God's own strength, so brilliant it turned black clouds to silver and ripped a rainbow across the sheeting rain. Some will say he shouted his mother's name; others that he called on God's son to guide him. They will *all* say he faced down the devil to save this crew, and much later, when he's come to his senses, Javier won't find it in his heart to deny them.

The truth is that as he surges forward to reclaim his place at the prow and to meet magic with magic against Belinda Primrose a second time, the ship pitches just so, and he's flung fifteen feet forward, as ignominious an approach as his retreat was seconds earlier. The truth is that the bolt of witchpower that crashes from him is little more than a desperate attempt to keep from flying overboard.

It does, however, do the things they later claim it did: it sears moon-coloured light through the storm, cuts rainbows across a landscape that has recently been a second cousin to Hell. It's good that others appreciate it: Javier himself is in no shape to.

He can't see Belinda, but he can feel her, a source of golden burning power in his mind. She might lie beneath him again as she did in his gardens, coaxing her first witchlight to life: that is the closeness he feels to her. She's not part of the Aulunian navy; there's a sense of solidity to her presence that even his own can't match, not while he rides the tempest-torn sea. He won't be able to drown her with her failing ships, but he knows now that she's near, and only has to reach land to find her and take a knife to her wrists and ankles and body before finally drawing a red weeping line across her throat. She will lie insensible, awaiting him; of that much he is certain. She fell once beneath his will, and he is stronger now.

BELINDA PRIMROSE

Witchpower surges at her, a lance flung through the tempest. It flies straight and true, and the woman she was six months ago would have fallen beneath it.

Today it might be a bit of straw, and she a kitten at play: she bats it away, and her own magic pounces after it, rolling it in her own will and bending it back toward Javier de Castille. She bent Dmitri; it is no great thing, now, to deny the red-haired Gallic king.

But she cannot simply cut him off from his power the way she did Dmitri: his awareness of the Cordulan armada is too useful if she wishes to drown those ships. So she falters, drawing the image in her mind: Javier standing above her, a spear in hand, thrusting down, and her own hands reaching to catch its haft in a desperate attempt to save herself. She twists silver power to one side, sending Javier stumbling; he recovers, and jabs again, and she flinches aside herself, letting magic slam into the earth around her. None of this happens on the physical plane: it's all within her mind, pictures to help her guide the play.

She split her willpower once while exploring talent with Javier, and he failed to see her attack until it was too late. It's more diffi-cult to do that now: the battle they fight for dominance is much more deadly than that game had been. But then, she's stronger than

214 • C. E. MURPHY

she was, and so a part of her mind goes to wrestling Javier while another leaks out along the latticework of conjoined sailing vessels.

The harshest part of the storm is over the greatest number of ships now, battering not just the armada but Aulun's own navy. She's lost ships while fighting Javier, the storm's uncaring hunger content with Aulunian sailors. Belinda splits her attention a third way, sending out tendrils of witchpower meant to discourage the high winds from smashing her ships.

Javier's power roars down on her, such strength that she drops to her knees, wide-eyed but unseeing on the storm-ridden cliffs. The picture in her mind loses focus, then comes clear again and now she's on a headman's block, and Javier stands over her as the executioner.

Belinda, with a whimpered apology to her navy, withdraws the magic meant to protect it, and flings up a shield as Javier swings an axe toward her slender neck.

Silver cleaves gold and there is a moment of joining and of erotic passion. It's filled with memory, with the trembling exploration of esoteric touch, and with the possibility of a future that neither Belinda Primrose nor Javier de Castille could have commanded outside of dreams. They are, for that brief instant, one.

The raging storm comes to a stop inside that moment, and a single thin line of entwined gold and silver unfurls itself through time, whispering of hope as it goes. Gold and silver and crimson: that slim thread carries Belinda's heart's blood with it, too, against her will and with it all at once.

Then it twists back, becoming wire, becoming a garrotte, and the cut it makes is around Belinda's heart, slashing it to pieces and leaving an aching hole inside her. Javier sees no pretty pictures in their tangled futures, and false dreams aside, Belinda has known that's how it must be. She did, after all, murder his mother.

Somehow there's humour in that thought. It enrages Javier and releases Belinda from her sorrow, leaving them a war to fight again. On the cliffs, Belinda gets to her feet again, slow joint by joint rising that's an act of defiance and necessity. Javier expects her to be on her knees; standing, she throws everything that she is into his teeth, and Belinda takes pride in that.

What she does not know is the storm has ripped her hair from its tight bindings, that it has torn her clothes and left her clearly a woman standing alone on the cliff's edge. What she does not know is that first one, then another, and now thousands of Aulunian soldiers have seen her, black-haired in the rain, white-skinned, lit by gold: an unearthly creature with her hands and face raised to the storm. What she does not know is that they have whispered it amongst themselves already, and that their story burns like fire through the ranks.

God, they say, may have lent Javier de Castille a gift of power, but He has sent the Holy Mother herself to watch over Aulun and her people.

Belinda, who would laugh at the idea, is blessedly unaware, and when Javier strikes at her again with his silver magic, she only lets a *tsk* of dismay through the shield she has created. She could fight the Gallic prince to a standstill, could dominate and destroy him, but wisdom, though it's come lately, has at least come to her. Her shield may be gold, soft rich metal that it is, but it's heavy and solid, and the more time Javier wastes trying to pick his way through it, the more time she has to pull his fleet down around him. She ignores his own bright boat for the moment, so as to give him no reason to stop trying to destroy her, and instead turns her attention to the ships doing battle with her own in the belly of the storm.

Most of them will never know what happened. Belinda's hands claw, and so does the wind-whipped surface of the sea. Heavy planks shatter under water shaped with human intent, holes smashed beneath the waterlines. A dozen ships are sunk before the others start to realise something is wrong.

She cannot drown them all. The armada is too vast, too spread out, but many of their ships are at the centre of the fight and the heart of the tempest. Belinda reaches for those closest to Javier's, following his latticework, and comes upon a familiar presence.

Marius Poulin is on board one of those ships, and his terror is fresh and strong. A cramp seizes Belinda's heart, taking her breath and proving there's weakness in her after all. Marius has been badly used, both by herself and by his king. Whether it's mercy or foolishness, sympathy stings through her, and she releases his ship from the gold-laced network that drags the armada into the sea. Marius deserves better than a death by drowning, and that much, at least, she can give him. She can do nothing about the guilt that surges through him when his ship crashes to the top of the waves while others around it are drawn inexorably down, but there's the price of war: no matter how and no matter why, those who survive will bear a burden of self-inflicted censure.

Another price is paid for that moment of mercy: Javier's realised what she's doing, and has unleashed his awareness of the other ships the better to focus on keeping his afloat. It's hardly a heroic response, but Belinda finds it commendable: he's the serpent's head, and without him the amassed Cordulan army will wither and die.

He is also the particular threat to Lorraine's throne, and so Belinda stands, indecisive, for what feels like hours in the lashing rain. But in the end there's more damage to be done to his army's morale, and more safety for Aulun, if the armada is destroyed. She has a sense of her own navy's ships now, having singled them out as the ones not connected by Javier's awareness, and she can continue to lash out and sink the invading ships without fearing for her own.

Whether it's the storm that loses strength in time or herself, she's not sure, but a block of sunlight falls through clouds that are white from releasing rain. Shocked by the brightness, she lets witchpower fall away from herself, and only a lifetime of stubborn practise keeps her from staggering with exhaustion. She stands where she is, wishing she had a staff to lean on, and watches the Aulunian navy sail back to harbour. Their cheers are audible from a half-mile away, and she lifts a fatigued gaze to the horizon, as if she could see the armada's remains limping back to Gallin. Javier has survived, but his fleet has not. It's a victory worth bringing home to Lorraine.

Weary beyond belief, Belinda turns from the view and hobbles away from the cliffs, entirely unaware that she's leaving behind a legend in the making.

SEOLFOR
† *in Alania*

It's with an old man's chuckle that he kicks his feet off the stump they're resting on and hitches himself upright with the help of his staff. By evening he's packed mules and carts, chortling all the while, and by sunset, he's making his slow shuffling way out of the village that has been his home for forty years, to finally begin shaping this small blue world.

14

JAVIER, KING OF GALLIN
4 June 1588 † *Gallin's northern shore*

There were too many drowning men to save.

The *Cordoglio* had tried, pulling those she could to the safety of her decks. One such had been Sacha Asselin, so rudely snatched from Poseidon's clutches that he had vomited seawater when they dragged him on board, and whose cough still sounded wet and pathetic. Javier had refused to leave his side until he was delivered into a physician's hands, and had agitated until assured that so long as Sacha kept warm and dry, no illness should set into his lungs. Even then he'd not wanted to leave, and sat for a long time with an arm around Sacha, as if he could keep death away with a firm hand.

Marius and Eliza had come to shore safely as well, their ship unscathed, though Javier'd only half-heard the story of their escape while they all huddled around Sacha. When sleep took the stocky young lord, Javier left his friends, returning to the beaches to stare down their length as afternoon turned to evening and the storm faded away.

Bloated bodies washed up every minute or two. It would be the same across the straits, with soldiers rolling against the cliffs and deposited on sandy stretches, there to rot. Cordulan survivors, if there were any, would count themselves lucky to disappear into the Aulunian populace; most would likely end up in prison, awaiting the end of a war that Javier had meant to begin so decisively that its end would be brief and inevitable.

"You've done your duty in mourning and watching the sea for survivors. Attend the mass for their souls, but we have a war to fight, Javier. The weather turned against us this time, and Aulun will come on the storm's heels, bringing the fight to us."

"It wasn't the storm." Javier kept his eyes on the sea, surprised to hear his uncle's voice, surprised it had taken a full six hours from the *Cordoglio* staggering back to port before Rodrigo came to remind him of his duty.

Now the Essandian prince stepped up beside him, no longer pretending the diffidence that had kept him behind Javier and out of sight. "The woman, then?" He sounded unexpectedly calm, while fear and fury rose in Javier's breast.

"Yes, *the woman*. Belinda. Witchbreed bitch. That storm was hers to command."

"Had you meant it to be yours?" Genuine curiosity coloured Rodrigo's voice, no censure and no concern. "I hadn't known it was in your power."

Black rage burnt a line behind Javier's breastbone, filling his breath with bitterness. "Nor had I. It had not been my intent." He spat the admission, hating it. "I—"

"Then our enemy has a weapon for which we were not prepared," Rodrigo murmured. "This is war, Javier. This is the way of war. Your own attacks, were they effective?"

"No." Bile in the answer, loathing so deep Javier couldn't say whether it was for Belinda Primrose or for himself. "She shielded against them. She ought not have been able!"

Rodrigo's silence drew out long enough for Javier to know it was measured, that the Essandian prince was choosing his words carefully. Useless anger beat inside him, that Rodrigo should have to, and yet had his uncle spoken carelessly he would have struck at him, his own impotence so vast as to need an outlet.

"You've spent these last months extending your gift's aspects. So, it seems, has she. We shouldn't be surprised."

Javier whispered "But her strength" with more despair than he wanted to own to. "I was stronger than she, in Lutetia, uncle. She fell easily then. She is only a woman."

"Words your mother would slap you for," Rodrigo said drily. "You taught her. She was still new to her magic, but it's been almost a year, has it not? Since you began with her?"

Javier nodded, a sullen jerk of motion, then lifted a hand to his face. His fingers were still cold and swollen with water; warmth, if it ever returned, seemed a long time coming. "She sees her power—saw it—as internal, a thing that benefits a woman. I had not imagined it might . . . expand."

A flush heated his face, making his hand feel colder still. His own magic had changed in the past months, giving him hints of the emotions in those around him. Clarity deepened his blush: such a development could all too easily be considered a womanly thing, appropriate to the fairer sex. If he could learn that, then he ought to have anticipated Belinda might better herself in active uses of the witchpower. He mumbled, "I'm a fool," and to his irritation and surprise, Rodrigo chuckled.

"War and women make fools of all men, nephew."

Javier's embarrassment fled, replaced by a more righteous anger. "How can you laugh? We've taken devastating losses."

"I'm old," Rodrigo said, droll once again. Then, less so, he added, "And laughter diffuses the rage that makes clarity difficult to achieve. Aulun will come for us, Javier. We must ready the army, and move them."

"Move them?" Javier snapped a hand toward the straits. "They'll come across the water. We can meet them here on the shore, and burn their ships with fire-arrows and cannon. We'll slaughter them before they're past the beaches." Silver certainty rose in his mind, making him loosen his sword as though the Aulunian army already approached.

"They know we have an army gathered here, Javier." Rodrigo found a stick and drew in the sand, idle sketches that became the shape of the two countries' coastlines. A mark slashed their location before Rodrigo stabbed holes in the earth, one to the north, where the straits were narrowest, and one to the south, where another sharp jut of land brought the two countries close together before the straits ended and turned to open sea. "They'll come there or there, and make for Lutetia as we would have made for Alunaer."

Javier kicked sand over the lower point, scoffing. "It's ten days' journey from Brittany into the capital if you're feeding an army. They'll want to ride their victory directly into battle, not waste time marching."

"They'll want to win. They're outnumbered and know it, so chasing us here is a tactical disaster. You were taught tactics, were you not?" Rodrigo might have been born of desert sands, so dry was his voice. Insult coloured Javier's cheeks again, but he made himself scowl at the rough map in the sand.

"It's a losing tactic for them regardless of what they choose. We could split our forces and still meet them with even odds at either of those places. Or we could wait here until we know where they're coming from, and meet them in battle outside Lutetia." Javier sucked his cheeks in, still sullen. "That would be to our tactical advantage."

"So you *were* paying attention. The army rides under Cordula's banner, but they're yours to command. What's your will?"

Guilt surged through Javier, burning away insult and sourness alike. Rodrigo's expression gave no hint that his words were meant to be loaded, and Javier wished, briefly, that the small skill he'd developed in sensing emotion might burgeon, so he wouldn't have to grasp his uncle's shoulder to see if that innocence was real. Asking him his will, after months of struggling to leave men their own, seemed a purposeful cruelty. Javier made a fist, and his voice, when he spoke, was rough and tight. "I'll hear the mass for the dead before I decide."

Hear the mass for the dead, and bend a penitent knee to Tomas so he might hear the priest's advice. He was king, and his will meant to be law, and yet the thought of it stated so directly sent hummingbird wings of fear fluttering in his chest. His will must be that, and nothing more: his, without bending others to it, not even if the Pappas had graced him with God's blessing. It was a test, as every moment of his life had been a test. He had failed a few bitter times, but not again. Tomas would guide him. Tomas would tell him what to do.

Sacha Asselin

It is not only Rodrigo who notices that, rather than go to his lifelong friends, Javier de Castille turns to the beautiful Cordulan priest after the mass. Sacha Asselin, still bundled against sickness and grateful for the warm blankets, sees it, too. He's been longer separated from his prince, now his king, than the other two, and when Javier hurries after Tomas rather than so much as glance their way, Sacha turns to Marius and Eliza with confusion written across his features.

Marius is the one who makes a gesture of acceptance. "It's been this way for months, Sacha. Since he arrived in Isidro."

"Javier's changed," Eliza says quietly. "More than the crown on his head, it's . . ."

"The *witchpower.*" Sacha grates the words out. Watching his king these last few days, it seems to him a gift that Javier told him about the witchpower himself, rather than let Eliza and Marius do it. It shouldn't be a gift: it should be something so matter of course as to be utterly unquestionable; there should be no relief or surprise that Javier took the trouble to unfold his secrets to his oldest friend.

That it feels like a favour knots a black rope around Sacha's heart, and draws it tight.

Marius sighs, but before he can make an excuse for Javier, Sacha cuts him off. "He's always been reluctant to stand tall. Now he's hiding behind the priest's robes rather than—"

"Rather than what?" Eliza's bold enough to interrupt; Eliza never has had as much sense of propriety as Marius is burdened with. "He's afraid, Sacha. He can do things no man should be able to." A hint of pink washes along her cheekbones, though the way she continues speaking gives no hint that she knows, or cares. Sacha, though, notices, and jealousy indistinguishable from anger scores him. Eliza doesn't notice that, either, as she says, "The Pappas has blessed him now, but he's spent his whole life fighting this power of his—"

"Instead of embracing it and becoming the power in Echon that he could be!"

Eliza stares. "He's leading the combined might of the Cordulan armies in a fight for the abandoned souls in Reformation Aulun, and he's only just past his third and twentieth birthday. What else would you have him do?"

"He should have moved for Sandalia's throne years ago, when he reached his majority. Then he'd be a respected and known quantity amongst the crowned heads—" Sacha has always been frustrated with Javier's unwillingness to put himself ahead of his petite mother. Now, knowing that Javier refused not only that, but his own astonishing power, sends flashes of rage through Sacha's vision, even when he speaks with Eliza.

"Oh, aye," Eliza says dourly, "because as an untried youth he's had such difficulty in convincing Cordula's crowned kings to support him. If he needs Tomas's faith to shore his up—"

"It's more than that," Marius murmurs, surprising the other two into silence. "Tomas can resist the witchpower, at least for a little while. Like Bea—Belinda—could. It draws Javier, moth to flame. He's spent a lifetime not bending others to his will, though we all know well enough that we couldn't say no to him."

"He's royalty," Eliza says with a sniff. "He doesn't need magic to be irresistible." There's the briefest pause, one in which the corner of her mouth turns up as if she has a secret, and she adds, "At least, I never thought so."

Marius glances between Eliza and Sacha, then drops his gaze again before Sacha can read the merchant man's thoughts in his eyes. "That's true. So resistance of any kind is appealing. He finds in Tomas something he's never found in any of us."

"And so we're to be replaced?" Acid spills through Sacha's question, and Marius shakes his head.

"Perhaps. Perhaps not. We might have feared the same from Beatrice's arrival, but in the end she wasn't . . ."

"She wasn't what she said she was," Eliza says flatly. "She wasn't what he needed. She wasn't us."

"Neither is Tomas." Marius sounds calm, utterly certain of himself. "Tomas is a thing Javier needs, but he can't replace us. Not even Javier's witchpower can fit Tomas into his life the way we're a part of it. Let him take the time he needs to build confidence in him-

224 • C. E. MURPHY

self, Sacha. The witchpower is . . ." He crooks a smile. "Alarming, and he's spent his whole life fearing it was the devil's gift. He'll come back to us, as much as he can. He's a king now. Things change."

Anger blooms in Sacha's breast. "We shouldn't change this much. He needed us on the *Cordoglio* as it came into Lutetia. He needs us still. He should be able to see that, and come to us."

"My love for him won't change," Marius says steadily, quietly. "He knows that. If we can go through all that we have gone through, if we can find forgiveness over bitter matters—"

"Belinda," Sacha spits, and Marius exhales, then nods.

"Belinda, and . . ." A thought seems to come to him, and he pushes it away, changing his mind about speaking aloud. Sacha draws breath to pursue it, but Marius shakes his head and murmurs, "It doesn't matter. Belinda can be named the sum total of the deepest cuts between Javier and myself. The rest are details, and I will not be bled dry by them. He's certain of us, Sacha. That's what he needs, to never have to doubt that we stand beside him, loyal and loving. Let the priest guide him through difficult times, and perhaps we ourselves can learn something of standing against our king from Tomas. It seems he wants that as much as he needs faith."

Silence takes them after that, and it's a long while before, by unspoken agreement, three old friends rise and go in search of a drink. To avail themselves, without asking, of the king's finest wine, and to wonder if Marius is right, or if their fourth is already lost to them.

BELINDA PRIMROSE
4 June 1588 † *The Aulunian Straits*

With the storm's passing, Belinda drew what vestiges of magic she had left around herself and let the witchpower hide her from sight. She didn't move beyond that, other than to sit on the soggy ground and draw her knees to her chest as she stared across the straits. Her heartbeat, a constant low thud in her ears, told her she was alive, but everything beyond that passed her by. She could see that wind stirred grass and dirt, that seagulls rose and fell on it along the cliffs' edges. The birds opened their beaks to cry, but no piercing sound reached her ears. Exhaustion numbed her until she couldn't say if her fingers and toes were cold, or whether her skin itched where drying hair lay plastered to it.

She believed that she could, if she must, draw shreds of composure around herself and become the primrose assassin she'd always been. Her will would stretch that far: she had made a life of insisting that it did.

That, though, was if she must, and only Lorraine's direct order might command a *must*. Witchpower didn't so much as hunger for sex, as it had done the only other time she'd emptied her reserves so far. That stirred faint astonishment: the power had been bound to sex, had fed from it and been replenished by it, since the moment Belinda had broken through the barrier in her mind. To find it unlinked now, to have no hunger in her body demanding renewal through passion, opened a lock within her, and her next breath came more easily. Dmitri had said sex and power were not one and the same: to have them uncoupled could only become a strength.

One to explore later, though. It was enough to sit and not feel the cold, not feel the damp, and to watch as the navy, unexpectedly triumphant, returned to port. The first ships brought a smile to her face, cracking the mask of weariness that had settled over it.

Thumps of satisfied relief broke her facade further as the whole of the fleet came into sight, their joy at victory a palpable thing, even over the distance. Belinda watched until their nearness was eaten by the cliffs' height, and then, smiling, put her head against her knees to gather warmth and savour her triumph.

That was how Robert Drake found her, a full two days later.

His hand was shockingly warm on her shoulder. Belinda hadn't known she was cold until his touch told her otherwise; she hadn't, indeed, known anything until that moment. She lifted her head to see an afternoon like the one she'd closed her eyes against, only with greater heat in the air, and no lingering weight of a storm on the horizon. Other things were different, too: a stiffness in her body like that of sleeping on hard ground, though she had no recollection of doing so. Witchpower was replenished in her mind, golden, strong, and calm, demanding nothing. The fleet anchored offshore was whole and bright and proud: when last she'd seen it, sails had needed mending and the men on deck had needed rest. Now ships had full sails and were littered with soldiers in their bright red coats, awaiting the tide so they might make war on Gallin.

"The queen is waiting for you, Primrose." Robert sounded oddly gentle, a voice she hadn't heard from him since she was a child. Not since before she began the game of stillness; since before Lorraine had visited Robert's country estates and Belinda had been denied seeing her. That he should use such a voice now seemed both strange and worrying, though worry itself lay too far outside of where she still was to take much root. It took a while for her to put words together: speech had become remote and unimportant as she'd sat on the cliffs.

Finding it again told her she needed water: her throat was parched and sticky, and her voice was that of a querulous old woman's. "The queen has given me orders to ride with the army."

"Things have changed, Primrose. Things are different now. Here." Robert crouched beside her and offered a wineskin.

Belinda took it and sucked the liquid down greedily. It was watered to the point of having almost no flavour, but it moistened the membranes of her throat and tasted as sweet as anything she'd ever known. Remoteness faded as the wine washed down, bringing her back to the world and rooting her in it again. "Different how?"

"Come back to the city," Robert said. "You'll see."

There were horses a little way from the cliff-top, both with saddles meant for riding astride; only as she mounted did Belinda notice her clothes were shredded and torn. Robert tossed a cloak her way and she pulled it on, glad that it was lightweight under the summer sun.

They came on the gathered army outside the city walls. Robert rode through them with easy confidence, but Belinda reined in, following more slowly as she took in the men around her, and their icons of faith.

The Madonna was everywhere, bathed in blue, her face not unlike Lorraine's, though her hair was dark. Her sign graced their armbands and their banners, and Belinda rode by artists making sketches as quickly as they could. Soldiers walked away a ha'penny the poorer and stuffing the queen of Heaven's likeness into their shirts and coats. More finished pieces of art littered shields and tent-sides, the haloed Madonna standing at a cliff's edge, hands raised to the heavens and holy power streaming from her. Some of these did dare to make Her as titian as the Aulunian queen, nearly a blas-phemy in the Reformation church. Indeed, for a faith intended to strip away the Ecumenic pomposity and worship of idols, to see so many men clinging to the Madonna bordered on heresy.

It would be worse still should someone somehow recognise the young woman who had proven the inspiration for those drawings. Belinda, half horrified and all astonished, tightened her cloak and drew up its hood despite the warmth of the day. She kicked her horse to speed and caught up with Robert, who said nothing, and said it loudly. Chastened, she fell back a length and rode into the city with him in silence. Everywhere it was the same: an uprising of faith in Aulun's rightness, in the Madonna, in Lorraine, the virgin queen so clearly beloved by God. Belinda wondered what they would say to learning of her existence, and how she gave lie to the pure and untouched image Lorraine had worked so hard to create.

Robert brought her to the palace, but through the servants' en-trance, and held his tongue until they reached chambers that Be-linda knew were his own, a gift from a doting queen. They were sumptuous, more so than Belinda would expect from her father, but then, it would have been Lorraine's decree that had decorated them. Not even Robert would dare to refinish the room against Lorraine's tastes. Belinda's gaze went to heavy tapestries and old paintings that could easily cover spy-holes, and, half mocking, mur-mured, "We are unobserved?"

Thickness filled the air, turning it to a kind of hiss: the same off-kilter feeling and sound she might have gotten from stuffing bits of cloth into her ears. Robert, drily, said, "We are now," and Belinda was surprised to hear him. He said, "Sit, Primrose," and gestured her to a chair before a low-banked fire. Belinda threw off her cloak and did so, looking for wine; Robert poured a glass and brought it to her before sitting as well.

"Do you know that Belinda Primrose is dead?" he asked after a sip. "Beheaded by Sandalia, while Robert Drake was ransomed?"

"I had heard." Belinda stilled her fingers, not allowing them to touch her throat. She had imagined more than once that her life might end on a headman's block, and for a few brief hours in a Lutetian prison, had thought it would be sooner rather than later. But some other unfortunate girl with similar colouring had met Belinda's fate that day, and she could find no guilt within her for surviving. "I envy your escape."

"As well you might, but the whole of it may give us an opportunity." Robert tapped a finger against his wineglass, then set the glass aside and leaned forward, elbows on his knees, hands folded together. "Heed me well, Primrose, for this is how it shall go."

BELINDA PRIMROSE
4 June 1588 † Alunaer; the queen's court

She had come to court twice as a child: once to murder du Roz, and a second time some seventeen months later to observe the way courtiers danced around one another, manipulating and pressing advantages, falling back and regrouping. It wasn't until she was older that she saw the parallels to battle in their interactions, but at thirteen she hadn't needed to. She had come to learn, so she might be able to participate in those dances herself, should the day come when it proved necessary.

Lorraine had been on holiday during the six weeks Belinda was at court, and not many, if any, would remember the ordinary girl in the unremarkable gowns. She dressed better than a servant, as she required access to the upper classes, but for a girl who was the adopted daughter of the queen's favourite, she drew surprisingly little attention. Only now did Belinda wonder if Robert's witch-power had had a hand in that. She wouldn't ask: to her mind, doing so would give her father a subtle edge in their own game, and she was already too many steps behind.

This, then, was the third time she'd come to the Aulunian court, and only the second with Lorraine in attendance. The first time she'd been dressed fashionably but modestly, wearing brown velvet that looked well with her hair and skin tones, but which didn't draw the eye as a more sumptuous outfit might.

This afternoon she blended in in a different way, wearing a dress so much like those half the court women wore that she wasn't certain she'd have picked herself out of a group, much less expected anyone else to. It reminded her vividly of the last gown she'd worn to court, the magnificent, binding green dress Sandalia's best tailor had sewn her into only a little while before all her plots and planning in the Gallic court had come to a disastrous end. There were no similarities at all between the one gown and the other; this one had the broad boxy skirts and puffed sleeves that Lorraine favoured, rather than the impossibly thin lines of the Gallic dress, and was a variety of bejeweled and embroidered colours, making the fabric stiff and heavy. No, there were no similarities save they were both prisons in which she was caught, making escape from inexorable fate virtually impossible.

She had been positioned barely ten feet from Lorraine's throne, manoeuvred there by Cortes, the thin middling man who played the part of the queen's spymaster. Lorraine was, of course, not yet present, and beneath the brocaded gown Belinda's skin itched with awareness of curious eyes on her. Courtiers tended toward their own subtle ranking system, with those who fancied themselves the most important—or who could convince others they were—nearest the throne. A scant handful of the most ambitious put themselves at the other end of the long hall, that they might catch the queen's eye in the first moment she entered, but aside from them, the gathered court went from most powerful to least down the length of the room.

Belinda, unknown, not astonishingly beautiful, not extraordinarily dressed, broke all protocol in standing where she did. She could feel animosity gathering and preparing to break over her, and for a moment considered welcoming it: lifting her gaze and meeting accusing eyes with the untouchable centre of witchpower. She would win any such battle of will.

And she would lose any friends she might have within the Aulunian court. Whether dressed in servant's garb or the finest gown, it was of no use to make deliberate enemies where friends might be had instead. Belinda dropped her eyes, caught her lower lip in her teeth, and sent a shy glance to the nearest handful of glowering courtiers before looking down again. *Yes,* that look was meant to say, *I know my place and it isn't here. But I've been put here, and what else might I do but stay? Forgive me: I mean you no harm.*

One of them—an earl of some renown, born to the Branson household and a likely contender for Lorraine's throne after her death—relented in his glare. Belinda was, after all, only a woman, and a young one, probably some cocky courtier's wife, being used to draw the man himself closer to Lorraine's attention. *She was pretty,* Branson thought, and his thoughts ran to Belinda, clear as a mountain-fed stream: she was pretty, her shy glance bespeaking an easy mark for bedding. He'd welcome her, all right, and her cuckolded husband wouldn't dare protest, not if he wanted to gain access to inner circles. Then when Branson had used her to his satisfaction, both she and her hapless lord would be dropped, shut out as thoroughly as though they'd never been given leave to enter.

Belinda, her eyes still lowered in a show of proper modesty, thought she might kill this one for herself, in the name of all the times she'd been used that way, and, piously, in the name of all women who were so used. Her small dagger lay bound against her spine, unusable but symbolic: she would use violence if Branson had the audacity to lay a forceful hand on her.

Cortes had left to carry messages while wolves circled the woman he'd left behind. Belinda kept her eyes downcast, only daring glances at the courtroom, which was aggravating. Well over a hundred men and women littered it, and she wanted to see who they were, what kinds of power they wielded and what kinds they imagined they did. A sting of witchpower entered the room and Belinda's heart clenched as she forbade herself the luxury of looking up sharply and searching out her father.

No, not Robert. *Dmitri,* her own witchpower senses told her an instant later, and then she glanced up after all, curiosity stronger than wisdom.

A bearded Khazarian dressed in the rich colours of his countrymen stood in the place she expected to see Dmitri. He had more breadth to him, more width of face and perhaps less height than the witchlord, though his hawkish nose and deep-set eyes were similar to Dmitri's. Confusion cascaded through Belinda, a frown marring her forehead. She turned her gaze down before her consternation became obvious, then smoothed her brow and made calmness the sum of what she felt.

The second time she looked his way she did it with witchpower and witchpower alone, her gaze still turned to the floor. Dmitri's thick black power, as mutable as his eyes, was unmistakable: she could taste the channels she'd left in his mind, places where her power had subverted his and made it her own. It was active, that magic, active in a way that felt like the stillness and yet didn't: it drew attention to certain of his features and sent attention away from others, a whirling, constant flow of power that said *notice this, do not notice that.* The stillness asked only that no notice be taken; Belinda hadn't imagined it could be mirrored and used in another way.

She lifted her gaze again carefully, focusing on what his witchpower said not to see: the narrower cheekbones, the prominence of his nose in comparison; the slender height that seemed redistributed into bulk. Her vision protested, sending a spike of pain through her head: she could see two men standing in one space, one Dmitri's familiar form, the other what he wanted others to see. Eyes closed again, Belinda turned her face away, both in awe of his power and unsure why he used it so.

Trumpets blared and Belinda started, an embarrassing lapse of control as she faced the long hall's end. Her skirts rustled in the silence that hung after the trumpets, whispers of fabric all along the hall the only sound. Even breathing seemed on hold for the moments it took Lorraine Walter, queen of all Aulun, to enter from darkness into light, the same pageantry she always used to draw her court's attention.

She wore white today, brocaded in silver, with bloody curls piled high and a tiara of diamonds sparkling amongst them: even aging, she was regal. She paused within the portal of dark to light, tall and slim and commanding, and then with grace and poise, did something that she had never done before.

She put out her left hand, and Robert, Lord Drake, her longtime consort and oft-rumoured lover, put his hand beneath it and stepped forward with her, squiring her through the door.

Shock rippled through the courtiers, a wave so palpable that it slammed into Belinda and all but sent her staggering. She dipped a curtsey with the others, but her breath was gone and her heart churned sickness into her belly. Emotion burned her cheeks—her own, the court's; even Lorraine, a brilliant distinct spark amongst the rest—all too high to call colour back; too high to allow her to be the cool, collected creature she had been shaped into being. Her hands clenched in her skirts and Belinda couldn't make herself release them.

Whispers followed hard on Lorraine and Robert's heels, astonishment so profound it couldn't be held back. He escorted her to her throne, guided her to sit, then stepped back with a bow so deep it bordered on insult, though no one watching believed it was meant as such. Robert stepped aside, not far: he took up a stance to Lorraine's left, just out of reach, the most unsubtle position of support and power a man had ever taken in the queen's court.

The courtiers were moving now, positioning themselves, jostling to see better, managing to whisper and wait with bated silence all at the same time. Dmitri, heading a small contingent of Khazarians, came forward, and grumbling courtiers let them. Other dignitaries from foreign lands joined him, making themselves a presence near the throne. Of them all, only Dmitri was flushed with witchpower, a magic Belinda could feel making points between herself and the two men. It was constrained in all of them, but potent, and for a fleeting moment Belinda wondered what would happen if they, Javier, and the imperator's heir were all to unite as comrades with a single will.

It was a fancy not to be pursued; she could hardly imagine what might bring them together in such a way. The thought dismissed, Belinda unknotted her hands one finger at a time, heart still slamming so loudly she thought it must be audible to those around her. No one displaced her, surprise in itself, and just as well: fighting to retain her spot seemed like an insurmountable effort.

Lorraine, as though utterly unaware of the stir she'd caused, put out her right hand expectantly. A wide-eyed scribe placed a parchment browning with age into her white fingers, the contrast burning a vivid picture into Belinda's memory.

"We are of a mind to share secrets today." Lorraine's voice was wonderfully cool, so full of disdain as to wipe away the import of any secrets she might tell. She brought the scroll up and tapped it against her cheek as she glanced over the gathered court. Belinda, witchpower under wraps or no, felt a hint of amusement from the icy redhead, amusement at how her people held their breath and leaned in, ready to dance at her whim so they might hear whatever hidden thing she intended on sharing.

Lorraine dropped her voice to a murmur, leaning forward a scant inch herself, the better to draw her audience in with. "We set a game in motion twenty-five years ago, a secret and silent game that we have decided must come to fruition today, as Aulun stands on the brink of war."

Belinda's too-hard heartbeat slowed to a more regular pace as her own amusement at the queen's theatrics burgeoned, then jolted high again as Lorraine sat back, her voice suddenly full of thunder and power. "We stand on the brink of war and are faced with a young rival who is a pretender to our crown. We know that our people are concerned that we have no heir, and that is the matter which we will now address."

Excitement erupted over the courtroom, sharp babble of voices too astonished to leave the queen her say. Branson, still no more than a few feet away from Belinda, said nothing, but ambition shot through him, brilliant as a blazing arrow. Belinda kept her eyes on Lorraine, not wanting to give in to the emotion soaring through the room. Robert was a bastion against it, but Dmitri smouldered with ambition.

Lorraine waited for the first edge to fall off, then spoke again, clear and crisp with an expectation of respect. "Lord Branson, come forward."

Blinding triumph poured through Branson as he first bowed, then came forward to kneel before Lorraine. She smiled, winsome as a girl, then offered him the aging scroll. "We would ask you to rise and read what is written here, my lord."

"Your servant, majesty." Branson had a good voice, soft, but with enough depth that said softness overlaid steel. He accepted the scroll, then stood as he unwound it, taking a few steps to the left so

234 · C. E. MURPHY

he might not block the court's view of their queen. It was well done, except it blocked Belinda's view of Robert. Not that she needed to see Robert to read him: his presence remained steady, touched with his own amusement as Branson moved between him and the court.

"Let it be writ that on this day, the fourth of May in the year of our Lord fifteen hundred and sixty two, that—" Branson faltered, eyes darting ahead of his speech. Faltered, then fell silent entirely, a dangerous crimson rising along his jaw before he read on. "—that Lorraine Walter was wed in secret by myself, Father Christopher Moore, a priest of the true faith, to Robert, Lord Drake, who . . ." His voice fell away again, colour climbing higher into his face as he repeated what had been made obvious: "These are marriage writs, my queen."

"Yes," Lorraine all but drawled, clearly enjoying herself. She put out a hand and the wide-eyed scribe dropped another scroll into it. The queen leaned forward to offer it to the earl, her smile that of a shark's. "And these, sir, are writs declaring the birth of our true and legitimate heir."

15

Heed me well, Primrose, for this is how it shall go.

They were not words that had ever preceded anything but truth; each time Robert had said them to her, things had gone as he declared they would. After a lifetime of such promises playing out as commanded, Belinda might have believed that this one, too, would come to pass.

Somehow, she had not.

The earl read out the name, *Belinda Walter,* in a voice shaking with rage. Belinda trembled, too, though more from disbelieving astonishment as she sank into a curtsey that brought all eyes to her. She had been exposed once in Sandalia's court, but this was declaration, not exposure. Her heart fluttered too fast, and she remained bowed a long time.

Robert, if he'd had his way, would have kept her behind a curtain, gowned in white and made to look fragile and innocent. Lorraine overruled him, insisting that Belinda look the part of one of the people, that she seem one of the courtiers. She intended to levy the illusion that Belinda had always been there, invisible, unnoticed, uninteresting, and yet a desperately important part of the court.

Of course, had she been there, *someone* would have noticed her, and so while she looked the part of an ordinary courtier, Belinda also finally understood why Lorraine had sent her to the convent. There was no better or more obvious place for a daughter of the throne to be raised in secret, to be educated and taught politics while kept safe from the harsh world her mother belonged to. No better place for an heir whose presence meant the queen could no longer dance beaus on a string, hinting at promises that came to nothing. For a woman and a queen like Lorraine Walter, a convent was the perfect place to hide a daughter until she became convenient.

Belinda Drake, Robert's adopted daughter, was known to have joined a convent at age thirteen: a decade later, Belinda Walter had emerged from one. It was a game so long in motion she could barely fathom the foresight it took to prepare for this day, for this move, unfolding so very many years after it was set in motion. The fraction of her that was still given over to calm stillness wanted to raise a toast in admiration of the woman who had birthed her, but she remained where she was, bent in a deep curtsey, and wondered a little at the chill in her hands and her shortness of breath.

She rose at the queen's subtle command, took the steps toward the throne slowly, as much for effect as barely trusting her feet. Tumultuous emotion filled the room, disbelief and excitement, utter belief and near-worship, ambition thwarted and ambition honed, rage and delight, all of it pounding at Belinda like a living tide intent on bringing her down. It exhausted her, and she tightened her belly, not wanting to rely on witchpower but unwilling to flag under the onslaught. Lorraine's voice cut through it, giving Belinda something to focus on, and for the second time, though she'd been told how it would be, she hardly credited what she heard.

"You all know that Sandalia, our lamented sister-queen in Lutetia, was for a brief time our own Lord Drake's host," Lorraine said. A smirk ran through the court at her polite language, but the queen's cool expression brought ugly humour to stillness, and into the silence she said, "You will have heard stories of why our beloved Robert travelled to unfriendly lands unescorted. You will have heard he went to rescue a daughter, even that he was made to participate in a mockery of a trial where a young woman of comely aspect was put forth as his child.

"That is nonsense." Lorraine's voice cracked over the gathered courtiers and garnered flinches from even the most resolute. "The woman on trial was a Lanyarchan noble called Beatrice Irvine, though Sandalia's clever prosecutor named her Belinda Primrose as well, knowing that was the name Robert had once used for his own daughter.

"They are both dead, Beatrice Irvine and Belinda Primrose."

A gasp ran through the court at Lorraine's cold claim, and despite her own heady connection to the story, Belinda felt a rush of horror as well. *She* was dead, very suddenly, with that statement: hearing it from Cortes had nothing like the strength of hearing it said in the queen's voice, and every new word that fell from Lorraine's lips further ended the life she'd known.

"Beatrice died a traitor to our Aulunian crown," Lorraine said softly. "Our spies now tell us she went to Lutetia to wed Javier de Castille and so to strengthen his claim on the Lanyarchan throne and on our own. But more, she incited rebellion against Sandalia herself, agitating for Javier to come to the Gallic throne, and so died for it. A traitor to one crown and a threat to another," Lorraine murmured. "Few of us have such lofty things said when we have passed away."

In the silence, Belinda heard breath being drawn in and held: no one wanted to stir the queen from her melancholic thoughts, for fear she would cease telling tales when she awoke from them. The instant before time had stretched too far, Lorraine raised grey eyes to the gathered courtiers and continued as though she'd never paused: "Belinda Primrose, beloved adopted daughter of Robert, Lord Drake, is dead because Belinda Walter now stands in her place. Secrets and protective fallicies have been set aside now, that we might introduce to you our heir, and that we might hope you will embrace her as we have so often longed to do over the years we have been apart."

Tentative cheers rose up, but Lorraine hushed them again, with a gesture of begging indulgence. "There is one more tale we must share with you. You know now that our daughter has spent these past ten years in the sanctuary of a convent, giving herself to God until the secular world sounded its call. What we have not yet told you is what came to pass three days ago, when the Essandian fleet sailed toward our shores."

Anticipation lashed the courtiers, whispers again: they had all heard talk of the holy Mother on the cliffs; they all, like the soldiers and sailors, believed God had intervened on Aulun's behalf, and if they didn't believe it, they had no better explanation. Now they leaned in hungrily, waiting on Lorraine's words, their gazes hot and heavy on Belinda herself. They knew: to a man they had dreams of what the queen would say, the shape of it if not the particular words, and their desire for their dreams confirmed was enough to stir well-dampened witchpower to waking. Knowing she shouldn't, Belinda reached out with tendrils of magic, seeking thoughts and tasting emotion.

Hope: so much hope it took her breath, and disbelief just as powerful, but begging to be given the lie. Stymied ambition, still, but in the moment there was more of a wish for God's hand gracing Aulun than there was of hatred focused on the young woman who had dashed many aspirations. Even that hatred waited in some to become love. Belinda held her breath and waited, too, to see whether Lorraine Walter could turn the tide.

"They had three ships to our one, five men to our one, for their ships were newer, larger, faster. We feared for our navy, sailing into the stormy straits, and so in the days before battle we called Belinda to our side, that we might pray together for God's mercy on our brave soldiers. I am a queen," Lorraine said, and her voice throbbed with sorrow as she slipped, all too deliberately, Belinda thought, into the singular. "I was unable to spend each waking moment on my knees, as I might have wished to do, but Belinda's steadfast faith never wavered. Never came I to my chambers but to find her in prayer, her head lowered, her hands clasped, entreating God to give our men safe passage. I was with her when the battle met."

Lorraine was on her feet suddenly, a creature of theatrics. The courtiers caught their breath and swayed back, then leaned forward, eager for her story, and the queen of Aulun reached out her hands and gathered them in. " 'There are so many!' she cried, and my heart tore to hear it, watching my tender child struggle under the weight of knowledge God granted her. 'So many! Mother— Mother, I must—'

"—and then she was silent," Lorraine whispered into a court-room so quiet it might have been empty. "She fell in a swoon, and when I laid her on the bed I saw her eyes were golden with the light of God's power. For hours she thrashed, not awake and yet not sleeping, with sweat on her brow and terrible wracking sobs in her throat. Not until the storm broke did she quiet and my heart beat more easily."

The queen fell silent, turning a gentle gaze to, it seemed, each and every face in her audience. Even Belinda waited nervously on the story's end, no less taken by it than were the courtiers. "She lay insensible for two days," Lorraine finally breathed, "and when she wakened, it was with confusion in her eyes. 'Mother,' she said. 'How came I here? I am certain I stood on the cliffs, with God guiding me to protect our fleet.'

" '*Our* fleet,' I said back to her, and said it with humour. '*Your* fleet, child, for with His guidance you have brought them safely home, and devastated the armada Cordula brought against us. They are yours, and you are their banner of hope, of light, of life, my child. I am only a vessel made to bring you into this world, so in the hour of our greatest need you might stand atop those cliffs and save us all.' "

It was as well a roar came up from the courtiers, hailing Belinda, hailing Lorraine, hailing God, for without it Belinda thought she might have lost all sense and laughed aloud at Lorraine's maternal modesty. Witchpower told her what the shouts and cheers would have anyway: the people believed. They'd heard stories of the Madonna on the cliff-tops, how she had appeared and disappeared; they'd embraced her as their saviour, and now were willing to embrace Belinda, raised as godly as a woman could be, as the embodiment of that saviour. It didn't matter whether it was true, not even to the cynical: it was *wondrous,* and that was better than truth.

Smug satisfaction bubbled beneath Lorraine's white-painted facade. She turned to Belinda and offered an embrace, shocking in its warmth. Twice, Belinda thought: twice before her royal mother had touched her, and now they held each other in a mockery of family compassion. It was not where she had ever imagined her road would end, the day she'd looked on Lorraine Walter and known herself for the queen's bastard.

"Where is the priest?" Branson's voice grated through the cheering, asking a question that should have been expected. Witchpower warned Belinda of Lorraine's alarm, though none of it showed on her mother's face as she looked at the earl. Looked down at him, perhaps with a hint of impatience, as though he were a bit of unpleasantness likely to stain her dress.

"Are you in need of one, Lord Branson? Have you sins to repent? A sin of greed, perhaps? A sin of pride?"

Mockery failed her: Branson's face twisted, but he refused to let it alone. "The same name witnessed wedding and birth. I think it not outside the realm of reason to ask that he come forward so we might hear these pages confirmed by the man who wrote them. Or is he conveniently dead, majesty? Dead, like your pretender daughter, so usefully murdered by a rival queen."

Before Lorraine could speak again, before she might give in to the anger and alarm Belinda felt boiling in her, another voice interrupted, soft and sorrowful: "He is dead, my lord. He died when I was seventeen."

Long moments passed before she realised, with surprise, that the voice was her own.

She extended the witchpower, unfurling it toward Branson with all the gentleness of a lover's touch. Doing so heightened her awareness of the rest of the court's high-running emotion, of their breath-holding anticipation that there would be war made here today, the Aulunian palace a new sort of battleground. What Belinda and Lorraine faced now would only be the first skirmish of many. The people and the army of Aulun would love the mythic story Lorraine had concocted out of half-truths, but there would always be men like Branson, hungry for a crown and unwilling to believe the word of a queen.

Defiance flowed from the man, prickly and determined. Robert remained a rock, steady and calm, but surprise piqued in both Dmitri and Lorraine, the latter tinged with relief. Lorraine had no easy explanation as to the priest, casting more of Belinda's doubt on the legitimacy of the papers her mother had produced.

Balance hung in the silence as Belinda took a few steps down toward Branson. She had never looked for the burden and gift she was being given; this was the moment in which she might make a lie of it all and free herself from its weight. A part of her wanted to: she had been raised in shadow, and even now her heart flew out of time, unregulated, terrified at being under the weight of so many eyes. Beatrice Irvine had been this exposed, and Beatrice Irvine was dead. It would be easy to draw the extended witchpower around herself and disappear, to avoid the life being thrust on her and become no more than she had been.

Duty, sharp and agonising, cut into her, and then witchpower ambition, and Belinda knew she would never retreat.

"His name was Christopher, after the patron saint of lost children," she murmured, "and he was the closest thing to a father I knew in my sequestered years. I would see him of a Sunday, when he was allowed to visit the abbey chapel and bend an ear to hearing the labours of my studies each week. In the summer and on fine winter days we would walk and argue doctrine, both religious and political." She wove the fiction from the life she had known, growing up under Robert's fond and distant tutelage, and from a dream of what might have been. That dream, laced with witchpower, drifted toward Branson, wrapping around him gently so it might settle against his skin and become comfortable before Belinda exerted her will behind it. It reminded her of Javier's casual expectation of obedience. She'd never imagined she might one day command the same influence.

And it was a different thing than she had done to Marius or Viktor; then, she had relied on the sexual link she shared with each man, able to control through it and it alone. But she was stronger now, much stronger, and breaking Branson would be too obvious, especially in front of so many witnesses. He required seduction; they all did. They required the vulnerability of a young woman raised away from the world, telling a story about death: about the death of the only person she'd thought loved her. They needed to believe it would never occur to her to lie—and they needed to trust that despite honesty, despite vulnerability, that she was not an easy target, ready for crushing and throwing away. Impatience swam over her, a sudden disdain for politics and an impulse to simply dominate, force them all to her will. Too much danger lay in that desire; despite Lorraine's promises, witchcraft would see Belinda burnt, and such a demonstration of power would be seen as witchcraft, not the Madonna's generous influence.

"He was tall," she said, and felt her own gaze grow distant, as though she looked back through memory. Indeed, she felt as though she did, while Lorraine's concern still spiked at the corners of her mind, and Dmitri's curiosity washed over her. "Tall, at least, to a child," Belinda added with a brief smile, then passed a hand over her eyes. "No, tall in fact: as a girl I often had to run to keep pace with him, and even when I reached my growth I looked up to him. Sharp-featured, with black hair, and he told me of the monastery where he'd studied."

Belinda had no doubt that, by the time Branson got a man there, there would be records of her imaginary priest, brothers who remembered him, a story of how he enjoyed gardening, their regret at his passing; all the things that made up a life, real or not. The world seemed a cruel place, that a man who had never been could take on more permanence than many who had been born, lived, and died without regard.

Lorraine, who had in all the brief times Belinda had enjoyed her presence, been a master of control, emotionless to Belinda's witchbreed senses, was now, beneath her painted face, full of disbelief; full of a growing concern that bordered on terror. It rattled Belinda, distracting her from the spell she tried to weave, and in a moment of inquisitiveness, she turned a few degrees back toward the throne.

"He told me of my mother, not of the queen, but of the woman. She who had wed and created life in secret, knowing herself to be the most valuable piece she had to broker, yet knowing she couldn't risk leaving her throne empty after years of playing suitors against one another. He called her bold and clever, and"—Belinda smiled quickly—"and apologised for it, for who was he, a humble priest, to pass such comment on a queen? But he gave me what he could of the mother who had to hide me."

Belinda reached out, trusting, sweet, hopeful, toward that mother, and wondered if there might have been a time when she would have done so and have it be less than the act of showmanship it was now.

Lorraine, even knotted with fear, was a consummate actress: when the daughter she had long been separated from reached for her, it was instinctive to take her hand, creating a line of compassion, of family, and of new beginnings between them.

Creating the link of touch that had always made stealing thoughts easy for Belinda Primrose, ever since she had awakened to her witchpower under Javier de Castille's guidance.

The girl knows was the underlying thought in Lorraine's touch, half incoherent with confusion. A flinch ran under Belinda's skin, an unexpected wound opening at how Lorraine thought of her: *the girl*. She had no name in her mother's mind, and that cut unfairly deep. Only in the past few days had Belinda often allowed herself the luxury of thinking of Lorraine as her mother; those were thoughts too dangerous to be reflected, even in her own mind. She was *Lorraine,* or *the queen,* and despite her skill in weaving stories, Belinda could hardly imagine a day might come when she would call the queen *Mother.* It ought not hurt that Lorraine thought of her similarly, rather than by dangerous words like *daughter,* or by her name.

Ought not, and yet it did. Belinda put the hurt away: there would be time to nurse it later, and she had only a few brief seconds in which to steal Lorraine's thoughts and find the source of her consternation.

Words came clear again within the constraints of Lorraine's mind: the queen was disciplined, her mouth curved in a gentle smile as she looked on Belinda, her gaze tender, with no hint of the rushing, bewildered thoughts behind her eyes. *How can she know, but then how could she know that I was her mother, and she knew that as well. Knew herself for the queen's bastard and made nothing of it, so perhaps she'll make nothing of this, either, that the priest who oversaw her birth—*

An image came into sharp focus: a hawk-faced man with black hair and deep-set eyes, with a sensual mouth and long hands. The kind of man Lorraine might have considered for a lover when she was young and not yet a queen. By the time she took the throne she knew better than to dally with the church. She was head and heart of her religion, and would allow no churchman above her.

All of that, all of it and more came with the picture of Dmitri

Leontyev in Belinda's mind. For all her control, for all the life she'd spent honing discipline, when Belinda smiled shyly and turned from Lorraine to once more address Branson, her gaze went first to the disguised witchlord in the courtroom.

There was nothing of concern in Dmitri's eyes, nothing of the amusement she could feel beneath his surface. He knew himself a stranger here, an envoy of Irina Durova's court, there for no other reason than to make polite of the failed attempt to build an alliance between Aulun and Khazar. Lorraine couldn't recognise him; the witchpower saw to that, misdirected both her eyes with the changes it had worked on his countenance and her memory, so that even if a hint of suspicion came into her mind, it would fade away again. As ever, Belinda had no words from Dmitri, only smug satisfaction that allowed her to understand the direction of his thoughts.

He'd been there at her birth, and Lorraine thought him dead.

"I can't speak to his age," Belinda said to Branson. She trusted the life she'd led to give her voice the right timbre, to show youthful uncertainty and sorrow even when she herself barely attended the words she spoke. "His hair was dark, but not all men lose their colour as they age, and he seemed old to me. That winter a cough took him, and he grew frail." Tears filled her eyes and she glanced to the side so she might brush them away in a semblance of privacy; a semblance watched by all the court. She would believe her, if she were they; such performance was what she was made for. "When he died I was alone."

A single thread of her attention was taken up by awareness of rising sympathy: the courtiers were half in love with her, in love with a romantic idea of a lonely girl destined for a throne; in love with the thought that they might now warm her and make her welcome. Mothers with marriageable sons plotted how a convent-raised princess might be best seduced; mothers with daughters considered how a crowned novice might need friends and guidance within the court. Younger women sighed in melodramatic compassion, imagining if only they had been the secret heir, and so it went, all through the court, all making a place for Belinda within their hearts. The romance would fade soon enough, leaving politics and manoeuvrings behind, but now, as she stood on the throne dais beside Lorraine, they warmed to her.

And she all but ignored them, her gaze on Branson but her thoughts on the two witchlords and the Aulunian queen. An energy crackled between them, nearly a quarter century of secrets kept. Belinda had no need to look over her shoulder at Robert to feel that he, too, was remembering the day of her birth, and the priest who had overseen it.

Bloody curls over translucent skin: that was the easiest memory for Belinda herself to draw up. The warmth of Robert's hands enveloping her, and the command: *it cannot be found out.* Robert's voice replying, promising that it would not be found out. And another command: *attend her.* Another response, a man's voice agreeing, and in the present, in the courtroom, hairs rippled on Belinda's arms, bringing a chill.

Dmitri, agreeing. Dmitri, promising to attend the queen who had just birthed Belinda, whose memories stretched all the way back to the moment of her birth. He had, so often in her life, awakened witchpower magic; she wondered now if his presence all those years earlier had helped shape the strength of her recollection, even before she could form coherent thoughts.

Lorraine, outside the weight of memory that burdened Belinda, but carrying her own fears, still performed the show they'd set in motion. Belinda had reached toward her once; now the queen reversed the offer, putting a hand out toward Belinda, and Belinda, as much the actor as her mother, took it.

"Not alone," Lorraine murmured. "Though it may have seemed you were for all those years after Christopher's death, you remained in our hearts. Our greatest regret is that we have been unable to know you, and we hope that God will grace us with at least a few more years in which we might become family."

For the second time, she drew Belinda into an embrace, and while courtiers shouted cheers and threw their hats into the air, clear memory, stolen from the queen's touch, thundered into Belinda's mind.

Afterbirth still rippling her belly: that, Belinda remembered herself, in the moments before Robert turned away and took her from the first and last glimpse of her mother for over a decade. But what Lorraine remembered and Belinda did not, that Robert did not, was the unexpected pain of another labour contraction, more violent than she thought to expect with passing the afterbirth. She had gasped with it, and the priest, rightfully concerned, came to her side.

It was he who delivered the second child almost an hour later. A boy, noisier in his entrance to the world than Belinda had been, and a source of appalled horror to the woman who'd birthed him. Robert was gone with the girl; with the bastard heir upon whom Lorraine had decided to risk everything. Lorraine had been pleased the child was female; she, after all, had done well enough as a woman alone, and fancied the idea of a daughter coming after her.

A son threatened everything, on every level. One bastard child was risk enough; a bastard son, should he learn his parentage, would consider himself rightful heir to a throne Lorraine intended on being Belinda's, if it should come to that. And the people would support him: no matter how fond they were of their virgin queen, a woman on the throne sat badly with many of them, and they would raise a banner to her son.

It was maternal instinct, oh yes, but not the instinct so lauded by men, which made Lorraine Walter thrust the squalling babe into her priest's arms and say, flatly, "Drown him, stone him, leave him to die in the forest, but do not let him see the dawn, priest. It cannot be found out. More than the girl, this cannot be found out."

In memory, Dmitri took the child and silenced his cries with a rag dribbled in water so the boy had something to suckle, and left the queen of Aulun to attend to herself.

Minutes later, pale, regal, trembling, she came barefoot to her guardsmen's door, and from there commanded them ride after the priest in secret until the ninth hour, and then to put him to death. They, without question, saluted agreement and left Lorraine alone again for the second time.

Alone, exhausted, but confident it would not be found out, she returned to her chambers, and with the ninth bell of the morning murmured a prayer for the priest's soul and for that of the dead boy, then emerged from the shadow of her father's death to take up her crown and sceptre again as an uncontested queen.

Lorraine released Belinda from their embrace and smiled; Belinda returned the expression without hesitation, and heard nothing of what Lorraine said next. The queen was wise to be afraid: should it be known she sent a son to his death, her people would never forgive her.

A curious spot of emptiness grew in Belinda's belly at the thought of a brother she hadn't known, chilling her in a way the stillness never had. She knew regret well enough to recognise it, but this was something else, a calmer and steadier aspect to that emotion, if such a thing was to be had. Not sorrow that needed regret, and she had too little attachment to a befuddling idea to regret it as of yet. Disbelief, maybe; a simple thing, that she might not have been so alone as she'd always been, had the world been just a little different. Yes: there, she knew it now. The coolness inside her was that same thick wavering glass through which she'd always seen the other side of her life, the one where she'd been born legitimate heir to the Aulunian throne. It was a curiosity, barely worth considering in one part for its unattainability, and in the other, for the rage she might have felt if she permitted herself to dwell on it. That was the shape of her dead brother inside her, and all wisdom said it should be left that way, impossible to touch.

Instead she sent an unfelt smile over the courtiers, catching gazes for an instant here and a moment there, until with witchpowered precision, her eyes met Dmitri's.

She had stolen only snatches of emotion from him, no clear thoughts or memories the way she could from one who wasn't witchbred himself. But the satisfaction beneath his changed demeanour lay in parallel to Lorraine's thoughts: they shared a source, one that inspired fear in the titian queen and smugness in Dmitri. His mind was guarded against hers, too familiar already with Belinda's ability to subsume his will and demand his power be used to her satisfaction. But she'd changed yet again, not only in holding the power of the storm, but in riding the high emotion that now lashed the court. If it could affect her, she could draw it in and make a needle point of it.

Suddenly impatient with half-answers and untruths, Belinda gathered her will, gathered the overwhelming support of the courtiers, and slammed through the feeble walls of darkness that Dmitri threw in her path.

DMITRI LEONTYEV
15 March 1565 † *Brittany, north of Gallin*

Dmitri Leontyev does not want to be here.

Oh, in the day that it happened, he was happy enough to be there. More than happy: delighted, smug, crafty. But it's not his will that makes him linger in memory now, and so his thoughts are tainted: he does not want to be here. This is anathema to his people: one does not rape the memories of another, and rage boils in him below Belinda's inexorable examination. She has no right, and he'll teach her the lesson of that when he's broken free. A creature vicious enough to tear apart his thoughts and invade old and quiet memories is not one worthy of veneration or of teaching, but should only be ruthlessly destroyed.

Belinda dismisses his rising fury with casual strength, holding him apart from the power that would allow him to fight back. He acquiesces suddenly: this is not the time or place for challenges. Struggle abated, his thoughts splash down a rarely-travelled path, and Belinda's satisfaction rises with Dmitri's clear and vivid recollection.

He left Lorraine barely an hour after the boy's birth, trusting the Aulunian queen to gather and garb herself appropriately. She's no longer his concern, although the horsemen coming behind him to take his life are. He approves: Lorraine should have sent them. He cannot be suffered to live, not with what he knows. Not with a sullen, hungry baby boy tucked under his cloak in the small hours of a greying morning.

The child should be dead by now, its brains dashed out against a rock somewhere, but if Lorraine wanted the child dead, she ought to have given him to someone else. Not to Dmitri, and not to Robert, either, for he'd no more sacrifice a child of their blood than Dmitri would. Lorraine, of course, doesn't know this, and doesn't need to.

A glade comes up along the path he travels, and Dmitri turns his horse loose to graze a little while as he and the baby wait for the men who are coming to kill them. In a moment of unusual precaution, Dmitri draws a veil around himself, making him hard to see: it will keep them from using arrows, if they're of a mind to do murder from a distance. The baby's muttering might slow and confuse them, but they'll see nothing until Dmitri wants them to.

Dramatics insist he kill them before they kill him, but practicality stays his hand. Lorraine will expect them back with word of his death, and to leave them dead on the roadside gives too much credence to the idea that Dmitri himself is still alive. He has no wish for the Aulunian queen to think he, or the boy, lives, and so when her men come on the glade he merely convinces them that they've done their duty, and left his body to rot in a shallow grave well away from the edge of the path. Even stubborn human minds are easy to deceive, and these two are used to being told what to do without comprehension.

Very shortly thereafter, Dmitri Leontyev mounts his horse again and rides hard for Lutetia, five long days away. There he slips into another queen's night chambers and presents to her a son to replace the one she lost in early pregnancy, as he was bidden to do so many months ago.

16

BELINDA WALTER
7 June 1588 † Alunaer, the queen's court

Ice cascaded through Belinda, wiping away even the stillness and running so deep that witchpower was quelled beneath it. Nothing in Dmitri's expression had changed, no shudder of repulsion or twitch of horror that told him he understood as clearly as she did what his memories had spelled out for her.

She had known, had known for months, that Javier de Castille was not his father's son. Never once had she dreamed he was also not his mother's. Had known that Robert knew nothing of Javier's parentage, for all that he, too, was witchbreed, but had not, could not have, put those pieces together and come up with the answer that lay before her now.

Lorraine was still speaking. Belinda heard none of it, heard nothing at all. She was accustomed to controlling her body, but shivers wracked her, sickness roiling in her belly until sweat stood cold on chilled skin. Her hands were blanched, and she could well imagine that her face had turned ghostly, too.

Amusement curled the corner of Dmitri's mouth, and bile rose to burn Belinda's belly and throat. He had known, and had failed to warn Robert; had let her father send her to Lutetia. Sent her to seduce the one young man in Echon so much like herself.

Had let her, by doing so, fall in love with her brother.

A remnant of dignity, of hard-won stillness, kept her upright and sober, though her eyes burnt with unshed tears and her stomach heaved so violently she thought it must be visible even under the corsets. Her hands remained quiet at her sides, trembling with the effort of not scraping at her own skin, as though she might be able to escape herself if she did so. She, who had done murder innumerable times without remorse, felt the need to confess as a bladder bursting inside her. Words, like tears, choked in her throat, every last fraction of control working to both protect her and, she thought, destroy her. She could not live thus burdened, couldn't face the morning, much less herself; the idea of what she had done, what she had been tricked into doing, would tear her apart before the night hours began to toll.

Witch, harlot, slut! rang in her thoughts: names she'd been called many times without them ever taking root. Never before had it been her own voice hissing the recriminations, inescapable in the confines of her mind. Javier's face swam in her vision, blurred by water she couldn't allow to fall. Slim face, long features, thin grey eyes under ginger hair, all so much like Lorraine, now that Belinda knew to look for it. She should have seen it, must have seen it—

Could *not* have seen it, had no reason to see it, would never have seen it had witchpower strength not stolen the truth from Dmitri's memory. For an instant Belinda hated the power, rage burning away her revulsion.

In the brief freedom from horror, a thought kindled, then winked away again, too quick to be grasped. Disgust swamped her again, drowning fury and leaving her shuddering. She would kill, she would plot, she would bring down a throne, all without care, but to lie with a man who was her brother, to find love where she ought to have shied away; there, it seemed, lay the line Belinda Primrose's conscience could not cross.

Clarity flickered again, tiny splash of comprehension through body-wracking abhorrence. This was a thing she would not have done. It was a thing done *to* her, if not by Robert's will, then by Dmitri's uncaring hand.

It was a thing done to *them*. To Javier de Castille and to Belinda Primrose, all unknowing and all as part of a plot to serve a foreign queen so far beyond Belinda's understanding she'd allowed herself not to think on it, to not try and comprehend. A queen of whom Javier knew nothing, and yet whom he was expected to serve, as she was, both diligently and well.

An answer was to be had within those thoughts, but Belinda put them away, forcing a lifetime of training to bend to her call. Lorraine had been speaking; Belinda searched her memory for echoes of what the queen had said, and found it in herself to curtsey with some small degree of grace before lifting her own quavering voice. "I would beg a boon, majesty."

"We can deny our daughter, the saviour of Aulun, nothing." Lorraine's smile was beatific, her confidence supreme, and only Belinda was close enough to see how both the smile and her eyes went flat as Belinda whispered her request.

"I have been raised in a convent, and am unaccustomed to the world, much less the grandeur of what I am now gifted with." She made a tiny motion, smoothing her hand over her gown in example. "I would beg that I might retreat to the convent until the Yule celebration, so I might gather myself and become more fully prepared for this role I'm soon to fill." Belinda gauged her hesitation, giving the courtiers time enough to hear her request but Lorraine too little to respond. "From there I might more fully pray to God to support our army and navy as they make war on wretched Gallin, and perhaps from there He will hear me with the clarity He chose to three days ago when the armada fell. I beg this of you, majesty. Let me retreat a little while to consider my new place, and to entreat God to keep our soldiers safe."

She could not have been refused, not then, not like that. The audience had concluded more rapidly than the spectators might have wished, and Belinda, no longer on display and in need of playing a role, had lost herself in icy tremors as she and the queen were escorted to private chambers.

Private indeed: Lorraine caught her arm and thrust her toward the secret room, forgoing her own rituals of greeting to snap, "You've not done as you were told, girl," and make a sharp gesture toward Belinda's torso.

Belinda flinched with the gesture, as though Lorraine had flung a knife and driven it home in her belly. She ought not have flinched; she ought not have shown such emotion, especially when her thoughts were white with noise, as though the sea had rushed in between her ears. Grey washed over her vision, turning the world to fog and leaving her blind and deaf. It took what little control she had to not fold her hands over her belly; to not sag against illness that churned her belly and weakened her legs. She had never sought to capture a king by way of a child, but it was the easiest route any woman might take in trying to better her position. Had they not had the witchpower in common. . . .

The child was not Javier de Castille's. Belinda swallowed, feeling cords stand out in her throat and knowing herself helpless to mitigate such signs of strain. The child *could not* be Javier's: her courses had come without fail once after Dmitri had come to her bed, and for all the months before that. Clinging to the thought, she answered without hearing herself; without much care for Lorraine Walter's exalted position. "There's been no time."

"How long can it take?" Lorraine sniffed, and Belinda pulled herself from a stupor to stare at the queen without mercy.

"To brew and sip a tea? Little enough. To wait for the child to become unrooted? Tell me, when your blood still came, did it do so gently, or were you bent with pain as some women are? Aborting a babe can be like the worst of those days, and I think, majesty, that you would rather I stood strong and steady against the storm than fell to my knees bleeding while Aulun died on the seas."

Lorraine's eyebrows lifted. "My little witch has grown a wicked tongue."

Belinda, through her teeth, said, "It has been a trying day."

"And you did well, Primrose." Robert entered on the end of her words, bowing to Lorraine and offering Belinda herself a rare smile. She nodded in return, too aware that such a smile would have once thrilled her in its assurance of her place in her beloved papa's eyes. Now it barely cut through the cold in her, cold that was the only thing preventing outrage from erupting in witchbreed fire.

She gathered her skirts and with them her will, and with both of those things in firm grasp, executed a curtsey of grace and beauty;

a curtsey that made her malleable, the good daughter, the well-shaped weapon. "Thank you, your highness."

Surprise shattered off Robert, and offence off Lorraine, though the former turned his to a booming laugh. "Highness, am I? It's been a day for elevations all around."

"I should think it the proper term," Belinda said to the floor, and, with care, awakened a note of humour in her voice. "Her majesty has not confirmed her lord husband as king, but surely as her majesty's consort you might aspire to such a worthy title as 'highness.' "

She shouldn't allow herself to be so sharp, she knew that, and still allowed herself the luxury. Better to offend a queen—and what had she come to, that upsetting royalty was the best of her options—than to dwell on the appalling truth that wanted to pull her down. Javier's thin face, his slim body, insisted on appearing before her eyes. For months his image had been an indulgence of wistfulness; now it seemed to mock her with what she hadn't known, and could all too clearly recognise now that she'd been granted the eyes to see it. She didn't want those eyes, nor the burden of knowledge that came with them, but neither could be erased. If she found even the slightest release in pointed words, in playing herself as almost an equal to the two she shared a room with, then she would take it, and for once trust herself too valuable to be thrown away.

Robert turned to Lorraine, full of good nature and wide eyes. "Primrose has a point, majesty." He took in Lorraine's tight mouth and stiff carriage, and softened both his words and his mood. "I have not sought a crown or title, Lorraine, not even in the staging of this particular play for these especial ends. Surely you know this, after all these years." He knelt, and to Belinda's eyes, to her cold witchpower senses, there was nothing but honesty in the action. "I am honoured to be named the queen's husband, and need no pretty titles. If you will call me Robert, and the rest of them Lord Drake as they have always done, then I'll count myself a favoured man."

Lorraine sniffed, a sound denoting pleasure, but her gaze was still hard as she looked toward Belinda. "And you, I suppose, will want the title of princess, as is your due."

"All I covet is a place as a novice again, my queen, that I might adjust to the awe of my new position under God's watchful eye, and amongst women who will not be impressed by my change of status." Belinda rarely indulged in sarcasm, and never with her superiors, but her tongue and tone had minds of their own today, and she could not control them.

Lorraine's expression went flat, but Robert, climbing to his feet, chuckled again. "She reminds me of you, Lorraine. Come now," he said to the look she gave him. "It's no secret you're known for your quick tongue and ginger temperament, majesty."

Another sniff said Robert had diffused Lorraine's pique for the second time. "The girl has not the hair for it."

Neither does her majesty, anymore. For a horrifying instant Belinda thought she'd spoken aloud, and bit her tongue against the inclination to do so. Newly made heir or not, stomach-sick with knowledge or not, there were boundaries she shouldn't even dream of crossing, and mocking Lorraine's physical aspect was unquestionably one of them.

"There's no need for her to enter the convent again," Robert was saying with a casual wave of his hand. "She can stay in the palace and study—"

"No." Inexorable cold, the same chill Belinda felt within herself, cut through Robert's easy plans. He stopped and looked at her with genuine astonishment, and she tried to remember when, if ever, she'd refused his intentions so flatly. "Unless I stay in this chamber, I can't go unnoticed in the palace, and even here there will need to be food brought, and drink, and chamber pots emptied. Unless her majesty wishes to field rumours on how she has begun eating and eliminating twice as much, it seems a bad idea. Besides, the courtiers are enamoured of my seclusion. We want them to love me, not think me a sneak."

Robert, drily, said, "You are a sneak."

"All the more reason to not let them see it."

"You enjoyed your time at the convent so much that you hasten now to return there?" Lorraine was as dry as Robert, and for a moment Belinda admired them as she might a set of horses. One might be bay and the other brown, but they were a matched pair for all of that, a lifetime of working together making them excellent complements to each other.

"It was your majesty's idea that I should be so pious as to gain God's support in our sea battle against Gallin." The coldness was dropping away, leaving strips of anger where it fell. "I can emerge from the convent more and more regularly as the months go by, becoming part of society without leaving behind the impression of purity. Your majesty knows the value of such illusions. At Yule I can finally be bold enough to take my place, and by then, majesty, we should have some clear idea of who are our enemies within the court and who will support us."

Lorraine's painted eyebrows shot up. " 'We,' girl?"

"Your majesty, his highness, and myself," Belinda said shortly. "I do not put myself so high as to use a royal plural. This life is still on the wrong side of a looking glass to me, *Mother*, but I do have some skill in making a place for myself where I was once unknown." The barb hit home, Lorraine tensing satisfactorily at Belinda's use of the familial honorific, tensing in a way Robert had never done when she had called him "father." She might never earn that reaction from Robert, not now, but to cut it from Lorraine was worth sacrificing it from Robert. "I would never presume to tell your majesty what to do, but it might be wise to permit me to do what I do best."

"Murder?" Lorraine asked archly, and for one exasperated moment, Belinda found herself tempted.

Robert intervened, his palms turned down as though he quieted a room full of squabbling old men. "Primrose has a point," he said a second time. "One I hadn't entirely considered. Perhaps she should be permitted to arrange the details of her coming out. She has both experience and reason to make it work, and . . ."

And, Belinda concluded, if she failed in endearing herself to the people with her slow exposure, then that, too, would be something of use for Lorraine and Robert to know. They bickered a little longer, but the answer was foregone. Lorraine eventually drew herself up and turned a hard look on Belinda. "Whether the public do or not, *we* will see you in a week's time, girl, and the matter of which we spoke had best be resolved."

Robert shared a look of open curiosity between the women as Belinda tightened her jaw and curtsied to the queen. "Majesty."

There was no other word she trusted herself with, no other response that could both satisfy and forbid bone-deep horror from spewing across the floor. Lorraine nodded, content, and together the three left her private chambers.

Belinda Walter emerged from the queen's apartments in a novice's grey robes and with her hair pulled back tightly, making nothing glamorous of who or what she was. Lorraine went with her to the palace doors, there to embrace her for the third time, and Robert, clearly amused at his role, kissed her cheek with great solemnity. Belinda curtsied to them both, and a procession delighted by her humility came together around her and made an escort of itself as she was returned to the abbey.

The eager young sister greeted her almost before the abbess, and a shy touch to the girl's cheek washed away any lingering memories of nights spent together. The girl, awed and delighted by Belinda's status and by the grace of her touch, turned pink and ran off to make a confession of pride so happily Belinda nearly laughed, the first time such humour had risen in her since the courtroom.

She could not, in this place, make confession. Not to the abbess or anyone else; the girl they'd taken in was an innocent, not one who knew any man's touch, much less one who had all unknowing spread her legs for her brother.

The thought brought another flinch, awakened the *witch, harlot, whore* singsong in her mind again. Belinda set her teeth and whispered a request to the convent's holy mother, and that brisk old woman led her to the chapel where she could kneel and fold her hands in prayer. To the world around her she was a penitent overwhelmed by her new standing, thanking God for it and asking that she be guided in His light for all her days. That was what they wanted to see, and Belinda was happy to let them see it. A part of her did, indeed, pray for the souls and bodies of the soldiers who were going to war, though she had little faith that prayers would protect any of them.

But mostly she knelt in silence, head bowed and, if not empty of thought, at least as unfocused as she could make it. The song of recrimination swam through her mind time and again, dismay and disgust turning her body to ice even when heat rose inside her as though she might sick up. She had made a lifetime of using people and things and had not loathed herself for it; now, having been used in a way inconceivable to untwisted minds, she thought there was a cleanliness to using people in begetting death. Death left scars on the survivors, but those scars healed: dying was part of life, not a sin, but what she and Javier had done was, and Dmitri had allowed them to enter it. *Ill winds ride in Gallin,* he'd said to her a year past, in the Khazarian northlands. He had known where Belinda would go and had known what her mission there would be, and he had warned neither herself nor Robert that a wickedness beyond comprehension lay in her path. No, there was no honesty to Dmitri's machinations, the way there was honesty in death. Belinda had no doubt that keeping such secrets furthered some end of Dmitri's own; he and Robert were at odds, though perhaps only one of them knew that.

Only one of them, and Belinda herself.

Slowly, slowly, through the chaos of thoughtlessness, a plan made a shape in her mind. She had knowledge and she had power: all she lacked were allies. Robert was not an ally, not in this, and Dmitri never would be. Whatever his plans, she would thwart them, and destroy him if she could. If that furthered Robert's goals, it was a price worth paying. But a cruel knot of surety held a place in Belinda's thoughts. Robert hadn't known, still didn't know, whose child Javier was, because he had been surprised at the Gallic prince's witchpower.

And yet cold, dreadful certainty whispered that if he had known, he still would have sent Belinda to seduce and murder, with no care for their consanguinity or the cost against their souls for brother and sister becoming lovers. That his loyalty to his foreign queen was far greater than any worry for an ungodly union between two witchbreed children. From Dmitri's words about siring heirs to continue their world-changing plans, Robert might in fact have welcomed another child born to the witchpower, even if that child was issue of an affair no human morality would condone.

That, though it was all but beyond her comprehension, there was something alien enough in her father as to make him into a singular concept that she could grasp.

An enemy.

With the calm of horror cloaking her, Belinda drew stillness around herself, then rose and left the chapel, left the convent, left the country, and went in search of Javier de Castille.

JAVIER DE CASTILLE
8 June 1588 † *Gallin's northern shore*

The messenger came through a sleeping camp long before dawn, riding a horse for all that the distance between the camp's centre and the nearby ocean channel was barely a mile. The gondola boy, who rarely seemed to sleep, but who was unwakeable when he did, roused Javier bare seconds before the rider arrived. Eliza dragged a robe over her own shoulders and belted Javier's sword around his waist before he staggered, bleary with sleep, to meet the agitated courier.

The man all but fell off his horse and dropped to one knee, shoulders heaving with breathlessness. "My lord, there's an Aulunian heir."

For an eternity the words made no sense. Javier stared at the top of the man's head—he was balding, with sweat rolling through thin hairs—and then transferred his gaze to the island nation invisible with distance and predawn light. "An heir?"

He was king of Gallin; he should be wittier than that. Shock, even coupled with a half-sleeping mind, should clear more quickly and leave him more able to accept and ask clever questions. "Lorraine of Aulun has declared an heir?"

"One of her body," the messenger gasped, and dared look up. Javier gaped at him, too thick-headed to even echo the man. Either emboldened by his king's silence or sympathetic to it, the messenger continued. "She has produced writs of marriage and of birth, my lord king. Marriage twenty-five years ago to Robert, Lord Drake, long since known as her paramour, and the birth two years later of her daughter. The girl was raised as an adopted niece by Robert until her thirteenth year, when she entered a convent. Yesterday in the queen's court she was presented, your majesty. Her name is Belinda Walter, and she is the Aulunian heir."

That had been seven days ago.

Too many points had made a line that morning: Beatrice Irvine, who was also Belinda Primrose, had given the truth to her bloodline when Robert Drake's witchpower had stood against Javier's in the Lutetian court. The Aulunian heir, it was said, stood on the cliffs of Aulun and called God's light to her, and in so doing destroyed the Essandian armada. Beatrice Irvine, spy, whore, witch, and traitor, was Belinda Walter, daughter of the Titian Bitch.

Javier de Castille had bedded, and nearly wedded, the heir to the Aulunian throne. Even now, in the midst of battle, when that thought came to him it came with a tang of bitter irony. How Sandalia would have adored that coup: she, who had stood against his marriage to Beatrice, might have handed Javier her rival's throne without a drop of blood spilled if she had only encouraged their union.

He had been poor company this past week, had Sandalia's son. Rocked between betrayal and a twisted admiration, he had drawn the lines for his friends, for Rodrigo and Akilina, and most of all for himself, struggling to see if he might have understood the truth before it had fallen from a messenger's lips.

He could not have. The wiser part of him knew it, but the knowledge had emptied him, and then it had filled him with rage. She had played him for a fool since the beginning, and that was a game she would pay for.

Blood tasted of metal. His nose was full of thick scents: more metal, more blood, viscera, and once in a while the startling clear salt and fish smell of water off the straits. When that faded the sun-rotted stench of everything else seemed all the worse, and Javier heard others around him coughing and gagging in the same way he did.

He was the king of Gallin, and he was not meant to be in the midst of a battlefield, spitting blood and blinking sweat away.

Aulun had come to Gallin at the southern jut, in the northern

Gallic province of Brittany; the very place Javier had argued to Rodrigo they would not try for. The two countries' proximity there had made the province a contested stretch of land for centuries; Aulun claimed it and Gallin refused to give it up. Lorraine even had holiday retreats in one or two of the area's more beautiful low valleys, and as Javier knocked away an Aulunian sword and skewered the man carrying it, he had the brief vicious wish that someone had simply slipped into one of those rarely used manors and done away with Lorraine on one of her visits. He would not now be numb with exhaustion from the ears down, had someone been so foresightful, and would be enjoying a blazing summer afternoon instead of desperately wishing for water and a lull in the fighting.

They had the numbers to defeat the Aulunians, some forty thousand Cordulan soldiers and Khazar's massive contingency of seventy thousand troops soon to join them. Rodrigo had sent the larger part of the Cordulan force to Brittany, convinced Lorraine's army would take the longer march in an attempt to surprise Lutetia by coming up on its southwestern side instead of from the north and east. It was the harder journey all around, not just for distance but because the Sacrauna protected the city on its southern border, but Rodrigo had been certain, and Javier had taken his uncle's lead and thirty thousand men to Brittany.

Aulun had not been marching on Lutetia as expected. Lorraine's army had been nowhere in sight, not marking the land and not distant on the sea. Javier, cursing, had posted a rear guard and retreated to ground that would give him the advantage when they came. *If* they came; he couldn't help but think of Rodrigo and the smaller part of their army to the north, perhaps taking the brunt of Aulun's attack.

They waited for three exhausting days for pigeons to wing back and forth, bearing messages of battle. Rodrigo, to the north, was at war, while Javier waited in boredom for an army that had turned its attentions elsewhere.

The fourth morning, they broke camp, and that was when the Aulunians came.

There were too many to have hidden, and sentries had been posted each night. Whispers of witchcraft followed the first battle, and witchcraft it had to be. Not even Javier had realised his eyes were fogged to the ships that suddenly appeared offshore, or his ears to the sounds of an army edging itself into place around his own. He had the high ground, and yet the Aulunian army swept around them, a collapsing wedge that drove his men into a narrower and narrower line of defence. He had never intended to fight amongst his men, thinking it wiser to wield magic from a distance so he wouldn't terrorise his own soldiers.

Caught in the midst of the Aulunian attack, he found himself with no choice, and then found his men to be happy to have a witch—or God—on their side, too.

Since then he had fought with them, revelling in the first gut-wrenching moments of panic and in how that fear faded into a noisy drive for survival. He had fought innumerable fencing matches, learning his skill with a sword, but had never known the moment that went beyond exhaustion, where his weapon's weight became as nothing, and he himself became a warrior who could fight forever. He had learned to rally men with a cry, and when they fell, to whisper a prayer over a dozen bodies without his own ever stopping its endless slash and stab and cut. He had learned, too, to be agonisingly grateful for the times when a retreat was called or an advance succeeded; times when he, like those ordinary men around him, could sink down, gasping for air, and take a moment to be astonished that he was still alive.

Such a moment had not come in some time, and wouldn't until one side or the other took a significant loss. They had fought since the morning, and with sunset's late arrival in the middle of June, it was all too possible they might continue on until twilight turned to darkness. They fought over a bit of land that meant nothing in absolute terms, but should Javier's army fall beyond it, they would no longer be able to see the straits. Aulun would have pushed them back from the water's edge, and that would strike a scar against his men's hearts.

"'Ware, Javier!" Sacha's bellow cut through the cacophony somehow: they fought only a few feet apart, but voices were nothing more than part of the indistinguishable noise of war. When one came clear it was as startling as the cold breeze off the distant water.

Instinct responded to the warning more than thought: witch-power flared, almost invisible in the brilliant afternoon sunlight. Flared not just around him, but around dozens of men close by, and when a cannonball smashed into the shielding, it sent Javier staggering, but it sent the men to cheering even as they ran from its explosive finale. That, too, Javier contained, and in doing so saved not only his own men's lives, but innumerable Aulunians as well.

That had not been a sought-after effect, and it had less sway on Aulunian morale than Javier might have hoped. They did not, and had not any of the half-dozen times he'd made such a rescue, suddenly flock to him, proclaiming him God's chosen one and the right and true king for whom they should fight.

Instead they jeered, unimpressed with even the safety of their own lives: all he could do was stop a cannonball or two, where the newly revealed heir to Aulun's throne could beg God's will in directing the weather to favour Aulun and her navy.

Storms, it seemed, were more impressive than cannonballs.

Not for the first time, Javier unleashed a volley of power as devastating as the cannonball itself, but vastly more selective: those men of a different army whom he'd just saved crashed backward, breaking against one another, collapsing in heaps that no longer had much in common with bodies.

He had learned very quickly that his own men would accept injury, would even accept death, when he dealt it to the enemy with his power, so long as it was clean. Broken bones, broken necks: these were acceptable, and if he could lance men with silver witchpower the way he might with a sword or arrow, that, too, was a show of power his army would rally behind. But the uglier aspect of war, the damage done by cannonballs ripping limbs away, caving in chests, smashing faces—all easily replicable with an unfocused burst of magic—were not things his people would rally behind. There was too much to fear in an ugly kill, and within the first minutes of their first battle Javier had felt that fear growing in the soldiers around him, and had changed his tactics. They wanted the devastation he could wreak, but only in the deepest bloodlust could they drop their worry about what it meant that a man could do what Javier did. Battle was the heart of bloodlust, it was true, but even now, even in its midst, Javier feared the witchpower's strength, and preferred to protect his men from its worst horrors.

Belinda, if she was out there in the battlefield, and she had to be, still seemed inclined to use her magic less visibly. The thought twisted a smile across Javier's face: less visibly, indeed. He didn't believe she could cloak the Aulunian navy, much less its army as they crept through Brittany to prepare traps for Cordula's combined might, from the distance of Alunaer. She would be amongst the army somewhere, very likely unbeknownst even to their generals. They might give thanks to their feeble Reformation God, but it was the witchbreed woman creeping around their edges who gave them the stealth they needed to have counted coup against the Ecumenic forces.

Cordula's army was not *losing*. Javier reminded himself of that with a ferocity bordering on desperation. They had the numbers and now that his army knew the Aulunians were there, they were easier to see, even when touches of witchpower magic helped to hide them. Belinda made no effort to disguise them during the day: there was little need, when the armies were met on battlefields, everything about them raw and direct and bloody. It was only at night when scouts came searching that Javier could feel whispers of magic, and even that never came close to him. If he were of another mind, that would be pleasing: his ability to reach beyond himself and sense other emotion, other use of power, was growing. In time he might seek Belinda out without ever leaving his post as king and soldier.

Seek her out, and end her in his mother's name.

For a time that ambition drove him: pushed him forward, in fact, and though he didn't see it, those around him did, a fiery-haired young king filled with silver rage. Aulunian soldiers fell back and his men advanced, all of them in a resounding mess of cannon-fire and swordplay and witchlight. Javier noticed Sacha in a moment of clarity, the sandy-haired lord grimacing with battle joy as he slammed his way into a formation of Aulunians. Then, very suddenly, there were no more, and the view to the sea was open. A cheer rose up around them and Javier put a hand out so that a banner might be thrust into it. He drove its pole into the earth, and witchpower gave him the voice to shout *"Hold this ground!"* so that all his people, and aye, all the Aulunian army, too, might hear the claim he made, and the challenge inherent in it.

A guard, more pragmatic than passionate, put himself between the Gallic king and the retreating Aulunian army, and took an arrow in the chest before Javier could give thanks or motion him away. Javier's hands went cold, youthful surety of survival collapsing with the guard, and while a roaring, insulted contingent of his men surged forward to take vengeance, Javier himself was pulled back to safety.

Eliza did not, quite, slap him for his bravado. Not quite: a slap, a proper slap, the kind she clearly wanted to deliver, would have stained a handprint across his cheek; instead she only hit him alongside the head, sending drops of sweat flying from his hair. Then she kissed him, and then she hit him again and stormed away, leaving Javier staring after her in befuddlement. "I knew there were dangers in bringing women to war, but I never realised I might lose my head to Eliza's ministrations rather than the Aulunians'."

Sacha growled, "You should have left her behind," from a few feet away, no farther than he'd been all day. Now, though, he was bent over a tub, sandy curls dark brown with water as he washed grime out. He'd stripped to the waist against the heat, and a handful of minor cuts scored his stocky body. The gondola boy, forever in the way but lithe enough to avoid being booted, washed away dirt and muck, then stuck bits of plaster against the small cuts. Sacha growled again and the boy scampered away, dragging his washing cloth through the cleanest water he could find before attacking Javier's own unimportant injuries with it.

Javier lifted an arm, letting the boy do his job, and hissed a sharp breath before exhaling it with a shrug. "Then I should've left her in Aria Magli. I don't know how else I might have kept her from coming to war. Throw her in the dungeon?"

"At least she'd have stayed safe." Anger boiled off Sacha, a different flavour of it than drove him on the battlefield. There was glee in that rage, a revelling in battle lust with no room left for anything else. Out of fighting's heat, though, it was tainted with something else.

Javier waved the gondola boy off and got to his feet, brow fur-rowed until the pinch of it made his head ache. The witchpower had done this to all of them, damnable stuff that it was. Useful, perhaps, but damnable, and not worth the price of friendship. "Sacha . . ."

Sacha snapped his head up at the difference in Javier's tone, spraying water across the open tent they shared. Wet curls fell in his eyes, making him look the part of a youth. Javier smiled, suddenly hopeful, and felt that hope die at a spike of bitterness from his old-est friend. "Is it the crown or the witchpower?" he asked very softly. "Which of them has changed what we had?"

"Neither." Sacha snatched up a towel and rubbed his hair into a tangle, cutting off conversation, but Javier waited on him, bringing surprise and consternation to his face when he lowered the towel again. "Neither, Jav," he repeated, then threw the towel away. "Nei-ther, or both, or all of it. You woo Eliza," he said abruptly, as though the words surprised him, and then in a smaller voice, an even tighter voice, added, "You'd have never done that, before."

"Because I was a fool. I've learned a little, perhaps. Someone was going to," he said more softly. "Woo her, or wed you, or me, or Marius. We may have all denied it, but we were never going to go into our age unchanged."

"You must know she's barren." Sacha's gaze sharpened on Javier, judging to see whether he did know, and when Javier inclined his head, angry triumph blazed in Asselin's eyes. "So she can be noth-ing more than a means to your ends. She deserves better, Javier."

"I have a little hope," Javier whispered. "A little hope that the witchpower may heal what the fever took. One's no less God's will than the other, no? And you need heirs, too, Sacha, making her no more an easy choice for you than myself. Of all of us, Marius might have most logically gone to her, but I think he was the least likely."

"Clearly," Sacha spat. "And she's only ever had use for me when she was drunk. Sober, she's never looked beyond you."

"Then be happy for us," Javier said, still softly. Asked: to his own ears it was a plea, hardly given voice at all.

Sacha lowered his eyes, murmuring "Yes, my lord" with such meaningless subservience as to light rage in Javier's breast. There was nowhere he could turn without engaging Sacha's anger, and his own temper lashed out, words low and harsh: "I could command you to be. I could shape your will to mine, so your heart was as happy as mine has been."

"And what a hollow victory that would be, my king." Sacha lifted his eyes, hazel gaze cool with anger. "Because I might not know the difference, but there's no one to bend your memory to suit. You know I've always wanted you to pursue your birthright. Now you have, and these are the prices we all pay."

He turned without being dismissed and walked away, stopping at the tent's far edge to snarl a handful of words over his shoulder: "I'll send you your priest. He should ease your pain."

17

Tomas del'Abbate
15 June 1588 † *Brittany, north of Gallin*

Tomas knows that he's watched as he goes to Javier's tent. Most of the gazes on him are friendly, seeing him as God's guiding hand on the young king's shoulder. It's what he'd like to imagine he is, though what hastens his footsteps isn't an interest in theological teachings, but a hunger for the fire that is Javier de Castille. He has not, he thinks, kept Javier on a righteous path, but has rather fallen from it himself; he has no other answer as to his eagerness to spend time in the king's burning presence.

Other eyes are more judging and less kind. Sacha Asselin, who brought word that Javier bid him come; Marius Poulin, whose gentle heart has brought him to working the hospital tents rather than doing battle on the fields. Marius straightens from someone's sickbed to watch Tomas go, and if Sacha watched him with resentment, it seems Marius's gaze is full of sympathy and regret. He's the quiet one of their foursome, the one whose faith in Javier seems strongest, and he's lost his place at Javier's side to Tomas. He knows it, and so, too, does Tomas, who also knows he should relinquish that place to Marius again.

It is the better, not the greater, part of him that knows that. He looks away, not wanting to meet Marius's eyes, and hurries past the field hospital to enter Javier's tent.

The king is half-dressed and sprawled across a chair, blood seeping from a thin cut on one shoulder. Always pale, the blue undertones of his skin make him look hollowed now, as though whatever life once animated him has fled and left a still-breathing corpse behind. Tomas hesitates at the tent's open front, and glances back to where Sacha Asselin delivered a message with daggers in his voice.

It's a moment before Tomas realises what the young lord has done. "You didn't ask for me."

"No. Sacha condemned you to me, or the other way around." Javier lifts a hand, twirls his fingers against the setting sun, and Tomas, as though he were a servant boy, releases one of the ropes that holds the tent flaps open. Shadow falls across most of Javier's body, making him even paler, but the darker light is more flattering to him than sun: he looks less unwell, and the colour in his hair becomes richer. "He's growing to hate me, Tomas. Are they all?"

"Not Eliza." Tomas moves to let the second flap fall, then thinks again and leaves it as is: there's no need to spend candlelight while the sun can still brighten a room. Javier shifts until he's entirely free of sunlight. He seems healthier, taken out of direct light, and Tomas wonders how the sun was so kind to Javier when he sailed into Lutetia. All light is God's light, of course, but when one walks in God's light one walks in sunshine. It's curious to him that Javier seems so drained by it. But then, they're all drained by days of battle, even those who don't take up swords themselves, as Tomas does not, as Marius does not, as Eliza does not.

"No, nor Marius," he adds, because Javier seems to take neither hope nor extrapolation from what he's said, and for all his jealous dislike of sharing the king, Tomas also doesn't like to see him in despair. "They only worry for you," he says in a rush, and wonders at his own pettiness, and what he imagines he'll gain if he steals all of Javier's time for himself. Whatever wish he might hang on a star, it will not come true: there are too many duties a king must see to, and Tomas's knowledge of the world too small to be a good counsellor in all matters secular. He wants Javier for himself, but not at the expense of the king's reputation.

A blush curdles his cheeks at that thought, thick discomfort that he doesn't dare let himself follow through on. He's grateful the sun is at his back, so Javier won't see how his face has heated, if even he should care.

"I threatened Sacha," Javier says dully. "Threatened to make us what we'd been, to force my will on him so he remembered only what I wanted him to."

Tomas opens his mouth to condemn the idea, and instead says, "Can you do that? You only forbade my tongue from speaking that which you didn't want said, not took away my memories of your talent entirely."

Javier shrugs one shoulder. He might be a sculpture, so pale is he in the half-light, but his movements are fluid, and Tomas can see blue veins and a pulse in his wrist when Javier passes a hand in front of himself. "I've never tried, but yes, I think so. Shall I?" An eyebrow quirks up, small expression somehow made of cruelty. "Try resist me, priest, and I shall bend your will until it breaks, take secrets of you, and leave you with no memory of the violation." He shudders, for which Tomas is grateful. Strengthened by that small show of revulsion, he pours Javier wine, and then a cup for himself before settling beside a blood-and-grime-stained tub of water.

"What is it you want of him?" he asks after several emboldening sips.

Javier holds his cup in long fingertips, not drinking as he stares out the open tent flap toward a battlefield he seems not to see. "Faith, I suppose. His faith in me, but in the end it's you who shows it. You, whom I used most badly."

"Perhaps God's grace has helped me to forgive."

"Perhaps it's easier to forgive a near-stranger his trespasses, no matter how bitter they may be, than a brother."

"Your majesty, if you'll forgive me a certain brashness . . ."

Javier waves his wine cup and turns a silver-eyed glower on Tomas, contradictory answers in his body's speech, but Tomas takes the first to be permission, for he has a thing to say and, having embarked on it, is of no mind to have it turned away. "Royalty is expected to be capricious, but none of those three see you as their king, not first. You're their brother, their friend, and only then their sovereign. You may never have forgotten your royal birth, but you've allowed them to. Everything has changed, from your position to your—"Tomas hitches over the word, hating it, but it's Javier's, and not his own: "To your *witchpower*. Lord Asselin may have thought he was prepared for those changes, but I think he wasn't."

"What should I do?" Javier drinks deeply of his cup and scowls when he comes to its base.

"Nothing." Tomas finds the hardness of his reply unexpected. "The choice must be his. He'll serve you because you're his king, but to hold on to friendship in the face of all these changes may be impossible, my lord."

"Have I asked too much of him?"

Tomas wets his lips, sips his wine for courage, and dares an answer he's uncertain Javier will like: "I haven't the years of friendship, but you've not turned your witchpower on any of them in such a . . ." He draws a breath, searching for a word, and Javier lurches out of his chair to catch Tomas's wrist in a heated connection.

"An intimate manner?" Grey eyes are gone entirely to silver, the weight of Javier's witchpower making the air leaden and hard to breathe. "I dream of that moment, Tomas. It disturbs and excites me, leaving me tangled in my sheets like a love-torn youth. The pleasure of your acquiescence, letting me fall into you as though I bed a woman. Do you dream of it, too?"

He lets Tomas go as quickly as he caught him, breath coming short, and he makes a fist of his hand as he looks away. "It dances on my desires, this witchpower magic. Wakens them where I had none, hungers for them when I would have them lie in quietude. Too often I fear that it controls me, and not the other way around. Tell me again." He reaches for Tomas's wrist again, but this time takes his hand, and turns a beseeching gaze on the priest. "Tell me again that this is God's gift, and that you've found it in your heart to forgive me what I've done to you. Tell me," he whispers, and there's no weight of compulsion in the plea, only desperation. "Tell me that I will not be abandoned by all those I love."

Heartbeat riding in his chest too fast, heat rising in his cheeks again, Tomas whispers, "The Pappas has named your magic a gift from Heaven, Javier de Castille, and though I don't share the years of friendship you have with Sacha, you've turned your power on me more intimately than any of them. And still, I forgive you. If I can, then I dare say you haven't asked too much of him." He crosses himself, and then Javier, and shivers when the young king kisses his knuckles.

Shivers, and wonders if it's forgiveness he's granted the king of Gallin, or simply blind worship better due to God.

"Stay," Javier breathes. "Stay a while, and pray with me, Tomas. Help me keep to the light."

Tomas touches Javier's hair, then, with regret, loosens the king's hand from his own, and rises to draw back the tent flap he's closed. Sunlight floods the room and takes away all the secrecy of their meeting, but makes a symbol and a sign of hope. They go together to kneel in light, and all down the hill, across the fields of tents and open fires that make up the Cordulan army, Tomas can see that the soldiers, led by their king, make a knee to God.

If Javier de Castille is truly damned, then God has a perverse sense of humour indeed, and is vastly more baffling than Tomas del'Abbate can ever hope to comprehend.

MARIUS POULIN
15 June 1588 ✝ *Brittany, north of Gallin*

Marius, like many others in the camp, joins Javier in prayer. Unlike most, as he bows his head he wonders if Beatrice Irvine—Belinda Primrose, or Belinda Walter; no, she has too many names, and he will think of her as Beatrice, for simplicity's sake. That was the façade he fell in love with, and though he knows she was nothing more than an act, there's still an aching fondness for her in his heart. He thinks, briefly, of Sarah Asselin, Sacha's sister, whom he was meant to wed three months past. He was in Isidro then, and when he returned Madame Asselin chose not to bind her daughter to a merchant boy going off to war. It's all right with Marius, who suffers a confusing blur of lust and disinterest when his thoughts fall to Sarah. But it's Beatrice, not Sarah, who might be on the battlefield somewhere, might be leading her own army in prayer, for they've heard stories of the new Aulunian heir, and how God has graced her.

There's an exhausting irony in that, for surely God can't have graced both Gallin and Aulun. There's no clear victor if He has; no mandate that assures His chosen people they're in the right. Marius, who has always had at least a little faith, finds himself kneeling and wondering about the witchpower that both Beatrice and Javier share. Wondering, if God has offered it to both of them, whether there's not meant to be a victor; wondering if God intends them to find a brotherhood amongst themselves and put aside war for better things.

Sacha would call Marius a fool for such sentiments on the best of days, and on the worst, which these seem to be despite their foursome being together again, his old friend would name Marius a coward, and Marius would flinch to hear it, but not argue the point. A braver man would take blade and armour and walk onto the battlefields with his brothers, but Marius has put aside his sword after the fight on the straits, and will not be convinced to pick it up again. He knows himself, now, to be unlike Sacha; unlike Javier, even, though the king lacks Sacha's ruthless ambition and willingness to make war. For Javier, Marius thinks, this is a necessity, perhaps a glorious one, but had Sandalia not died so badly he doubts very much that his king would have reached so far as Lorraine's throne.

And now it seems to Marius that, with witchpower on both sides, either God intends they should annihilate each other or He intends they should be too evenly matched for either side to win. Either is a possibility that should be spoken in Javier's ear, for all that Marius is sure the king won't want to hear it.

He can almost hear Javier's argument: that the Pappas has blessed Rodrigo's marriage to the Khazarian dvoryanin Akilina, and in so doing has shown them all that it's God's wish that the Khazarian army join with Cordula. Their numbers, Javier will say, are the mandate Marius is looking for; they're the deciding factor for two armies otherwise well-matched. And Marius, who is only a merchant's son, and knows little of war, will have to agree or find himself feeling the fool. He's sure of it, and yet he climbs to his feet, brushes his knees free of dirt and grass, and makes his way toward Javier's tent. There is, after all, always the chance that his king will listen.

Sacha's voice cuts across his path before he gets there, sharp and disillusioned: "Don't bother. He won't hear a word you've got to say, not with the priest there."

"A priest you sent to him," Marius says mildly, but comes and sits

274 · C. E. MURPHY

beside Sacha at a campfire made of little more than embers. The night doesn't need heat: the fire is only for roasting a rabbit over. Marius gives the beast a poke to see how close it is to done, and upon burning his finger and getting a noseful of stomach-rumbling scent, decides to wait a while before calling on Javier. "He still hears us, Sacha. He's the king now. He was always going to turn to advisors other than we three."

"Advisors are one thing. Priests are something else."

"What," Marius asks, suddenly droll, "men with their own agendas? Not that, Sacha; certainly not that. If we're to surround him with folk who've nothing more than his welfare on their mind we'll have to retreat to the farthest reaches of the Norselands and hide amongst the reindeer." He picks up a stick to poke the rabbit with as he speaks. "Even we have agendas."

"What's yours?" Sacha demands, and Marius looks up from the rabbit in genuine surprise. The truth is, when he said "we" he was thinking most of Sacha, and he finds himself without an answer.

"To keep us strong, I suppose," he says after a moment. "To keep us stable, so Javier has someone to turn to when needs be."

"He doesn't need us anymore. He's got that pri—"

"For pity's sake, Sacha, let up. My God, man, what if we'd taken such offence every time you found a woman to dally with? If one of my hopeless romances had turned my head for longer than a week, or if Liz had found a confidant outside of our foursome? Through childhood we were all things to one another, perhaps, but we're adults now, and Javier is king. Are you really so jealous as all this? What are you afraid of? A family such as ours is less easily broken than this, Sacha."

"And if it's not? If he's too besotted with his priest and his power and his crown to look to us anymore?"

"Then we accept it." Marius stares across the fire at his old friend. Disbelief and dismay flutter through his chest, knocked about with each heartbeat. The idea that Javier's outgrown them is unfathomable. Yet even if it's true, it hardly matters. That much, if nothing else, is blindingly obvious to Marius, and he can't imagine how it's anything less to Sacha. "He's our friend. He's our king. We give him what he needs, whatever that may be."

"Why? If he turns from us, why should we stand by him?"

Marius's jaw drops and he gapes at Sacha, waiting for the laugh; waiting for anything that says his old friend is less than serious. Finally, when Sacha makes no excuses, Marius speaks again, his voice strained. "Because he's *the king,* Sacha. We need no other reason."

Sacha, it seems, doesn't hear him at all, anger distorting his answer. "You're a man, Marius, not a lamb to the slaughter. You can make a choice. Do you not deserve better than this? Do not we all?"

"Better than what?" Marius isn't made for debates or for politics. He can be clever with words when he has to be; has been so even under the duress of Javier's witchpower, when his king didn't ask precisely the right questions. He had sex with Beatrice Irvine, shared intimacies with her, but Javier skirted the direct words with euphemisms, and those allowed Marius a few lies of omission. So he can be clever when he must be, but now, gawping under Sacha's anger, he's got no cleverness at all, only bewildered astonishment. "Better than to have Javier steal Beatrice away? Better than to watch him confide in a priest when I might have hoped my friendship would do? Better than to be fighting a war when I might have been newlywed and safe at home in Lutetia? Of course. Yes, of course, we all do, but at the end of the day none of that matters, Sacha. He's our king and he needs our friendships." He's about to make a platitude, an excuse: about to say, *I'm not like you, not a warrior, and the fight is too much. The best I can do is be there when he needs me,* but Sacha mutters something that sends a chill of alarm down Marius's spine. "What did you say?"

"Nothing." The answer's another mutter, sullen as a child, and Sacha spits at his low-burning fire. "Eat the rabbit. You and it deserve each other." He surges to his feet and stalks into the failing evening light, leaving Marius, the rabbit, and a handful of treacherous words behind.

Serve him if you will, he'd said. *My loyalty deserves more.*

RODRIGO, PRINCE OF ESSANDIA
16 June 1588 † Gallin's coast, well north of Lutetia

Rodrigo de Costa is married to a viper.

This is not in and of itself news—he knew the devil's bargain he made when he said his wedding vows—but he had not quite imagined to find himself in a battlefield hospital tent with a long shallow cut across his ribs, politely refusing the drink his wife has brought him out of a not-irrational concern that it might be poisoned. There are easier ways to rid oneself of a husband than by infection setting into a wound, but in war, there are few ways more inevitable or acceptable for a man to die. Rodrigo doesn't trust Akilina to not press the advantage of his injury and parlay it into his sudden, tragic death.

Furthermore, he can see amusement in her black eyes: she's followed his train of thought, and takes a healthy swallow of the wine she's brought before offering him a sip again.

Well, either she's taken an antidote or it's clean. Annoyed with himself for showing so much mistrust, Rodrigo accepts the wine and admits, privately, that it's an excellent vintage, far better than might be expected on a battlefield. But then, this is Gallin, and they pride themselves highly on their wines.

"I've had word from Chekov," she says when he's drunk his wine. Interested, Rodrigo pushes up on an elbow and a passing physician smacks him on the shoulder with absolutely no regard for his rank. He glowers; the doctor glowers back, and, somehow chastened, it's the prince of Essandia who retreats. Privately—very privately—he might admit that relaxing feels good: the wine's not yet done its work, and a cut across the ribs tells a man how much he uses those muscles without ever realising it. He can fight if he must, but it would be better not to, and he's put in his show as a virile leader, still able to take on the enemy. There are men who will tell tales the rest of their lives, about how they were at Rodrigo's side when he took an injury fighting the Aulunian army in Gallin.

He gestures for Akilina to continue, and sourly wonders why those who'll tell such stories weren't there to help block the massive sword that had cleaved through armour and left a score on his ribs. But that's unfair: in the midst of battle most men do well to not fall to their knees and sob for their mothers; it takes seasoned soldiers used to fighting together to protect one another's backs, and Rodrigo hasn't fought alongside an active battalion for decades. He had hoped to live the rest of his days without seeing another war, but, ah, God laughs when men make plans. "Chekov," he says aloud, as much to remind himself as prompt Akilina. "Your commanding general. They're close, then?"

"South of Lutetia, and awaiting orders on where to ride."

"To Brittany," Rodrigo says without hesitation. "The bulk of the Aulunian army is there; they've only sent enough here to keep us fighting, keep us distra—"

Satisfaction is glinting in Akilina's eyes, and anger cuts through the discomfort of Rodrigo's ribs. The change from Essandian to Khazarian is instinctive, a way of protecting what he says from curious ears around them. "You've sent the orders."

Akilina widens her eyes in a mockery of concern. "My husband was indisposed for some time this afternoon, and I thought swift action was best. Was I mistaken?"

Khazarian's a better language for hiding anger in than for pretending innocence, but Rodrigo doubts the shift in language has hidden their tones from anyone listening. He says "You were not" in as civilised a manner he can, then lowers his voice further to warn, "You aren't here to command, Akilina. You're here to give the Khazarian army a figurehead and to keep waters smooth with Irina. I will send you back to Isidro if you overstep your authority again."

Oh, she's a viper, yes, and, perversely, Rodrigo admires her for it. She's a woman in an unprecedented era; not even Javier's vaunted many-times-great-grandmother Gabrielle seized and held so much power as the three great queens of this time. Lorraine and Sandalia and Irina have set a dangerous precedent.

But Sandalia is dead and Lorraine, God willing, soon will be, leaving only Irina. Their time is coming to an end. Akilina will have to satisfy herself with one throne, and a prince above her. And to that end, Rodrigo *will* cut the wings of her ambition, by sending her back to Isidro in shackles if he must.

Though she's sitting, Akilina manages a curtsey, ducking her head so it hides her expression for a critical second or two. When she lifts her gaze again it's full of beguilement, as though Rodrigo might be a youth susceptible to such games. "I meant only to hasten our inevitable victory, husband, and spoke not in my name, but in yours. Forgive me my boldness; I know now not to extend myself so far."

Each word a literal truth, Rodrigo thinks: Akilina's not fool enough to give orders in her own name, even if the Khazarian army would accept them. And now she *does* know not to extend herself so far, but she was willing to test the boundary. "Then we understand each other," he says, and for a moment falls silent, considering the changes in the world around them.

Sandalia is dead, yes, with Lorraine soon to follow, but Lorraine has pulled a trick that Rodrigo never expected. She has produced an heir after all, a woman grown, and a woman whom the Aulunian people believe to be God's favoured child. It's at her feet their victory at sea has been laid, and she, near-mythical creature that she is, is now beloved to the wet island nation. He wonders if she would be even more loved if they knew it was she who'd poisoned Sandalia's cup.

He cannot yet decide which is stronger: the impulse to enact vengeance and claim Belinda's life, or the desire to end a war and put Javier on the Aulunian throne by political means. Weddings between mortal enemies have been a matter of state so long as there have been states to matter; Rodrigo is thinking not of Javier's happiness, but of lives spared and bloodshed averted, all while achieving the same ends they reach for now. With his nephew on the Aulunian throne, and Aulun folded back into the Ecumenic church, Cordula's reach would span from Parna down the length of the Primorismare, and all around Echon's western coast. Reussland, the Prussian confederation, the icy Norselands, and all the smaller city-states and mountain countries in Echon's belly would be caught between the Ecumenic empire and allied Khazar.

Best of all, perhaps, is that the lives not wasted on the field in Brittany could be turned to the church's expansion wars in middle Echon. Reussland is vulnerable now, with only women left as heirs, and could easily fall to the Cordulan faith.

It will not be as smooth as that; it never is. But the idea has merit, much more merit than a war that could go on for months or years before the Aulunian crown is placed on Javier's head. Ignoring the pain in his ribs, Rodrigo sits up and reaches for a shirt while speaking to the ward in general—someone in a position to act will hear him. "Leave a small battalion here to deal with the encroaching Aulunians. We ride to join our brothers in Brittany."

DMITRI LEONTYEV
16 June 1588 † *Alunaer, capital of Aulun*

Dmitri's knees ache.

He's been on bended knee on a hard floor for what has extended past politeness, past any mark of respect, past anything but pettiness and belittlement, and he has been thus because Lorraine Walter is punishing Irina Durova for allying herself with Essandia. Unfortunately for Dmitri, Irina is hundreds of miles away, and a sovereign queen besides, so it is he who assumes a position of subservience and holds it until he is bruised and sullen.

More annoyingly yet, he knows what's in the letter that Lorraine is deliberately filling her time with idle chat and banter in order to avoid reading, and once she's read it, all this nonsense will be over. When she's read it, he will suddenly be her closest and dearest friend, and she'll be full of solicitous concern that he has not knelt too long or felt much discomfort, and he, of course, will have to lie about it.

His people, with their rarely broken psychic links, don't play games of this sort. Just now, Dmitri wishes humans didn't either.

On the other hand, it's not possible to play his own people off one another the way it can be done with these courtiers and kings. Dmitri is not above admitting that when he's the one controlling the game, he rather enjoys mortal politicking. He suspects that's a very human perspective, and is pleased by it: the person he'd been before submitting to the change was a creature entirely of loyalty, of no especial original thought beyond serving his queen. He'd been clever, yes; that was part of why he'd been chosen. Robert was steadfast, and so became the leader of their three, and Seolfor, well. Seolfor was as close to a dissident as their people knew, a thing of creativity and curiosity that served ends beyond those the queens dictated.

Dmitri understands Seolfor far better now than he ever did before. Before, serving the queens was an end of itself, and a satisfying one. But it took surprisingly little study of humanity to begin understanding ambition, and by the time they had perfected the genetics of their new forms, an idea had shaped itself at the core of his mind. He kept it small, not fanning it in any way while he retained his original shape; it was all but impossible for his people to keep confidences, and the best way to do so was not to think about the things one wished to leave private.

The human mind, limited in its ability to communicate with others, was wonderfully liberating for someone with a secret.

Over the millennia the queens had developed a method of deciding their breeding partners. They were long-lived, his people, four and five times the length of a long human life span, and they gave cold birth: eggs by the hundreds, kept warm and safe by the queens and their lovers. With the near-infinite space between stars, and the comparatively few worlds suited for their needs, they had become a space-dwelling race, and obliged to constrain their breeding to what was appropriate for a ship to support. The queens only bred after the successful domination of a resource planet, and they chose the fathers from the genetic material left behind from the changed. The most successful of the changed became fathers to new generations, a genetic legacy made to children they'd never see. It was natural that the leaders, the steadfast ones, the organisers, of each small infiltration sect, should be the anticipated fathers.

Dmitri intends a coup.

The idea has flamed in his mind since taking this new shape. Robert follows staid old plans that they've used since the beginning of time: war to drive innovation, to keep populations off-balance; technological leaps great enough, over short enough times, to leave the infiltrated people numb with the shock of change. Time has proven these tactics create strong slave races: ill-educated and stupefied, a people don't need to understand how or what they're doing in order to provide goods to what may as well be their gods. But

Dmitri believes a unified, thinking populace is of even greater use to his queen, that a people raised to fully understand their technology are more likely to be inventive, and to offer new choices and greater potential to a space-faring race that has spent millennia at slow war with other resource-hungry peoples.

It is, he's willing to concede, likely to be a slower path than Robert's brutal means to an end. But if he can guide this small planet away from the war-ridden industrial future Robert intends, give them a freer hand in their own development, and in doing so provide new resources to his queen, then the time will be well spent.

The gamble is enormous, but if it succeeds, Dmitri, not Robert, will father the next generations, and his innovations, not the old ways, will inspire his children.

Yes, Dmitri understands Seolfor better than ever before, and a part of him disdains the so-called rebel of their society, for he's seen nothing of Seolfor's hand in changing the shape of this world's future. He himself may fail, but if so, he'll do so gloriously—and that's a very human thought indeed. He's seen Robert succumbing to those same kinds of human weaknesses; seen it in his failure to recognise Belinda's burgeoning *witchpower,* as she calls it, when she was a child; seen it in Robert's loss of control in Khazar; and sees it in Robert's fondness for Lorraine, who's replaced their alien queen in his mind. Dmitri likes to imagine he has no such failings himself and, knowing that's unlikely, tries to guard against them. He knows Ivanova is coming into her own witchpower, and has trained her if not in the actual magic, at least in the thought patterns that will help her develop it. He is far less enamoured of Irina than Robert is of Lorraine, though the few brief months he spent at Sandalia's side, playing the part of her priest and her lover, still waken a hunger in him, all these years later. It's as well that she, like Lorraine, set murderers on his trail after he delivered Javier; both queens thought him dead, and while it meant a long time before he dared rejoin either court, even in such a disguise as the witchpower now lends him, it's still better by far to be dead than a dangling question in their minds. He might have grown soft on Sandalia, had he stayed near her, and he prefers the sweet memories of a lifetime ago.

Lorraine, finally, is turning her attention to the damned letter. Dmitri has not been watching, not blatantly; that would be too obvious, and the longer he watched the less likely she was to read the thing. She opens it with a frothy indifference that would be charming in a woman a third her age, and which looks absurd in her. Seeing that he watches, she allows her attention to drift elsewhere, but her eyes come back to the letter with surprising alacrity. She caught a few words, then, before beginning her game again, and what's written there is more interesting than any playful foolishness.

She reads it through once, gives him a sharp glance, then reads it again before letting it roll closed so she can tap its column against her cheek. She says "Very well" petulantly, like a child whose playtime is spoilt, and gestures her doting courtiers away. "If we must to work, then we suppose we must. Our dear friend from Khazar has brought us news, and we must speak with him."

This tells the court of the letter's importance: Lorraine stands and leaves the throne dais to greet Dmitri herself, to raise him up and make all the false apologies he predicted she would. Then she laces her arm through his and demands, prettily, that he walk with her; at least, it would be pretty if she were thirty-five, and her breath not wretched with sweets.

"You've read the letter," she says the moment they're beyond reasonable earshot. There are no doubt listening-holes all over the palace, even in the broad corridor down which they walk, but Lorraine's boxy footsteps and the echo of the uncarpeted hall will help to disguise some of what they say, and as for the rest, it needs not be kept secret.

"Of course, your majesty." Dmitri rather likes the heavy Khazarian accent, but would keep it in place even if he didn't: it hides any familiarity the titian queen might have with his voice. It's been twenty years and more since the priest he was took away the son she'd borne, but the time was a momentous one: she might well recall the voice as well as the face.

"We find it . . . unexpected."

It would be entirely wrong for Dmitri to grin, and so he doesn't, but it's a near thing. "Her Imperial majesty thought you might, majesty. And yet she feels she ought not compound a mistake already made."

"Few of us, queens or not, accept such truths with grace," Lorraine murmurs. "Our sister in Khazar is to be admired. We have been . . . concerned," she says, again with the pause that speaks volumes in understatement. "We had thought ourselves to hold a special place in our sister-queen's heart, given that we are so alone in holding our thrones as we do, and the Essandian alliance has brought us distress for that reason."

"I am instructed to beg forgiveness for any heartache her majesty may have caused your majesty." This dance could go on forever, but Dmitri takes the steps, trusting that once form is met, Lorraine will become more forthright. If not, he'll grind his teeth and carry on, because protocol can't be ignored, whether in a mortal court or among his own people. There are things they have in common, his people and these; there are points all the sentient races have in common, though rarely enough to build an alliance on. That, in fact, is as alien a thought as any other: those who reach the stars conquer and infiltrate and control, but they rarely, if ever, ally themselves with one another. The known galaxies might have a very different shape if their peoples were inclined to cooperation. "As your majesty knows, the combined Cordulan armies, and the Ecumenic faith, are of a size to be concerning, even to an empire as great as Khazar's. Provided the opportunity, your majesty can surely understand why prudence dictated her majesty should build an alliance with a navy as powerful as Essandia's."

"Yes," Lorraine says, and she draws the word out, because here's the crux of the matter: "But Essandia's navy is no longer master of the sea."

Dmitri offers a slight bow, not enough to disrupt their sedate walking pace. "And now it's my imperatrix's concern that if their mighty navy can fall so easily, so, too, might their army. An alliance that looked healthy only months ago, your majesty, seems suddenly to be a burden. Her imperial majesty sees a change in the tide, and hopes you might forgive her for the caution that guided her hand in previous undertakings."

Lorraine's voice changes, becoming both sharp and arch: "We

will have command of the Khazarian army that now marches through Gallin?"

"As is written in her majesty's hand," Dmitri murmurs, and Lorraine smiles.

"Then we forgive our sister all trespasses, and embrace our new alliance."

18

IVANOVA DUROVA, THE IMPERATOR'S HEIR
21 June 1588 † *Brittany*

Her mother is missing her by now. Will have been for weeks, indeed, because Ivanova Durova rode with her army when they left Khazar. She has watched pigeons race back from the generals' tents: pigeons carrying no-doubt frantic tales of how military men cannot find one young woman amongst the thousands of soldiers who march on Gallin. There have been inspections and spot checks; it even seemed, for a little while, that the entire army might be called back so the imperator's heir could be found. Ivanova wrote her mother a note of her own then, promising she was well and promising, equally, that she intended to go to Gallin and watch war happen whether the army continued on or not. Better, surely, to have her protected by the troops than to have her riding alone.

Do not, she had also written, *send more men to try to find me. They will fail.* Irina knew nothing of the power Ivanova commanded: not even the priest and counselor Dmitri, who had trained her thoughts to shape that power, realised how much she'd come in to what she privately thought of as magic. What else might it be, this influence that let her change men's minds or slip among them unseen? It was that talent that had permitted her to join the army; had even left an impression of herself behind, so her whirlwind maid and others about the palace had vague recollections of seeing her even in the days after her departure. That simulacrum had faded with the fourth day: she'd felt it, and not long after, messenger birds had begun winging their way back and forth between the capital city of Khazan and the generals leading the march.

Ivanova knows perfectly well she oughtn't be as bold or as gleeful as she is: the price for her daring will be high. But it will also not be paid today, and in very little time her army's long journey will be over. She stands in her stirrups as the regiment she rides with crests a hill, and suddenly there's a battlefield before her.

Aulun and Cordula clash in a broad valley between low hills: Ivanova can see glimpses of the straits beyond those hills; glimpses of the ships Aulun sailed on. They're resplendent, the Reformation soldiers, wearing their red coats as they rush in from the north. Ecumenic Cordula's soldiers are a rainbow of discord, uniformed in green and blue and mustard yellow as they ride from the east and south. There were more of them, before the armada: the Ecumenic church should have commanded enough bodies to overwhelm Lorraine's troops, but no more. They are close to evenly matched now, and for a breathless instant Ivanova sees patterns in the chaos of war, surging back and forth like a living creature. Her own army comes from the east, down the rolling hills and into the field, and Ivanova, like her brother soldiers, shouts with raw enthusiasm as they race to change the tide of war.

JAVIER DE CASTILLE, KING OF GALLIN
21 June 1588 † *Brittany's battlefields*

The Khazarian army swept through the countryside and slammed into the back of Javier's army with the force of a hammer to the anvil. Those who were meant to be reinforcements arrived as mercenaries at best, traitors at worst, and what had been planned as a ruthless crushing of Aulun's army turned into the pulverisation of Javier's own troops.

Javier stood on a hilltop and watched it happen: watched Aulun, bewilderingly, rally themselves when they *knew* Khazar was encroaching. Watched them attack with the confidence of a young bull, smashing into Javier's front lines, thinking, perhaps, to kill as many of the weary Cordulan soldiers as they could before facing the fresh Khazarian troops. It was an idiot's ploy: they'd be exhausted by the time the lines opened and Khazar poured forward to meet an Aulunian army that had nothing left with which to defend themselves. Javier'd saluted the brave and stupid men and sent a curse toward their generals: they might be the enemy, but wasting lives in that manner was an affront to God. Tomas had begun praying for the souls of the dead, and had yet to stop.

Khazar's army was visible from miles away, tens of miles, if he'd had the height to see them, but even on nothing more than a hilltop, the distance turned brown with dust rising, and began to shake with the impact of tens of thousands of feet. They had come a terrible distance to fight this war for Javier, and they would be given no time to rest before meeting their first battle. He had saluted them as well, in honour of their determination and in thanks for the overwhelming favourites their presence would lend his victory.

And then, screaming their queen's name and cursing Rodrigo's, the first ten thousand soldiers had crashed into the Cordulan army's unprepared flank and obliterated them.

Even now if he closed his eyes Javier could see it, the way so many men literally overran his army, flattening what had been tents and food supplies and camp followers; bowling over soldiers who had seconds ago stood cheering their arrival.

It shamed him how long it had taken him to react, though recounting the moments said it couldn't have been more than minutes, and perhaps not nearly that long. No, Javier was certain it had been that long, his slow thoughts reeling with incomprehension. There was no doubt they were the Khazarian army: they flew banners bearing the complex knotwork that was a symbol of Khazarian pride; they wore the black uniforms with brightly coloured epaulettes that made streaks of brilliance even through the dust and the distance. Those who rode did so as though they'd been born to the saddle, with such grace it seemed impossible that the crimson flying from their swords was blood, or that the men who fell before them did so of anything other than awe. They were all the things the endless Khazarian army was meant to be: great and terrible and strong.

And the enemy.

That, ah, *that* was what Khazar had always been: the enemy, a force too vast to be defeated, and Javier's heart went cold and sick in his chest as he stepped out of himself and saw for the first time what he and Rodrigo had done: invited an unstoppable army into Echon, all the way to its western coast. Horrifyingly, that empire could now consider Echon to be in its clawed grasp, with nothing more in its way than a few armies of smaller proportion by far than their own.

Javier unleashed the witchpower.

Belinda had stood on shore, *on shore,* the Aulunians said, and had brought down his fleet, miles away in the midst of the straits. Miles from where she could see them, and Javier could see the leading edge of the Khazarian army, could see more than that as they boiled over low hills and into the flats that had become the battleground. If she could affect what lay out of sight, he certainly could destroy what he could see.

Silver lashed out, brighter than sunlight, and rolled into the Khazarian army with all the destructive willpower that Javier could channel behind it. He had held back for the sake of his men's morale, had listened to their fears of an invisible magic as deadly as cannonballs and had made his magic a thing less terrifying for their sake. Now, for their sake again, he let go of that gentleness and revelled in wanton slaughter. A release sweet as orgasm shuddered over him, and then again, as though the witchpower rewarded him for using it.

Bodies turned to red mist on the battlefield below when his magic hit them, and the wind caught that fine crimson fog and sprayed it across his army and the Khazarians alike. Part of him heard screams, some of agony and others of blood-mad joy. Later he would hear stories of how men in his army smeared pale streaks across the blood drying on their faces as they'd heard the Columbian savages did, and, mad with battle lust, threw themselves into the Khazarian front.

Threw themselves against an unstoppable force and, to a man, died, but their story became a thing of legend.

Others, their swords and pistols lost in battle, scooped up limbs torn from bodies and literally beat their enemy to death; Javier felt that, too, riding back on the waves of power he flung toward the attacking army. His vision burned red, even the silver magic drowned in blood, and all the helpless rage he'd felt at his mother's death, at Belinda's betrayal, at the unstoppable shaping of events, poured out of him to tear the Khazarian army asunder and to lend his men the will to fight.

It went on for almost an hour, the Khazarian masses too many, too determined, or too stupid to crumple in fear and drop their weapons. Each volley Javier sent forth felt like the one that had destroyed Rodrigo's oak doors, nothing more: there was no more horror in taking life than that. Indeed, the ongoing rush of power wracked him as might the pleasure found in a lover's body, making him feel astonishingly alive.

If this was giving in, he had been a fool to struggle so long. He'd been wrong to argue with Rodrigo over the best use of his magic, had been wrong practising tentatively with Belinda, had not needed to hide himself all his life. Witchpower pounded through him until he thought that if he cut his skin, his blood would run silver. This was God's gift, not the devil's, for surely such pleasure could come only from the king of Heaven.

The first sign that something was wrong troubled him no more than a tickle in the throat, a tiny cough that might stutter his voice. It stuttered his power, instead, so small it seemed meaningless. Joy still ran through him, far too seductive to stop even if that warning had meant anything. He extended his hands, lobbing vast balls of witchlight toward his enemy, and knew himself for a god among mortals.

Then exhaustion seized him, a cold black wall that overwhelmed silver power, and when he reached for another ball of light with which to destroy more Khazarians, there was no response from the once-boundless witchlight.

Panic surged, a flux of new energy, and for a few more seconds there was power to fling amongst the invaders. Relieved, Javier took a step forward, proving himself strong.

His knees buckled and he fell, hitting the earth hard enough to bite his tongue. Blood tasted unbearably bitter in the wake of seductive witchpower, and with the small part of his mind still capable of forming thoughts, he knew his gaze and eyes were blank as he turned them toward the Khazarian front.

Released from the onslaught of his power, that army surged forward again, and his own people began to die again, in terrible numbers. Javier reached for magic, reached to save those he could, and fell into a heap in the grass.

The skies rained blood that night.

He awakened to the sound of it, falling like any other rain from the sky. For a few seconds he lay still, placing himself: this was his tent, this the cot he'd slept in the last fortnight. The rain was a comfort, washing away sins, at least until Marius ducked into the tent, bloody streaks rolling down his cheeks. Javier felt his face give away his fear; until Marius said, abruptly, "It's not mine."

Relief slumped Javier in the cot before confusion pushed him upward again. He trembled with the effort, sending the cot to rattling, and Marius pushed him back down again easily. "You've been unconscious fourteen hours. Drink this."

Javier took the wineskin Marius thrust at him and coughed on the first sips. "The battle? The army?" His voice broke on the second question, recollection coming back to him more clearly.

"Lost," Marius said grimly. "Khazar crushed us, Jav. You held them for almost an hour, but when you collapsed . . ." He took the wineskin without asking and drank heavily himself. "Our forces are split, with the larger surviving side with you, and a smaller battalion on the other side of the God-damned Khazarian army. Aulun broke through our defences to the north and they've met in the middle. They're dancing on our corpses."

"The blood?" Javier gestured at the stickiness on Marius's face, and used the same motion to ask for the wineskin back. "I thought you weren't fighting."

"There was no choice, by the end of the day, but the blood's not mine." Marius handed the wine back and jerked his chin at the tent's front. "Go look for yourself."

Jaw set, Javier sat up, swinging his legs over the edge of the cot, then swayed. Where witchpower usually lay within him was an emptiness, so deep he'd never known he relied on the magic until it was gone. "Mari . . ."

His friend was there, an unexpectedly steady shoulder, a strong arm helping him to his feet. "I've got you, Jav."

"You always have." Javier put too much weight on Marius, barely able to move his own feet, but they stumbled to the door, and took a step outside.

The smell of blood filled the air, rain doing nothing to wash it away. Clouds turned the sky black, even in the height of summer, and Javier could see little more than pathetic campfires in the distance as water collected and rolled down his face. They stood there a few long moments before Marius said "That's enough," and pulled him back inside.

Only then, under the lamplight in the tent, did Javier understand. The water dripping from his hair was tainted red, tasting of copper and dirt. Witchpower fluttered inside him, low warm feeling of satisfaction that overrode, then sank beneath growing horror. Javier wiped his face, watched blood fill the lines of his palm, and whispered, "I did this?"

Marius shrugged, voice weary beyond disgust. "It's Khazarian blood. The rain's been carrying it all night. Yes, Javier. You did this. It's all right." A faint note of something familiar replaced the weariness in his words: a note of camaraderie and of pride. "You probably saved us all, Jav. It's terrible, but we'll find a way to make it right."

"Get me Tomas." Javier, still staring at his hands, barely heard what Marius said, glancing up only in time to catch a spasm cross his friend's face. "Get me Tomas, Marius," he whispered again. "I need the priest."

"Yes," Marius whispered, and even Javier heard agony and understanding in his voice. "Yes, I expect you do."

Javier was kneeling when he arrived: kneeling at a tub of water, scrubbing his hands until he thought they might bleed themselves. He heard a movement at the door and let go a cry of relief, making it to a confession: "I enjoyed it."

"Good," Sacha said flatly.

Javier flinched and turned, still on his knees, to stare at Sacha without comprehension. "I asked for Tomas."

"And I'm sure you'll have him soon enough, and as often as you like. But I thought that since you're awake now you might want to know what's happened out there. I'll leave you if I'm in error, my king." Sacha scraped the words out, grinding them into Javier's skin so he blanched again with each sentence. "Rodrigo is near, perhaps twelve or fifteen hours away. Birds have brought messages to him and back again, since the Khazarian betrayal. The last missives say they've broken for the night and will be here by afternoon. The troops must sleep."

"Of course. We'll need them fresh." Javier's voice came more roughly than he expected. "Akilina?"

"Under guard and in hysterics. She swears she knows nothing of it; that it's all Irina."

"Irina and Lorraine," Javier whispered. "On what basis?"

Sacha shrugged and came all the way into the tent, flinging himself into one of the chairs and taking up the wine Marius had abandoned. "Rumours are flying, most of them saying that God's shown Irina that Aulun walks the true path, but we have no answers yet. We're broken, Javier. Your army is split and your men are terrified. I'm the last to counsel caution, but you may need to sue for peace."

"No." Javier closed his fist on bloody water. "No. Today I learned what the witchpower can do."

"You overextended yourself and thousands of your men died for it. If you can't do better than that—"

"I can!"

A smirk twisted Sacha's face. "Then tell me why you're crying for your priest, and why your first words on my entering were a confession. You need strength, Javier, and if that means rolling in the stench of blood, then you'd better do it. Men are dying on your command. For an hour today you gave them hope, and then you fell and took all *their* strength. If you want to win this war, you're going to have to do better."

Javier, distantly, whispered, "You're cruel, Sacha."

"Because I see a man, my friend, my king, crawling when he should stand tall. Because you have power and you loathe yourself for using it. You have got to do better." Sacha was abruptly in Javier's space, kneeling before him, hands knotted on his shoulders. "We all depend on you, Javi. I depend on you."

"And his majesty is right to depend on God's guidance in what is right and what is wrong," Tomas murmured from the doorway. "Forgive me, majesty. Marius said you asked for me."

Frustration contorted Sacha's features and he held Javier even more tightly, bringing their heads together so he could whisper, "Don't let the priest weaken you, Javier. We need what you can do." Then he released Javier as though he'd grasped a hot coal and got to his feet, stalking by Tomas and crashing shoulders with him as he left the tent.

Tomas jostled with the hit, no hint of his thoughts marring his features as the door rustled and fell into stillness. "You did well," he finally said, quietly.

Javier croaked laughter. "Did I? Is the fall of blood from the sky not a sign of the end times? Tomas, I enjoyed it." Sacha's warning burnt him, but the all but empty place where the witchpower magic had been burned more deeply. "I've never known a woman as sweet, and in the heat of it I thought this must be God's grace giving me pleasure for doing his will. But the magic is gone." The last words came out a broken whisper, as if spoken by a frightened child. "I'm empty, and know nothing of how to refill this place inside me. What if I'm wrong and the pleasure is the devil's?"

"The Pappas blessed you." Tomas came to him, touched his hair, then knelt. "We must believe this is God's will, Javier, all of it. That the Khazarian betrayal is meant to test our resolve, and that we must push all the harder against Aulun."

"Sacha thought you would stay my hand."

Instead, Tomas took his hands, warm touch that brought a discovery of his own chill. "I've walked this far with you," the priest whispered. "We've entered Hell, and I'll not leave your side now. We'll pray," he promised. "God will replenish the magic, and you'll stand fast and take back the ground we've lost. Aulun will be our kingdom, yours and mine in God's eyes and in His name. Don't be afraid, Javier. Don't be afraid."

Javier, trembling, leaned forward into Tomas's embrace, and as the priest began to whisper a prayer, felt the hunger of witchpower begin to grow again within him.

BELINDA WALTER

Belinda should have reached Javier by now, a full fortnight after she slipped away from Alunaer. Should have, and didn't like to think that it was fear keeping her from making contact. There were reasons to have delayed: whispering the stillness around all the ships, drawing it close so that even eyes searching for them were unable to see them, had wearied her. The same trick again spread over the army as it left the water and penetrated Brittany's north shore. They moved in silent secrecy, an advantage her people would have paid dearly in blood had they done without. Worthwhile, but tiring.

She felt Javier on the edges of that secrecy, felt his awareness of her presence, and shivered under the intensity of his hatred. He would mark this war a success if it ended with her head on a pike, even if every soldier he brought with him died in putting it there. Even his ambitions on Aulun's crown would be satisfied by her death, though he clearly intended on attaining both.

Hiding an army from plain sight was more exhausting by far than hiding only herself. She'd learned in Lutetia how far she could push herself, and had grown far beyond those limitations now, but even so, without a *need* to drive herself forward and face Javier, without a mission assigned to her by someone else, she risked a few days of lingering and recovering while the first battles were met. Her confidence in her own witchpower was immense, but she respected Javier's as well, and preferred meeting him when she was at full strength.

It was not, she had told herself again, fear.

And then Javier tore the front lines of the Khazarian army apart, turned them to mist that lifted to the sky and came down as red rain. Standing under that hideous downpour, Belinda Primrose admitted fear, and for the first time in her life, stood stymied by it.

The weight of his power, its destructive potential unleashed, brought ice to her skin, red rain colder than it had any right to be. She'd found the play of his magic erotic, once; now, even beside the truths she'd learned, she could hardly imagine finding anything but horror in what he turned his power to. And yet she felt no maliciousness in it, not like how his anger became pointed and focused when he thought of her. The bloody rainfall was a result of war, a necessary evil: that was what cold red water collecting in her hair and in puddles around her feet told her.

Slowly, as the sky bled through her clothes and soaked her to the skin, she came to recognise the necessity of what he did in what *she* had done to the Cordulan armada only weeks before.

They were both monsters, and she took comfort in that.

It released her from her fear, gave her a direction to move in. The combined Aulunian and Khazarian armies had won the day, but sleeping under the falling blood of their comrades stripped away their bravado. They would need it come morning, and that, at least, was a thing she could help with.

Standing unnoticed in the midst of a war camp, Belinda turned her face to the weeping sky and reached for magic. Golden warmth chased the ice away, then stretched upward, though she tried to mute the witchlight itself. Tried, but with her eyes closed, could hardly know if she succeeded, and she had no intention of parting her lashes to risk blood drops splashing in her eyes.

After the storm and the armada, pushing a handful of summer rain clouds away from her camp seemed simple, little more than a whisper of concentration and an encouragement to empty themselves elsewhere. They had no will of their own, no personality, and yet she was inclined to assign them willingness or stubbornness, depending on how easily the wind bent to her call. She sent them out to sea, not just from over her camp, but from over Javier's. Her armies were distressed by the falling blood, and she thought Javier's might be shorn up by it, such proof as it was of their king's power. Better to take away their source of pride as well as her people's source of worry.

She waited, witchpower still extended, in expectation of Javier's response. They might fight the war themselves, sister against brother, Aulun against Gallin, Reformationist against Ecumenical, and leave the rest of the armies to return home, there to sleep safe in bed, to lie in the arms of lovers, to forget the savagery that had made up this day and those like it.

But there was no answer from Javier, no angry lash of power to match the outpour he'd made that afternoon. Recognition sluiced through Belinda, a suspicion without foundation: he had exhausted himself, as she'd done the first time she used her magic extensively; as she'd done, indeed, at the armada, and again in concealing Aulun's navy and army from Gallic eyes. Unlike Belinda, though, Javier had never needed to measure his ability to continue beyond the edge of exhaustion: what he faced now would be new to him, a frightening depletion of witchpower. The war, if it came down to them, would not happen tonight; if she was lucky, if her army was lucky, he would be days in recovery, and his confidence would be even longer in returning to form. With a little leeway, the newly allied forces could finish taking Brittany and move east to Lutetia.

And Belinda could face an unarmed Javier with her secrets and her plans.

Satisfied that the rain had stopped, hopeful of her deductions, she opened her eyes to find herself the centre of a gathering, all wide-eyed men struck with awe. She smiled, gentle as she could, and murmured, "You don't see me, my friends. I was never here."

For the rest of her life she would wonder what they'd seen that night, and so, for the rest of theirs, would they.

Javier had recovered by morning.

Belinda knew it the moment she awakened: the air tingled with released power, far more controlled than it had been for an exhausting long hour the day before. She left the camp, taking high ground a mile or two away, and from there saw Javier standing alone in a column of silver.

It washed out from around him, ripples that cascaded over his people, shielding them from the Khazarian onslaught. Only sometimes did he lash out with a witchlight bomb, and after the first time she recognised the building of power in him, and so aborted the explosion's power.

He flinched as though he'd taken a physical hit, just as he'd done months ago in his bedroom as they'd played at this game now made deadly. She was harder to see than he, her power less active; that, it seemed briefly, was how it had always been, Javier with a showy talent and herself keeping hers under wraps, more subtle. Dismay twisted her stomach as she saw how neatly those two things fit together, the one the half of the other, and again cursed herself for not seeing the impossible before. Dmitri would pay for the folly he'd led them into, she promised herself again, and then Javier's attack leapt across the space between them and she flung up a shield of her own.

She knew Javier's power better than Dmitri's, knew its shape and knew his thoughts, and yet when she followed his magic back, reaching for its source as she'd done with the dark witchlord, the knack of grasping it and cutting it off eluded her. Silver magic hammered her shields as she searched for that point of closure, until a blow slammed through and left her gasping.

Triumph rather than a second strike hammered through her cracked shields. Belinda pulled back from searching for Javier's weaknesses and strengthened her focus, sealing up her own frailties as she might plaster gapes in a wall. Javier smashed down with his magic again too late, and she felt his shock as strongly as she'd felt his exultance. For all that she'd drowned his armada he still thought of her as weaker than himself, easily overwhelmed as she'd been in the Lutetian courtroom. His next attack came with more anger behind it, verging on frantic: she wasn't supposed to be able to resist him. Mouth pursed, eyes gone vacant as she stared across the distance at her rival, she let her idea of a strong front fade, trying to make herself appear weaker than she was.

Javier's magic jumped at the chance, crashing down with all the force he had to muster. It rebounded again, less strongly, but Belinda's hand lashed upward, as though she threw a knife, and with that idea pitched her own power back at Javier.

He staggered, visible action, across the flatlands. More ready for his weakness than he'd been for hers, Belinda flung a second, weightier ball of witchpower after the first, gold attacking a weak point in his silver shield. The impact felt to her as profound as a cannonball, and for the second time, the Gallic king stumbled. On the battlefield, her army surged forward, taking whole yards of land and beating down the enemy as Javier's shields faltered.

Delight surged through Belinda: so long as she could distract

Javier, her armies had the advantage of numbers and of position. She need only keep him occupied while the shields he'd built to protect his people failed. Aulun would triumph without effort.

Javier realised his mistake only moments after she did, and she felt the sharpness of his rage before he pulled back from their battle to turn his attention to the larger one below.

She was tempted to taunt him into another sally, as caught up in the game of war as any of the soldiers on the fields below. She could take him: she knew she could, and in doing so could bring Gallin's ambitions to an end. It was in all ways what the queen's heir should do; it was what duty whispered she must do.

Carefully, deliberately, Belinda drew her own power back, turning it to nothing more than the containment of Javier's witchpower bombs. They came more rarely as he began to understand what she was doing and saw that his expenditure of magic got too little result. But her own golden power flared in outrage, as though it wanted to respond to Javier's blatant use of magic; as though the part of her which fanned ambition would never rest so long as anyone else dared their own aspirations. She, and she alone, was meant to inspire loyalty, as much as she was meant to be loyal to her queen.

Belinda's hoarse laugh scraped her throat. Robert and Dmitri and their far-off queen had made of her a bewildering thing; a thing she barely understood herself. Childish logic told her that loyalty built from peasant to lord to king to God. No one walked at the head of such a chain without both owing and owning loyalties. By that reason she could be Aulun's heir and demand her people's loyalty, and still bend her own to her queen.

Witchlight, seductive, warmed her as she held to that thought, then cooled again as she whispered, "To Lorraine."

There were wars on the battlefield, and wars inside her. Loyalty to Lorraine meant destroying the young witchlord who stood miles away, drawing on his own power to protect his men.

But Javier de Castille—against all odds, against all reason—was not her enemy. Dmitri was. Robert was. Their unknowable queen, too; they made up a triumvirate of power stretching beyond the obvious, beyond the sensible and beyond the practical. Loyalty, bred into Belinda's bones, lay stretched between two needs, and that she had come this far should have made her path a clear one.

Serving Aulun had to mean betraying Lorraine.

Belinda slammed her hands into fists and pulled her power back, leaving the blended Aulunian and Khazarian armies unprotected, and leaving, she hoped, the thinnest of bridges on which she could cross the distance between herself and Javier.

He would very likely kill her on sight.

Belinda lowered her head, tucked herself in stillness until she was all but impossible to see, and amended her thought:

He would very likely *try.*

Rodrigo's arm of the Cordulan forces, eight thousand strong, rode into the back of the Khazarian army at sunset. Belinda watched, holding her magic in until it cramped her belly and made her hands sweat with the need to act. It was little more than a salvo on Rodrigo's part, an announcement of his arrival: the day had gone on too long already, and no one had the heart to fight. A few men died on both sides before falling back from the battle, exhaustion driving them to rest.

A hundred and fifty thousand soldiers would come to battle in the morning. Two-thirds of them were the allied Khazarian and Aulunian armies; they should, by rights, defeat Cordula's troops through numbers. But her army was wedged between two forces of almost-equal size now, and retreating to present a unified front would only give Javier's men a chance at their backs. No, it would have to be done through numbers; watching campfires light up, Belinda was glad she wasn't a general, obliged to move men like chess pieces and watch plans fall awry.

She had left crossing into Javier's camp until nightfall: witch-power or no, walking through a battlefield invited more trouble than she wanted to risk. They weren't so very far apart, the Gallic king's camp and her own watching-place in the woods. But Belinda left her safe place with more trepidation than she'd felt since childhood, since Robert had come for her in the middle of the night and set her on the road to murder. Then, as now, all that she was hinged on a few critical moments at the end of her journey, and then, as now, she was uncertain of how that ending would play out.

This is how it shall go, Primrose. The memory of Robert's voice echoed in her ears so clearly she thought, for an instant, that he'd spoken in her mind in the same manner as a few months earlier. But the echo came again, rising from within her, not from an external source. *This is how it shall go,* and with that promise came her own confidence. The words this time were hers, as was the plot. "Heed me well," she whispered to herself. "For this *is* how it will go."

ROBERT, LORD DRAKE
22 June 1588 † *Alunaer, the queen's private chambers*

Of all the things that should not be dancing through Robert Drake's mind, Irina Durova's beautiful face is high on the list. But the imperatrix's image is there, bringing with it a humour that Lorraine, queen of all Aulun, would not appreciate at all, which is why Robert is biting his tongue in an attempt to keep laughter at bay.

It is, as he's observed before, easier to be angry at a plain woman than a beautiful one, but Lorraine's wrath makes it quite clear that a woman of failing beauty is still very capable of being angry at a man. Any man, but most particularly himself in this time and place, and if he were asked, Robert would admit Lorraine has the right of him.

He, after all, taught Belinda Primrose to be a sneak.

Another girl has been wimpled and put on display for the moment, an event she should revel in as the most exciting of her brief life, because it will almost certainly be the culmination of it. Lorraine's brother, who died little more than a child, was so ruined by the disease that had wracked him that another pretty blond boy took his place as the funereal body, while the young king himself was buried in a shallow grave in the middens. A family of such pragmaticism is unlikely to allow Belinda's double to live long after Belinda's safe return.

A return, Robert hears, which he is expected to expedite. He brings his attention back to Lorraine, and against all wisdom smiles at her. "Forgive me," he says, and though he's cheerful, there's honesty in the request. "I should say I expected this, but I didn't. Belinda's been a well-directed tool all her life, unaccustomed to taking her own rein. I didn't think she would."

"My experiences with the girl say she's impetuous and—" Lorraine breaks off with a muttered curse. "And clever. But I thought her loyal, Robert. I thought her loyal beyond question."

"She is." Robert says that with easy confidence, and rises out of his kneel to emphasise it. "You set her a task, Lorraine." He's made much freer with the queen's name since her revelation of their long-ago marriage, a stunt so well-considered and oft-discussed that even Robert barely remembers whether it happened in truth or in fiction. "You told her to keep her people safe. I've never, not since she was a child, given her the *how* of accomplishing her duties, only said they must be done. You may be her queen—"

"And her mother," Lorraine snaps, but Robert shrugs dismissively.

"That, too, but the one holds more weight than the other, and it should, given how we chose to raise her. Either way, I think she's chosen her own path to fulfilling the job set to her."

"We did not grant her permission—"

"How often," Robert interrupts, greatly daring, "have *you* waited on permission, my queen?"

Lorraine stares at him, and stares hard. Robert smothers another smile, far too pleased with the girl-child he raised and feeling a little sorry for her mother. Belinda's presence in Gallin isn't something he counted on, but it, and her stormy relationship with Javier de Castille, will drive the war in dramatic waves. This is what Robert wants: the more passion and the less reason, the longer it will last, and the more room he'll have to push forward leaps in technology. These people have guns, they have metalworkers, but they have no automation, and he requires a level of automation beyond what they can currently imagine. He admires their blue jewel of a planet, but he'll turn its skies grey and let its people forget the colour of the sun, if it will help to arm his own people for their long nights between the stars, and for the battles they find there.

"Are you suggesting," Lorraine finally says, icily, "that your Primrose is . . .'' She can't, it seems, finish the evidently appalling thought: Belinda may be her daughter, but Lorraine is unaccustomed to thinking of anyone as being like herself.

"You're a force unto yourself, my queen," Robert says both smoothly and truthfully, but then he allows that smile to encroach. "And she's admired you her entire life, Lorraine. She will do anything for you and for this country. Don't worry. I'll go to Gallin and bring her back, but don't worry for her safety or her methods. If she's bold, she comes by it naturally."

"For me," Lorraine says, still coolly. "For me, for Aulun, and for you, Robert. Her loyalties don't begin and end with me."

"But mine are yours to command." A wash of foolishness heats Robert's jaw and creeps up his cheeks at the simple truth of those words. His other queen may wait beyond this world's moon, preparing for the time when humans break far enough away from their small planet to shuttle ore and minerals and fuel to her ships, but in the here and now, a very large part of Robert Drake is given over entirely to the red-haired queen of Aulun. Still flushed, he bows deeply and takes himself to the door, trying to shape his thoughts to a journey across the straits, and to finding a wayward daughter.

"Robert." Lorraine waits until he's turned back, then says, "Take the Khazarian ambassador with you. I want one of Irina's chosen men on the front lines, as much to oversee her troops and report to her as to be seen and reported on. We are unified, Aulun and Khazar, and the world will see it in my lord consort and Irina's ambassador standing arm in arm."

"Your will, my queen." Robert, more than satisfied, bows again and leaves the chambers with a lightness in his step.

19

JAVIER DE CASTILLE, KING OF GALLIN
22 June 1588 † *The Brittanic battlefields*

Javier had hardly believed Rodrigo would arrive in time. *In time,* as though the Essandian prince's fragment of an army could break the Khazarians' backs, as though there was some terrible and wonderful difference another eight thousand men could make to their cause. Javier had let almost all of his magic go when Rodrigo's troops did finally come over the hill, not because they deserved less of his protection, but because he was only barely on his feet, and permitting someone else to take the brunt of the allied attack was the only way to retain consciousness for the night's remainder.

Rodrigo himself rode up the hill with the last rays of sunset behind him, making a tall beautiful slim line of masculinity against golden shadows. Javier saw Belinda's power in that colour, then bared his teeth and shoved the thought away: she was out there, but not to make Rodrigo of Essandia look heroic as he gave the Cordulan armies a modicum of hope.

Akilina rode with him, evidently free, until Rodrigo dismounted and strode to his wife, lifting her from her horse. There was stiffness in his movements, speaking of an injury, but he was gentle with Akilina, and as he set her on the ground Javier saw the ropes that bound her wrists. Red scrapes said she'd been wearing them a while now.

"Surely," Javier said with all the steadiness at his command, "this is unnecessary, uncle."

Anger flashed in Rodrigo's eyes, and with it Javier's intuition leapt: the anger was for binding his wife, not for Javier's question. "The generals will have it no other way. It seems they doubt an army's ability to keep one single woman under watch without subjecting her to such indignities." He put an arm around Akilina's waist, steadying her as they went into Javier's tent, where more of those generals waited to argue strategy and tactics and to make accusations of betrayal and perfidy. Javier stood where he was, swaying with the wind as it wrapped him, and gave half an ear to the arguments already rising in the tent.

There was nothing new to them—there would *be* nothing new. They were old women gnawing at old bones, trying to find marrow that had long since been sucked away. Blame was flung about as though it were a cannonball itself, its weight crushing where it couldn't be deflected. Low anger, tainted with silver, rumbled in Javier's belly, and he stood waiting for the inevitable phrase that would push him into action. He would wait until then, would wait until emotion ran so high that the witchpower could simply seize it and direct it as he wished, and if that was a sin against God, so be it.

Javier closed his eyes and listened to the mounting debate in the tent, and repeated those words to himself: *so be it*. He was king, he was God's chosen, he was blessed—or cursed; it no longer mattered which—with the witchpower, and between Tomas's faith and his own need, Javier de Castille no longer gave much concern to whether God approved of his decisions. Better to be damned trying to save souls than in not acting.

A bitter laugh coughed up from his chest, a thick wet sound. Sacha would be proud. Finally, Sacha would get the ambitious liege-lord he had always wanted.

Someone inside the tent snapped, "Rumour from Lutetia is that Akilina herself poisoned Sandalia's cup."

Javier lifted his chin, opened his eyes to watch the fading horizon, and waited a little longer. Not much longer now. Anticipation strengthened and excited the witchpower, though it seemed that all such emotion belonged to the magic, not to himself. There was only the nausea of dreaded necessity in his own thoughts, the discomfort of determination. It would be better to revel in the witch-power's enthusiasm, and perhaps later he could. Too much lay at stake now to enjoy his choices.

Rodrigo, so softly, said, "I would not say such things if I were you," to the offending general, but another voice took up the first officer's cry.

"First Sandalia dead and now the Khazarian army our betrayers, and Akilina Pankejeff a very common link, your majesty." The honorific was a tag weighted with sarcasm, questioning Rodrigo's worthiness to bear it. Javier closed one hand into a slow fist, waiting, still waiting. Witchpower anger began seeping through him, heating resolution into passion.

A third took up the call. All of them were voices Javier knew, men he could put names to without seeing their faces. Men who ought to have been more unquestioningly loyal, and who ought not dream of saying what this one did: "The woman's well-known in Khazar as a witch, Rodrigo, and she's naught but bad luck to all of us here. There's a sure answer to this problem in the sharp of my sword."

There: there were the words Javier had waited on. He heard breath catch in every throat in the cloth-walled room, and demanded, without speaking himself, that no word be said. Half a beat later he threw open the tent doors and stalked inside, all of it so quick he might not have needed witchpower to stay their voices. Might not have, and yet he flexed it, uncaring of the right or wrong in using magic to silence objections. "We will hear no threats of a queen's neck on a cutting block. We have lost enough royal blood already and are not eager to lose more. Akilina is not the problem here."

Emotion so strong it might have been his own rose up in all the men and the solitary woman in the room. It was sweltering inside the canvas walls, torches thickening the air as they offered light, and the night was already warm. Coupled with outrage, with disbelief, with insult, and with a soprano relief over all that masculine fury, the heat poured sickness into Javier. It sprang out as cold sweat on his lip and clogged his throat. For a terrible moment he thought he would lose all control and become a fool in front of half-rebellious generals. He *could not* let that happen.

Witchpower answered that need, all of its anger turning cool and soothing. It coated his insides and spilled outward, lending him strength and a confidence bordering on eroticism. He would have his way, and the thought gave him the same comfort and delight he'd felt in raining blood on his enemies.

"Akilina is a charm, nothing more, a thing dangled in front of Essandia in order to give the Khazarian alliance a pretty face. She hasn't the power to reforge that alliance, and if you made use of your minds instead of retreating into childish fears of witches you would know that. Only Irina could have made the decision to ally Khazar with Aulun at this late hour. Our navy is crushed and now Khazar stands with Aulun on Echon's western border. Irina could not have foreseen the armada's defeat." That much, at least, Javier was certain of: none of them had foreseen it, and even if he'd known Belinda's powers were increasing, he'd never have fathomed they'd grown to such devastating effect. Irina Durova couldn't have known the Cordulan navy would suffer such a loss.

He left a silence, both to gather his thoughts and to lend weight to what he'd said, and no one broke it. Silver magic told him no one could, that witchpower held the generals' tongues even as they fought for speech. Hands planted on the map table, Javier levelled his gaze toward men resentful but unable to stop listening. "She couldn't foresee it, but I think we face a tactician more talented than any of us had realised. There was always a chance, however small, that the navy might fall. Irina didn't send a man to strike a bargain with Aulun after the armada. He would have been there, waiting for word to offer the Red Bitch the alliance she's always wanted.

"Sixty thousand of Irina's army are already here, and as many again remain in Khazar. She has Echon in the palm of her clawed hand, and Aulun at her side. These two queens need only break our back here in Brittany and then they'll move across Echon in their own names and for their own heathen gods. Gentlemen, we have been outplayed by women, and I will not have it.

"In the morning we will bring our army back together, regardless of the cost. God has offered me a blessing and I'll turn what small talent I have toward easing our reunion pangs, but it will be your skill, generals, that will win the day. The combined Cordulan armies are a formidable force, even in the face of the Khazarian alliance. Reuniting our men will give them heart, which I deem more valuable than any flanking tactics we might manage to manoeuvre out of our current positions. Our armies will be one, and then with our strength united and God's mandate driving us on, we will defeat Aulun and drive Khazar back to her frozen northlands, and Echon will for once and all bend knee to Cordula's church!"

The uproarious agreement came so quickly and with such pleasure that it might have been born of honest emotion, rather than relief at finally being able to speak, rather than Javier's implacable willpower directing them toward cooperation. This was an easier battle than with Tomas, if it was a battle at all: these were men who wanted a fight, though they might not have chosen it in the manner Javier did. There were objections, but they came in the form of how best to implement his plans, not inherent opposition to what he demanded. Javier sat down, fingers steepled, and watched old men bicker over strategy as they rushed to do his will.

Out of them, Rodrigo remained silent, watching Javier. His opinion was a note in the crowd, a sentiment that stood out more clearly than the others. There was pride in the Essandian prince, but more, there was curiosity, and Javier didn't need clearer thoughts to know his uncle wondered if the generals acted of their own accord or his. In time Javier met his eyes and shrugged a shoulder; it didn't, in the end, matter, and Rodrigo pursed his lips before giving an acknowledging shrug. Only then did he get to his feet and go to Akilina, taking a blade to cut apart the ropes that bound her wrists.

Though her hands must have been numb, she gathered her skirts as she stood and made a curtsey toward Javier: thanks, he knew, for distracting the generals and sparing her life—as much thanks as he was likely to get from a woman unaccustomed to subservience. He tipped his head toward the door. The Essandian queen was better off out of sight, and Rodrigo quietly offered her an elbow. They left together under the cover of arguments, a royal pair too unimportant to notice.

AKILINA, QUEEN OF ESSANDIA

Rodrigo murmurs "I'm sorry" the moment they're outside the strategy tent, and what's more, he does it in Khazarian. Akilina, whose pride is keeping her from rubbing her wrists or hissing in pain as blood comes back to her fingers, is not so prideful that she can't be made to trip over her own feet in surprise, and in regaining her balance promptly loses the battle to keep her hands still. She wrings her wrists and stares at him in astonishment, and Rodrigo de Costa, her husband and the prince of Essandia, repeats, "I'm sorry. I shouldn't have let them keep you in ropes, but I believed you were safer that way."

"I was." Akilina can't tell which she begrudges more, that he's right or that she's admitting it. "Rodrigo, I did *not*—"

"I know." Rodrigo rolls his eyes so dramatically his eyebrows move, giving him the look of a much younger man, there in the Brittanic moonlight. He turns a rueful smile down at her, and says, "Well, you might have, I suppose, if you'd imagined six months ago that Sandalia would die, that three countries would unite under Cordula's banner to take revenge on her murderer's throne, that you'd be bartered in marriage as a piece to wed a tremendous army and an unstoppable navy together, and that that navy would be drowned in the first battle the war saw."

"Irina did." Akilina sounds bitter to her own ears: she had not imagined Irina Durova to be so foresightful.

"No." Rodrigo shakes his head and turns toward the battlefields. They're aglow with campfires now, and the wind carries voices speaking half a dozen languages up to them, an unintelligible blur of humanity that he speaks over without heed. He seems to Akilina a perfect monarch in that moment, literally above the concerns of ordinary men. "Irina saw a chance to ally herself with the Essandian navy and its trade routes, all for a price far less than her own hand or Ivanova's in marriage. But Javier's right. She holds her throne with an iron grip, and would never close channels with Lorraine completely. She'll have sent an envoy to Aulun to smooth the waters and to be there waiting, orders in hand, should the alliance our marriage built go sour in any way. Anything less makes an enemy of Lorraine, and with Sandalia gone, Irina will want her sister queen to side with her. They have only each other now."

He glances at her, a darkness in his eyes, and Akilina, seeing where that comes from, dispenses with everything but the truth: "If Sandalia had died by my hand, husband, I wouldn't have been there to scream over her body."

Rodrigo's eyebrows quirk upward, and then a second time, making something of a shrug. "No. No, you wouldn't have been." He puts the slightest emphasis on *you,* giving Akilina credit that amuses her. Lesser killers, that emphasis suggests, might have been at Sandalia's side to watch her die, but not Akilina Pankejeff. She's wiser and more subtle than that.

Of course, so is Belinda Walter, who *did* murder the queen of Gallin, and who has managed to earn herself the heirdom to a throne through it. Akilina's admiration for the young woman knows no bounds, and she looks forward to an opportunity to kill her. There's an amber rose that she carries with her, a jewel Belinda wore for a few very short hours after Akilina gifted it to her. It had been meant to go with her to the grave, but instead Akilina rescued it from the aftermath of the bloody mess in Sandalia's courtroom six months ago, and has kept it nearby ever since. It had been beautiful at the hollow of Belinda's throat, and that's where Akilina will place it again, when she finishes the game between herself and the Aulunian heir.

There's a new and interesting side to that particular game, now that Akilina is the Essandian queen. If Belinda is dead, then Javier is all the more likely to gain the Aulunian crown as a pretender to the throne, making him king or heir to half of Echon. He's as of yet unmarried and without children, and so there's a chance Akilina might be able to set her child as heir to the lands he'll claim.

Javier de Castille will, of course, have to die childless to solidify her child's claim, but it's no more outside of bounds than Javier's claim to the Lanyarchan throne through his mother's first marriage. The gaining of thrones is a delicate matter, born of politics and cleverness, and if Akilina Pankejeff can topple a row of dominoes, it will make her queen of an empire to rival Irina's.

That would be ambition realised to a glorious degree, and that, if anything, would be safety. It's a complex path to security, but the risk is worth it.

"You should return to the generals and their strategies," she murmurs, as though that's the only topic she's been considering.

"Not until I've seen you safely back to our tent." Rodrigo pulls a thin smile. "We may be among friends here, but I would prefer not to risk my wife or her child to someone bitter over Khazar's betrayal."

"Allow me, my lord." Sacha Asselin comes out of the dark, looking broody. It's not an expression well-suited to his sandy hair and light eyes; Marius would wear it better, though from what Akilina knows of him, Marius doesn't tend toward brooding.

Rodrigo makes a sound of pleasure and surprise and embraces the young lord, then steps back to tease him: "Have you been hiding here waiting for the chance to squire my queen, Sacha?"

Sacha loses some of his sulkiness to smile at Rodrigo. "For weeks, my lord, ever since duty called me back to Gallin." Then the smile falls away and he glances toward the strategy tent; toward, more precisely, the unseen red-haired king within.

"He'll be free soon enough," Rodrigo promises quietly. "If I can entrust Akilina to your escort I'll herd those old women out of there on the good sense of all of us needing sleep before tomorrow's battle. It'll be good for him to see you, Sacha. It's hard, being newly come to a crown."

Sacha turns to Akilina, all politely mocking concern. "Is it true, majesty? Is it difficult, bearing the weight of a crown?"

Akilina, who a day ago would have played along, finds her throat sour with bile, and lifts her hands to show the red raw marks around her wrists. "More difficult than I had imagined, Lord Asselin."

Sacha blanches and actually drops to a knee, hand fisted against it. "Forgive me. I was foolish and meant no offence."

"Get up, Sacha," Akilina says gently. She's not angry; indeed, she could almost feel sorry for the young man. "You meant no harm. I know that."

"I should be wiser than this." Sacha gets to his feet, but his hands remain balled, and Akilina wonders if it's her pain or his embarrassment he feels the most for.

"That much," Rodrigo says lightly, "is true. Keep her safe back to our tent, Sacha. There will be trusted guards posted, so you needn't stay. Javier will wait on you."

"My lord." Sacha's voice is barely a whisper, and he offers his elbow to Akilina with all the attitude of a whipped puppy. Rodrigo nods to them both and removes himself to the strategy tent, while guards—trusted escort or no, there are always guards—fall into step ahead of Akilina and Sacha to bring them to the battlefield tent that's the home of Essandian royalty.

"You've lost the look of pleasure you had about you in Isidro, Sacha." Akilina speaks in Khazarian; Sacha has enough of the tongue to be passable, and the guards are Isidrian. She can say anything she likes without fear of being understood by those who should not understand. "Are things not well with the king?"

"He's besotted by his priest." God, the bitterness in Sacha's tone! Akilina has the lighthearted impulse to bring his hand to her mouth and lick it, to see if he tastes as sour as his words. Instead she squeezes his forearm, perhaps imparting comfort, but more important, offering solidarity. She and Sacha are in this scenario together, and she would choose him over Rodrigo if she could: these are the things she wants him to believe. For an amusing moment, it occurs to her that the latter, at least, is true: Sacha's easier to control, and Akilina prefers men to bend at her whim. Lips pursed, she walks a little way, considering that, and decides she's glad she hasn't had Sacha murdered yet. He's close to Javier, and if she should need to have the young king killed, Sacha might easily give her the way in.

But that's not where her thoughts ought to be resting, not now. "Does the priest weaken him?"

Sacha makes a derisive sound. "He's been weak all along. I never knew how weak, not until I learned about the power he's been granted. He's had this his whole life, and still he hid behind his mother's skirts, and now behind Tomas's cassock. He doubts his every step and begs forgiveness from a God who gave him power to be used. And nothing I do or say seems to sway him, not anymore. Not with the priest on hand."

Akilina barely thinks about her response; doesn't think at all, but

lets the obvious fall from her lips: "Then the priest must be removed."

The young Lord Asselin, who is not as pragmatic or hard as he
likes to imagine he is, comes to a stop and stares at her as though
she's voiced the unthinkable. Akilina widens her eyes and, if they
were not in public, would put her fingers against his chest, mould
herself to his body, make of herself an innocent and sweet thing
ripe for the taking. Sacha's an easy mark, and will agree to anything
if he believes she'll be his reward. But they are in public, and she's
not fool enough to throw over a throne in favour of a crude
lordling with tall ambitions. She jostles him into walking again,
quickly enough that it should look only as though one or the other
has put a foot down wrong, and when they're once more in pace
she says, "Would it not solve many problems, my lord? His majesty
has been led astray so often this past year, looking for salvation and
answers in newcomers. You three must know, though, that you're
his heart and his guides, if only his eyes can be cleared. Beatrice
Irvine is gone. Without the priest, who else can he turn to but
you?"

"It would be better." Sacha's speaking to a dream, not to Akilina,
but that's all right. They've reached Rodrigo's tent, and the guardsman there—Viktor, poor Viktor, so besotted and bewitched by Belinda Primrose that he has, in the months since she broke his mind,
become little more than an automaton. Akilina had hoped he
might heal with Belinda's death, and so brought the wretched man
to watch the beheading Sandalia had staged. But no, the axe fell and
some poor girl's head rolled, and Viktor let go a terrible shout and
fell to his knees, face in his hands as he cried, "She is not my Rosa,
she is not my Rosa, *she is not my Rosa!*" He has said nothing else
since, not in Akilina's hearing, and yet she's kept the guardsman on,
waiting for some thread of sanity to work its way through his fractured mind. It may never, but the dvoryanin is curious, and it does
her no harm to have a guard who never speaks. So it's poor Viktor
who pulls the tent flap aside and allows them entrance, and Viktor
who lets it fall again without any thought as to whether the Essandian queen ought to be left alone, in private, with a man.

Which gives Akilina all the opportunity she could want to tuck herself against Sacha's side and sigh the sigh of a woman bereft. "If Rodrigo were not so sure he would return soon . . ."

"I've done my duty by you both," Sacha says, not for the first time, but without the smug attitude he once displayed. "Cuckolding's one thing, but asking to be caught for it, that's something else. Not even a queen's that fine a spread."

Someday, Akilina is going to stuff a knife into Sacha Asselin's guts, and smile as he bleeds out.

The thought cheers her, and she turns a toothy grin on the youth. "Nor is any young buck, my lord Asselin." Then, because she doesn't want him off her hook, she softens her expression and smoothes her hand over her belly as she adds, quietly, "But Rodrigo's not a young man, and children need fathers."

Sacha's gaze snaps to her stomach, then returns to her face with such neutrality it screams of ambition. Akilina smiles again, then lets her eyebrows draw together and says, gently, "Think a while on the priest, my lord. Find us an answer."

JAVIER DE CASTILLE

There would be no battle, come morning. Not of the usual sort; that was agreed on. The day's duty was to unite the splintered aspects of the Cordulan army, and, those tactics decided, the generals and Rodrigo had left Javier to his tent. He doused torches with witchpower will, too weary to get to his feet as a normal man might, and sat in the dark a long while, his eyes gritty with exhaustion.

No one—not Gaspero in Parna, not these gathered generals tonight, not Rodrigo—had struggled against his will as effectively as Tomas del'Abbate. Simplicity told him he should be grateful, that the young priest and his faith in God had greater strength than any of the other men Javier had tried to overpower, or that Javier's magic had grown to such strength that these men were easy to break. Here, at least, they were of a mind to fight; he hadn't needed to push them in an unnatural direction. And yet that they acquiesced so easily stole his confidence, rather than enhanced it.

Nothing, it seemed, could satisfy him. Javier opened his eyes to the muggy black tent, of a mind to call for Tomas and guilty at how many times he'd interrupted the priest's sleep. Surely he could find comfort elsewhere for a while; Tomas carried enough of Javier's troubles on his shoulders. Sleep might be enough for Javier himself, at least for tonight. He shoved out of his chair, trusting his feet to know a safe path through the tables and seats strewn about the tent.

"You faltered." Sacha's voice cut through the darkness, a thick growl of accusation.

Javier looked up blindly, exhaustion filming his vision as much as night did. "I didn't see you come in." Witchpower only twitched sluggishly as Javier reached for Sacha with it, and subsided without bringing him any hint of his friend's intentions. That was all right: words had done well enough for all of them, most of their lives. Javier passed a hand over his eyes, trying to wipe away the haze, then picked out what sense he could from what Sacha'd said. "I faltered? When?"

Concern washed weariness away while he thought of the day's battle, then sagged. "At the end, when Rodrigo came. I know. I was . . . so tired, Sacha. I should have tried harder."

"When *Rodrigo* came?" Sacha spat the words hard enough to send a cramp through Javier's shoulders. "I watched you this morning, Javier. After yesterday, we all know you can make concussive blasts with the witchpower, but you gave up on them almost before the battle was met. You threw a handful, no more, when you might have decimated the enemy troops."

"That—" Javier's voice cracked on the single word and he searched for wine in the dark tent, then gave it up and swallowed instead. "Sacha, I—"

"What did the priest say to you?" Knives had duller edges than Sacha's questions, and fire, less heat. "I begged you to be strong for us, Javier. We needed your power today, and instead you were a woman on the field. What did he *say* to you?"

"He said nothing! Sacha, you understand nothing!" Javier crashed into the table, sending pages and quills to rattling. The witchpower awakened again, pounding silver through his veins, feeding on his anger. "There was no point in bombing—"

"It was what we needed you to do!" Sacha flung a chair aside, crashing it into others to underline his shout. "It was what I asked you to do, Javier, and what am I to the king if my pleas fall on deaf ears? How can I advise a man who won't listen? How do I lend boldness to the troops if our king, with his God-granted gifts, shivers and shies at shadows? How—"

Witchpower roared in Javier's ears, louder than blood. He moved with its tide, taking long steps toward his oldest friend with no thought in mind but to silence him. Sacha, unafraid, forthright, stood his ground, still bellowing accusations that he refused to hear answers to. Javier would *make* him hear, make him hear at any cost, and seized his shoulders with that intent.

"Leave off, Sacha." This time the unexpected voice came in a shaft of moonlight, Eliza pushing the tent flap open far enough to admit herself. Sacha bit off his fury with a snap, and Javier flinched, suddenly too aware of what he was about to do. Too aware that in another breath he would have snapped Sacha's will, would have proven himself, once more, untrustworthy amongst his friends. A blade gutted him, bright and mocking: his own power, stronger than he was, and Tomas not there to lend him the hardy faith he needed to stand against it.

Silver clarity brightened his world, witchlight anger filling the tent because it had nowhere else to go, with Javier's will to dominate abated. *Everything* was illuminated: each action they'd taken in the last weeks had been well-lit, forbidding them to hide their darkest thoughts in shadow. Only the night of the blood storm had been a black one, and that, too, seemed as it should be. Heart hammering, witchpower still surging in him, he released Sacha and turned toward Eliza.

No light was unkind to Eliza Beaulieu. In witchlight she was porcelain, short hair grown long enough now to tuck behind her ears and frame her face, making her eyes larger and darker than ever. There was insufficient strength to the blue moon to make a shadow of her body within her clothes, and witchlight only offered promises and hints, but Javier imagined her lithe curves so easily it seemed he could see them. So, he thought, did Sacha, and there again lay a sword between friends, one Javier had never intended to forge.

"Destruction has a price, Sacha." Eliza left the flap pulled open so light spilled in and came between them in fact as well as figuratively. Fingertips on Sacha's chest, she pushed him back a step. "The skies rained blood, and we survived, but at what cost to Javier's soul? We need a warrior, but we also need him to come out a king on the other side of this war, and I'm not sure anybody can do what he did for long and hold on to what makes him human. Is your pride worth that price? Go on." She jerked her chin toward the door, dismissing him more crudely than a king might, but with as much finality. "Get drunk if you have to, but sleep it off and come to your senses, Asselin. He's going to need you in the morning. We all will."

"Women and priests." Sacha looked beyond Eliza, looked to Javier again, and his mouth twisted as he hissed the words. "If this is what you are, Javier, I've been a fool all my life."

Eliza patted his cheek and used a voice of sugar and honey, teasing as if they were still children. "Yes, Sacha. You are. It's not news to any of us, my friend. Now go drink yourself stupid—if it's possible to be duller than you already are—and get some rest."

Sacha curled his lip and left them alone in a tent suddenly full of silence.

"Will you make a light?" Eliza asked after a long time. "Or shall I get a torch?"

"Belinda is out there," Javier said at almost the same moment, then flinched with a spurt of embarrassment. "I can see. I forgot you couldn't." Witchlight spilled through the darkness with a soft glimmer, changing the quality of his sight. He couldn't remember the magic offering him night vision before, but nor did he remember needing it to. It reminded him now of the shadows he and Belinda had cast the first evening they'd lain together, working magic and losing themselves in each other's bodies. When it lent him, and him alone, sight, it was of a more ethereal quality, more as though he saw spirits and souls than true forms. Even now the witchlight trembled, trying to retreat into him where it could replenish and face another day. "Find candles, please," Javier whispered. "I'm more weary than I should be."

Eliza ran to do it, striking flints and lighting a candle or two before moving papers off the map table so she could set the waxworks down safely. Only then, watching the flame, did she say "Belinda?" with great caution.

Javier sank down into the nearest chair, his head a heavy weight in his hand. "It wasn't weakness or fear or Tomas's warnings that stayed my hand. Belinda Primrose—*Walter*—is out there some-where, fighting for her people, and one of the first things we learned to do together—"

Eliza snorted loudly enough to get a tired chuckle from Javier, though he left it alone otherwise. "Was to catch each other's power in a shield, rendering it inert for such purposes as I'd been using it for. She contained the witchpower bombs, Liz. There was no point in wasting my energy creating more of them, not when I could be shielding the men and trying to keep them from harm. It wasn't weakness. But Sacha . . ."

"Sacha's in no mind to listen. I'll try to tell him for you, Javier." Eliza pressed a fingertip into softening wax, then looked over her shoulder at him. Candlelight wavered along her jaw, turning her to a creature of shadows again, but this time of warmth and comfort-ing secret places, rather than the cool moonlit goddess of earlier. "I thought you were the stronger."

"Of Belinda and myself? So had I." Javier rolled his head back, closing his eyes to capture Eliza's image behind the lids. "She's grown more talented since we last saw her."

"When I last saw her I thought her only particular talent was in getting a prince between her legs," Eliza said drily. "Javier, I am— I'm sorry that she wasn't what you thought she was. For what it may be worth, I'm sorry."

Javier put a hand out and heard Eliza move before the warmth of her fingers covered his. "I thought you loathed her."

"I did." Eliza kissed his fingertips, then slipped onto his lap, warm comforting weight. "And do, even more than before. But if she'd been as she appeared, and had made you happy . . . the part of me that's more generous than a penny-stealing street rat would have been glad for you. So I'm sorry that she was other than as she seemed." She kissed his throat, full mouth forming a smile against his skin. "And glad that through all the convolutions you were made to see me, my king. Had Belinda not come amongst us you might never have done so, which makes it hard to hate her entirely."

Javier scowled. "Women are bewildering."

"Yes." Eliza bumped her nose against his, amusement in her voice. "Accept it. We're complicated creatures, able to love and loathe with equal ease, even when the object of such varied emotion is a single person. I should think men can too, but that they prefer not to think about it."

Javier opened his eyes, meeting Eliza's bright gaze. "Men, perhaps, are obliged to choose one emotion to act on. I may go into battle afraid, but I show courage, or we all lose heart."

"I think I would rather be a woman." Eliza smiled, making herself merely lovely, instead of the beauty she could be. "Especially a guttersnipe woman on the arm of a king. It affords me such freedom. Tell me, king of Gallin. If your witchpower is so muted as to leave you trembling and frowning at calling a little light, does that mean the woman in your lap, ungraced by God as she may be, has the better of you tonight?"

Javier groaned and sat up, gathering her in his arms as he tucked his nose against her shoulder. "You've had the best of me all along, Eliza, and if it's not God's grace that's put you by my side, then I've nowhere to lay my thanks."

"Never fear." Eliza slipped out of his arms and took his hand and a candle, leading him to the curtained-off area that was his private space in the battlefield tent. "I know just how and where to lay your thanks, my love, if that's the name we're giving it now. The rest will come in the morning," she said more softly. "Explanations and battle, but for now, Javier, come to me and rest."

20

Not until noon, with the sun overhead and sweat pouring into his eyes, did Javier think of bridging the space between the two halves of his splintered army with witchpower.

Tomas heard his curse and glanced at him with curious concern that Javier shook off. He already held shielding in place, with rare attempts at witchpower bombs aborted early by Belinda's magic. Eliza had been unable to find Sacha that morning, unable to explain Javier's tactics before the armies came together in a terrible clash. She was with the doctors now, as safe as anyone could be on a battlefield. Marius and the gondola boy were with her, and if Javier concentrated he could pick out the notes of their determination amongst all the others. It was a poor use of his attention, though, and he'd only tried it once.

As he would only try this trick once. If his luck held, Belinda wouldn't recognise what he did until it was established, and would be unable to break it. She might be his match, even his better, in power now, but he thought he could hold her off, so long as he had nothing else to do.

Witchpower extended in two shimmering walls, creating thin silver shields for his men as they struggled against the enemy and struggled toward one another. Aulunian troops made a broad river of red coats between those two banks of power, crashing against them with all their might. They were too many to hold back entirely: they found weak points and surged through, or Cordulan soldiers forced their way forward too quickly for Javier, trying to see the entire battle at once, to account for. Men died despite his efforts, but not, perhaps, in the numbers that they might have.

The fleeting idea to capture Aulun's army in a bubble danced through Javier's mind and he put it away again: they were too many, and he would have to stand against the full might of their cannons trying to bring his shields down. Better to be more clever, and perhaps reunite his army before Aulun saw what was happening. The corridor had to be a narrow one, slender enough that it would go unnoticed for a while. More than one would be better, though the thought made him wince with anticipation of difficulty. One at a time, then: that would suffice.

His instinct was to shove Khazarians and Aulunians aside, actually clearing a path for his men, but he fought it, instead slithering a thin point of power across the river of redcoats toward its opposite shore. Not until his fingertips touched, making a triangle, did he realise he was building the shape with his hands even as he tried to build it in his thoughts. Physical action begot magic: he extended his hands, palms placed together to make a needle of his fingers, and when he had reached as far as he could, power melded with power and a silver line shimmered through the midst of the Aulunian army. Eyes wide on the battle below, Javier parted his hands a few inches, edging his corridor open. Keeping it permeable as best he could: they would notice, had to notice, if a sudden wall of air knocked them aside, and he wanted subtlety where it was possible. It only had to be a few shoulder-widths across to accomplish his ends.

His fingers flexed, almost uncontrolled, a surge of tension that brought the soft witchpower walls up to strength and cut off a thin red line of Aulunian soldiers from their brothers.

For long seconds, nothing changed on the battlefield: men shoved and pushed and slew, moving back and forth over small distances, and then one of the Aulunian soldiers died. Another took his place, and then another, each falling back a step as a trickle of Cordulan troops pushed their way into the corridor.

A moment later there were no more red-coated men standing within it, and Cordulan warriors roared triumph. Javier heard the same cry tear from his own throat as men began spilling through the tunnel he'd made, joining their brothers on Javier's side of the shielded battle.

It wasn't so much as a tide turning. Javier, a fist clenched in victory, reminded himself of that. He had to hold the passage and his divided army had to work its way through so they could fight together against the combined might of Aulun and Khazar. It wasn't yet anything decisive.

But it was a beginning. Breathless, elated, Javier risked opening the floodgate a little more, then bent his head to the task of keeping it strong.

ROBERT, LORD DRAKE
23 June 1588 † *The Aulunian Straits*

Dmitri has been at Robert's side for two days now. It shouldn't have taken Robert this long to press the matter, but it's only now, with the recognisable flavour of Javier de Castille's power pouring off the Gallic coast, that the newly named queen's consort turns to a still-disguised Khazarian envoy and says, "I never imagined Seolfor had it in him."

Dmitri tucks his chin, black beard masking his face as well as a woman's veil might. "You sent him to Essandia, Robert. Lutetia's on the way, and Sandalia was a pretty woman."

"Mmn." Robert turns back to the ship's rail, examining the distance. "But it leaves the boy untrained, and for all his renegade ideas, I wouldn't have thought that in Seolfor's nature."

"Isn't that the very definition of a renegade? Besides, you left Belinda untrained," Dmitri says, and there's a hint of smugness in his voice. Robert stills the impulse to knock him overboard; he'd be rescued soon enough, but he would also see the action as a sign of Robert losing control.

As if Javier's existence isn't proof enough of that.

He doubts, doubts in every way, that Javier is Seolfor's son, and yet there's no other explanation that fits. Dmitri was Sandalia's faithful priest and lover for a little while, but not lucky enough to father a child on her. Robert himself never tupped that queen, no, nor Irina, either, and for the briefest moment there's a sting of genuine human envy and amusement in him. Men would count coup on those conquests, and find Dmitri the victor, with two queens to his bed and Robert having only one. Akilina wore a crown now, but to number her among the royal women Robert had bedded seemed somehow cheating.

Perhaps this is why, and how, he's come to lose control: he allows himself to tumble down streams of thought like this one, making mortal games out of what ought to be serious duty. He shakes off some of his musing and answers Dmitri with an argument, though he's not sure the other man's wrong. "She was too young when she came into her power, and did well enough shaping her own mind for its release."

"Think what she might have been if you'd seized on her talent when she was a child."

"Think what happens when you give children gunpowder to play with. She's of more use adult and less skilled than she would be dead from playing at witchcraft when she was nine. Or is the imperator's heir so controlled that she's hidden all signs of the power you've taught her since she was a toddler?"

Dmitri's face flushes under his beard. "She's slower to come into it than Belinda was, is all."

"As have been our children on a hundred worlds," Robert says, deliberately soothing. "We thought short human lives meant quick development when she hid herself in shadow, but she's probably only precocious, a fluke. Ivanova and," he sighs, "Javier, I think, make that clear. He had no noticeable presence until lately. He's Belinda's age," Robert adds more softly. "Seolfor would have had to have come north to court Sandalia. He was in the mountains by then, already waiting."

"What better time to do it than when she stood to wed the Gallic king? He'd failed with Rodrigo already. Perhaps the secrecy was to protect himself if he failed again."

"Rodrigo." Robert's lip curls. "Half a decade and more wasted trying to get that man to marry anyone, to bed anyone, so a child might be gotten, and he waits the better part of a half-century and weds himself an army without warning. I would give my teeth to know what finally persuaded him."

"He's been cautious since childhood. Since before we came here; since the days when we only watched and learned. He fought two wars before he took his crown, and a third not long after. He's dedicated himself to a lifetime of peace since then, a lifetime of building treaties rather than one of conquering." There's something unusual in Dmitri's voice; it takes Robert a moment to place it as respect. "I think, given his choice, he might have selected an heir, another man of wisdom and careful consideration, rather than trust his sister's son to wear the crown thoughtfully. I think Rodrigo de Costa would have chosen never to go to war again, if the world had let him alone."

"If *we* had let him alone," Robert says almost mildly. This is a side of Dmitri he never dreamt existed, a creature of quiet regret for what's been made of a mortal man.

Dmitri shrugs. "If we'd let him alone, yes. But Sandalia is dead, and not even Rodrigo could allow that to go unanswered. And if there was to be war, for the first time since he was a youth, he needed a wife, a possible heir, someone whose claim might go uncontested while he risked neck and blood on a vengeance he couldn't afford to deny."

"You admire him." Robert truly is surprised; he'd thought Dmitri admired no one but himself and his own cleverness.

"He's tried a path of rationality and reason against all odds, against every history his people know. I think he has daring, and I think he has vision." Dmitri quirks an eyebrow, suddenly himself again, and adds, "I think he'll die for it, but yes, I admire him."

Robert, despite himself, grins. "Shave that hideous beard, Dmitri. Give us your own sharp face back. Lorraine won't see you again, and Sandalia's dead. There's no chance of discovery."

"When we put in. I'd as soon not risk my throat to a razor and an unexpected wave." Dmitri turns his attention toward the distant Gallic shore, where a battle rages out of sight. "It's not just Javier's power at work out there, Robert." It's nearly a test, an almost-question investigating whether Robert is still too blind to his daughter's talent.

"No, it's Belinda, too, and with more finesse in her wielding than she had a few months ago. How much did you teach her?"

"Less than I would have liked," Dmitri says with unusual forth-rightness. "More than I might have thought. She has no grasp of science. There's no rhyme or reason, in her mind, to what she can do. Trying to teach her to heal . . ." He snorts and waves a dismissive hand. "She can do it, brutishly, but there's no understanding of how the body works, how to create unity in what's damaged. She's better with emotion and weather. I think she imagines the clouds and wind to be human, somehow, and can shift them accordingly. But if she's precocious I'm as glad Ivanova isn't, because Belinda's a queen in her own right, make no mistake." He goes silent a few moments, then glances at Robert. "What did you tell her of our purpose here?"

Robert breathes laughter. "Tell her? Nothing. She stole a little, more than she could understand. Not enough to worry about, because it's beyond her. It's beyond all of them."

"Stole it." Now Dmitri's surprised, and Robert curses the impulse that led him to telling the truth. The other man's surprise fades, though, fades into a warning, which is unlike him: "Watch yourself, Robert. She'll usurp your power."

Two answers come to mind: one is that for Belinda to do such a thing is both unthinkable and natural, with the latter carrying more weight as he considers it. Unthinkable only because she's been shaped for loyalty; natural because she's female, and has that touch of his queen in her, enough, perhaps, to whisper to her that she has what these humans would call a *divine right* to be worshipped. Robert keeps that thought to himself, because the other is the more interesting. His voice is dry and curious as he asks, "And would you know, Dmitri?"

"Better than I should." Dmitri clips his answer short enough that Robert hides a grin: he's meant to take the bait, and he will, out of interest in the game, if nothing else.

But he's probably not intended to take it by saying, drolly, "You slept with her, then."

Dmitri shoots him a startled look that turns into thinned lips. "She equates sex with power."

"With good reason. But you, with your so-wise ways, don't, and so when she slipped under your guard and put a noose on your witchpower, it came as a shock, didn't it?" Robert sees angry agreement in Dmitri's eyes, and shakes his head. "You should know better than to play with that kind of fire. What the females see as power *is* power. All the cleverness in the world won't undo that. What did she take of you?"

"Pleasure," Dmitri says, sourly enough that Robert coughs on a laugh. Seawater sprays up from below and gives him an excuse to wipe a hand over his face and do away with his amusement.

"Most men wouldn't look so grim, Dmitri. My primrose is pretty enough, and well-trained in bed. What else?"

"She can command my skills as though they were her own, Robert. Snatch memory from me if she wants it, and now it seems she's done the same to you. I know you've intended her to take the throne, but is she under as much control as you believe?"

"Is she not?" Robert's interested in the answer, suddenly focused on his second. "Have you stolen thoughts from her in turn, hints that she's set herself on a new path?"

Dmitri's "No" seems to come reluctantly, though he repeats it with more certainty. "No, but her grasp of the situation—that we serve a 'foreign queen'—has made her uncertain of her own place, and she resents that you haven't trusted her with the truth and the details."

"Rightfully, you think."

Dmitri spreads fingertips against the ship's rail, a shrug of sorts. "I'm inclined to believe the burden of knowledge is more compelling than the weight of ignorance. I'd have begun her training earlier, and offered more secrets."

"As you will with Ivanova?" Robert's careful with the question; Khazar and its ruling family are Dmitri's to deal with, but Robert will face the consequences of Dmitri's choices.

And the look Dmitri gives him says the other man knows it. "In a few more years, by your leave. She comes into her place in the imperatrix's court this autumn, with her fifteenth birthday, too young yet to grasp the subtleties of what we do here. But Belinda's twenty-three, a woman fully grown, and I think your control over her would be all the greater if these past five years she'd been a student of our plans."

"These past five years and more she's been an assassin and a seductress," Robert points out. "I've needed her where she was. Ivanova is different, not a secret. Still, I'll watch for any resentment, any seeming change of her heart." Sharpness takes his breath as a woman's face comes to his mind's eye: Ana di Meo, dark-haired, olive-skinned, with lively eyes and a bent for wearing outrageous colours that few could carry off. She was set on Belinda to watch for those very things not quite a year ago, and she has been dead these last six months, dead at Robert's hand, for the troubles that came to her in the watching. He's good at putting the past away, but Ana has the capability to haunt him, and will, he thinks, for the rest of his days. "Thank you," he adds more roughly, and hopes the unusual gratitude will end the conversation.

It does: Dmitri nods, and both men fall silent, leaving Robert's thoughts room to run ahead of him, rife with speculation. Dmitri will not have shared this out of concern, but rather to sow dissent: his witchlord brother is ambitious, as, Robert supposes, are they all, those who have come to this world to change it. But Dmitri's looked for years to see signs of Robert's weakness, and sees them clearly enough in how he's handled Belinda. Sees them in Javier's existence, still a thorn in Robert's side. The easiest thing to do would be to kill the boy, but that's foolishness and injured pride speaking: simply because he's unexpected and unknown doesn't mean he's useless or dangerous. Indeed, Javier is *witchborn,* as these people would call it, and Robert can no more seriously contemplate murdering him than he might consider committing suicide. There'll be a use for Javier yet—that's a wager Robert would make.

That use might be in controlling Belinda. Ana said the girl was lonely, and had watched love grow up between prince and secret princess. With Sandalia's death, Robert doubts Javier still has such tender feelings toward Belinda, but she may well harbour affection for him even yet. The threat's a useful one to keep in mind, should Robert need to bring her in hand.

A faint smile creases the corner of his mouth. He's doing what Dmitri wants him to: making plans against the chance Belinda has turned away from him. And yet, manipulated into it or not, it's better to face the possibility that it's necessary, and be prepared to control her, than to be blindsided. Dmitri may not have intended doing him a favour; very likely intended on driving a wedge deep enough between them to create trouble where currently is none, but Robert imagines himself a better gamesman than that. Preparation is a different matter than antagonisation, and he loves his daughter too much to force her into an opposing position on their board.

Chills lift bumps on his arms, an all-too-human admission of emotion, for it's not the wind off the water that makes him cold. He's fallen prey to weak emotion in the past, most especially in the matter of Lorraine, conflating her with his alien queen and worshipping, loving, them both, and fell again with vibrant Ana di Meo, so gently it wasn't until she had to die that he saw the mark she'd left on him.

Love is not a name he's often given to his feelings for Belinda Primrose either. Pride, yes, and amusement, and delight, and all those things put together are something larger than he likes to think on. She's a tool, not meant to be adored, and yet the truth of that sentiment is hot enough to bring blood to his face. He loves his daughter, and that's a dreadful admission.

It changes nothing; it can change nothing. But Robert, shaken and suddenly cold, turns away from the railing and retreats under the deck, there to wait out the little time before they come to Gallin in silence and concerned consideration.

BELINDA WALTER
23 June 1588 † *Brittany; the front lines*

An absurdity held her in place, nothing more. For two days Belinda had pushed forward and Javier had pushed back, power flexing with the mindlessness of a river wearing at its bed. Without her witchpower in play, she was one of thousands trying to push through the wall of Javier's magic and being rebuffed; *with* it in play, she became a focal point, a place where his power solidified and became stronger. She thought it was instinctive, as no deliberate destruction rained down when she brought witchlight to bear. Either ignorance or sentiment stopped him, and Belinda doubted it was the latter.

She had come onto the battlefield at night, not expecting Javier's shielding to still be alight when he must surely lie unconscious with exhaustion himself. But she met resistance as she walked the front, and felt as though shackles closed around her when she tried pushing through witchpower shielding. It was cold and sharp, that magic, sharper than she thought of his power as being, but perhaps a sleeping mind shaped it differently. Unable to press through and unwilling to retreat to the hills, when morning came she took a blade from a dead man and went to war, golden sparks sheering off her when her bladework was overpowered and magic became her primary defence.

That night Javier's witchpower shield had been even harder, an iron maiden made to surround her and her alone. Only after trying to break through left her white and cold with sweat did she fall back, curling in a huddle under a tent flap where she could steal a bit of warmth and finally some sleep.

The second day she was a soldier the field changed. She felt Javier's power rearranging the troops around her, but without the vantage of height her sense of what he did was muted. Pushing against his power to explore his intentions hardened his shields and made the men who fought around her all but useless. Frustration and admiration tore at her in equal parts: she'd believed herself unstoppable, and yet with little more than casual pressure, the Gallic king stymied her.

She didn't know how, precisely, the tide had changed. Its flow had altered, that she knew, but toward early evening something fundamental shifted, and the direction of battle went from two fronts to one. Cordula's armies let go a united roar, and Belinda scrambled away from the chaos of fighting to find a hillock, so buried in bodies that it made a spot of higher ground. Teeth set against disgust, she clawed her way over dead men whose flesh gave and squished with her weight, then turned her eye to the battlefield.

Yes, the splintered Cordulan armies, in their greens and blues and yellows, had become a single mass that stood against the allied red and black of Aulun and Khazar. They were still outnumbered, but the success of their unification attempt gave them heart, and Belinda wasn't surprised to hear horns call the Aulunian retreat. Cordulan troops chased her army, but not far: the day had gone on too long, and they had cause to retire and rejoice. Tomorrow's battle would come soon enough, and their triumph deserved a night's celebration and sleep.

Without clear thought, she slipped and clambered down the hill of flesh and began walking forward through troops returning to their camp. Stillness came to her slowly, making her feel as though she faded away, insubstantial as a ghost, and none of the tired, bloody faces around her seemed to notice. Javier's witchlight shield still shimmered across the field, so faint with weariness she was surprised it stood at all, and yet when she reached it, iron clamps seized her and held her still.

Aloud, unconsciously, she said, "I'm trying to make a kind of peace, you foolish bastard," and then coughed a laugh at the unintentionally accurate description of her brother's parentage. *Her brother.* The thought came more easily now, though it still sent revulsion itching through her. Even that grew so familiar as to be edging on tiresome in its reminder. It was a thing done to them, she told herself again, and with that truth in hand all desire was dead.

Most desire. She still carried a wish in her heart, a very strong one, to end one vendetta so another might begin, and that, she whispered to the iron-clad power that held her in place, *that* was why she must be allowed to pass. There were no soldiers to keep safe now, not with the retreat sounded and sunset creeping up on them. She and she alone had a need to cross, and not for the sake of war.

She felt a mote under an alchemist's glass, cold iron witchpower examining her, searching for truths she had no need to hide. He hadn't been so cold, before; war, Belinda thought, was not good for Javier, if this was what it made of his witchpower. It was good for none of them, perhaps, except Robert and his dreams of conquest, and that was an idea that pulled another rough laugh from Belinda's chest. She, in all meaningful ways, had begun this war by poisoning Sandalia's cup, and had thought it the best and wisest course to keep Lorraine's crown safe. Irony tasted as bitter as the cold power that held her in place, and she wondered if everyone who set wars in motion later wondered at the rightness of what had driven them to do so.

Witchpower relented, and Belinda stumbled onto enemy territory feeling very alone.

JAVIER DE CASTILLE
23 June 1588 † *Brittany; the Gallic camp*

"Javier." Tomas's voice broke through a rush of silence so loud it could only be witchborn: silence weighted with silver, pounding in his ears like blood. Javier shuddered, and Tomas's hands closed on his shoulders, warm and strong. "Javier," the priest said again. "You've done it, Javier. It's over. Rest."

"Over?" Javier lifted his head, neck muscles screaming protest. "The war?" Heat patched his face at the foolishness of the question, but Tomas's smile held sympathy, not mockery.

"The battle, at least. The day. Look you to the fields, my king. See your army as one." He stepped aside but stood close, as though rightfully imagining Javier would need support.

The river of red-coated soldiers had become a sea streamed with black: Aulun and Khazar together, retreating now from a wall of witchlight so feeble that Javier doubted it would stop a robin, much less an arrow or a sword. His men, an ocean themselves, but of many more hues, surged forward to heckle their fading enemy. Witchpower went with them, rolling just ahead of their blades, and Javier staggered where he stood, strength draining from him. *Belinda,* his hateful thoughts whispered, *Belinda* had drowned a whole armada, and yet he could barely keep his feet after a day of shielding his men from the worst brunt of war. She had grown so much, and he had fallen so far, all in such a short time.

Still, it was her army that withdrew, not his. That was worth taking pride in. Javier managed a smile and its weak presence brought a light of satisfied relief to Tomas's golden eyes. "I don't know what you did," he murmured, "but you changed our luck. Come back to the war tent now."

A king shouldn't lean so heavily on his priest; the idea weighed on Javier's mind as Tomas fitted himself against his side, shoring him up. Shouldn't, and yet this king couldn't stop himself: he didn't trust his own feet to carry him the few hundred steps back to his quarters.

Songs of triumph greeted them as Tomas shoved the tent door

open. Generals surged forward, catching Javier's shoulders, slapping his back, pride in their voices, as though they'd never doubted him. Their accolades left a tangy taste, flatter than blood, in the back of Javier's throat, and he searched the tent for a gaze that didn't hold him in adulation.

He found it in his uncle, sprawled in a chair, long legs splayed out and fingers templed in front of his mouth. Rodrigo only nodded, a small motion of approval, and if the corner of his mouth shifted in a smile, it was all but hidden behind his hands. Javier nodded in turn and looked for a seat of his own. Finding none, he gave up any pretence of strength and leaned more heavily on Tomas, who ducked his head. "Let me find you somewhere to rest, majesty."

"No." Javier shook his head wearily, but smiled. "Their ebullience will keep me on my feet a while longer. Just stay near and be ready to catch me if I fall."

"Always."

Despite the promise, Javier was torn from Tomas's side and pulled into a throng of generals and admirals too pleased with their coup to worry, yet, about tomorrow's battles. Someone thrust a cup of wine into his hands and he drank greedily, then ate what was offered with as much abandon, heady from both wine and pride. He caught glimpses of Tomas and recognised the priest truly was almost always close enough to catch him if he fell. Touched, he raised a toast that the others followed heartily.

"To God's will," Javier said throatily. "To our victory in God's name, and to Tomas del'Abbate, whose gentle spirit has guided me when I've needed it most these past months."

Ruddiness crept over Tomas's olive skin and his eyes turned to fire, shyness and delight both manifest in his gaze. He opened his mouth to speak, and a blast of cooler air rushed in with the opening of the tent doors.

"The gentle priest" came on the air, words harsh and sarcastic. "Our gentle priest who's given our warrior king such counsel. Our army is one again, a gift indeed. This power of Javier's is God's gift, priest. Why counsel him to such moderate measures as reuniting our army, when he might have shattered the Aulunians with cannonballs of his own magic? Perhaps you don't want us to win, or perhaps you fear the gift's not God's at all, but the devil's own."

Javier twisted around to find Sacha at the door, Marius and Eliza flanking him, though their expressions told tales of horror as he spoke. Shocked silence swept over the room, broken by Eliza, who'd never cared for propriety. She barely bothered to lower her voice as she snapped, "What's gotten into you, Asselin? This is a celebration."

"A celebration of a minor victory that might have ended this war, had our king moved boldly. It *rained blood,* Javier, and this is what you follow it with?"

"Your fight is with me," Tomas interrupted softly. "Your hatred's not for Javier, but for me and the wedge you see me as having driven between you. Show some pride, Lord Asselin. Bring your war to the one who's your enemy, and leave your friendship intact." He came to stand at Javier's right, not blocking his sword hand, but placing himself slightly forward, as if he could protect Javier from Sacha's daggered words.

Sacha strode forward, leaving Eliza and Marius to scramble along behind, though to Javier's eyes they didn't so much follow him as put themselves into the circle of contention. Marius took a place just beyond Tomas, and Eliza hung back on Sacha's left, one hand half-outstretched as though she could drag him back and knock sense into him. Beyond them Javier was aware of the silence, of gathered generals and warriors all holding their breaths, waiting to see how disaster would unfold. None of them, not one, stepped forward to diffuse the scenario, to try to calm Sacha or silence Tomas. No, this was too important for that. This was a moment in which they could test their king's mettle without forcing a confrontation themselves. Almost he admired them, for their audacity in waiting.

Almost. Near-exhausted witchpower began to gather, working itself up to strength, and Javier was uncertain whether he'd rather turn its lashing on his passive generals or on Sacha's bubbling hurt. Even without the witchpower he knew that was what drove his oldest friend, that displacement had pushed Sacha this far, a thing Javier had never dreamt could happen. "What would you have me do, Sacha?" His voice was edged with enough regret to last a lifetime. "I do battle against another who wields the same kind of power. My attacks are stymied, and it seems to me a better use of talent to unite our army so we might fight as one than to wear away my strength in a fight that will only end in a stalemate. I have tried to tell you this."

"The Aulunian heir," Sacha snarled. "How can she share your power, Javier? You can't both be God's chosen. The Pappas has blessed you, and so we know your magic to be God's gift. Hers must be born of a bargain with the devil. This priest dooms us all by urging you to caution. You've got to stop hiding behind his skirts, unleash everything you have, and destroy our enemy. Or do you cling to fear and weakness because you can't trust that your power is God-given?"

"You speak foolishness." Tomas's face flushed with passion. "A day ago we were lost. Today our army is one, and tomorrow our united strength will wage war against the infidels. God's hand is in this."

Javier raised his palm, silencing the priest. "I fight to the best of my talents, Sacha. If I'm weak it's because I've spent a lifetime rejecting this magic, afraid it was a temptation laid before me by the fallen one. With the Pappas's blessing and Tomas's steady hand I can trust it's God who's granted me this skill, and walk unafraid."

"What of us?" Sacha asked, voice low and distorted. "What of those who were your family before this magic came to life, before this priest came to your side? How can you not trust us, Javi?"

He broke on the last word, sending a lance of pain through Javier. That nickname, *Javi,* was reserved for Sacha alone, a bond between him that he guarded jealously. To hear him use it in company meant he was more uncertain of his place than Javier had ever wanted him to be. "I will always trust you, Sacha. How can you doubt that?" His own voice dropped as low as Sacha's had. "Can you not forgive the part of me that needs the priest's faith and guidance? It's never meant I don't need you, my friend. It only means I need him, too."

Betrayal rose up in Sacha so quickly it swept over Javier like the riptide, pulling him down and drowning him in it. "You *need* us," Sacha snarled. "The priest is only a crutch. Damn you, Javier, what must I do to show you?"

BELINDA WALTER

Witchpower, heavy as thunder in the air, rubbed Belinda's skin as, confident in her invisibility, she slipped through the last few guards and pup tents that made up the body of the Ecumenic army. The royal tents, the strategy centres, and the accommodations for high-ranking military lay beyond the common area. Of all of them, one was largest and cleanest, and that was the one she made her way to. She would have known it as her quarry had she been blind, such was the power building there, and she tightened the stillness around her before entering, making certain she would remain unseen until she had well and truly studied and understood the situation within.

She pushed aside the tent door in time to watch Sacha Asselin draw blade and fling himself toward Javier de Castille.

21

Love, in the end, tells all.

Belinda Primrose ought not be in this room at this moment, but she is, and every part of her that is thinking and rational knows she should let this game play out. But that's not the part of her that acts: that part is, perhaps, Beatrice Irvine, who is divorced from the truths Belinda's come to know, and whose heart still beats too fast at the thought of a ginger-haired prince coming to her bed. Belinda has fallen, fallen further than she knew, because the queen's bastard would let Javier die, but the woman she is now slams a witchpower shield around the young king, and throws all her strength behind it, so there's nothing left for herself.

And realises, less than a breath later, how very badly she's chosen.

Marius is there, suddenly, terribly: a physical shield far more visible than the one she's offered. Marius is there, between king and killer, and Belinda's scream isn't the only one to fill the war tent. The sound Marius himself makes is dreadful, a gasp of pain and surprise so soft Belinda shouldn't be able to hear it, especially under her own scream; especially under the bull's bellow of horror and rage that Sacha Asselin shouts out. His back's to Belinda, blocking his hands, blocking Marius's belly, but she knows there's blood there, draining the colour from Marius's face.

Guardsmen are there now, between Belinda and the others, swords raised to strike at Sacha, and Belinda is reminded of Ilyana's death, six months ago in a Gallic courtroom. Sacha will die the same way, skewered by long blades, and the only sorrow she has is that she doesn't wield them herself. Her heart has stopped: stopped, she thinks, the moment she entered the tent, and it may never beat again.

But she's wrong, and the contraction that comes next is the most painful thing she's ever known, gutting her, cutting her own throat, weakening whatever strength she had.

Because another scream belongs to Eliza Beaulieu, who has somehow got herself between Sacha and the guards. She staggers now, white-faced, under the plunge of their swords. One man struck from on high, cutting down from her shoulder at such an angle that it can barely have missed her heart; the other has struck through her gut, the same kind of blow that Marius has taken for his king.

The three of them, two men and a woman, fall to their knees, so slowly as to be a dance. There's grace inherent in this death, but only for a moment. Marius, perhaps, knows what Eliza's done; Sacha does not, and his howls are for the man he holds in his arms, his dying friend. One of the guards, horrified, yanks his sword back, and Eliza screams again, folding herself over the blade that's left, the one thrust into her belly. That guard has let his sword go, has fallen to his knees himself in apologetic supplication, and Belinda has the momentary clear thought that he pulled the strength of his blow, else he'd have driven through Eliza and pinned her to Sacha, taking both their lives. She wants to commend his swiftness in doing so, but even if she could draw breath beyond the icy cut of horror in her own throat, she knows he's killed the beautiful Gallic woman. There is nothing to commend.

All of this, all of it, has taken almost three seconds.

Javier de Castille

It was inconceivable that Sacha could lift a blade against him. If Javier had any clear thought, it was that: Sacha *could not* raise a blade against him, and therefore must mean it for someone else.

Tomas, who stood at his right hand. Tomas, whose faith strengthened his; Tomas, toward whom Sacha's shoulders were squared. It was the smallest thing in the world, and yet it was everything: those

few inches in difference between where Tomas stood and where
Javier did. No one else could possibly see it; their stances were
wrong. They would see a friend displaced by a priest, outraged at
his fall in status, determined to take vengeance on the man who
had belittled him. They would see a king in danger, and think nothing of those around him.

He had so very little witchpower left at his disposal, but it was
enough to throw a shield around Tomas del'Abbate. It was easy, in
fact, guarding a single man after days of protecting an army. Nothing, not even the largest cannon Aulun might bring against them,
could shatter that shield; Tomas, standing at Javier's side, was utterly
safe.

By the time Javier understood that he should have wrapped
everyone in witchpower, shielded them all from one another, refused them the ability to move, it was much too late.

Marius had been no more than a few feet away; Javier knew that
in the same way he knew where his right hand was. It was a mark
of his own shock that he didn't know Marius would lurch forward
until it was already done; clear thought might have told him he
would do such a thing. It was a graceless act, desperation leaving
beauty far behind, and it seemed impossible that the merchant man
could move as fast as he had, or that the end result of such quick-
ness would be a soft wet sound and a point changing the shape of
his shirt in the back.

Metal rasped around the room, promise that someone would die
as the price of an attempt on another life.

Sacha would die for the attempt of taking another life.

A woman had screamed in that first moment, when Sacha had
thrown himself into action. Eliza, the only woman there, and out of
all his old friends, she's the one Javier might have imagined could
move so quickly and so smoothly. She was a guttersnipe and a thief,
and needed all the grace and speed at her disposal.

Her second scream was full of pain, a wholly different sound
than the first one, and it made no sense. Not until Sacha, horror
stricken across his face, crashed to his knees with Marius in his
arms, and Eliza, behind him, fell just a little more slowly. Two guards
stood beyond her, one with a bloody blade lifted in his hand and

shock greying his skin, and the other empty-handed and staring at the sword stuck through Eliza's gut as if he didn't understand how it got there.

Javier's heart went cold and still in his chest, a weight of iron bent on killing him, and soundlessness rushed through his ears. The world was nothing more than those five figures: Marius, dying. Sacha, a murderer. Eliza, dying. Two guards, bewildered, who in doing their duty in protecting their king, had surely written themselves a death sentence.

All of it, *all* of it, had taken perhaps three seconds, and no more.

Tomas fell to his knees as though he, too, had been gutted, but his attentions were for Marius, whom Sacha would not release. "Give him to me, *give him to me,*" the priest demanded, "give them both here, their last rites must be given before God takes them home."

Javier said, "No," and Sacha said, "Both?," each of them in the same numb tone, and under it, Marius whispered, "Eliza," to Sacha, pain aging his voice. He coughed blood and drew a ragged breath before whispering, "How strange, that. The two of you in rivalry over her so long, and yet it's me she'll go with at the end. Liz, oh, Liza, our sister."

There were guards in the way, men trying to pull Sacha off Marius, trying to make order from the chaos in the room. Somewhere outside of Javier's immediate awareness he knew people still shouted, still screamed; that soldiers were flooding the tent and shoving people aside, trying to protect their king. He pushed them all away with a gentleness born from incomprehension and disbelief: witchpower rolled out of him and extended the shield he'd built for Tomas, until it encompassed king and priest and three people whose friendship lay bleeding out onto thirsty ground. Tumultuous noise faded, and, as though the sound itself had kept him on his feet, Javier knelt, far more slowly than had any of the others who had fallen.

Sacha twisted, tears tracking clean white lines through dust and mud staining his face, and gave a cry like a dying stag when he saw Eliza crumpled over a sword. He reached for her and Marius slipped in his arms, begetting another cry, and Javier, full of cool horror, put a hand on Sacha's shoulder to keep him still. Eliza seemed not to breathe, but Marius still took short, pained gasps. Tears stained his temples, too, falling back into his hair and making his eyes so bright they seemed full of life, not death. Javier bent over him, struggling for words as hot water dripped from his eyes. He ached from his very core, agony radiating out, and could only loathe the weakness that thought himself in pain when Marius lay dying.

"You have deserved so much better than what I've given you," he managed to whisper. "I'm sorry, Marius. I'm sorry." And then, out of weakness, because he should be looking to Marius's hurts, not salving his own, he asked, "*Why?*" and wondered if he wanted to know the answer.

"My king." Marius shuddered. "My brother. My friend. Always, Jav. Always. You need . . . Tomas's faith. Couldn't let him die."

Javier closed his hand on Marius's so hard it hurt even him, but Marius gave no sign of new pain, only turned his head a little toward Tomas, who whispered ancient rites even as tears spilled down his own face. "Take care of him, priest. Take . . ."

"Marius. *Marius! Eliza!*" Words turned to insensible shouts as Javier bent over Marius's still form, then in a panic released him and scrambled toward Eliza, sick with anticipation and despair. Tomas let go a hoarse cry and reached after him as though to pull him back from an even-greater blow, but his fingers slid off Javier's shirt, and Javier came, on hands and knees, to Eliza's side.

Came to find the sword taken from his lover's belly, and to find, impossibly, Belinda Primrose on her knees beside Eliza's body, her wrists bloody and forearms strained over hands hidden in Eliza's gut. She withdrew one hand from Eliza's wounds and seized his wrist with bloody fingers, rage and determination turning her hazel eyes to fiery green as she whispered, "I can save her. *I can save her, Javier. Lend me your power.*"

BELINDA WALTER

Something screamed inside Belinda, white-hot and bloody, scoring her innards and rendering them blazing streaks of pain, nothing more and nothing less. Marius Poulin should not be dead, not in any world that had any kindness to it at all, and that she, *she,* of all people, should think the world owed anyone a bit of kindness, said how deeply her fury ran. Not since childhood had she dreamt there were such things as fairness and unfairness, not since Lorraine the queen had ridden away from Robert's household leaving Belinda still a secret, forbidden the chance to meet the icon of the Aulunian throne. It was neither fair nor unfair: it only was, and each day of every man's existence passed in such simplicity.

But it was *not fair* that Marius Poulin, whose greatest sin was loving those who were unworthy of it, was dead, and Belinda Primrose would not, *would not,* let another confidant die from the jealousies born of an unfair world.

God, it would be better, it would be easier, with Dmitri there; with his ineffable understanding of the smallest components of human flesh, with his rich black power hers to command. She was brutish in healing; Dmitri'd told her that, and she had no reason to doubt it. Even now the ghosts of his understanding teased at the edges of her mind, incomprehensible and tantalising. He'd thought in terms of delicacy, layering one level of healing over another until the whole became whole again, and there in the dirt and blood in Javier's tent, Belinda struggled for the same light touch.

And failed. She knew little enough of failure, really: to do so now reminded her of her youth, when she'd begun the game of stillness. She'd failed more often than not in the beginning, flinching when she cut herself with her tiny dagger, crying out when fire raised a blister on her hand. Success had come over months and years of practise, but Eliza had seconds, minutes at most, and Belinda would never become the healing artist that Dmitri was, not in that time; perhaps not ever.

Stopping the flow of blood was easy, no more than capping witchpower in broken places, just another use of a shield. But then the blood backed up, mixed with things it shouldn't, and even with her hands buried in Eliza's belly Belinda couldn't imagine the fine level of detail that Dmitri had used to heal and excite her. She used great sloppy stitches instead, forcing things together and melding them, *melting* them, with the heat of witchpower. It would work; it had to work. She could command a storm; she had to be able to heal a single woman.

Through blood, through sweat and dirt and viscera, a familiar scent caught her attention, and, enraged, Belinda lifted her eyes to meet Javier de Castille's shocked silver gaze.

Time turned to nothing, a bolt of understanding outlining Belinda's thoughts so sharply she thought the tent might come alight with it. She was the creature of stillness, of internally focused power, and Javier the one whose lifetime of witchpower practise had taught him to overrun the will of those around him.

But she had commanded the storm, a vast and violent and profoundly external thing, and it was Javier who had learnt the subtlety of influencing people in such a way that they didn't so much as recognise what he'd done; it was Javier who had changed his own shields so they were wide and strong enough to guard an army. It was delicacy on an enormous scale, shaped in a way that even she'd been unable to break through.

Two halves of a whole, she thought, with furious clarity. Each of them with strengths the other lacked. Feeling afire with rage, she took a hand from Eliza's gut and seized Javier's wrist with bloody fingers. "I can save her. I can save her, Javier. *Lend me your power.*"

For the shorter part of eternity, he resisted. Belinda felt the struggle, so deep and clear that under other circumstances she might have laughed. Wisdom told Javier to command her capture and her death; but then, wisdom had loosened its hold on Javier de Castille in this time and place. His friend was dead and his lover lay dying, and intellect crumbled before the terrified hope that Belinda Primrose, creature of lies that she was, might this once be telling the truth.

Even she, manipulator and murderer, might have risked trusting herself this once, because if she failed, she'd pay for it with her life. She might well pay for success with her life, too, but with the memory of Marius's heartbreak and gentleness in her mind, she could, she *would,* do nothing less.

And Javier, as though he might have in turn read those thoughts and intentions from her, capitulated in totality, and opened channels of silver power to her for the taking.

Their familiarity snatched Belinda's breath, and she wasn't certain if she knew his power so well because she'd grown up in her own under his tutelage, or if she had known it from before birth, when they'd shared a small red room of safe rumblings and warmth. Memory didn't stretch so far back; no, she remembered that warm dark place as barely a dream, one from which she awoke into cold brightness and warnings that shaped her life, but the dream was only that, with no surety to it.

It didn't matter. What mattered was she knew his power, and he hers, and that sharing it—aye, sharing it, rather than the thieving she'd done with Dmitri's—bloomed and opened a fineness of control that Belinda'd never known with her own talent. There was so little to Javier's power that it startled her: he was worn thin, her brother, had pushed himself to the edges of what he could do, in order to keep his people safe. Belinda admired him as much as she felt disdain: even in her worst moments she forbade herself the weakness she felt in Javier now.

But their sharing went two ways, with her witchpower flooding to fill what Javier had lost. He drew a breath that seemed to make him larger, and because she came to this meeting with the intention of holding nothing back, the gold of her magic folded under and came up again silver, one need fed by another.

Javier had no more learning or understanding of healing than she did, but his implacable will had a feather-light touch to it. Teeth buried in her lip, Belinda subsumed her broad impulse beneath the delicacy of Javier's power, searching for a way to communicate what Dmitri had taught her.

The will to offer, it seemed, became the offering: Javier grasped a concept that slipped from Belinda's mind, that small things made up even the liquid of blood, and that to heal they must be bound back together. She was out of control, heat building under her hands, silver power raging through her as blood stretched and reached and stuck to itself, and then tissue and muscle and skin on top of it. It felt like the building of a wildfire, one she couldn't pull away from, and when it erupted it was with a sharp cry torn from Eliza Beaulieu's throat.

Eliza surged upward with the strength of a newborn foal, clumsy and desperate to be on her feet. Javier caught her, his voice a sob, and Eliza crushed her eyes shut as she held on for a few brief seconds. Belinda sagged, hands planted in the mud, head dropped, and disentangled herself from Javier's silver power. She knew she should draw the stillness close, cloak herself from the noisy, fascinated onlookers. Instead she sat where she was, head hanging, half-seeing Javier and Eliza pressed against each other, and seeing, far more clearly, Marius's still and silent body just beyond them.

There was another man, too, young and strong-jawed, with black curling hair and eyes that had looked too long into the sun: its golden light seemed burned into his soul. He wore a priest's cassock and an expression of both love and despair as he looked on Javier de Castille and Eliza Beaulieu. A note of sympathy struck itself and became a chord within Belinda's breast, and that was absurd enough to get a tiny, harsh laugh from her. To find herself in commiseration with a Cordulan priest over the heart of a man they were forbidden to have was too rich and bitter for words.

"Sacha?" Eliza's question, small and raw, feared the answer.

Misery twisted Javier's features as he set her back a few inches. "Alive. But Marius, Liz . . ."

Bewilderment struck home and Eliza pulled away to see Marius's body. The sound she made scraped Belinda's spine and took up residence at the base of her skull, a low moan of sickness that would never leave her. Belinda stuffed bloody fingers against her mouth, trying to keep from echoing it.

"He died protecting—"

"Me," the priest said thickly. "He died protecting me."

"And I—" Only then did the fact of her well-being raise confusion in Eliza's voice. She made a fist at her belly, fingers clutching her bloody shirt as she searched for the injuries that should have taken her life. "Javier?" Confusion edged her voice toward panic. Emotion ran raw and red over all of them until Belinda wanted to weep with it, but her eyes were dry and hot, refusing tears. One hand dropped back to the earth, scraping dirt away, as though she might dig herself a grave to lie in and let the world's misery pass her by. Marius should not be dead; it was a cruelty not even she wanted to face.

"Belinda saved you." Javier spoke with a terrible neutrality, so calm that Belinda knew he, too, could bear no more crushing emotion and only retained the edges of sanity by refusing to look at or believe what was going on around him. She could share his pain if she wanted to, reach out with witchpower and know what he felt, but instead pulled magic into herself and held it in as small and tight a knot as she could. Her own heart felt of nails driven into flesh each time it beat; she had no need to experience that same feeling in those around her.

Eliza's delicate beauty fell to pieces beneath tears reddening her eyes and streaking her face. The expression she turned on Belinda was mystified, so confused as to forget anger; that, Belinda had no doubt, would come soon enough.

She heard herself say, "Marius was too far away," as though it would explain everything, and opened a hand in a plea for forgiveness. That was a betraying action, a weakness, and she ought not have permitted it. But the world had been turned awry, and it was months now since she'd hidden all the things she was meant to hide. Dull with grief, she turned her gaze on Javier. "I need to speak with you, king of Gallin, soon and in private."

"Are you mad?" Eliza's despair turned to anger inside a heartbeat, so swift Belinda felt envy: she would give much to have a target to lash out at, a target such as she herself provided for Eliza and no doubt would for Javier. "You come here, *here,* after what you've done, and you think any of us will let you be alone with Javier? Why not cut his throat ourselves?" Her lovely face blotched as her eyes swelled with tears born as much from rage as sorrow. "Why not just let Sacha—" She broke then, sobs hiccuping through her speech.

Belinda lowered her gaze, acknowledging Eliza's rightness, then looked back at Javier. They were all still kneeling in the mud, kings and royal heirs and street rats alike, all of them brought low and made level by the one constant companion Belinda had known since her twelfth year. Death gave no quarter and no care, coming for all of them in its own time.

"Please," she said, and wondered when the last time she'd said that word outside of playing a role had been. Not within easy memory, and that may well have meant never at all. "You know I wouldn't be here if I didn't have to be, Javier."

Javier whispered, "That name is not yours to call me by," but there was no conviction in his anger, sorrow still too heavy upon him. "You will be my prisoner," he said, and then, bitterly, "Can I keep you?" which, not long ago and asked another way, might have spasmed hope through Belinda's heart.

Now, though, she only shrugged and shook her head. "Perhaps, if it's all you were given over to doing, but I haven't come to offer you that kind of challenge. Put me in chains if you wish. The only thing I won't let you do is take my life."

She looked to Marius and closed her eyes against his death, as though doing so might wipe away her knowledge of it. "I would . . ." It took a second try, a wetting of her lips and a rough hurtful clearing of her throat, to whisper, "I would stand at his grave while he's buried, if you'd let me. I . . . cared for him, Javier. I would not have seen this done."

"No." Javier's harsh reply lanced misery through Belinda's belly. He had every right, every reason, to turn her away from Marius's grave, and yet somehow she'd imagined he would show her that small compassion.

It was a mercy she'd in no way earned. Sandalia's petite form swam behind Belinda's eyelids, vivacious and full of life; she would have been stricken and blue with pain, fingers clawed at her throat and eyes bulged with poison, when she died. No, Belinda deserved no quarter and no kindness, not in any way that Javier could take from her. She was lucky to still be living, lucky that no overeager guard had stricken her down in the moments of chaos after she arrived, or had taken her head from her shoulders when she'd knelt by Eliza's dying form.

Lucky, in fact, that no one did so now, out of misbegotten or honest duty to their king. Belinda looked up slowly, aware of the noise surrounding them but also, finally, aware that it was heard at a remove, as if all the people pressing so close were in truth a hundred feet away.

Only then, with the searching for it, did she see the silver sheen of witchpower that kept everyone away from the foursome huddled on the floor. It had been there all along, had to have been, in order to keep their conversation and actions untroubled by those around them, and a discordant note shimmered through Belinda's own power. After days of being trapped at the army's leading edge, she'd crossed Javier's witchpower boundary without a whisper of trouble when she'd moved to save Eliza's life. If intent informed Javier of what he would and would not let pass, it seemed strange that she, who had had no plans to cause harm, had been forbidden to come closer to the Cordulan camps.

Javier said "No" again, shaking her from her thoughts, and making her meet his eyes. "I think you wouldn't have seen this done. I think if you had no abhorrence of what's happened here that Eliza would lie dead now, too. For that," he grated, "for that you have your stay of execution, and for Marius's sake you may come to his grave and say your good-byes when the rest of us are done. He would like that, and so for him, I'll give you a last few minutes at his side. And then we'll talk, Belinda Walter. Then we shall have words."

He got to his feet with all the stiffness of an old man. His clothes were ruined, black and red with blood, and he put a hand out for Eliza, whose rise was tremulous and relied on his support. "Take her away from here," he said softly, and no one doubted he spoke of Belinda, not Eliza. "Don't bother binding her. Just take her away, and give her somewhere decent to rest." His mouth curled against the words, as though they were unsavoury but he too much the gentleman to say otherwise. "If you give me cause to regret this. . . ."

Belinda bowed her head and let herself be hauled to her feet by two guards, who jostled her roughly, perhaps trying to make up for having failed Javier already today. Pins and needles stung her feet as she was taken away, and the last she heard from the king of Gallin was a weary, miserable question: "Where has Sacha gone?"

Akilina de Costa, queen of Essandia

Screams from the near distance drive Akilina from the tent she shares with Rodrigo, and good sense kept her from plunging headlong into the chaos erupting in Javier's tent. She is alone, then, as alone as a woman can be in a camp full of soldiers, when Sacha, weeping with blood, staggers from Javier's tent and breaks into a shuffling run, taking himself away from the noise and terror within that tent.

Akilina snaps "Stay here" to her guards, and because one of them is Viktor, they'll listen; Viktor has done nothing but obey the most direct and simple of orders the last six months, and will permit no one within an arm's reach to do otherwise themselves. Her second guard, an Essandian, inhales to protest, looks at the big Khazarian, and, with a sigh, lets Akilina go.

She's already gathered her skirts and begun to run, moving more lithely and quickly than Sacha. Still, they're well beyond the boundaries of the camp when she catches him; the royal tents are set up on the back edge of the line, at the greatest height, so generals and kings alike can watch the battles as they go on below. Forest backs them up, and if it were not for the thin moon in the sky, Akilina might lose Sacha entirely.

But she comes on him in a clearing, fallen to his knees and muttering in words so broken that even her excellent grasp of Gallic is frustrated by them. She breathes, "Sacha?" and touches a hand to his shoulder, as if he's a horse in need of gentling.

He flinches, and she comes around him, kneeling a few feet away, where he can't fall forward and smear blood over her. "Tell me, Sacha," she whispers. "Tell me what's happened."

"It was supposed to be the priest." Sacha's words come clear, and send a sick thrill of worry into Akilina's belly. There are two people it cannot be: it cannot be Javier, and it cannot be Rodrigo. News of their deaths would have flown to her ears even while the screams still went on. The blood is beginning to dry on Sacha's sleeves and chest, and so it is neither king of Gallin nor prince of Essandia. Her heart hangs between beats, unwilling to contract again for fear the sound of doing so will overwhelm Sacha's whispers. "It was supposed to be the priest," he says again, and impatience slams through Akilina.

Her hands claw in front of his chest as though she could pull the words from him, but she tries to keep her voice soothing and soft. "Who is it?"

"Marius," Sacha whispers, and crumbles on himself, sobs wracking his body.

Relief sags Akilina. Marius is no one, except a king's friend. His death means nothing to her. All she needs is a certainty that Sacha won't compromise her when he confesses to the reasons behind attacking the priest.

More's the pity that she's unarmed. She might easily have made a story of how she saw Javier's oldest friend running from the chaos and out of concern followed him, only to face his killing rage and be forced to defend herself. But she reminds herself that it's better that the Essandian queen should have no blood on her hands, and instead takes another tactic in silencing his tongue. "Sacha. Sacha, listen to me. My heart aches for your loss, Sacha. I wish it had gone as we meant. But you must run or you must be prepared to face their wrath."

"*I.*" Sacha spits the word through his tears. "Why not *we,* lady? Why should I not condemn you when I face Javier? Had you not whispered treachery against the priest in my ear—"

Akilina whispers, "Because the babe is yours, Sacha, and condemning me means your son won't sit on the Essandian throne."

Sacha Asselin's every movement stops: he doesn't breathe, he doesn't blink, he doesn't sway where he kneels in the soft earth. He only stares at Akilina, utterly arrested, and for a moment she wonders if apoplexy will take him and he'll collapse.

Then the pulse in his throat flutters, so hard that she can see it even in the moonlight, and he draws a breath that sounds sharp as knives. "How do I know this isn't a trick to save your own neck?" Despair's gone from his voice, replaced with something so harsh that Akilina thinks her skin might disintegrate under the sound.

"You don't," she says, trusting a raw show of truth to score him more deeply than charm or dissembling. "You don't, but you've suspected since the beginning, and the chance that I'm telling the truth is too high for you to risk damning me. You're Javier's oldest friend, and you drew on a priest, not on him. He won't have you put to death, not even if Cordula demands it. You may lose stature, but in the worst of all worlds you can become an ambassador to Essandia, and play uncle to your son. He'll love you," she whispers, "and he'll be born to a throne. Is my denunciation worth that price?"

Sacha's shoulders slump and his expression turns dull with hatred for a moment. "Are you a witch, Akilina? Does the devil guide your steps and leave you unscathed in the worst of moments? Sandalia dead at your feet, and a crown to wear for it. Marius dead by my hand, and an heir to pay for him. Javier's power makes him weak and needy of a priest, but I wonder now if that's not a safer bargain to make than dealing with you."

Akilina gathers her skirts and stands, wishing Sacha were not covered in blood. She would have him, otherwise, let him bury himself in her in despair and shame and desperation, and with that passion bind him to her ever more strongly. She is not a witch, not in the way of folklore, but she's a woman of strength and ambition, and that, in the end, may be the same thing. "Plead a madness of jealousy," she says, rather than answer his questions. "You've been Javier's friend all his life, and many will sympathise with a displacement that drove you wild. Javier's guilt will hold him more closely to your side, and the priest will lose some of his hold. In the end you'll guide Javier and in time you'll guide your son, and hold power behind two Echonian thrones. Come back to the camp before dawn, Sacha. I'm sure they'll bury your friend at sunrise, and he deserves for you to be there. But tell no one I found you tonight; what we have, you and I, must be kept a secret."

She turns and walks back through the forest, leaving Sacha Asselin alone with his thoughts.

22

JAVIER DE CASTILLE, KING OF GALLIN
25 June 1588 † Brittany; the Gallic camp

Cannon roared with the first light of dawn, lead balls smashing through troops on both sides of the war, and for the first time in days, Javier did nothing to mitigate their strength or damage.

He had slept, but only because his body was weak: his heart wanted to stay awake, as if refusing sleep would somehow refuse the truth of Marius's death. As if, if he faced the morning without rest, he would be rewarded for vigilance by Marius's return. But neither had happened; he'd slumped over Marius's body, tears staining the shroud until exhaustion claimed him, and when he woke it was to his friend's cold, unmoving form, and to his own lack of stomach for further war.

A pity, that, and he knew it, for what he'd set in motion wasn't going to end with an easy suit for peace. It would go on until either the Aulunian crown sat on his head, or he was dead. A numb place sat inside him where ambition had burned: nothing was worth this cost, not even Sandalia's vengeance, and yet now the price was paid, and nothing could be done but to carry on.

Eliza was curled at his side, a weary ball of heat, like a kitten searching for comfort, but he had none to offer her. He'd wakened her with a touch to her hair, and before she earned so much as an early-morning smile, tears filled her eyes and she put her nose into his ribs, each of them holding on as though answers or relief might be found in clinging to each other.

THE PRETENDER'S CROWN · 351

Tomas found them that way when he came for Marius. They three and Rodrigo, who joined them as the sun broke the horizon, lifted the shrouded body together, and went a silent, heartbroken trudge to the hilltop grave that had been dug in the night. Akilina waited there at a respectful distance, present but not intruding on a grief she wasn't fool enough to pretend was her own. The gondola boy, unexpectedly, was nearby as well, unrelenting misery twisting his features, though he'd clearly forbidden himself permission to cry. Javier's heart knocked as though he'd been hit, suddenly close to coming undone by a child determined to be a man in the face of sorrow.

He looked away from the boy to find Tomas waiting on him, waiting for a signal that Javier couldn't yet give. He turned half-blind eyes to the hills and the horizon, waiting himself, waiting for a thing he wasn't certain would come to pass.

"There." Eliza's voice came softly, little in it but grief and exhaustion. Javier looked for the shadow she saw and found it: Sacha, whose arrival tore at Javier's heart. He should be there; he should be there because Marius was his friend and for penance, and at the same time a black rage rose up in Javier that he dared to attend. Eliza touched his hand, and he loosened the fist it had made. Loosened it, because he feared what a fist might do when Sacha got too close, and because Marius wouldn't want them fighting over his grave. Marius wouldn't harbour the rage that clenched Javier's own heart; Marius would call it all a mistake, and find a way to forgive. Javier couldn't bring that much kindness to the fore, and only gave Tomas a fractured nod, inviting, commanding, him to begin.

There was no comfort in ancient words of ritual, or in the quiet recitation of the things that had made up Marius Poulin's life. Tears burned Javier's eyes and made his stomach sick, but wouldn't fall; he could not, it seemed, allow himself that weakness in face of morning's light. Marius would have cried; Marius had always been softer. Eliza stood beside him silently; only her quick gasps for steady breaths told him her tears fell. Sacha, standing a little distance away, was dry-eyed and haunted, and that, Javier thought, was as it should be. And Rodrigo, well, Rodrigo was there out of respect, and his expression was steady and grim. No one else attended; no one else had the right, so far as Javier was concerned.

He bent to cast the first handful of dirt into the grave himself, its thump and rattle the most final and dreadful sound he'd ever encountered. They worked together then, two monarchs and a priest and a guttersnipe, to fill in Marius's grave, and all the while Javier felt Sacha's aching gaze on his back. Even if Javier'd made the offer, there weren't enough shovels: this was not a duty their friendship's fourth would be allowed to participate in. That was a cost of what he'd done, and Javier counted it low enough indeed.

When the grave was fresh earth mounded high, Rodrigo put a hand on Javier's shoulder, not trying to make words fit a space where silence said enough. Then he called Tomas to him and walked away, joining Akilina before taking their leave of the three remaining friends. The gondola boy walked a few steps with them, head lifted as if he were royalty's equal, then took himself in another direction. Only when they were gone did Sacha edge forward, uncertain of his welcome.

"You should have been with us last night, to sit vigil." Javier spoke to the raw dirt, and barely knew his own voice, strain making him sound like an old man.

Sacha turned his face away as though he'd been hit, eyes closed and his answer dull. "I was afraid."

"You should have been," Javier said again, and this time wasn't sure if he meant to repeat his first sentiment, or if he was in agreement with Sacha's fear. "Go away, Sacha. I'm telling myself Marius would want us to drink to his memory together, that he'd consider what has happened to be nothing more than a terrible, forgivable mistake, but I am not Marius. I am not that good. Go away, fight in this war, and when I have the stomach for it I'll see you again. You are forbidden to die valiantly," he added in a whisper. "You will live, Sacha Asselin. You will survive, because death is too easy a path for you."

"Javier—"

"Do you think it makes it *better*?" Javier thundered, all too sure of what protest his oldest friend would make. "Is it *all right* that you meant that knife for Tomas and not for me? That Marius died to save my faith rather than my life? You attempted one murder and accomplished another, Sacha, and do you think that's *acceptable*? You live, and live free, because you are my oldest friend, and for no other reason. Any other man would be arrested, would be hanged or beheaded as fitted his rank, for what you have done. Do not test me with your explanations and your excuses. I'll have Madame Poulin to answer to," he finished in a whisper. "Give me no reason, no reason *at all,* Sacha, to hand her the vengeance she'll rightfully demand."

Sacha bowed, the deepest and most honest genuflection Javier had ever seen from him, then spun and ran, rough long steps taking him toward the battlefields. Eliza, silent, came to Javier's side to put her hand in his, and he flinched. "Don't. Don't tell me I was too harsh, Liz, don't—"

"No." She tightened her fingers around his until they both trembled from her grip. "I wouldn't even if you were, not with Marius d—" A gasp swallowed her last word and she began again elsewhere, rather than give voice and therefore a kind of acceptance to the matter. "If he was anyone else I'd have seen him dead before dawn. But because it's Sacha it would only make it all the worse. We'll find no justice in this."

"Did I . . ." Javier swallowed, wanting to unask the question before it had more than begun. But it was too late: giving it any voice at all had let it form fully in his mind, and it would gnaw at him if it went unspoken. "Did I do this, Eliza? Is this my fault?"

He wanted her *no* to come quickly enough to absolve him. Instead she stood quiet, looking at Marius's grave, and finally sighed. "Part of me wants to say yes, Jav. To lay the blame somewhere. But I'm not sure you did. We've been together so long that it's not easy for any of us to watch you need another. You must know that. I only bore Beatrice out of love for you and at your explicit request. Marius . . . felt displaced by Tomas, but he was kinder than I am. Than Sacha is. He saw, perhaps, that Tomas offered you something that we secular three couldn't, and I think he didn't . . ."

"Hate me for it?" Javier asked thickly.

Eliza nodded. "He understood. His loyalty to you was unshakable."

"I thought Sacha's was, too."

"Sacha's always been more jealous." Eliza's fingers were cold in

Javier's. "Jealous of me, jealous of your crown, jealous of Marius's money, for all that he's noble-born."

"I'd think you'd have been jealous of Marius's wealth, if any of us were," Javier whispered, more to keep his mind from burgeoning guilt than conviction of his words' truth.

Eliza chuckled, soft sound made mostly of sorrow. "I had so little that there was no room for envy when you gave me so much. If anything haunted me, it was the fear it would prove as my father thought it would, too good and with too high a price. I had nothing to lose. Sacha saw himself as having everything to lose. Sees himself, perhaps, and so seeing a fifth come into our friendship . . . Beatrice was easier. She was only a woman. But Tomas is a man, and worse, awakened the ambition, or the will, in you, to do the things that Sacha's long since agitated for. No," she finally said, quietly. "I don't think you did this, Javier. You might have been able to stop it, but . . ."

"But?"

Eliza straightened her shoulders, lifted her chin, small signs that told Javier he would have been better pleased had he not asked, because she would answer with a truth he wouldn't like. And she did, after taking a measured breath. "You have blindnesses, Jav. Maybe born of your rank, maybe born of your power, I don't know. There's an arrogance about you, an assumption of your infallibility, and a—"

"I am not perfect, Eliza." Javier's voice cracked in horror. "I've spent a lifetime *afraid* of my fallibility—"

"You've spent a lifetime afraid the witchpower was the devil's gift, and afraid that giving in to it was the path to damnation. I'm talking about something else. You're self-centered, my love, and it makes you bad at reading the hearts of those around you. You asked," she added even more gently, then shook her head. "Maybe you could have seen this thing being shaped, maybe you could have stopped it, but maybe any of us could have and none of us did. I wouldn't lay the blame at your feet, but at Sacha's, if it must be laid. I think you would come back to us," Eliza whispered. "I believe that in the end you will always come back to us, because we know you better than anyone else. Sacha's jealousies and fears took that belief away from him, until Tomas's death seemed the only possible course. We've all paid." She closed her eyes and put her temple against Javier's shoulder as she drew a tired breath. "We've all paid. There's no use salting the wounds."

"Aren't you angry, Liz?"

"Of course I am." She turned her face into his shoulder. "But I'm more afraid of what becomes of us if we let the anger eat us whole. I don't want to become what Sacha's become."

"You're good for me, Liz." Javier put his arm around her and buried his nose in her hair, willing tears not to fall at the familiar scent of her. "It took me too long to see it, but you're good for me."

"I know." Eliza tipped her chin up to give him a watery smile, then wrapped her fingers at his elbow and gave him a heartless tug. "Come away for a little while. You promised one other the chance to say good-bye."

BELINDA WALTER

Given that she was in essence a prisoner of war, Belinda spent the night in surprising comfort. Better by far than the last time she'd been a guest of the Castille family: then she'd huddled in the darkness of an oubliette, stripped naked and awaiting a dawn that would surely see her dead. By comparison the small guarded tent and bedroll she'd been given were luxury, and she made no attempt to escape or slip away from her tent to listen and learn what she could of the Cordulan camps. War rarely offered the chance for uninterrupted rest, and yet she slept soundly as a child while in the heart of an enemy camp.

She awakened to the sunrise cutting through a gap in the tent walls. Cannon roared in the distance: her army was wasting none of the long summer day in making war. A boyish voice, familiar but displaced, spoke outside the tent, his Gallic broken yet full of confidence. A moment later the tent door flew open and a child walked in, slim and strong and haloed by the sunrise, making him unearthly and beautiful.

Then her jaw dropped and her eyes goggled, an expression Belinda felt mirrored on his own face as the boy blurted "Fine lady?"

in Parnan, and then repeated the words in a gleeful crow: "Fine lady! You have come all the way from the city of canals to see me! See how brave and handsome I am, and my banner that I carry for Cordula!"

He whipped a length of fabric from his waist, unmaking a belt and turning it into a long flag marked with Cordula's red cross of war. He draped it across his shoulders and struck a pose, chin lifted and gaze distant with pride before excitement caught him again. "The king tells me to fetch the woman to visit the grave, but he has never said the woman is my friend! I told the man nothing," he said, eyes still wide but now serious. "The blade-faced man who came to look for you, lady; I told him nothing of you. I am very brave, no? And you will walk with me now so all of this strange dry country can see that I have the love of a fine lady for my handsomeness and my bravery."

"But what are you doing here?" Belinda asked beneath his rush of words, and despite everything, despite the deaths, despite the lies, despite the truths she'd learned, despite all of it, she laughed, and sat up from her bedroll to haul the gondola boy into a rough hug. Oh, she didn't know herself, didn't know the woman who would let herself do such a thing, but for a moment within the madness of the world she clung to a momentary gift of joy. "You shouldn't be here," she whispered into his hair. "There's a war on, and a boy so handsome and brave as yourself should be far away, safe in his boat on the canals. Your father will be missing you, my friend. Or will your eight brothers and sisters be enough to keep him from noticing you're gone?"

"Fourteen," the boy said into her bosom, happily.

Belinda laughed as she set him back, countering with, "Twelve," and he shrugged with all the good nature in the world.

"What is one boy out of so many? He will miss the coin I bring in, but there is one less mouth to feed, and when I go home I will have tales of making friends with the king of Gallin, and many other beautiful people, too." Some of his mirth fell away, leaving brown eyes large and sad. "But one of them is dead, fine lady. Marius, who was kind to me, is dead."

"Yes." Tightness caught Belinda's throat and she coughed, trying to clear it. "Yes. He was kind to me, too. Javi—the pri—the king . . ." She trailed off, the boy's tumble of words finally coming home to her. "The blade-faced man?"

Worry spasmed across the child's face. "He came in the coldest month, just after the new year. He looked for you, told me your face and your dress and your manner, but I said nothing to him except lies, fine lady." He faltered, then looked away, guilt as clear as the worry of seconds earlier.

"What did he want?" Belinda's heart had become a hammer in her chest, determined to break through bone and fall to the floor a betraying, beating thing.

"To know who paid me to meet you," the boy whispered. "To know the name you went by, and to know who you met when in my beautiful city. I lied to him, fine lady. I told him nothing."

Just after the new year. Belinda closed her eyes, thoughts flying ahead of words, making leaps that had little to do with what the child had said and everything to do with what he kept from her.

Secrets learned in Aria Magli just after the new year could come by pigeon within a week to Lutetia. A pigeon could carry word of Belinda Primrose, called Rosa, and of Robert Drake, who had paid this boy to find Belinda and ferry her through the canals. A bird could carry all those stories and more to Akilina Pankejeff, who had stripped Beatrice Irvine away and left Belinda Primrose naked on the Lutetian palace's courtroom floor eleven days after the new year began.

She had thought herself betrayed by a kiss shared with a courtesan, but heartbreak had not moved Ana di Meo against her. No, the cards had fallen another way, and now, unasked for, she learned the truth of the pattern they'd made. It shouldn't take her so hard; the *how* hardly mattered now. Yet she couldn't help but look through the glass that warped the life she knew from the one that might have been. Had she silenced the boy when she left his gondola, the world she now walked through might have been a very different one.

"He came back," Belinda said quietly. All her delight had drained away, leaving her to feel untethered, as though she floated on a slow and inexorable river of fate. "This blade-faced man came back, and because you are brave, very brave, but not stupid, when he came back you told him what he wanted to know. I'm surprised he let you live." She shouldn't let him live: should wrap her slim fingers around his throat and crush the life from him, rectifying a mistake made months ago.

"My friend was there," the boy said miserably. "He is a gypsy man and clever and quick, and the blade-faced man looked at him and decided no, that I was too small a thing to matter. I'm sorry, fine lady. I'm sorry."

Belinda touched the boy's hair, numb with a grief that came from somewhere deeper even than Marius's death. "So am I."

"Will you kill me now?" He straightened his shoulders, made himself look unafraid and accepting, and an ache took Belinda's breath from her.

"No." Once she would have: perhaps even so recently as a day earlier, she would have. But she could see no reason for it now; the boy had owed her nothing, and had done more to protect her than reason dictated. In the end, he'd done what he'd had to survive, and she was too familiar with the weight of such decisions. "No," she said again, and swallowed against a tight throat. "You've answered questions for me, told me how the blade-faced man's mistress found me so she could work against me. I'm to be queen of Aulun someday, did you know that?"

The boy's jaw dropped again and he shook his head, making what Belinda had thought of as rhetoric into a weighty confession of its own. "Queens and kings," he whispered. "And I only a gondola boy. How did I come to this place, fine lady? How am I part of it all? How can that be?"

Belinda laughed again, a tiny fractured sound. "So you can be impressed after all. I thought such a fine brave handsome boy as yourself thought all of this only natural. I don't know," she added far more quietly. "I don't know, only that this world is smaller than it once was, and perhaps even queens and kings need a forthright and sensible gondola boy to see the world with. I'll be queen," she breathed, "and a queen can grant a pardon. Please." She got up and put her hand out to the boy, calling witchpower to hide them both from prying eyes. She had hidden an army: to shield one small boy took almost no more thought than secreting herself in the stillness and silence. "Take me to Marius's grave," she whispered into the quiet that surrounded them. "Take me there, and all will be forgiven."

He left her there, kneeling in fresh dirt with the sound of cannons shattering in the distance. Men screamed and died, faint distractions under the warming morning sun. Belinda curled her hand in the earth, wondering at the emptiness inside her. An innocent boy had broken open the secrets that had led to Beatrice's destruction, that had led to Marius's death. The boy wasn't at fault: this was a chain of events that stretched back to before his birth, one that came, perhaps, to this inevitable end, with Belinda bowing her head over a lover's grave and questioning whether she had any tears to shed. She doubted it: tears were an indulgence that only left her weaker, and she had had enough of weakness.

Nothing more esoteric than Javier's footsteps told her of his eventual arrival. Ordinary humanity, and nothing else: it seemed a lifetime since she'd relied on something so simple. It made her spine itch, made her aware of the small dagger she wore there as she was rarely aware of it anymore. Moreover, it whispered of her vulnerability, and that woke witchpower inside her. She knotted it down, and gave herself over to trust.

The king of Gallin stayed behind her a long while, weight of his regard heavy enough to make her want to squirm. Stillness wrapped her out of habit, tamping the urge to twist around and meet his gaze, proving herself, as always, to be stronger than the things around her. She thought he waited on her use of witchpower, waiting, hoping, that her fear or discomfort would shatter and make her reach for him in some manner. It would be all the excuse he needed; if she stood where he did now, it would be the weakness she would seize on. But there was no magic in the stillness, and she could wait forever in its grasp.

In time—a long time; the sun marked a noticeable distance in the sky as they waited on each other's resolve—in time, Javier came to stand on the grave's far side, putting the sun behind him so a thin streak of shadow fell across where Marius lay and splashed on Belinda's kneeling form. "For Eliza's life," he said very softly. "For Eliza's life I'll listen."

Belinda inclined her head, one more moment of solitude and gathering herself before saying, "This is not a frivolous question, and I don't ask it to test your patience. Do you remember your birth, Javier?"

Even without witchpower senses extended, she felt his anger flare, and heard his sharp inhalation before his teeth snapped together. "No one remembers their birth."

"I do." Silence, more silence; this was harder than she thought it would be, and she hadn't imagined it might be easy. "I had a glimpse of Lorraine, just one, before my father took me away. It didn't mean anything to me until I met her just before my twelfth birthday. I recognised her, *knew* her, and I've known since then that I was the queen's bastard."

"The marriage wasn't legitimate?" Javier seized on that, as she knew he would, but Belinda shook her head, pushing it away.

"I didn't know about the marriage until a few weeks ago. I've always thought of myself as a bastard."

Javier, against all likelihood, lifted his gaze and shot her a look so dry she almost smiled. But humour faded even more quickly than it was born, and she took another steadying breath. Bad enough to speak those words aloud, admit to anyone that she was Lorraine's daughter, when she'd kept that secret so close for so long. But she'd managed that; it was the next part that made her mouth dry and her hands icy cold. "The same day Lorraine announced she and Robert were wed and I was her heir, I learnt she'd borne a second child that night. A boy, whom the attending priest was told to drown."

Shocked anticipation flooded her, Javier's emotion riding too high to be ignored, even with her magic tied down. "He wasn't drowned? There's a male heir to the Aulunian throne? That—"

"Changes everything? Gives you a worthy rival to make war against, instead of simple and infuriating women?" Belinda caught herself, bit her tongue and reined in her temper. "Did you know I was born here? In Brittany? At one of my grandfather Henry's estates, where Lorraine had retired to mourn the anniversary of his death. And her priest, when he took the boy, had only to ride a week to the east to bring the child to Lutetia, and to a queen who'd lost her babe when word came of her husband's death in the Reussland border skirmishes."

She waited then, waited for the inevitable incomprehension, then the necessary leap of Javier's thoughts, and then for the response she knew he'd make, his voice sharp: "You lie."

Belinda lowered her gaze, waiting. That denial was the easy one, the simple disbelief that he could be other than his mother's son. There was more to come as he faced the possibility of truth and what it meant that they had lain together.

She ought to have expected the colossal witchpower blow that knocked her aside, flung her a dozen feet from the graveside and made her head ring with agony. She *did* expect Javier's furiously repeated "You *lie!*," and when his second witchlight attack came, she did nothing but curl on herself and keep the assault from landing. Through his outrage, through the pummel of power, she heard him shout, "Fight me! You must *fight me!*" and a crack of misery within her chest made her feel as though she might shatter into a thousand pieces. She knew his horror too clearly, and it was inevitable that the only person she could share it with would want her destroyed.

"I remember hearing her say 'It cannot be found out,' " Belinda whispered. Whispered, and for all that there was no way Javier could hear her under the rain of magic he threw down on her, she had every confidence that he would. "Before I even knew what words were, I heard her saying that, and they've been a part of me all my life. I said them to you once, Javier." Flawless memory was a gift and a curse. "It was snowing, and I stood on your balcony and you pulled me back. Warned me of discretion, and I said *It cannot be found out.* Do you remember what you did, Javier? Do you remember how you felt?" She remembered, too clearly: discomfort had flared in him, and he'd moved away, leaving a sense of unhappy and inexplicable recognition as his legacy jostled awake in those words.

"Like a clarion bell had been struck under my skin." The witchfire had lessened as she spoke, and faded into a faint prickling in the air when Javier answered. "Like I'd heard them before, like they were familiar, but I couldn't remember why."

"She said them again when you were born. When she gave you

to the priest. Javier, we're secrets, you and I. Not even Lorraine knows you survived." Belinda lifted her head a little, unwilling to make herself much larger, but witchpower pushed at her skin from the inside. It whispered of uncomfortable truths, making every word she spoke too clear and too real; pushed by it as she was, she doubted she could speak a lie to Javier and make him believe. "You have her look about you. I . . . saw it, once I knew."

"*Once you knew.* Does your heathen church even *care?*"

"Yes!" Heat curdled in her face and she struggled to bring her voice down, words tight in her throat. "The Reformation church is not so different as that. And I— I cannot get clean enough since I have learned the truth. I . . ." A shudder crawled over her, revulsion revisited before she exercised command over her body and her thoughts. "You believe me."

Javier laughed, hoarse angry sound, and sat down, the grave mound half hiding him from Belinda's view. "I wanted Rodrigo to have the witchpower. When I went to Isidro, knowing your power came from Robert, knowing it ran in the blood . . . but Rodrigo is only a man. *This cannot be!*"

"It cannot be found out," Belinda agreed wearily. She pushed herself up, got to her feet, and came around the grave to kneel a few feet away from the Gallic king. "Three of us know this secret, Javier. We two, and the priest who made this happen. He lives, and he didn't stop me from coming to Gallin and to your bed. There's vengeance, if you want it."

"He can't live," Javier whispered. "No queen would let him live, not when he carried such secrets as these."

"They would if his witchpower led them to believe him dead."

She had him then, had him so thoroughly that for an instant she wished she played a game. Javier's gaze snapped to hers, grey turning silver with outrage and confusion. "Robert?"

"No. His name is Dmitri, and he's of Irina's court, and probably Ivanova's father. He and Robert . . ." Belinda thinned her lips. "They serve a foreign queen, so strange I barely understand. And they're harbingers of war, not just between Gallin and Aulun, but between . . . between continents," she finally said, faltering. "A war for the world, Javier. I've snatched thoughts from them, just enough to see—"

"You've always been able to do that, haven't you?" Javier threw away the rest of what she'd said with a gesture, focusing on the witchpower use she'd named. "I've only just begun to read emotion in others, but you've been able to since the beginning. You used it to convince me to release you in Lutetia."

Belinda's jaw clenched, but she nodded. Javier stared at her as though she'd become a foreign thing herself, then slumped, arms around his drawn-up shins and forehead touched to his knees. "I should say you're doing it now, but I think you can't anymore. Not to me. I'd know it now. The world can't go to war, Belinda. It's too big."

"Look to your battlefields," Belinda murmured, "and tell me that again. All of Echon fights there today; all of Echon and so many Khazarians. The world's already at war, Javier, and my father's worked to orchestrate it."

"So have you," Javier said sharply, bitterly.

Knots tied in Belinda's belly, admission of guilt that made her nod. "He wants us fighting each other. War drives us to advance in *technologies.*" She spoke the unfamiliar word slowly, struggling to latch concepts stolen from Robert's mind and ideas half-explained by Dmitri to solidity and sense. She felt as though she tried to grasp water: it looked to be a whole, united object, but when she plunged her hands in it to take it up, it slipped apart into droplets and spilled through her fingers. Such was her comprehension of what Robert was, what Dmitri was, what she and Javier were, though to perhaps a lesser degree. "He wants us fractured but dangerous, so when his queen comes to us we'll make good soldiers but not good generals. We're being used, Javier." That much, at least, she was sure of, and desperation deepened her voice.

"Dmitri sent me to Gallin knowing our heritage and knowing I would find my way into your bed, and he *didn't care.* He did it so this war would come about, and if those are his means then I'll do everything I can to destroy his ends. I've spent a lifetime unquestioning and loyal, but this is too much. This is further than I can bend. They want a war, Javier. They want our guns and science to advance while we fight one another, so that when their queen comes we have weapons she can use, so she can make us her soldiers without losing any of her own."

Three weeks; three weeks and longer, it seemed, the idea had been burning in her mind as an answer, a vengeance, a plan, all to seize back a far-flung destiny. "Bastard or heir, I am the daughter of a queen, and I will not let men who have sent me to lie with my brother turn my country into a breeding place for foot soldiers for a monarch from foreign lands. I cannot break them without you, Javier. I can't take the shaping of our futures from them on my own. It needs both of us, and it needs Ivanova if we can get her, and it needs Dmitri Leontyev dead."

JAVIER DE CASTILLE, KING OF GALLIN

Everything he'd known of Beatrice Irvine was a lie. Her name, her presence in Gallin, her very existence was a story meant to bring her closer to him, a fabrication to allow her access to the queen, his mother, so that Sandalia might die. The love Beatrice had professed for him was a lie because Beatrice herself was a lie: everything, *everything* about her, a lie.

Everything but the witchpower.

Falsifying it was impossible. It was a part of her as much as it was a part of him, inherent in their beings, a solitary truth shared between them that could not, in any way, be undone. It could be used, manipulated, shaped, but not unmade, and it lay between them like a blade, cutting everything else away. Hate was numb beneath grief already, but against the vibrancy of the witchpower even hatred faded. Logic aside, sin aside, he wanted collusion with the one other being like himself.

So much like himself. That they shared witchpower when no one else did carried too much weight: Belinda Primrose, Belinda *Walter*, spoke the truth when she named him Lorraine's son and her full brother. That Robert Drake was their father, both of them . . . the bitterest dredge was that in a cold, gutted part of him, it made sense. Sandalia had been strong and witty and bold; Rodrigo was all of those things still, but neither of them burned with the magic Javier carried in his blood, and Rodrigo had confessed with a word that Louis, Javier's father in name, had nothing of the witchpower in him. His power was born of something else, some*one* else, and he had met its progenitor in a Lutetian courtroom half a year since. Had met Robert Drake, a big man who had left little physical mark on Javier, but who had left him everything in the realm of magic. There was far more chance of truth in that story than in God's hand selecting him to carry a banner of silver magic against His enemies in war. He was only a bastard, a secret, a thing made use of by men whose end game lay beyond his comprension.

He was precisely as Belinda was, and for a single shattering moment, he believed all she had to say. Believed she'd known none of what she'd just confessed when she came to his bed; believed, even, that Beatrice Irvine had loved him, if Belinda Primrose had not.

The question spilled out unexpectedly, an entirely wrong thing to say to her quiet, passionate speech of freedom and determination. She was proposing an alliance and a war against an indeterminate enemy, and instead of giving a yes or no, he said, "*Did* you love me, when you were her?"

He had learned already that Belinda was a consummate actress: the memory of her performance in the courtroom struck a note even as astonishment filled her eyes now. He shouldn't believe her display, but now, unlike then, he could open witchpower senses to her and taste the truth behind her act.

"How can I answer that?" Belinda jerked her gaze away. "My answer condemns me either way. If I say no I'm the betraying whore you think me, and if I say yes I'm both and a pervert besides. Yes," she added far more harshly, and witchpower flared in her as though she expected an attack.

Pain and regret lanced Javier, and a loneliness worse than any he'd ever known. The fire he'd wanted was there, a core of passion and desire that had become despair, all of it driven by the beating of Belinda's heart. Surprise washed after those rich emotions, muting them for a few seconds as he realised it was his own, that he hadn't believed she'd answer honestly, or that she'd once loved him. He drew breath to respond, but she continued, still harsh with inwardly directed anger.

"Yes. And for a few minutes when you took me from the oubliette I believed I could do as we whispered to each other. That I could turn my back on my duty and my loyalty and give myself to you. But I was too much the creature my father'd made." Her mouth curled as though she tasted something foul. "I turned my hands to blood crawling back to my duty because I didn't know how to leave it behind. You were the first crack in my armour, and now it's shattered apart." She extended a hand, expression grim with determination. "I can take memories from others with a touch, and if you're learning to sense emotion . . . take what I can offer. If I didn't love you, it was only because I couldn't name what I felt. It was wrong, and perhaps now we're damned, but I swear to you, Javier, *I did not know.* And in not knowing, I loved, and in loving, everything that I was has come to an end."

"I believe you." Silence rode the air between them, heavier than words. Belinda kept her hand extended, waiting. He stared at it, then at her. "You still murdered my mother."

"Yes."

He stared harder, then pinched the bridge of his nose. Too many things were changing, the footing he'd always stood on shaking loose. Robert Drake was his father, Lorraine Walter his mother, and conniving, manipulative Belinda Primrose his twin.

But Sandalia de Costa was his family. She had known he was no blood of hers, and had made him her son. Drake may have granted him the witchpower, but the older witchlord was not, would never be, Javier's *father.* The thought was calming, but he feared looking at it too closely, certain he would shatter under its weight. Power rose, soothing and stabilising, and he held on hard to its silver comfort before dropping his hand. "You might have lied just now. Blamed Akilina, as Lorraine has done."

"You'd have known. And I'm trying not to lie to you." A desperate sort of humour coursed through Belinda's exposed magic. "It doesn't come naturally, so perhaps you'd consider not encouraging me to my more usual half-truths. I liked Sandalia," she said more roughly. "There was even a moment when I wondered why I'd want her dead."

"And then?"

Belinda's extended fingers curled in a loose fist. "Then I wondered why I wouldn't. I was trying to protect my mother's throne, and I didn't understand the scope of Robert's ambitions. I still barely do. It's too strange, too . . . alien to comprehend."

"A foreign queen," Javier said carefully. He was too tired for rage, too tired for hate, and too full of uncertainty to try to burn weariness away and give those darker emotions their due. He needed Eliza on hand to spur him to anger against Belinda, or Sacha to build unfocused fury.

That thought sparked heat after all, and he saw resignation and defeat crumble Belinda's face. "No," he said aloud, surprising himself. "Tell me your intentions. I'll bend an ear to listen, at least."

23

Belinda Walter

"Do more than bend an ear." For the second time, Belinda extended a hand. "I'm speaking in riddles, not to confound you, but because the truth I've had from Robert's mind is beyond my comprehension. Spoken aloud it'll only sound like dreams. Take my hand, please, king of Gallin. Without witchpower sharing none of this will make sense."

"Here?" Javier made a short gesture toward Marius's grave. "Should this not be done in private?"

"You would bring the Aulunian heir back to your own quarters?" Belinda asked, exasperated. "Here your people will give you privacy to mourn. Back in your tent you resume your duties. Thought shared with witchpower is the work of a moment." More softly, she said, "Take my hand, Javier."

Javier scowled, then set his jaw and seized her hand all in one swift motion, clearly belying his instincts in doing so.

Static shot through the touch, witchpower flaring in a burst that lifted hairs on Belinda's arms and sent a thrill of excitement through her. Too familiar, that taste of desire. Javier jerked back, but Belinda knotted her fingers around his, refusing to let him go as she grated, "This is how we know each other. You woke my power with passion. If we're to win over this thing we must learn each other again, go beyond this already-known need and find another path."

"You're a *witch,* you've done this deliberately, you—" Javier broke off with a strangled sound, one too close to release for Belinda's liking. Fire sizzled through her, golden power bubbling and surging until her body ached and heat melted the core of her.

Sex isn't power. Dmitri's words came back to her, an unlikely source of salvation. He'd been both wrong and right, but now she snatched at the ways in which he'd been wrong. Commanding the storm hadn't been born of sensuality, nor did she any longer require that sexual pulse to steal emotion and thought from those around her. Sex and power could be divorced: for the sake of her soul, they *must* be divorced.

She'd drawn on rage and on raw determination to power the magic in the past; now panic proved a new and capable way to feed it. She had always claimed more faith in Lorraine than the Reformation God, and yet faced with knowingly surrendering to desire in the arms of a man she'd learned was her brother, Belinda found she had a little faith after all: faith that God would not forgive a passion so unholy. It seemed she wanted a chance at salvation, if a life such as hers might be forgiven.

Need burned out under that panic, witchpower steady and bright within her. Belinda shuddered and dared lift her gaze to Javier's. The silver-eyed king looked back at her with a mix of revulsion and loss that sent Belinda's vision hot and swimming. She whispered, "It isn't fair," then laughed at herself, rough sound of pathos. The world had never been fair, and yet hers had shifted so dramatically that such protestations seemed in order. And those changes hadn't yet come to an end; she must, indeed, pursue them with all diligence, make certain they came to pass.

Javier gave her a thin smile in return, his emotion more controlled than her own. At its core was confusion and hatred: he had no call to love her, and every reason not to. But the edge had gone, even when he thought of his mother. His world had, perhaps, also changed too greatly to let old anger hold sway, at least in this moment. Where rage once burned, sorrow now lay: sorrow for Sandalia, and more freshly, for Marius. Guilt, too, guilt so deep it coloured everything, even his command of the magic inherent to his soul. He feared the witchpower in a way Belinda didn't, saw it as condemnation even when the Pappas, the father of his church, had named it God's gift. He had stolen free will from too many men, and saw that as an unforgiveable crime, as deadly as the one he and Belinda had shared, to ever be comfortable with his magic.

"Enough." The sharpness of his tone caught her out: her feelings would be as clear to him as his were to her. Discomfited, she wondered what she'd betrayed in those few seconds, but he cast off her concerns with an angry burst of words: "Show me this stuff of dreams. Show me the enemy you say we have."

The demand shaped her thoughts, spilling them into as near a semblance of sense as she could manage. A hint of resentment splashed after it and she bared her teeth, not liking that his command could get such a ready response from her. They had to be equals in this, or fail.

Then there was no more time for petty resentment, the fractured images she'd stolen from Robert washing through witchpower and sharing themselves with Javier de Castille.

JAVIER DE CASTILLE, THE QUEEN'S BASTARD

Fire rained from the sky.

It seemed a brief eternity before he realised that no, fire rose *into* the sky, streaky smoke trailing behind vast blasts of heat as incomprehensible machines flew toward the stars. They strove for the moon, for *ships* made of metal that hung in the void between heavenly bodies. Men piloted the vessels that left streaks across the sky, working to serve an overlord they knew nothing about.

His vision reversed, turning from the sky to the earth, where terrible pits, deeper and broader than any salt mine, scored the surface, and where men rode in monstrous metal contraptions that hauled ore and dirt toward the wide crater edges.

Distant from the mining sites lay cities, great square buildings with uniform windows and tall smokestacks that belched black muck into the sky. The men and women who worked them looked weary, ill-fed, grey with smoke as they guided ugly chunks of precious metal down rattletrap belts that led to processing centres a thousand times larger than any forge Javier had ever dreamt of.

Heat boiled out of them, turning the sky to hazy waves and bringing the very depths of Hell to life.

His voice cracked, pushing aside the pictures: "If this is what they want, they must be stopped—"

"Wait."

Another ship sliced through the sky, and this time fire *did* rain from it, huge slabs of light slamming into the ground, into buildings, into the mines, and killing men by their hundreds. Belinda whispered, "I've seen inside their ships, Javier . . ."

With the whisper came the image of a man, though that simple word fell away into nothingness as the creature came clearer. It was man-shaped in the way a peddler's monkey might be, with a misshapen head atop a central column, but nothing else in its makeup said *man* in any way. The face was a snarl of rage, eyes set wide apart and swiveling independently of each other, and too many brutish limbs manoeuvred the controls of its ship. It had half again the bulk of any man Javier had ever seen, so thick and fearsome it might forgo its radical weaponry entirely and simply pull its enemies apart. Even as nothing more than a picture in his mind, it stank of something that made his bowels turn to water, as though it could crawl inside his head and trigger a primitive terror that undid any rational thought and strength of character he might cobble together.

"What . . . ?" Horror lay somewhere in the depths of his question, but bewilderment was what coloured it.

"Invaders from a foreign land," Belinda whispered. Her voice and her magic were both laden with uncertainty, not in what she shared but in how it could be. "They come for our . . . our salt and our metal and our land. These ones are Robert's enemy, the enemies of his queen. They fear them in particular because the witchpower has so little effect on them."

"In particular?" Now horror did break through, Javier shaking off the images to stare at Belinda. "There are others?"

"Dozens. Dozens of races, all in need of the same resources, as we need what we take from the Columbias. Some are more easily defeated." Belinda put her hands along her temples as though she tried to hold her thoughts together. "Some fall before the witchpower easily. Those ones pursue other paths of exploration, staying away from Robert's kind. The space between the stars is almost infinite, and they rarely meet anymore. But those who can fight the witchpower will come on Robert's heels, will come to strip this world of its iron and water and greenery. Robert means for us to feed those resources to his queen, to advance us so far as to deliver them what they need while they never soil their . . . hands."

Another picture rode with the last word, a great silvery scaled monster with no more hands than an insect might have. It cried of *dragon* to Javier's mind, though only because no mortal creature he knew had such size or such sheen: it looked less like a great wyrm or terrible lizard than a giant, segmented insect, oddly fragile for all its enormity. "My father's people consider themselves delicate invaders," Belinda whispered. "They make slaves to do their bidding rather than destroy populations and take what they desire. The ones who come after them would simply wipe us from our homes as if we were rats."

"But what are they? Where are they from?" Not *why*—the *why* of what the things Belinda told him of made sense, in a remote and unemotional way. His people raided the Columbian continent for goods and raw materials; the idea that someone else might invade them for the same seemed only reasonable. But those who might come for Echonian resources should be Khazarian, or Aferican, not monsters encased in ships that cut through sky instead of water. Cold crawled over Javier's skin and inched its way to the bone, carrying disbelief beginning to border on refusal.

Belinda laughed, soft sound of near panic. "I don't know. Alien. Inhuman. Things I never dreamt existed. God hasn't peopled only our world, Javier, even though your church or mine would burn me for the heresy of saying so. But what I've taken from their mind is real. No one could imagine it."

"But he's—" Javier choked, unable to put voice to the idea that Robert could be other than a man.

Belinda swallowed, so strained he felt it through the witchpower. "The soul leaves the body at death, transcending to Heaven or Hell. They have a way of capturing it, giving it a new body and a new life." Her uncertainty rose through the witchpower, not in doubting that something like what she described happened, but unable to comprehend how. "It has to do with the witchpower, with their ability to make magic with their minds. It defines them, more than it defines us. We see our talents as powerful, but they consider what they can do here to be weak. But it's strong enough to slip into a few places and to shape our countries and our continents so that we'll be raised up to serve them. And if we don't allow this shaping we'll have no defence when their enemies come. We'll have no way to fight back against any of them."

"So you would play both sides against the middle," Javier said slowly. "You would hide from Robert Drake the fact that we move against him even as we embrace the changes he brings?"

"We don't dare turn to him for help. He'll use his witchpower against us and bend us to his will." Belinda's argument rang with unshakable surety. "You said I'd hidden my power behind walls of womanly fear, but it was Robert who locked it away. I was too young, my power developing faster than he was prepared for, so he placed that wall in my mind. I remember him doing it, though I didn't understand all that it meant until I met you. And he stopped your power in Lutetia, stopped it without effort. He could well be able to do it again."

"We're stronger now, both of us." Javier spoke without knowing whether he was truly entertaining Belinda's madness or simply drawing it to its inevitable conclusions. "We might be less easily taken now."

"And if we defeat him only to learn he reports to his foreign queen? We can't know what she might expect of him." Belinda sank back, face pinched. "I know a thing or two about living in the shadows, Javier. About shaping events from there, and the wisdom of moving subtly."

Javier bared his teeth, anger coming to sudden light inside of him. "If we can do nothing about Drake, then—"

"Dmitri," Belinda said in a low vicious voice. "He's under Robert's command, a servant to the general, and he has in more ways than Robert used us badly. He has strength, but I know his secrets now, and with him removed Robert will rely on me all the more, giving us a place of power inside his plans."

"Us. The day when we were *us* has long passed. Why are you

here, telling me this?" Muscle tightened in Javier's jaw, anger fanning higher. "What good am I to you in this power play?"

"I need allies. This battle is larger than Gallin or Aulun, larger than Reformation or Ecumenic law. I might succeed in the shaping of one country, but to stand against what's coming we need a continent of a single mind. A world, if we can make it."

"No." Anger burst over Javier's skin, driving away the cold and leaving him staring down the Aulunian heir with fresh loathing. "This madness is of your own making. This *war* is of your making, in the shape of my mother's death." He threw those words at her, claiming Sandalia as family; the ties there were far stronger than the story Belinda had spun, no matter how much truth he felt in its core. "These plots are yours to unmake, not mine. You don't need allies, not to fulfill your ambitions, not to murder this Dmitri or trick your Robert. You want friends, people to salvage whatever desperate fraction of yourself still has a conscience. I owe you nothing, least of all that. You say we've been used, but *I've* been used, and by you. Your nasty truths, the things you've learned, they change nothing. I'll delight in crowning myself the Aulunian king, knowing in my gut that it's no pretender's crown, and you, my enemy, will die on a hangman's tree, nothing more than a fast-fading memory."

Honest astonishment filled Belinda's eyes, and she was silent a few seconds before saying, "But the things I've shown you—"

"Are madness. Even if they're true, they're madness, and lie so far beyond my grasp that I cannot even pretend to believe we could face them."

"What if you're wrong? What if we can?" Belinda leaned forward as though she'd catch his hand again.

Javier pulled back, denial and rage filling his motions as he spat, "Then Belinda Primrose can save us all. You can give me nothing that makes entertaining your games worthwhile." He climbed to his feet, all but stumbling over Marius's grave in his anger and his haste to be away.

Belinda's voice followed him, hard with desperation: "I can give you a child."

Belinda Walter

This time she was prepared for the witchpower lashing that came down on her, and shielded herself from it. Disgust and fury drove that blow, and she weathered it, knowing she'd spoken so poorly as to earn the burst of temper. "I am pregnant," she said beneath the storm of his anger. "Not by you, but by Dmitri, and so will bear a child who is fully heir to the witchpower. Eliza can't have children, Javier. If you mean to make her your bride, you'll need an heir, and she can't give you one."

"And you would—" Javier's barrage of wrath ended in a sputter of unwelcome hope. *"Why?"*

Breathing hurt, as though she'd been laced into a corset tightly enough to damage her ribs. Despite that, despite too little air, her heart beat much too fast, flooding her body with heat. This was a devil's bargain she'd never dreamt of making, and it twisted tears through her, though they didn't rise so far as her eyes. No, they only reached her throat, making her voice small and tight as she answered. "Because you're still outside Robert's easy realm of influence. Because to get a controlling hand in your court, in your life, he'll have to send or become someone else, and you can sense the witchpower if it comes close. Because you need this, and it's all I have to bargain with."

She dragged in a deep breath and felt something pop in her chest, a shard of pain that loosened a little of the tightness that bound her. Everything she'd said was true, but this last was perhaps truest of all, and most risky to admit: "Because I'm Lorraine's heir and I won't be permitted to bear a child out of wedlock. If I can only stay free long enough to bear it, this is my child's best chance to survive."

"You would be well off a prisoner of war, then." Scratchiness filled Javier's tone, making him sound as rough as Belinda felt. Hope lanced her, a blow so hard she folded with it before forcing herself straight to meet Javier's gaze.

"Help me orchestrate these next few days and weeks of war, and I'll come to your war camp a willing prisoner. Lorraine and Robert know by now that I've left Alunaer. They'll have some poor girl playing my part until I can be returned, and won't make a public spectacle of my being missing. It looks too clumsy, as if they can't control me. You can negotiate the terms of my release under that cover, and be satisfied with them a month or two after the child is born."

"Or I could just have you killed." Javier sounded almost curious, so matter-of-fact as to be dismissive.

Witchpower rose in her like a tide, seeming slow but also inexorable as it turned her vision to gold. "You could try."

Javier chuckled, though his own silver power made no effort to respond to Belinda's flat anger. He'd tested her, then, nothing more, but even knowing that, she wanted to spit fire at him, to crush him and his ambition where he stood. The impulse still rode her as he asked, "Why would I give up the Aulunian heir? Particularly when I desire her crown?"

"Because Aulun will show you no quarter if Lorraine believes me dead at your hand. We have the Khazarian alliance, and Irina's army is endless. A sweet enough bargain will have Gallin sandwiched between the army already here and a new force sweeping in from the east. You're already outnumbered. Gallin would be destroyed." Belinda's nails cut into her palms, a luxury of reaction she once would never have allowed herself, but she no longer cared. A lifetime of stillness had done its duty, had made her invisible and had permitted her to excel at the tasks she'd been set, but she was coming into a different life now. She was no longer a secret, and should a crown be placed on her head the knack for hiding thought and feeling would be useful, even crucial, but her role would be to be seen. She could permit herself the indulgence of emotion now, and a part of her revelled in it.

"And with Gallin your child."

Belinda's smile felt sharp enough to be a snarl. "*Your* child, for all they'd know. Aulun would show grace and kindness toward the babe and toward her enemies, and rescue the wretched tot, adopt it and raise it up, and the Gallic throne would become Aulun's after all. We can do this dance all night, Javier, and I have no more patience for it. Will you take my bargain?"

"And let you walk free to sow chaos on the battlefield? You're here now. It wouldn't be my wisest move, to let you go."

Belinda stood, finally making herself an equal to the king across the grave. "Do you think you can stop me?"

"No," he said after a long moment. "No, I don't suppose I can. This plan of yours . . . needs Eliza's blessing."

"Oh," Belinda muttered, "this will be rich."

ELIZA BEAULIEU

The only clever thing Javier has done is to not bring Belinda Walter with him to propose their mad alliance. Eliza might have ended the entire question with a thrown dagger, if he'd been that foolish, and a very large part of her wishes he had.

Instead, she has a knot in her gut, one that draws her heart and her bladder and her stomach into a single knocking spot, so every time her heart beats she feels the need to both vomit and pee. It might be funny, if it didn't weaken her legs and set a tremble in her hands, which reminds her of the fever that nearly took her life and did take her ability to bear children; and that, somehow, brings her back around to where she is, staring at Javier de Castille as though he's put a knife through her.

"How can you even be thinking this?" is what she finally asks, though it barely begins to scrape on the things she wants to say. "You want me to raise *her* child? Is it *yours*?"

Javier shudders and shakes his head. "No. No. Thank God, no. She says the child's due at Christ mass, and so it can't be mine. I wouldn't wish that it was. But it is—" He catches her hands in his and holds on too tight, not quite hurting her, but as if letting her go might set him adrift. "It's perhaps our only chance," he whispers. "It's—"

"This is far more than asking me to live with her as your spy," Eliza snaps. "Even if I were to bear your child, Javier, nobody would care if you got a bastard on me as long as you also wed a proper princess and make a litter of children on her."

"I want to marry you," Javier whispers. "Eliza, how much must I pay for being a fool? Marius is dead—"

"And you're plotting how our lives will go on without him with him not a day in the grave!"

"I have to!" Javier lets her go with a burst of energy, propelling himself backward. "Eliza, if we're to make this thing work it needs to be decided now. *Now*, yes, in the midst of all this hell. We are given no surcease."

"Why does she even suggest it? Out of love for you?" Bitterness fills Eliza's voice and she can't stop it. Javier, though, only sags and takes the anger as though it's his due.

"Because she wants the babe to live, and Lorraine can't have a bastard grandchild. Giving it up to us saves its life and gives us a chance to be together."

"And what does she care if we're together? She wanted you for herself, once. Why not seduce you and claim the baby's yours, and end this war with a marriage between Gallin and Aulun?"

Javier, drily, says, "I'm not quite so easily led as that, Eliza." Some of the dourness fades and he looks away. "She took Sandalia's life. Perhaps she offers us this one in exchange. It's not a fair price, but perhaps it's not a bad one either."

"She saved me, too." Eliza slides fingers over her belly, feeling a place where not even a scar remains. "That blow would have killed a child in my womb, Javier."

"Not if God's blessing was on us both," Javier whispers. "Our army could use a miracle."

Hurt stings Eliza, making her feel childish and sullen. "That isn't fair."

"No. But then, none of this is. I can't begin to find the moment when it all went wrong."

Eliza takes a breath, then holds her tongue. She has an answer to that, a too-clear answer that harkens back to the moment Marius Poulin walked Beatrice Irvine into the prince of Gallin's favourite gentleman's club. The world began an endless tumble toward horror then, and hasn't righted itself since.

But had Marius done otherwise, Eliza herself would not now be the king's lover, and despite the prices that have been paid, that's the one thing she's wanted all of her days. Had she known the cost would be Marius's life she might have long since walked away, but there was no knowing; there never can be a clear picture of how the future will unfold.

A bowstring ties itself around her heart and contracts, a small pain accompanying a cruel thought: if there is any way in this world for Eliza Beaulieu to triumph over Beatrice Irvine, it may well be in taking her child, raising it and loving it as her own, and knowing that Belinda will never share that joy.

It's the wrong place to begin, adoption out of vengeance, and yet Javier's right in more than one way. It's the one chance they might be given, and if the babe is due at the Christ mass, then she and Javier have been lovers just long enough to make it possible. The Pappas in Cordula will be angry, and so will the Parnan king, but no one would condemn Javier for wedding and making legitimate the first child born to his body, not in a time of war. Most will rejoice, and count it a blessing.

How easy it is. Eliza falls back a few steps and finds a seat so she can drop her head into her hands. How terribly easy, to slip over the precipice from denial to belief. She's thinking already that the child is Javier's, and if it's Javier's then it can be her own as easily. And to be a mother . . . that's a dream she put away a long time ago, sealed it with lead edges and tried to forget about. "I have never been able to refuse you."

Javier lets go a rush of air and crashes forward to land on his knees before her, to hide his face in her lap. Eliza puts her fingers in his hair, her alabaster ring white against ginger before she bends to kiss his head. "This is madness, my love."

"Yes." Javier's answer is muffled and trembles on the edge of both laughter and tears. "I had better call for the priest, and for Rodrigo. Shall we be wed by noon?"

"A battlefield bride," Eliza murmurs. "What will you have me wear, Javier? My trousers and linen shirt, and my tall boots with a dagger at the thigh?"

"Do that," Javier whispers, and looks up with a laugh marred by tears. "And I'll wear one of your diaphanous creations, for my hair's longer than yours already. We'll flummox them all." He kneels up and catches her face in his hands, kisses her carefully, as though she's suddenly become fragile. As if, Eliza thinks, she truly is pregnant, and he, a man suddenly afraid that his touch might damage her or the child. Heart full of confusion and hope, she returns the kiss, then shoos him to find Tomas and Rodrigo so a wedding might be performed.

In the end she wears one of her gowns, and it's Javier in trousers and a linen shirt. Eliza forgoes her wig, so the short length of hair she's grown out is tucked behind her ears. It's pulled askew by the wind, and is echoed by the flutter and twist of her skirt around her legs and the dance of her heart in her chest. She's never truly imagined being married, has Eliza Beaulieu, and in the crux of it she finds she's terrified. Excited, but terrified, and she wonders if all women come to the altar in such a state.

Word runs to the troops, down to the battlefield, and for a short while at the noon hour, all the fighting comes to a stop. Eliza has no idea why, but as the allied Cordulan troops turn to watch distant figures on the hilltop, Aulun does not advance. Instead they all watch the handful of people presided over by a priest whose voice cannot carry to the men below.

It carries as far as Javier and Eliza, and to the prince of Essandia who's come to stand witness, and to Belinda Walter, who watches from the safety of her witchpower stillness, where no one can see her. Her heart's strangely full as she watches this marriage, giving it most of her attention.

Most, but not all: some of her mind is given over to a witchpower shield keeping Aulun from attacking Gallin's unprotected flank. She ought not: she ought to let her army crash into Javier's and watch the Cordulan alliance crumble under the strength of her army. But she won't have that, not today, not in this moment: that much, at least, she can give to Javier and Eliza de Castille.

When the vows are said and the kiss is made, the watching troops send up a roar of approval that must be audible across the straits. Rodrigo steps forward then, to kiss Eliza's cheeks and then to murmur something in her ear, something that makes her take knee, and before the world's armies, Rodrigo of Essandia crowns a pauper the new queen of Gallin.

Belinda, smiling and appalled at her sentiment, slips away, and spends the day doing what she can to mute antagonism between two warring factions, that a king and a queen may be given one brief moment in the heart of loss and sorrow and blood to find a little joy in the knowing of each other.

ROBERT, LORD DRAKE
26 June 1588 † *Brittany; the Aulunian camp*

Generals, messengers, soldiers; all are listless. It's not the aura Robert expected from an army with the size and strength to easily crush their enemy; he has come to Brittany expecting an enthusiastic victory and a tremendous welcome for the Khazarian ambassador who has given Aulun its overwhelming edge. They had the welcome, Dmitri uplifted by their effusive praise, but they've not had the crushing defeat Robert anticipated.

Instead he's watched a slow dance on the battlefields as the Cordulan army has worked its way back together, becoming a unified mass instead of huddled, disspirited troops. It's Javier de Castille's witchpower that's done it, and Robert has watched without interfering, almost too interested in the game to worry, for now, about the outcome.

But today the war's tenor has changed: today Aulun's army has lost its focus, seeming to no longer care that they've got an enemy on the field. Word has come through the troops that Javier has taken a bride, and Robert would think the audacity of marrying in the middle of a war might heat the Aulunian soldiers' blood. Instead they seem content to lay down arms for the day and let Gallin celebrate.

"It's Belinda," Dmitri says beside him, and Robert startles.

"Who's married Javier?" That thought hadn't occurred to him, and for a moment it brightens his day.

Dmitri snorts. "Not in this or any other world, I think. No, it's Belinda dampening their spirits. Can't you feel it?"

"Oh," Robert says, "that." Now that Dmitri's put the words to it, he can, of course, feel that it's witchpower weighing down Aulun's troops. Belinda's dangerous to him, her witchpower too much like his own, perhaps, for him to notice properly, and that's a thing he doesn't dare admit to Dmitri. "I wonder why."

"I suppose she harbours feelings for him still, though I'd think they'd drive her to send her army storming his when he showed a moment of weakness. Shall I clear it away?" Dmitri asks airily, and in asking insinuates that Robert's incapable of it.

"Let them have their rest. Tomorrow will dawn another day."

"You trust her implicitly, even if she quells the army's fighting urge. What if she's turning against you, Robert?"

"What if all the stars should fall from the sky?" Robert gives back, with as much concern for the one as the other. "She's one of us, Dmitri. Loyalty bred in the bone. She's never reached beyond the limits she's been given. Not even now, when she's been made heir to a throne, has she striven beyond it. This is her duty and she'll follow it through. If sentiment's taken enough hold to make her soften our troops today, then tomorrow she'll have shaken it off, and will make war with the strongest heart of any of us."

"How can you be so certain?"

Robert looks the scant distance down at Dmitri, bemused. "Because she's my daughter."

Dmitri ducks his head, evidently satisfied, and after a moment leaves Robert alone to watch the quiet battlefields.

BELINDA WALTER

The distance from Javier's wedding site back to the heart of the Aulunian camp seemed less when she had no witchpower shields to fight against. It was a mile or two, no more, and Belinda traversed it within an hour of the wedding. She felt safer on her side of the Aulunian line, and was glad to climb the hills that gave her a view of the battlefields from the south.

Gossip amongst the troops warned her that Robert was there, and she came on him speaking with Dmitri. She hung back, listening with mild curiosity until the Khazarian witchlord left. Only then, without dropping the blind she'd wrapped around herself, did she ask, "Do you know why he doesn't trust me?"

Robert didn't flinch, which perversely pleased her: he shouldn't have known she was there, and yet a part of her wanted him to be the infallible father, looking through her veil of deception as he had when she was a child. "Either he's built a plot with you, or has been unable to," her father said. "If it's the former, he knows you're un-trustworthy; if it's the latter, he hopes to make me think you are. Which is it?"

Belinda loosed the power that kept her hidden and, smiling, stepped up to Robert's side. "He believes you serve your queen poorly. That this war is wrong, and that alliances must be built in-stead. He thinks a people inspired by peace and education will leap forward more quickly than a people ravaged by war. He would take your place in the line of fathers, by proving himself wiser and more clever than you."

"Really." Robert sounded astonished. "I didn't think he had it in him. He shouldn't. What did he offer you?"

Belinda gave a laugh that belonged to someone she no longer fully recognised. She knew her role so well that it could never falter, and yet the light note of sarcasm and dismissal in her voice felt harder than she wanted, anymore, to be. "A crown. A kingdom. All the things I never coveted, and which patience has brought to me anyway. I sought none of this, Robert. How can I be who I am, what I am, and have truly never reached for what lay beyond the glass?"

"Because you're a good girl," Robert said seriously. "Because you've been given tasks and duties and have been happy to fulfill them, knowing yourself a vital and integral part of the dark mo-ments that keep a queen safe on her throne. We live in a world of ambition, my Primrose, but there are those who truly wish only to serve. I'm one. I've raised you to be, too."

"And Dmitri?"

"Dmitri." Robert fell silent a few moments, watching the fields below. "Dmitri ought to be. How much intelligence have you gath-ered on his plots, Primrose?"

"Enough to know he means to use me to displace you." Be-linda's forehead wrinkled, the thought difficult to pursue, even still. "He thinks my ambition, whetted, will push me toward ridding us of you, because he'll tell me more, teach me more, and give me more than you might."

"And you think?" A cautious note sounded in Robert's voice, so faint Belinda might not have heard it if she hadn't spent a lifetime attuned to his hints of approval and censure.

"I think I'd like to know. But from childhood what has mattered to me is that I serve my queen as best I can. I never asked," she added, almost lightly. "Du Roz was sent to plot against Lorraine, and I never asked what part a young Gallic noble might play in her downfall. Perhaps I was too young then, or perhaps it never mattered. What mattered was you told me it must be done for the queen's safety, and asked me to do it, and I would rather have died than disappoint you. So would I still."

"Ah, du Roz," Robert said. "Du Roz meant nothing to anyone. He was only convenient, and I needed a man no one would miss to see if you could do murder and walk away unscathed. The haste I came for you in was born from his intention on returning to Gallin in a day or two, having spent only enough time in Alunaer to pride himself on walking through enemy courts." He threw the man away with a gesture of his hand, and in so doing left an empty place of astonishment in Belinda's chest. "Dmitri, though; Dmitri could do us harm."

"No." Belinda's voice sounded thin to her own ears, though it was unmarred by the tremours shaking her body. Du Roz had been a fop, a tool used to shape her, and nothing more. Not an enemy, not a criminal, not a threat: only a man barely beyond a boy's years in the wrong place at the wrong time, where he could die to make Belinda Primrose the queen's most secret assassin. She called stillness and was dismayed at its lack of strength, at how it all but deserted her when she stood at her father's side and needed it most. "Dmitri won't be a problem. He trusts me," she said with a smile as thin as her voice. "Let me teach him the folly of standing against his queen's desires."

"That's my girl." Robert smiled, a bright and genuine thing she would have given her life to earn as a child, and he pulled her into a powerful embrace. "I'll leave it in your hands. Keep him alive if you can bend him to your will, but if not, better dead than a troublesome thorn in our sides."

"This is how it shall go." Belinda curtsied, smiled, and left Robert on the hillside so she might find a private place and fall to her knees in horror of what she had been made into, and how.

24

She emerged at dawn, having spent the night hidden in stillness. The world had gone away from her, no cold, no breeze, no biting bugs; no witchpower or politics pushing or prodding her in any direction.

Now, with the first morning light, she felt Javier's joy in Eliza, and felt, too, the cold iron will that had kept her from crossing Gallic lines. She admired that he could separate his attention so thoroughly, and do so much with his divided will.

Robert was closer, a waterwheel of power, running deep and fast and utterly self-absorbed. That, perhaps, defined him in a way Belinda had never realised: all that he was, was meant to serve another, and the single-mindedness of that duty allowed him to look no further than his own needs and ends, with no care for the cost it might extract from others.

But then, she was little different. She'd come out from hiding clear-eyed, clear-minded; clear of all difficult and weighing emotion—or that was what she told herself. The why of du Roz's death didn't matter: it was a thing done long in the past, and if it had shaped her, then it had done so that she might slip across battlefields inciting both wars and alliances. Come the end of the day, she was as she needed to be.

So, at least, she told herself.

Belinda curled a lip at her own softness and wrapped her arms about her shoulders, ending with a hard shake, the sort of thing a frustrated father might visit on an aggravating child. For a lifetime

she'd embraced what she was. Becoming coy and shy about it now
bordered on absurdity. Doubt had to become action, a truth that
had been made vividly clear when she'd squatted to pee: her belly
was beginning to swell, and she had almost no time left in which to
implement her plans and retire to the comparative safety of Javier's
war prison. Dmitri had to be dealt with: that was foremost. From
there, she could turn her mind to other plots.

She had no immediate sense of where the dark witchlord was.
Perhaps he had deliberately tamped his magic, making himself invisible to her.

As though anyone whose bed she'd shared could hide from her,
much less a man whose own power she'd commanded more than
once. Incensed by the idea—and then, below that, faintly amused at
her own ire; the witchpower still, even now, tasted of its own opinions and ambitions, though at the same time she couldn't say they
were anything other than her own—she cast out a web of witchlight, watching it glimmer briefly in the early-morning sun before
it faded into nothing more than her will searching for a singular
and most particular presence.

She found it like a battlecharger riding her down, a wall of black
magic with no cracks or infirmities she could sense. Dmitri himself
stalked out of that black cloud, fiery, full of passion, beautiful in his
hawk-featured way. Oh, yes: even in repose this man was compelling, and when driven by ambition and anger, then whole continents might fall before him, ready to cry his name and take up his
banner.

"That has been my purpose," he snarled, and for an instant Belinda was taken up in his dream, a whole world united behind a
powerful leader whose vision led them to technological wonders
and mechanical glories. A world united behind *him,* venerating
him, lifting him to his queen's notice on their words of praise. Cordulan emperors might have striven for such adulation, and wept to
see how easily he commanded it.

Belinda's laugh came soft beneath that picture, making mockery
of herself as much as Dmitri. "I thought I was to be the leader
under whom this world rallied."

There was no apology in the rolling wall of Dmitri's power. To his mind she was a tool, easy to manipulate. "You turned against me, against our dream, and think to steal my child."

Belinda had an instant in which to gape, in which to absorb shock. Dmitri had not been meant to know about the child: she'd shielded her thoughts and taken her body from him before she thought he could know. Yet if he did know, reason followed that he would hold back his onslaught of power: surely a witchbreed babe was worth more than the cost of his plans betrayed to Robert Drake. Even as she thought it, though, threat formed as a black-edged weapon in the witchlord's hand.

New astonishment flooded her, though if she could build a shield with her magic, certainly a sword might be made of it, too, for shields were meant to be shattered by blades. Belinda shoved thought away, turning her attention to the needs of the moment, and Dmitri struck, a terrible crash of power that sent dark spider-webs over Belinda's golden magic. The blow came on as though it had struck through armour, blunted but still strong. She lashed back with a volley of thrown power like she'd used against Javier.

Dmitri caught those bursts easily, flinging them back toward her. They penetrated her shields, her mind and magic unable to distinguish between her attacks and her own power turned against her. Dizzy more with surprise than pain, she fell under the onslaught, and for a vivid moment saw herself, saw Dmitri, through the eyes of frightened soldiers around her.

Witchpower lanced back and forth, bright with gold and dark as death. It looked inhuman: *she* looked inhuman, blazing with more power than she'd ever imagined. Her hair was alight with it, answering to a breeze no mortal man could feel, and her eyes were vivid brilliance. A nimbus enveloped her, blurring her features so she was only feminine, and not any individual woman, and Dmitri, in turn, had become a black knife of masculinity, driving forward to strike at her. In witchpower regalia, they became gods, and for the first time Belinda fully grasped the power Robert's foreign queen could hold over Belinda's own people. If the witchblood could make her seem something so alien and magnificent, then a generation raised up under foreign rule would worship and fear their starborn queen, and never have the heart to stand against her.

Unexpected compassion broke in Belinda's breast. She might have spared the men around her this battle, might have drawn a veil of secrecy around herself and Dmitri, but she had nothing *to* spare. Envy sizzled through her, that Javier had learnt to hold shields even when he was distracted by other matters; it was a knack she would bend herself to in the days to come. All she could do now was scramble back.

Triumph slashed through Dmitri's attack, his view of her fall erupting as confidence in him. She'd stolen the upper hand a few times in Alunaer, but conviction soared toward her on his witch-power: he'd allowed it, had given up his own will in order to gain her trust.

Belinda, on her elbows and her arse in the dust, seized that open channel of magic to ride it back into Dmitri's core. That should have been her plan from the start, forcing a weakness in his de-fences. Power blazed through her, shaking off the images stolen from watching soldiers and bringing her to life. Darkness cracked under the brilliant shafts of her witchlight.

It opened astonishment in the witchlord; astonishment and dis-belief, too fresh to yet turn to anger. Belinda released the water-wheel rush that had once captured her magic and had more than once stymied Dmitri's, and then his amazement did turn to rage. *You are not my match,* Belinda whispered, uncertain of whether she spoke aloud, but certain that he heard her. *You aren't Robert's match, much less mine, and you will bend until you break beneath my will. You—*

Cold iron slammed into Dmitri's power, and black crumbled to dust with nothing more than a gasp of bewildered pain.

Belinda flinched back with a cry, sickened to meet a terrible nothingness where Dmitri's presence had been; afraid of the silence that took his place. Witchpower faded and cleared into morning sunlight, and Belinda, icy and confused, jolted to her feet so she might see and understand.

A girl stood where Dmitri had been, his body at her feet. Her head, crowned with thick black hair, was lowered, and her breath came in short hard gasps as she worked her fingers once, then again, as though they were alien to her and needed exploration. They were red with blood, and a knife wound opened Dmitri's throat, blood beginning to slow now, with no heartbeat to pump it forth. His power was as nothing, all the potential and all the possibility, all his promises and all his lies turned to sable dust that scattered across the surface of Belinda's power, and faded away.

Skated, too, across the girl's witchpower, which sheeted off her, a cold iron magic of unexpected familiarity. Not Javier, after all: that iron will had belonged to another, and all of Belinda's begrudgment fell away as the girl lifted her gaze.

She would have her mother's beauty: that, even more than the magic, struck Belinda. A strong square face and large eyes with crackling hair framing them; a sharpness to her nose that would come from her father, from the man who lay dead at her feet, but which only served to heighten how extraordinary her features were. It would be years yet before the pieces came together in a stunning whole, but even now, those who had the eyes to see it would know Ivanova Durova would become extraordinary.

She could be no one else: not with those features; not with the power that fitted her like a cloak, comfortable and certain of its place. She had the slenderness of youth, as she should: she wasn't yet fifteen, and at a cursory glance her slim form, clad in soldier's garb, might have been taken for a boy. With her hair tucked up, the illusion might have lasted a few seconds longer, but looking her in the face, Belinda couldn't imagine that Ivanova could ever be mistaken for other than what she was: the imperator's only heir, a girl, and a beautiful one at that.

The witchpower, then, had kept her safe from curious eyes; kept her safe for months as she travelled across Khazar and Echon with her army. Belinda stifled the impulse to throw her head back and crow with delight: this child didn't belong here, and yet she had taken a life with the ruthless efficiency of a trained soldier; with nearly the same cool calculation that Belinda herself might have shown.

Voices were beginning to buzz around them as Dmitri was recognised; as fear and anger began to set in over what seemed a coup in the heart of the Aulunian camp. Ivanova stepped forward, fully comfortable in drawing attention as an unfriendly gathering turned their eyes to her in preparation for forgiveness or mutiny, and even Belinda knew not which.

"This man who has been the ambassador from Khazar has come here to strip the heart of our alliance." Ivanova spoke Khazarian in a sweet voice, a soprano that Belinda thought would deepen with age, but it suited her now, fresh and young and light, and it won the attention of all the soldiers around her. Caught in the moment, Belinda translated Ivanova's words, the girl breaking often to let Belinda's speech echo her own. "I have suspected him a danger, and I have come with my mother's army to watch over you all. You saw the evil that swarmed from him; he had made a bargain with the devil, and now that dark contract has cost him his life. I only regret that he was not made to stand trial and burn, but time was short and I could not risk this—"

Her gaze fell on Belinda, who shook her head a fractional amount, not wanting to be exposed as the Aulunian heir. Almost without pause, Ivanova continued, "This dearly held alliance's failure by allowing a man like that to murder a fellow woman who has come to war. We are expected to stay at home and pray for our men," she whispered, and Belinda recognised something of true frustration in the girl's voice before Ivanova lifted it again and cried out, "But we are as made for war as you are! I have come to show you that the imperator's heir is not afraid of battle, and to command and know my brother soldiers in the fields! Now," she said more conversationally, beneath the roar that answered her rally, "now I think we had best retire, you and I, and speak of what's come to pass."

What a spy the imperator's heir would have made; what a spy! Belinda had known few enough instances in her life when she'd been given over to veneration; there was her childhood with Robert, and her esteem for Lorraine the queen. Beyond that, though, she could think of no other time when she'd sat in open admiration, fighting the smile that crept over her face.

For the moment Ivanova's power lay tucked so quietly within her that Belinda had no sense of it: the girl sitting across from her might have been any ordinary child. Any ordinary child, at least, who had secretly worked her way across fifteen hundred miles to be where she now was. Belinda knew with a touch of envy that her own magic was not nearly so well hidden.

"It's a discipline of thought," Ivanova said in her light voice. She seemed unimpressed with herself, unconcerned with the blood recently washed from her hands. "Father Dmitri was my tutor since childhood. He'd taught me the rules of logic that give the power a channel."

"Father?" Belinda's surprise broke the word as though she were a boy whose voice was changing.

"He was my mother's priest," Ivanova said, and an untoward relief snapped in Belinda's chest. The girl didn't know that Dmitri was her father in fact, and it wasn't a burden Belinda would lay on her. Sentiment, again; such sentiment, but she was a little enamoured of Ivanova's cool containment, and had no wish to risk shattering the girl's calm. Murdering a mentor was one thing; patricide something else, even if in the moment it was unknown.

That thought spiralled too near her own sins. Belinda deliberately opened her hands, smoothed her skirts as if they were emotions, and exacted control.

"I think he never knew the magic was awake in me. I think he was waiting for it, to train me in it, but the talent's been there since I was—"

"Eight or nine?" Belinda guessed, and Ivanova nodded. Memory scoured Belinda: how Robert had quieted the power in her when she was that age, rather than offer training in the discipline of thought that would master the witchpower. Perhaps if he had, she might have been the precocious witchlord Ivanova was now.

"I thought at first he'd realise it, but time went on and he didn't seem to, and I grew more talented." Ivanova smiled suddenly, bringing all her youth to the fore. "I would sneak after the boys and watch them at bathing, or listen to councils my mother hadn't invited me to. And I came to war," she said more seriously, "because my father loved it more than his wife or daughter, and I would not be refused the chance to see what had drawn him from us. I didn't know then that there were others like me, with the magic."

"Witchpower," Belinda murmured. "Javier calls it the witchpower. You held me back when I would cross the Gallic lines. I thought it was Javier's power turned colder, but yours is iron and his silver." And her own gold: soft metals, compared to iron, which seemed more telling than she wanted to consider.

"I couldn't risk that you were going to kill him." Ivanova spread her hands, expression that of utmost reason. "I couldn't risk either of you dying before I even had a chance to meet you and see the magic that we share. I watched, when you went to him. I listened to it all." Her eyebrows drew down over dark eyes, a frown marring her forehead as though the expression could give her the talent to see through Belinda's soul. "You believe the stories you told the Gallic king. That the magic we're born to is . . . foreign."

"I do." Hairs stood up on Belinda's arms, tiny thing she couldn't control. "You listened to it all? Then you—"

"Know that my father was in all likelihood not Feodor?" Ivanova shrugged, the first stiff movement Belinda had seen her indulge in. "And yet I'm still his heir, as you are Lorraine's and Javier is Sandalia's. These witchlords of yours have woven a complicated game toward a nightmare ending."

"A nightmare that's all the worse if we don't arm ourselves to fight it." Belinda knelt forward, reaching for Ivanova's hands. The girl didn't accept, leaving Belinda in a position of pleading subservience. "Javier is my ally in this, but reluctantly, and only because I can give him—"

"Yes," Ivanova said impatiently. "I was there. He's a coward, your br—"

Belinda, already close to the younger woman, already with her hands extended, clapped a hand across Ivanova's mouth so sharply it might have been a slap. "Never say those words aloud."

Ivanova's eyes widened over Belinda's hand, outrage coupled with astonishment, and iron witchpower shot out, not quite an attack, but unquestionably a rebuff.

It crashed into Belinda's own golden magic and was absorbed without a ripple.

"You're clever," Belinda whispered. "You're talented, and you're skilled, and I like you. But you had the advantage of surprise against Dmitri, and you will never be able to surprise me. I may not be your superior, but I am your elder, and my life has been made of treachery and deceit. I believe you're right. I believe Javier de Castille is a coward, but the rest of it, little girl, the rest of it *will go unspoken*."

She loosened her fingers and Ivanova wet her lips to protest, "You can't. You can't . . . !"

"Of course I can." All the whispers of envy had slipped away in a tidal pull of golden power. Someday, someday this young woman might challenge Belinda's authority, and that, an ancient instinct told her, was as it should be: every queen, in time, gave way to another. But not while in their prime, and not to a youth, even one whose talents were manifest.

A more ordinary part of herself insisted that she needed Ivanova, needed her power and perhaps the diplomatic bridge she provided, and that part, by slow degrees, reeled her back so she sat across from Ivanova once more, both of them flushed with passion. "Some things are too dangerous to be spoken aloud," Belinda said as softly and with as much cajoling as she could. Witchpower tendrils encouraged Ivanova's anger to relent. This was something Belinda could no longer do with Javier, but Ivanova, for all her youthful strength, was still a stranger to Belinda and her magic. "We're not seeking to topple thrones, for all that that's my father's will."

Ivanova had a fine rage on her, all the insulted fury of childhood not quite left behind. But she was impressed, too; impressed and perhaps a little frightened, having never faced another woman with her talents. Ambition was temporarily quenched, and with it a degree of her certainty, though a slow bloom of confidence crawled up to salvage what was left of her pride. "You still need me as an ally to keep your father distracted. You shouldn't treat a needed asset so."

Amused, Belinda inclined her head in a show of apology. "You're right. I shouldn't, and I apologise. Panic struck me, and panic often asserts itself as domination. I do need you," she said, humour fleeing. "I'd like to have your belief, but your agreement will do."

"I'm not a coward." Ivanova lifted her chin as though she'd been insulted. "I can see the truth of what you've shown Javier, and can look on it unafraid. There are men from beyond the mountains and beyond the oceans who look different from me. Perhaps it's no surprise they might come from beyond the stars, too, and look even more strange to my eyes. I have met women they call witches," she added far more quietly, and sounded suddenly like a child. "They are women who know herb lore or who are unattainable, but with whom men still fall in love. They're old crones or great beauties, and none of them at all have a hint of the witchpower. This magic of mine isn't like anything anyone has ever known, and if it comes from a foreign, far-off place, then at least what I am makes sense."

"Is it so easy?" Belinda knew she shouldn't ask, but the question spilled out regardless. "You accept it that easily? I've—" She laughed with resignation. "I've struggled and fought for the past half-year, and can still barely grasp what we are, but you can turn it to sense in your mind so quickly?" Perhaps it was the malleability of youth; perhaps Belinda was too much the thing she'd been raised to be, but another sting of envy ran through her at Ivanova's shrugging nod.

"Our people—Khazarian or Aulunian, Gallic or Essandian—don't have witchpower. Either we are impossible, or we are blessed or damned by our gods, or the figments stolen from Robert Drake and Dmitri Leontyev's thoughts are true, and we're children of . . . foreign queens," Ivanova finished in a whisper. "That we exist negates our impossibility, and that our fathers wield this same power and attribute it to foreign masters rather than gods or demons gives credence to the third possibility."

"Dmitri did teach you clear thought," Belinda murmured, though a supposition she hadn't considered came on her as she spoke: perhaps Dmitri and Robert were simply mad, the stories they'd concocted were ravings of deranged minds, and their children were heirs to nothing more than insanity.

"The trouble is," Ivanova said, "that if we ignore these bits of dreaming and they're true, then we are wholly and terribly unprepared for what the future brings. If we listen and they *aren't* true, then we're ready for a war that may never come . . . but it's better to be ready than caught off-guard." She looked up, her eyebrows lifted. "Dmitri is dead. Robert Drake will rely on you. Tell me what we do now, and I'll go to share your intrigues with Javier de Castille."

"Primrose?" Robert Drake threw back the tent flap with enough force to set the room shuddering. He looked wilder than she could remember ever seeing him, eyes round with alarm and hair crackling as if alight from within. He had been a long distance across the camp to have taken so long to come to her side, even if he'd known instantly that Dmitri was dead, and she had no way of knowing if he had. If not, a runner would have gone for him, and even still, he'd not been quick in coming. No need to be, perhaps, when it had been his plan as much as hers to remove the dark witchlord from their plots.

She sat in a huddle on the ground, Ivanova wrapped in her arms. They had washed the blood from Ivanova's hands, but stained cloth lay at their feet, and tears welled and spilled from Ivanova's wide staring eyes. "She saved me," Belinda whispered. "In the heat of battle, she leapt on him and cut his throat, that the Khazarian-Aulunian alliance might not be broken. This is Irina's daughter, Robert. This is Ivanova Durova, and she has pledged herself to us in blood."

Heed me well, she had whispered into Ivanova's hair. *Heed me well, for this is how it shall go.* Had Ivanova not announced herself so dramatically—and, Belinda admitted, to such good end; the men who'd been caught up watching her fight with Dmitri had needed an explanation, and the imperator's heir suddenly amongst them was a thing of legend—but had she not done that, Belinda might have secreted her away, might have found her a hiding place or sent her to Javier, and made use of a soldier as the man who'd taken Dmitri's life while paying for the audacity with his own. She had faith in her ability to tweak memories just enough to let that be the dominant perception, even without the sexual link that made altering minds so much easier. That had been before: she was stronger, now.

But Ivanova had been announced, and to change memories that much seemed like too great a risk, especially when Robert Drake would see a malleable child in Ivanova's frightened eyes. He'd shunted Belinda's power into quiescence when she was younger than Ivanova; he would never imagine that Dmitri's daughter had already come into her own. Dmitri's loss would be more than made up for by the chance to shape Ivanova with his own hands.

All they had to do, Belinda whispered, was let him believe himself the mentor, the guide, the saviour of a girl shocked and horrified by the actions she'd taken.

Robert knelt, a show of both sympathy and honour due to the imperator's heir, and extended a fatherly hand toward her.

Ivanova gave a choked sob and flung herself from Belinda into Robert's arms: into the protective circle only a man could offer, and into an assumption of safety created by the world they knew. Robert gathered her close and murmured an assurance, then lifted his eyes to Belinda and smiled with obvious triumph.

Belinda returned the smile, returned pleasure, and kept all her own triumph hidden away where her father would never see it. "She should rest," she murmured after a little time had passed. "She was very bold in the face of fighting, but it drained her. Let me put her to rest a while, Robert, and then we'll speak on what her being here means."

"It means my friend is dead," Robert said after Ivanova was tucked into a warm corner and Belinda had breathed a command to sleep, or at least pretend to sleep, over her. "Was there no other way, Primrose?"

"Not to Ivanova's mind." Belinda poured wine and offered Robert a glass, aware that she had once more fallen into the position of servant. Better to keep to old and safe roles than to upset a balance she now needed. "How could she know I had the ability to defeat him, to bend him to my will and make him your subservient again? I saw a little of our battle from the soldiers' eyes, Robert, and even I would have thought it Heaven fighting Hell. Ivanov must have seen the Khazarian ambassador doing his best to murder the Aulunian heir. What could she do but try to stop him, and salvage her mother's alliance?"

"How," Robert said, "did she know who you were?"

Belinda lowered her wine cup and stared at the handsome bearded lord across from her. "Father." The word was spoken with acidic incredulity. "Half the Aulunian army believes me to be here, in spirit if not in physical form. I'm praying for them, remember? And God Himself graced me with the light and the power of Heaven so I might save the fleet from sure defeat against the armada. So when a woman bursting with God's light stands battling a man filled with black spite at the heart of the Aulunian camp, who else *could* she be?"

Robert pursed his lips, then shrugged his eyebrows and took a long draught of wine. "A fair point, I suppose. You're meant to be safe at home in a convent in Alunaer, Primrose. How am I to explain your presence here when you've been seen there?"

"My spirit has flown to war," Belinda said airily. "My physical form kneels in dutiful prayer and God gives my soul wings that I might lift the hearts of my soldiers to His command, and inspire a conversion to the Reformation church in all those who fall before our army." She smiled, and, clearly despite himself, Robert laughed.

"Ah, and damn the nurse who taught you cleverness, girl, for certainly I'd have instilled a civil tongue in your head."

Belinda all but dipped a curtsey where she sat, a smile still curving her mouth. "Of course, papa."

Robert's voice softened. "You haven't called me that in a long time."

"We haven't played at games of family for a long time. I've been too long a tool, and not at all a daughter. Perhaps things are changing now." She glanced toward Ivanova and then back to Robert, eyebrows lifted. "Things are unquestionably changing. I know you think it's unnecessary, but I need to understand. War brings innovation—that I can appreciate. But to make ships that sail through the sky, to dig pits in the earth so vast whole seas could disappear into them . . . these things are so far beyond us. How can we few shape a world that's worthy for our queen?"

"Our," Robert echoed, thoughtfully, curiously.

Belinda spread her hands. "Is she not? Is serving Aulun, and through Aulun, your queen, not what I have been made for?" She fell silent, looking away from Robert as she worked her way toward the right things to say. A lifetime of training had taught her to find them, had taught her to play silences and speech as instruments, carrying them each to the breaking point before shoring them up with the other.

"I understand so little," she eventually murmured. "Yet what I do know is that when I see the things that drive you, I see loyalty most of all. In my life I have been loyal and held faith and trust in you." She shook her head, almost dismissing her own fancies. " 'Heed me well, Primrose, for this is how it shall go.' Those words have always been true. Each time you've said them, the things you've named have played out as you've said they would, and Lorraine's throne has remained safe. You love her," Belinda said, so clearly it might have been an accusation. "I think you didn't mean to, but you love her, and I think that if your foreign queen's needs should damage Lorraine's own that even you might hesitate in fulfilling them."

"I'm fortunate," Robert said, "that the two have never run counter to each other. Nor will they ever; even if Lorraine should live to the greatest span of mortal years, her world won't change so much in that time that I'll find myself standing against her. I have been fortunate," he said again, and a note of sorrow deepened the words, proving him too aware that fortune was a fool's friend.

"So even if I look only to the things I understand, if I bend my head to my mother's crown and play the part she's given me, then I serve where and how I should. That's comfortable to me, Robert." The truth there made her heart hurt, even when filtered through witchpower ambition. Aspirations born of magic ran down certain channels, willing to serve one far-off and mighty figurehead so long as her own supremacy went unchallenged by the greater populace. Bending knee to Lorraine felt right, even still; bowing to a foreign queen was not anathema to one such as Belinda, who was made to serve. It was this other thing she'd become, with awakening and breaking free from the rigours she'd been shaped to, that fit poorly, and yet even as she spun her web for Robert, she knew she would follow the lines she cast out for herself, rather than be drawn into his intrigues. He and Dmitri had demanded too much, had pushed too far, and in doing so had unintentionally set her on her own path.

"If I look beyond those comfortable places then I see what I've seen all my life. My papa, guiding me toward something he understands more clearly than I do. I want to understand," she whispered, suddenly harsh. "I want these goals and intentions to be shared, I want you to think me worthy of that trust. But even if you won't give me that, I'll serve Lorraine with all my soul, and until the day I die, and in doing so, think I must give myself over to serving your queen. So yes, Robert. *Our* queen, whether she sits on a throne in Alunaer or in a ship amongst the stars." Her confidence wavered on the last words, but she brought her chin up, defiant of her poor comprehension.

A wave of pride broke over her, flooding from Robert with no evident care as to what he exposed. He offered a hand and Belinda took it, wincing at the strength he crushed her fingers with, and bemused at the witchpower wall that kept her from tasting anything of his thoughts. He'd learned, then, had learned to be wary of her, and that was as it should be, though she made no attempt to rob him of his secrets as she'd done half a year earlier in Sandalia's private chambers.

"This war will carry on a while yet, and in its time you'll come to see how we'll shape this world for our foreign queen. You're right: we're too far away from it now for its form to be seen, but in another year, in another ten, you'll begin to understand. Lend me a little patience, Primrose. I don't ask from a wish to keep you unschooled, but because you lack the experience to cast your imagination as far forward as I would have it reach. It is asking a child who's only seen a rain puddle to imagine the ocean, or asking the blind to describe the stars. You'll learn to see the ocean, Belinda. You'll learn to describe the stars. But give me a little more time in which to open your eyes, so that you're not staggered under the weight of vision."

She had professed her trust in him and had made much of being willing to serve, so she bowed her head in agreement, and for a moment held tight to Robert's hand. "Will we win this war?"

"It doesn't matter," Robert said, ruthless with honesty. "Whether Cordula's combined might wins or Aulun's Khazarian alliance takes the day, all that truly matters is that we force our hands toward advances that will help us surge forward in technology. I'll try to win it for Lorraine, of course; my loyalty goes that far, and perhaps even further. But in the end what I need from this fight are new weapons, and new ways of making them, and so I must make a need for them."

"You could give them to us," Belinda said slowly. "Why the subterfuge? Why force us to the advancements you need, rather than offer them to us as though a god might?"

"Why did I send you a dancing-master?"

"Because the grace learned for the dance floor stands anyone, woman or man, well on a field of battle." She reached for the stillness, wanting its cold comfort to hold her as she worked through Robert's question and its application, but she'd fractured her hold on it too badly, and found herself only able to sit and stare, unfocused, while a finger tapped her knee, visible signal of her scurrying thoughts. "A skill struggled for is more trusted than one that comes easily. The witchpower," she added softly. "It's simply there, and its unasked-for presence makes me wonder if I can control it, at times. A new weapon given to the world without men fighting to create and understand is less trustworthy than one that's been sweated and bled over. You want us to have pride of ownership in what we've done. A queen with thinking subjects is better served than one with mindless slaves frightened by the magical machines they use." She looked up, surprised. "Dmitri's intentions weren't so different from yours."

"Dmitri was eager for an egalitarian world, where everyone's education gave them room to stride for the stars and serve our queen. Education is dangerous," Robert murmured. "Less so when applied only to a certain class."

Laughter caught Belinda off-guard. "Educate everyone? Who would till the fields and fight the wars?"

"Disgruntled students and angry lawyers," Robert said, suddenly cheerful. "The latter might not be a bad idea. Do you see the trouble, then? Alliances are well and good, but it's in the heat of wartime that innovations are made, and amidst that chaos it's easier to seed fresh ideas to meet old needs and make them seem like natural progression. We can change a world in a matter of decades this way, prepare it to serve our queen, and yet not expend our own resources on conquering."

"Decades," Belinda echoed. "It takes patience to plan so far ahead."

Patience he'd instilled in her, it seemed; stealing his plans out from under him, changing her world to one that could fight and defend itself, wasn't a thing to be done overnight.

"The distances our queen has travelled are incomprehensibly vast, even to my mind. They become meaningless numbers, useless in any practical fashion. It takes time, a long time, to cross those distances, and even when our enemies pursue us at their quickest pace, we have decades and even longer to spare."

"Will they come here? What happens if they do? Will the queen we've learned to serve protect us?"

"Of course," Robert said smoothly, and Belinda knew it for a lie, not through the witchpower, but for a tone of voice that harkened back to her childhood, when he'd promised that when the time was right he would call for her to meet the queen, and instead left her, for thirty days, to stand by her door in hope, waiting for an introduction that never came.

Stillness finally settled around her, calming and comforting, the gift of a habit she'd begun the morning after Lorraine and Robert rode away without so much as glancing back. Robert would raise her people up to strip her world of its resources, to be near-slaves to his queen, and when his enemies came to them, he would abandon her world to their flying ships and terrible weapons, and, as when she was a child, he would never look back.

Belinda tightened her fingers around his and gave him a smile born of pure relief and gladness and utter mistruths, and whispered, "Then let us serve, Papa. Let us change this world."

25

JAVIER DE CASTILLE, KING OF GALLIN
3 July 1588 † Brittany; the Gallic camp

"She's betrayed us." Javier spoke to the sound of footsteps, not bothering to turn his head and see who approached. A week on since Belinda had slipped away, a week in which Aulun had steadily moved forward, crushing the Ecumenic army. Only his magic kept them from wholesale slaughter, and it seemed inevitable that that, too, would fail. He'd stopped sleeping, not from a lack of weariness, but from the gnawing hole in his gut that said too pointedly that God was not, after all, his benefactor or his blesser: Belinda's stories were the stuff of nightmares, and still somehow carried the inexorable weight of truth. He'd tried not to think on it, had made no confession; not to Eliza, not to Tomas, not, most certainly, to Sacha, whom he hadn't seen since the morning they buried Marius.

That was where he sat now, by Marius's grave under the thin light of a new moon. Marius knew all his secrets now, if anyone did, and Javier took small comfort in sitting with his friend in silence, no pretensions or lies between them.

"Who has, my king? Eliza?" Tomas's confused voice startled Javier, who looked sharp after all, then settled into a sigh.

"Oh, it's you, priest. I expected Liz coming to ask me why I wasn't yet abed."

"And the answer is betrayal? By whom?" Tomas sat down without Javier's leave, but then, until lately Javier would have thought nothing of it. He'd drawn away from Tomas in the past week and knew it: saw his need for the priest as what had cost Marius his life, and so retreated from what might have been solace offered in the friendship that remained.

There was Marius; and then there were Belinda's stories of foreign lords, too uncomfortably real when witchpower burnt away his fears. God hadn't graced him with magic: something far more incomprehensible had, and knowing that made meeting Tomas's eyes all the harder. It left Javier alone, with neither priest to confide in nor God to trust in, but better that than to find new prices to pay.

"The Holy Mother," he said, trying to stop his thoughts with words spoken aloud. The witchpower came from a source entirely other than God, so perhaps laying blame at the queen of Heaven's feet wasn't the blasphemy that it might be. "Aulun thinks she walks amongst them, and with their numbers and their victories, perhaps they're not wrong. Perhaps she's abandoned us despite our faith, and perhaps God looks to her lead."

"You can't believe such things, Javier." Admonishment and concern filled Tomas's tone, as though he knew the lines he was meant to say and the emotion he was meant to fill them with, but his own uncertainty crept through and made what he said truer than he'd intended. "God will not abandon his favoured son." Determination slipped into that statement, and Javier wondered if Tomas's conviction could sway God's mind.

"Of course not." There was nothing else to say, nothing Tomas would find acceptable, but sarcasm weighted the words and gave too much evidence of Javier's failing belief.

"Javier . . ." Tomas shifted, lifting a hand to touch Javier's shoulder, but it fell again and he settled himself. "You've not come to confession in a week, my lord. I thought perhaps it should come to you."

"To what end? Marius is dead at Sacha's hand and I have no stomach for any horror beyond that. My sins are so compleat as to beg no forgiveness." Belinda's face—and more—flashed in his vision, soft warmth and witchpower and the devil's own damnation. Oh, he had loved: how could he not, when met with a creature so much like himself. Disgustingly like himself, and done without wilful intent or no, God couldn't forgive that sin. Lust: he ought to have known not to fall for that most deadly of temptations, as Sacha ought not have fallen to green-eyed envy. Eliza, thus far, seemed unscarred by any of those terrible seven; if he could keep her clear, that, perhaps, might be a small salve to his soul.

"There is nothing God cannot forgive if you come to him truly penitent," Tomas whispered, but without the serene confidence he'd once had. Javier looked to him, curiosity piqued over self-doubt and flagellation, and more welcome.

"What have you learnt of unforgiveable sin, priest?"

"I've learnt that even man can forgive that which we might call unthinkable. My intellect tells me time and again that I should revile and fear a man who's stolen my will from me, and yet my heart harbours no resentment. If I, who am weak with mortality, can forgive, how can God, in His infinite compassion, see any darkness which He can't forgive?"

"You've forgiven what I can't," Javier said harshly. "Leave me alone with my sins, priest."

"Your sins and your betrayals? Are you certain you spoke of the Holy Mother, and not one closer to you?"

"What?"

"Eliza caught quickly," Tomas murmured. "Are you certain you've married a woman who's bearing your child, Javier, and not one who's taking advantage of some by-blow of a Maglian lover?"

Laughter seemed the wrong response, but it was the one that burst from Javier, wholly derisive. "If only you knew how certain I am."

"How can you be? Came she a virgin to your bed? A woman of such beauty, living in a city of whores?"

Javier slammed his hand out and caught a fistful of Tomas's robes, all of his laughter gone. "If you value the tongue in your head, priest, you will silence yourself now and no such further words will ever pass your lips. The time to voice your doubts was before we were wed, and I will have your respect now." Witch-power boiled, hoping for argument, for any excuse to overwhelm the priest and use him as it would. For once Javier had no urge to temper it, as eager himself to embrace furious insult as his magic was. It would be a release unlike anything on the battlefield, all intimacy and personal need. He fought for his troops out of duty, but Tomas would serve his pleasure.

"Forgive me." Tomas's voice came low, no hint of resistance in it. Frustration twisted in Javier, witchpower thwarted by acquiescence. "I should have spoken earlier," Tomas went on, still soft, still light; a lover's voice, all wrong in the thin moonlight. "I should have, but in the chaos of the day did not. Forgive me, my king."

Javier released him with a curse, turning futile witchpowered anger toward the distant hills, where it could unfurl itself without harm. "What choice have I, when you plead so prettily? But don't test me, Tomas. Don't let your thoughts or your tongue wander down those roads again."

"My lord." Tomas sat silent a moment or two, then got to his feet. "I'll leave you, my king. I hope your thoughts turn to happier things."

"Aye," Javier muttered to his departing steps. "So do I."

"Would it make you happier to know the Aulunian heir hasn't betrayed you?" A woman's voice, marked with a Khazarian accent, came out of the air, and for the second time Javier startled, this time jolting to his feet.

"Forgive *me*," the voice went on, and with it a girl's form came clear, only a few feet away. Witchpower tainted the air around her, a cold iron weight more implacable than Belinda's, or even Javier's own. Her magic had a feeling of certainty to it, like Robert Drake's: like she'd spent a lifetime ensconced in it, practising with no fear for her soul. "Forgive me," she said again, cheerfully, and without a hint of the repentance Tomas had voiced when he'd said those words. "I'd intended to show myself earlier, but your lovely priest arrived. I'm meant to go virgin to my wedding bed, but for a face such as that . . ."

A fist clenched around Javier's heart and pulled it askew in his chest, knocking breath away into dull sickness. For an instant his mind flew to the impossible, that witchbreed men and women were all around, and that not a soul in Echon was safe from their interferences. A cry knotted itself in his chest at the relief and despair borne with that idea, but it was another thing entirely that he said aloud: "You would be Ivanova. There is rumour in the camps that you are with the Aulunians, and Akilina has had a letter from your mother. She's worried about you, princess."

The artfully carefree expression on the girl's face spasmed into guilt. "My mother wouldn't have allowed me to ride to war."

"With good reason, and yet it seems she couldn't stop you." Javier made a short gesture at the night she'd faded out of. "I must learn to do that, to hide in the shadows. It seems a knack the witch-women around me have learned. What are you doing here?" His heart's beat had steadied, though shock still swam through him. Belinda had said she couldn't shape their future alone. *It needs both of us,* she had said, *and it needs Ivanova if we can get her, and it needs Dmitri Leontyev dead.*

All the armies knew Leontyev was dead, and now Ivanova Durova stood at the heart of his own camp, as if conjured by Belinda's will. It was not possible: the Aulunian heir had only said those words a week ago, and she could not have brought Ivanova here in that time. The girl had to have moved on her own in order to be in this place now, and Javier de Castille suddenly wondered if God's hand was in this after all. Men could orchestrate war across a continent—that, he believed. But for the scant handful of children who might stand against that war to gather through their own will and no other guidance—that smacked of destiny. Javier turned a slow astonished look on the girl before him, and she, standing under flattering moonlight that gave hint of the legendary woman she would become, answered him with a shrug.

"I've come as Belinda's voice, because Lord Drake holds her too close for her to slip away. There's no betrayal, king of Gallin, but the Ecumenic army should lose whether she intends it or not. You're too few, and we too many." She sat abruptly, graceless as a colt and wiping away the promise of beauty her youthful form held. Javier sat more slowly as Ivanova spoke, her words measured. "We'll come to war tomorrow, Belinda and myself, but most especially Belinda. We'll ride hard on you, coming to break your army's back, and at the height of it you'll do battle with Belinda herself. And you'll win, king of Gallin. This will be your chance to take the Aulunian heir prisoner, and turn the tide to your call."

"So easily," Javier muttered. "Will Belinda play her part?"

Ivanova shrugged again, loose and comfortable in her body. "Belinda acts out of duty, serving Aulun more faithfully than I'd have wagered possible. She sees this war and this gamble for the future as doing that. Aulun is perhaps subsumed by the needs of the world, but that's too big a thought for her, and so she serves Aulun and in so doing serves the world. She'll do what she must to those ends." Compleat confidence filled the girl's answer, enough so that Javier's eyebrows rose.

"Dare I ask what prompts me to act?"

Challenge lit Ivanova's black eyes. "I don't know. Dare you?"

Intrigue caught him out, for all that a quiet rush of wisdom said he might be happier ignorant. Still, Javier nodded, and Ivanova flashed a pointed smile.

"You're a king afraid of his power, a boy with only a few friends who's desperately afraid of losing them. One's dead, another betrayed you, and the third's become your wife, but the duty you owe your throne will force you to put her away unless there's a child. You'll make any bargain and forgive all sins so you might not be left alone."

Anger sharp enough to tell him the girl spoke truth shot through Javier, making his speech short. "You see very clearly."

Ivanova lifted a shoulder and let it fall, then turned her palm up. A ball of dull iron witchlight formed and blinked away. "The magic lets us see as clearly as we choose. We have little time for prevarication and pretty lies."

Javier stared at where her power had disappeared, then met her eyes. "And what drives you?"

She smiled, suddenly full of a child's wickedness. "I don't like being told what to do." Both smile and smugness faded. "You know royal lives are not ours to do with as we please. I've taken this chance to see war before I'm confirmed heir, and it will likely be the last truly free act of my life. I think it was necessary, but my mother will not agree. So this is the mark I'll leave, no matter what becomes of my life: I'll do what I can to help steal this world back from those who would take it from us. I don't like that they think they can make us unknowing slaves to their intentions, and if I can play the contrary and do a part to prove them wrong, then my life's well spent, even before I take a throne." She waited a moment, then arched an eyebrow. "Do you read me with your magic, king of Gallin? Do I speak the truth?"

Javier's mouth thinned, inadvertent admission that she did. Ivanova nodded, then leaned forward to put a hand over Javier's. Her fingers were warm, much warmer than his own, as if she burned with internal fire. The passion of youth, he thought, then smirked; he'd not reached an age himself that would be called anything but youth, and yet Ivanova seemed young to him. "Are you so certain this is a war we can win?"

Ivanova looked down her nose at him. Beakish nose, almost too sharp: it should've taken away from her beauty, but instead it added to it, giving her unexpected strength. Her smile, though, which came after that scolding look, was entirely a thing of ease and enjoyment with no worries for strength at all. "Unless you choose to fail on the battlefield tomorrow, yes. I don't know, king of Gallin. Are you content to be defeated by women?"

"Go away," Javier said as severely as he could. The girl had made him want to laugh, and he thought laughter should no longer be his companion. Not after the last week. Not, in truth, after this past six-month. "Go away," he said again, and got to his feet. "I'll bring you your battle come daybreak."

BELINDA WALTER
4 July 1588 † *Brittany; the Aulunian camp*

Wisdom should have sent Belinda to sleep hours since, but she sat in shadows, watching the distant Gallic campfires through a still-dark night. The sky would begin to grey with dawn in less than an hour, but for now she was alone with her thoughts and plans, more alone than she'd been in a week.

Robert had turned avuncular with Dmitri's death, suddenly making her his confidante and yet somehow conveying almost nothing to her. Curiosity had her in its grip, her tremulous understanding of Robert's world burgeoning into a desire to know more. It seemed to her that she'd tucked away what he was until a part of her mind had grown accustomed to the strangeness, and could make some rough sense of it. Struggling for words with Javier had helped: it had torn away her reluctance to face what little she'd learned, and Ivanova's ruthless, childish practicality had done its part as well.

Her father, though, would have no truck with furthering her comprehension. He'd asked for time and she'd agreed, afraid he might see through her plans if she pressed too far. Even so, witch-power ran in slow tendrils around her mind, pushing her thoughts, examining what she knew, and she was unsurprised when Robert crested a nearby hillock and came to sit at her side. He looked well-rested, as if he'd awakened from a comfortable bed at his estate, rather than being one man among thousands sleeping on a hillside under summer stars.

Feeling like a child, Belinda tilted against his side and murmured "Papa," which garnered a laugh from the big man.

"If you were eight, that trick might still work, my Primrose." Still, he put an arm around her and kissed her hair, playing the role of father he'd abandoned years ago. "Your thoughts are heavy enough to stir the air. What's amiss?"

Belinda ducked her head against Robert's shoulder. "We're a hard day's battle from victory, Papa. Give me the chance, and I think I can rout Gallin and its ambitions with a single blow." It had taken a week to lead Robert to this opening. Played too hard, she would lose the game, and neither she nor Javier would forgive her the slip.

"Can you?" Robert sounded amused; felt amused, through the vestiges of witchpower that danced around them both. Belinda wound hers more tightly, keeping it close and hoping she didn't seem to retreat by doing so. "What would you do, Primrose?"

"Rumours of my presence fly about the camp," she whispered. "The fight with Dmitri was unsubtle, but no one quite imagines the queen's heir is on the battlefield. There are stories that her spirit, imbued with the Holy Mother, is so bright and great as to have settled on a camp follower when the Khazarian ambassador took it in his head to end the alliance. They even say the Holy Mother brought Ivanova here, to protect Belinda Walter's spirit from that attack."

"That," Robert said in scolding amusement, "is inconsistent, my girl. Why would the Madonna choose a camp follower for Dmitri to attack, only to then send another champion to protect her?"

Belinda put her elbow in his ribs, comfortable action of the little girl she'd once been. "You, of all people, whose life is made up of spreading and starting and quelling rumours, should know that consistency is not gossip's strength."

"True enough," Robert said contentedly. "Go on."

"The army believes the Holy Mother rides with them. I think that come tomorrow's battle, she should. Let me become a banner for a few hours, to inspire them. My witchpower, unleashed, is gold as sunlight, pure as God's love. The troops will cross mountains to fight for the Madonna."

Robert pulled away as she spoke, turning an expression of astonishment on her. "You would propose putting yourself into the midst of battle? Need I remind you that you *are* the Aulunian heir, Primrose? What would we do if we lost you?"

Belinda sat back, expression stiffening with offence. "Surely you have more faith in me than that, Father." Beneath bubbling insult, she wanted to laugh: she was supposed to be vexed at the idea she might lose, but the emotion was real, ready to strike Robert down for his audacity in doubting her. Even the fact that she intended on losing did nothing to assuage her pique, and the contradictions struck her as funny in a moment when she should be entirely focused on performing the role she needed to. "You might rally the men yourself," she went on, still rigid with indignity. "But no one knows you're graced with the witchpower, and there are already channels laid in their hearts and minds to lay down their lives for the queen of Heaven made manifest."

"But the war must go on a while yet, my Primrose. We've had no time yet to push forward with the developments I want." Robert lifted his chin and looked out over the battlefields as Belinda's stomach plummeted, a chill running over her skin. "Perhaps it'd be best for you to return to Aulun. Lorraine's perturbed at your absence as it is."

"If you've a pinch of kindness in you, you'll at least let me take my glory ride before sending me back to that convent," Belinda said as drily as she dared. Her hands were steady and her breathing calm, but her voice wanted to tremble. She had not thought of how she might go forward should Robert refuse her suggestion. To act without his blessing was to strike out on her own far more than she'd intended. It would tell Robert her mind was her own, and that her goals lay at odds with his. Beatrice Irvine had been impetuous, but Belinda Primrose, in all her life, had rarely been. She cursed that for the first time: had she been in the habit of breaking rules and following her own fate, she might now go against Robert's wishes without stirring concern in his soul. Then again, had she made a lifetime of that sort of boldness, she would never have come this far.

Robert chuckled. "I'd rather face your wrath than Lorraine's, my Primrose. No, we've too many plans to advance to risk defeating them now, and I fear you're right: you leading them into battle would bring about the utter destruction of the Ecumenic army. Go back to sleep and dream of glory, but keep that pretty head safe for its golden crown."

"Yes, Papa." Belinda got to her feet as Robert did, and dipped him a curtsey as he walked away into the night. Darkness took him after a few steps, and she was left watching where he'd been, a clarion thought in her mind.

Robert Drake had not made ritual of his order. There were words so ingrained in her she doubted she could stand against him, but they'd gone unspoken: he had not murmured, *this is how it shall go, Primrose. Heed me well.* He had not locked her into that path with a phrase so familiar it might well have been a witch's spell cast to bend her will.

Carefully, carefully, Belinda stepped back into her tent, and knelt in its darkness to prepare herself to go against Robert, Lorraine, Aulun, and the life she had known.

RODRIGO DE COSTA, PRINCE OF ESSANDIA
4 July 1588 ✝ Brittany; the Gallic camp

It will be dawn in an hour or two, and Rodrigo should be sleeping. The morning is all too likely to bring the devastation of his army, and there is nothing he can do about it. A week has passed since

Javier brought the broken Cordulan army together into one, and that they've survived this long seems more luck than any blessing on God's part. Rodrigo would be grateful if an archangel would roar down and sunder the Aulunian alliance, and in so doing show His hand of approval for their war. As it is, it's easy to lose faith; Javier's witchpower kept the fight roughly even for a day or two, until Belinda returned fire. It took only a day of that onslaught for the Cordulan allies to fall back, and then again, and now Rodrigo stands at the centre of a storm, his army sleeping around him in what may be their last night together.

There's still a stiffness in his ribs where the long shallow cut has not yet fully healed, and a part of him is phlegmatic about it: as the days pass it seems ever more unlikely that he'll live much longer to worry about it. Still, Akilina has offered daily to tend the wound, and he's politely rebuffed her: he might yet survive the war, and would rather not be obliged to fight for his life against his wife's tender ministrations.

Rodrigo shakes himself, and steps away from his blind watch of the quiet front lines to duck into his tent. A map is spread across a table there, the same map that used to grace Javier's tent, but in honour of both his marriage and of losing Marius, the strategy sessions have been moved away from the young king's room and into the older prince's. Akilina, only a few months longer a bride than Eliza, is piqued by this, but the generals and officers of the army are not inclined to bow to her whim. She's been evicted from the sessions, even when they run late into the night, because no one trusts her, not even her husband.

Eliza has been a blessing there, has played a diplomatic part as though she was born to it. They have a small thing in common, the pregnancies beginning to swell their bellies, and while it hasn't made friends of them, it's given them grounds on which to build a camaraderie. While Rodrigo and Javier retreat to argue policy and strategy, the women sit and talk, perhaps sharing their hopes for their children, though Rodrigo imagines Akilina has some loathing for that topic, especially as she's still sick and pale, where the Gallic guttersnipe seems strong and healthy.

The Gallic *queen,* Rodrigo reminds himself: he crowned her

himself. And he likes Eliza, likes her quick tongue and her sharp mind. He thinks there's a pragmaticism in the young woman that Javier needs, and if she caught him by falling pregnant, perhaps it's all to the best. Gallin needs an heir, though if this war goes on the way it is, its heir will be Lorraine Walter's bastard daughter.

Bugs crawl over Rodrigo's skin at the thought. No: Akilina and Eliza will be sent to Lutetia, though Isidro is safer still. But either gives them some chance of bearing their children in safety, and one of them, at least, must.

That Akilina will never agree to go is beside the point. Within another week the heart of the Cordulan camp will no longer be safe. Looking at his maps, at the streaks of colour that are Khazar and Aulun's alliance, and the small retreating bands that are his own army, he wonders if he should wait so long as a week, or just have them sent away now.

"Prince! Essandian prince! I have words for you!" For all that it's the middle of the night, the gondola boy bursts into the tent, wide awake and pleased with himself. Rodrigo can't remember the boy being anything other than pleased with himself, yet still, in the midst of war, to see his shining face and bright confidence is worthy of mention every time.

The child's Gallic has improved far more rapidly than his care to use it correctly has: he still speaks like a water rat, and frequently in Parnan, trusting that the people to whom his messages have any importance will understand him. He is, of course, correct, which means he'll never learn to have a properly civil tongue in his head, but perhaps to have one would diminish his exuberance, and that's a price Rodrigo might consider too rich to pay.

He ruffles the child's hair and gets a dour look for it: the boy clearly considers himself too old for such treatment, and not too low to scold royalty. "The lady Eliza will make me cut it if you keep making it fall into my eyes, Essandian prince."

Rodrigo, trying not to laugh, says, "My apologies. I thought I was clearing it away from your eyes. You have a message?"

"Oh!" The boy draws himself up, affront to his hair forgotten. "There is a man here to see you, prince, a very old man with mules and carts and a look about him that you do not want to argue with.

I know," he said with great solemnity. "I have seen men like him before, and have been thumped by them."

"A man with mules and carts," Rodrigo says with some astonishment. "Here, in the heart of the camp?"

"Sí, signor prince. He is outside your tent, feeding his mules. One of them likes wine in his water, but the man says he never gets drunk."

"The donkey doesn't get drunk, or the man?" Rodrigo asks, bemused. "How did he—" Nevermind: the boy won't know. Someone will answer as to how an old man with a supply train of any kind has come unchallenged into the heart of the Cordulan camp, even in the small hours of the morning, but it won't be the gondola boy any more than it might be Rodrigo. "Very well," he says after a moment's consideration. "I suppose I'd better see this man of yours."

"Yes, or one of us will get thumped." The way the child says it suggests it won't be he who feels the weight of a thumping, and Rodrigo grins as he follows the child. Had he been able to guarantee a boy like this one, he would have wed with a fair mind to breeding heirs, instead of reluctantly and near the end of what any man might consider a long life.

The man with the mules puts paid to thoughts of his own long life so abruptly that Rodrigo's grin broadens. He's silver-haired and rheumy-eyed, carries a stick taller than he is, and leans heavily on a donkey who slurps at a trough full of pale pink water. He—the man, not the donkey, though the donkey's seen innumerable years himself—looks to be ninety if he's a day, and seems to have been carved out of already-gnarled wood over which a brightly-coloured sackcloth has been thrown. It's possible that not even Rodrigo would have stopped him from trodding through camp, because despite the gondola boy's warnings of thumpings, the visitor looks as though he's unlikely to keep his feet without the support of both staff and beast.

Indeed, he leans toward Rodrigo with a wobble bordering on the dramatic, and squints at him with those blue rheumy eyes. "King's man," he says unexpectedly, and in such a heavy mountain dialect it takes Rodrigo a few seconds to translate it into clear Essandian.

Then he blinks, too nonplussed to take offence. "Prince's man if any, grandfather. I—"

"Pah!" The old man waves his stick like it carries a banner; indeed, Rodrigo's gaze snaps to its top for an instant, looking for the flag that would give this old man such confidence. "Prince's man, sure enough, but 'king's man' has more strength in its sound. King's man, man's king, doesn't matter anyway, you're losing this war, king's man."

Now offence does win out, bitter ashy taste in Rodrigo's mouth. It's not that the old man's wrong; it's that admitting it openly in front of a gathering crowd of curious, sleepy-eyed troops is not to be done. But before he can give a diplomatic answer—before, thankfully, the gondola boy can give a less diplomatic response— the old man waves his stick again, this time all but under Rodrigo's nose. "I've brought you a gift, king's man. I've brought you a toy to turn the tide."

While Rodrigo is still looking for something to say, the old man steps back and with a flourish, tears the canvas from his wine-drinking mule's cart to expose the new way of the world.

That's what Rodrigo thinks when the canvas comes back to reveal a shining gun on heavy wheels: *this is the new way of the world.* It is clearly a weapon, and clearly not a cannon, though it's the size of one. But rather than a large barrel it has many smaller ones set in a circle, and at its arse-end, where a cannon fuse might be lit, there's a large box with slanted sides. Rodrigo's moving, climbing the cart wheel, staring at the gleaming monstrosity with an excitement that turns his knees weak and makes his breath come short. In a half-century of life, he's never met a woman or a man who had such an effect on him: if he had, he might have fallen prey to a marriage bed or mortal sin long since. But his eyes are for the weapon, and there's a crank within reaching distance; Rodrigo spins it, sending the barrels rattling in a circle.

Now he understands the box on top, or almost: he feels like a child exploring a hidden passageway as he climbs inside the cart and looks into the angled box; into the hopper that will feed bullets into a half-dozen barrels. His heartbeat is so fast his vision swims, and it's all he can do to stop from crowing as he spins the crank again and listens to the empty barrels chatter. "How quickly does it fire?" Oh, God *is* listening, God is concerned for the Ecumenic army's fate after all, and has sent an angel of war to Gallin in the form of this rickety inventor and his drunken donkey.

"Six hundred rounds in a minute," the old man says, "and there are five more like it. The trouble is making enough bullets, king's man. Set your men to it, if you want to win this war. A single man can only do so much."

"We'll need a whole new way of making them." Rodrigo kneels by his terrible gun, smoothing a hand down one of its long thick barrels, and when he looks along its line, he sees a future that didn't exist only minutes ago. He feels as though his mind's been opened, as if curtains he never knew were there have been drawn back to let sunlight in, and it makes him giddy. He's an embarrassment to himself, and he doesn't care. "Men can't keep up with that rate. Perhaps if we build a line to pour moulds, to quench the shells in water and have men pour gunpowder in at the end. The line could be run on a waterwheel and by men with bellows to heat the metal. Yes."

He might have done as much to make any bullet: that thought strikes him, and fades away without rancour. This opening of his mind is a gift, and if he looks backward there's no shame in having only thought as ordinary men did. But now, faced with a mechanised gun, the possibility of its components being created with the same efficiency as it would fire them seemed vivid and obvious. "How did you think of it?" he whispers.

The old man snorts dismissively, and in so doing shows his pleasure. "Old doesn't mean foolish, king's man. A cannon's slow to load and gets too hot to use, and pistols are worse. But the two together, and put on a crank to keep the barrels cool, now that was a bit of cleverness." He leans on his staff, age-lumped hands wrapped around it, and looks satisfied. "A forge and patience in the mountains, that's what it took, and a few dead cattle when I was wrong about how far the bullets would go."

"I'll make reparations," Rodrigo says drily, and straightens from his inspection of the gun to smile at the old man. "So? Will you show us how it's used?"

26

In the last weeks Belinda had become, if not enured to, at least accustomed to the sounds of warfare: the screams of men and horses alike, the thunderous crash of bodies and metal; the louder-yet roar of cannon and the reports of muskets and pistols. Those last were the rarest of the cacophony, too unpredictable in comparison to sword and arrow and cannon.

But what she heard now, what she had been hearing an hour or more since, was a different thing entirely. Gunfire shattered the night repeatedly, manifesting as bursts of white fire in the distance when she peeled back the tent door to search for the sound's source. She'd closed the door again and settled back into her place, trying to let the noise disappear into the night while she focused on her preparations, but it invaded her hearing time and again. If a hundred men could be taught to shoot a hundred muskets in succession, no misfires ever heard, it might sound a little like what tore from the Ecumenic camp. Men, though, would never be so precise, each rattle snapping off in flawless succession, and when it would briefly stop she found herself straining to hear it again, waiting for whatever portents it brought to come clear.

It was easier, perhaps, to concentrate on that than to let stillness take her and make herself face the necessary choices she'd made. Without the stillness, without her usual certainty, she felt adrift. If an overwhelming love would take her, a compulsion to do whatever she must in order to preserve her child's life, then she might act more freely, but she had no softening of her heart, no dewy-eyed romance to hold herself to. The babe had to survive, not from love, but from pragmaticism. Robert's alien war was coming, and a witchpower child of her own birthing meant a small hope that there would be aspects of that war beyond Robert's control, aspects that might do her world some good. So the child must be preserved at any cost, even giving it up to Javier de Castille. She had no other choice, and the woman Belinda Primrose had been a year ago would not recognise that decision or the woman who made it at all.

A year. Gregori Kapnist had died barely more than a twelve-month past, and Belinda's world had come unmoored in the time since. She would cut her last lashings today, and wondered what would be made of her in future days. Robert and Lorraine would never trust her again, and she might well pay for her decisions with the loss of her throne.

Dry humour curved her lips. So be it: she'd never sought the throne to begin with. Witchpower ambition itched with dismay at that, but settled again; it seemed that part of her was inclined to protect the unborn babe as well, and could ignore the middling detail of a throne until later.

"Belinda?" Ivanova spoke from her corner, quiet but fully alert. Belinda paused in collecting a soldier's uniform. She couldn't be ready to ride with the dawn, for fear Robert would visit before the battle began. Wisdom might have sent her from the tent an hour since, prepared to hide amongst the troops, but the sounds from the Gallic camp and her own need to sit a while and face the decisions she'd made had held her in place.

She turned to Irina Durova's daughter. "I'm about to cast myself to the wolves, and when I return I think I'll no longer be the favoured daughter. I wonder: will Khazar grant sanctuary should I require it?" The words were very soft, soft enough that listening ears wouldn't hear them, but she feared Robert's witchpower might reach forth to pluck her intentions from her thoughts. No quiet voice could stop him from doing that.

"Aulun and Khazar are allied," Ivanova said after a long moment. "We would be pleased to offer you a place in our home should you require it." She waited a moment, then sat up in the darkness. "Has something gone awry?"

"Robert intends on drawing this war out," Belinda said steadily. "My thought to bring victory by leading the troops today has been refused."

Ivanova caught her breath and Belinda lifted a hand against her concerns. "I'll ride, regardless. But Robert will know then that he doesn't control me, and—"

A new burst of gunfire rattled, drowning Belinda's voice even from the distance. Ivanova frowned, looking through the greying light as if she could see through the tent walls. "What is that? It woke me a while ago."

"It's the changing of our plans." The tent door flew open to admit an invigorated Robert, his eyes bright and actions full of energy. "Primrose, I'd almost dream you knew of this, with your plan for the morning. No," he said almost instantly, as a confused frown marred Belinda's forehead. "No, I see you didn't. It's Seolfor," he said with admiration. "It must be, after all this time. Forty years. He might have built enough to change the tide in that time, even without automation. They'll be enough to terrify the troops, at the least. Our men will run all the way back to Aulun without some kind of bolstering, and so you'll ride with them today after all, Primrose. You'll become the banner that denies their fear and drives them forward to capture the guns and win the day."

For all his fine words, Robert didn't release Belinda to the battle until the sun reached its zenith. By then the new Cordulan weapons were clearly visible: half cannon, half gun, they rained devastation and men fell under their onslaught like bits of straw. Even the Khazarians, with so many men to throw against the rapid-fire guns, cowered and then finally refused orders, falling back in disarray.

Panic shot through the Aulunian troops as the Khazarians retreated. Belinda, still a far and safe distance from the front lines,

knotted her fingers over a twisting stomach, her throat tight against
the need to disgorge fear in sickness. Half a day: half a day's battle,
and the Ecumenic army was wiping away the difference in numbers. More than two thousand men were newly dead, and easily
twice that number injured or dying.

This, Belinda reminded herself with crystal precision, this was
just the beginning of the future she intended to create. The part of
her that was the assassin trained from childhood wanted to stand
and watch and feel nothing, to envelop herself in stillness and become remote from death and destruction. For all its horror, it was a
necessary horror: without these terrible weapons, without more
like them, growing worse with each generation, when Robert's
queen and her enemies came for Aulun and Echon, they would be
left defenceless. This must be done, she whispered to herself, and let
go a small bitter laugh at the echo it wakened in her mind: *it cannot
be found out.*

That echo had the power to shatter her stillness, even if she had
the strength to hold it in place. Oh, she had it: a grim, deep-set part
of her knew that she could, if she must, draw untouchability around
herself and care nothing for the men who died. But they deserved
better than her cold calculations. They were dying for the choice
she'd made, and she would do them as much honour as she could,
by flinching and trembling and dreading each new burst of gunfire
as they did.

When the Khazarians broke, Robert legged Belinda onto a tall
solid mare and handed her the reins. Belinda gazed down at him a
long moment, etching his features into her memory. It would be
half a year or more before she saw him again, and the world itself
might change in that time.

One side of Robert's mouth curled up in a smile, and he nodded, paternal indication of pride and love. Then he slapped the
mare's hindquarters and sent Belinda into battle without a word
spoken by either of them.

Witchpower lanced out as the mare leapt forward, a golden
surge of light so brilliant it might have been born of the sun itself.
It carried all of Belinda's needs: the need to act instead of watch, the
need to keep a devil's promise with the red-haired king of Gallin,

the need to survive at any cost, so her world could be shaped to fight a battle none of them was yet able to understand. Magic scoured the earth in front of her, tearing it up, and her own men fell back as if they were afraid the new Cordulan guns had come up from behind, as well. A path opened all the way to the front lines, and only there did it crash against Javier's shielding, and reverberate, golden play of power against silver in a familiar erotic thrill.

Belinda bared her teeth and her sword in one gesture, each as much a warning to herself as a rally to the troops. Fury at seduction's hideously easy path dampened any desire to pursue it, but she hadn't been wrong in telling Javier that because they knew that route better than any other, they would have to find a way to force themselves past it when using their witchpower in tandem.

For an instant her perspective twisted, magic playing between herself and Javier, until she stood behind silver shielding and watched a golden rod of power race toward her. She could see herself in the red coat of an Aulunian soldier but with her hair left loose and long and free, could see the strong slim lines of her legs clutching the mare's bellowing ribs, could see her sword lifted and her face contorted with the energy of war.

She was, she thought dispassionately, quite beautiful, in the way of ancient goddesses riding to battle. She'd never thought herself beautiful at all, only pretty; prettiness was safer for one such as herself, because beauty would be remembered. Just now, though, seeing herself blazing with witchpower, with God's power, beauty seemed a gift she was glad to accept.

Javier himself had a deeper and more visceral reaction, rage and lust and fear all tangled until they turned to loathing, and it was with that deep hatred the witchpower snapped back and returned her vision to normal. With it came an awareness that her troops were rallying, that men were screaming the Holy Mother's name and falling in behind her with an eagerness to protect her or die trying.

Her magic and Javier's slammed together again as she crashed into the front lines, sword suddenly no longer aloft to win hearts but swinging and splashed with crimson. The mare screamed and struck out with her hooves and Belinda fought in time with her, leaning to slash and stab and strike with strength that seemed beyond mortal. That was battle, that was witchpower, and together they made her feel unstoppable. No one near her fell to the rapid-fire guns: her shields were as strong as Javier's, and bullets shattered against them. Cannon roared, trying to bring her down, and then faded away as guns were pointed elsewhere, taking on targets who would die as they were meant to. Her sword arm turned to fire, then to lead, and finally passed into the dull ache that she recognised from practise as a child. She could fight forever this way, if she must, but instead she flung herself, time and again, at Javier's shield, golden surges of magic slivering sparks of silver. She would break through; she had to. The larger part of her no longer recalled why, except that she was at war, and that was what one did in war.

It seemed to her, then, that she was the last to notice that the fighting fell away; that men of both armies were taking their distance from her and looking elsewhere on the field. Belinda threw a weary look toward the sun, though at midsummer its place in the sky told her less about the time than it might have. Midafternoon, at the least; she had been fighting for some hours, and only with the breather that came on her now did she wonder if she could continue on. But the men around her weren't looking toward the sun or toward the fast-guns that had, unobserved, fallen silent. Their attention was turned to the Gallic camp, and Belinda, belatedly, saw what had arrested them.

Javier de Castille came to war at last. He rode a grey horse, making Belinda notice for the first time that her mare was a bay. It ought to have been gold, she thought then; that would make her and her brother as different on the field as they could be. Unlike herself, Javier wore armour, but then, in armour no one would have seen her for a woman, and the point of her presence was to be the queen of Heaven's avatar, while the point of Javier's was to be God's warrior. He'd forgone a helm and his hair was afire in the sunlight, grown long enough to edge over the armour's neckpiece. Belinda thought if a sword should clip a bit of those locks from his head, the red strands would become talismans as precious as the Son's blood to those who snatched them up. He rode slowly at the head of a small spear of men, coming to war as Belinda's opposite in every way.

Forgetting that he was the enemy, forgetting that she would have to lose to him, forgetting everything but admiration for showmanship, Belinda stood in her stirrups and raised her sword in a salute to the Gallic king. Even across the distance, she saw surprise filter over Javier's face, and he echoed her gesture, raising his blade. Silver witchpower shot up, bright against the blue sky, and the Ecumenic armies erupted in cheers.

Belinda, grinning, swept her sword in a broad half-circle above her horse's ears, and golden fire ripped across the distance toward Javier and his men. He shielded, magic splattering across the field, and war was on them again, the respite lost under screams and blood and passion.

Javier rode for her, as she knew he would. His arrowhead contingent of riders lost its shape to the press of battle, but others joined him as they picked up speed and came to crash against the Aulunian front lines with all the strength they had to muster. The shock reverberated through her, rattling her shields, but she urged her mare forward again and shouted out her own war cry as swords clashed and rang together. The fast-guns began firing again, spitting death more rapidly than any sword could deal it. Belinda let herself forget again that she was fighting to lose, and kicked and bludgeoned and struck her way toward the king of Gallin.

He answered well before she reached his side: silver power came to bear, hammering her until she slipped in her mare's saddle. An opportunistic fool seized her arm and she backhanded him with her sword's hilt and the mare's weight behind the blow. His neck snapped, but his fingers, tangled in her sleeve, didn't loosen, and Belinda, yelling, fell atop a dead man.

Witchpower kept her alive a few seconds, golden shields shattering swords as they drove down at her. Belinda scrambled to her feet, shoving men away with her arms and her power alike, and came up on the defensive and subtly dismayed to discover she was at the heart of a Gallic push: not one of the men around her wore the colours of Aulun or Khazar. Teeth bared in another grin, she called a vestige of stillness to herself, trying to hide in its shadow, but at least one armoured rider saw her fade away, and shouted out a warning that drew attention all around.

Breathless, swearing, shockingly high with enthusiasm, Belinda let him ride her down, and when he swung at her, stepped beneath the blade's arc and brought her own sword up in a sweeping circle of its own.

Its tip slashed a long deep line through the horse's shoulder, but momentum carried the blow through, her sword slamming into the knight's belly and rendering his armour as though it was soft meat. He was past her then, nearly wrenching the sword from her hands, but she dug her feet in and hauled the blade back, cutting even more deeply and earning a scream from the metal. *Witchpower*, Belinda thought: she hadn't the strength for that strike without magic's help. Blood splashed over her and the knight was wrenched around to face her. His head dropped and his fingers came to the cut before he lifted his head and his visor to meet Belinda's gaze.

Sacha Asselin stared at her, genuine astonishment in his hazel eyes before he shuddered and toppled silently from his horse. One foot caught in the stirrup and the animal tried to shake him off, then began to run. Belinda's sword slipped in her hand, fingers numb as her thoughts as Sacha's body crashed and slipped alongside the horse, then finally fell to the ground and disappeared beneath the feet of fighting men.

War raged on around her, and the loose grip she held on her blade was enough to send a part of her mind screaming that she was a target, vulnerable, an easy mark. But intellect had no hold on her: she stared at the place where Sacha had fallen with dull incomprehension, and her clearest thought was that a mistake had been made.

Not in Sacha's death: she'd intended that for months, had sharpened the tiny dagger she wore at the small of her back and promised it its first heart's blood from the young Lord Asselin's breast. It pressed there now, scolding her for promises broken. No, the mistake was in his death being done on a battlefield. It was supposed to be personal, a gift from the queen's bastard to the prince's friend, and done this way there was no surge of satisfaction, no wicked pleasure. Murder was an art, and this only a crude means of survival.

Witchpower swept around her, and Belinda, stupid with disbelief, turned toward it to greet Javier's armoured fist with the side of her head.

Nausea came with waking. Belinda kept her eyes closed, already certain she lay in a tent; the light was too dim to be outside. At least one other person was with her, but the witchpower wouldn't respond and let her ascertain her companion. Javier, probably; maybe Eliza. Belinda wet her lips. "I'm surprised to be alive."

"You should be." Javier, yes, his voice torn with pain. Belinda was abruptly glad the witchpower lay quiet, that she couldn't feel his anger and agony. Fresh sickness rose on the edge of that relief: he'd hit her hard, hard enough that she might be pleased to have survived it, though her surprise came from not waking with a dagger through her heart. Pain swam through her skull, looking for a release of laughter: she would not, of course, have woken with a dagger through her heart. Finding that funny made her head ache all the more.

"Why am I?" Safer words than a declamation of intent in killing Sacha Asselin; she'd meant to do that, either in the need to live on the battlefield or in doing murder at a later time. Javier would see through any facade she tried to weave, and so it was better not to try at all.

"Because not even I knew Sacha was riding the front line," Javier said after a long time. "Because this is war, and a man in armour was about to kill you, and I think you could not have known who he was. Am I wrong?" His every word was precise, measured out in misery.

Belinda sagged against the cot she lay in, tension running from her shoulders and lessening the pain in her head a little. "You're not. I wouldn't have killed him that way, had I known." Her tongue ran too free and she was unable to stop it even when Javier barked a rough sound and said, "You'd have killed him some other way."

"In private, in intimacy. He deserved that. He'd earned as much." Belinda bit her tongue, wondering which phrase would get her throat cut.

Javier breathed the name of God and got up silently enough to tell Belinda he'd shed his armour. She dared open her eyes and stared at the ceiling, nausea edging around her again. The Gallic king might have all the secrets of Aulun of her, if he knew what questions to ask. But instead of pursuing them he said, "There's the other matter, as well."

The child fell heavily after those words, though it remained unspoken, and that, Belinda thought, was the truth of why she still lived. Had she not bargained the child away and had Javier and Eliza not already put in play their false pregnancy, she had little expectation that Javier de Castille would have stayed his hand over the matter of Sacha Asselin's death. He had lost too much too quickly, and that was a thought unusual to one such as Belinda Primrose. She sat up cautiously, vision swimming, and counted herself lucky she'd survived Javier's blow at all. "I'm your prisoner, as we intended. I'll do nothing to risk it. And I am . . . sorry for the cost it came at, Javier."

"Are you," Javier said, but not in a way that asked for her answer. He was grey in the dim lighting, his hair's lustre lost, his eyes hollow and face aged. Too many losses, Belinda thought again, and wondered if it was sympathy that spiked through her. "You will not be welcome at his graveside."

Belinda bowed her head. "I wouldn't presume to ask." Nor did the refusal dismay her, as it would have done over Marius; Marius had deserved better than his fate, but Sacha was a player in his own right. "What's happening?"

"Sacha will be buried at dawn." Javier spoke so coolly Belinda knew he chose to misinterpret her question deliberately. Only a moment passed before he relented. Not, she thought, out of kindness to her, but out of a desire to remove himself from her presence as quickly as he could. There would be mourning to do, and a great deal else to face before Sacha's funeral rites.

"Aulun retreated with your fall. Your father's sent an envoy to negotiate your return. The return of the Holy Mother's avatar," Javier corrected himself. "They don't admit to who you are. Perhaps it's to my advantage to flaunt the truth."

"No." Belinda winced at the sound of her own voice, too harsh and low. It scraped the inside of her head, shaking more sickness loose. "You hit me too damned hard," she muttered, then pulled her thoughts back in order. "If you make noise about Aulun's heir being your captive, they'll parade the girl playing my part in Alunaer so your lies can be dismissed."

"And of those who've seen your face? How will he fool them?"

Belinda shrugged. "They'll begin with the girl looking a great deal like me, but you can influence men against their will, and I can alter memories. Do you doubt Robert Drake can do these things, too? I'm his witchbreed daughter. He'll go far to bring me back under his control, and we need months in which to negotiate if this child is to be born yours. Don't rile him on this. Call me by whatever title he wants to give me and play at the game until we've finished this part of the bargain."

"Is it so easy for you?" Javier turned her way, not quite looking at her. "Is it all nothing more than deaths and deceits? You're so cold, and it's worse when I think of the woman Beatrice Irvine was. How can you construct a character of that nature and be so ruthless yourself?"

"It's the only way I can construct such a character," Belinda whispered. A dozen other comments came to her lips and didn't pass: Javier would neither believe nor care for the truths she'd come to face, that Beatrice had become too much a part of her, that what had once been easy was now matter for endless internal debate, that none of Beatrice's softness or Belinda's own questions took away from what must be done, regardless of the price. Out of all the things she might say, one wanted most to be spoken: *I didn't drown Marius's ship.* It would do no good; she'd drowned dozens of others, and Javier would have no pity or pleasure for the solitary act of compassion she'd engaged in that day. If Marius still lived, perhaps, but that she'd saved him only to see him die a few weeks later took the strength from a childish hope of absolution.

Javier gave her a hard look, then went to the tent door, not speaking until he'd reached it. "You'll be kept under watch, not because I think we can keep you from escaping, but for your protection, though God help the fool who comes at you toward any end. I go to treat with your father." He stepped through the flaps, leaving a bar of sunshine across the floor, and after a moment Belinda gathered herself to cross the dim room and look at the world from within the Gallic camp.

Sunlight splashed hard and white into her vision, turning Javier into a blur as he strode away. A wobbling old man leaning on a staff crossed between them, cutting away brilliance, and turned his head to give Belinda a querulous glower. Her headache flared, and with it a spike of light burst around the old man.

More than burst: even with her temple throbbing and a finger-tip touch telling her a bruise was purpling there, witchpower answered that burn of white, matching like for like. Belinda blocked the glare with her hand, squinting to get a clearer picture of the man.

There was more than an old man's height and breadth to him, though witchpower buzzed around him until it became a hiss almost indistinguishable from the sounds of the world. Within that cloak of power he was ageless and full of a mischievousness she'd never seen in her father or in Dmitri Leontyev. Unbidden, a name came to her lips, a name stolen from Robert, from Dmitri; not one she had known until this moment: "Seolfor."

It was too soft a sound; it would never cross the distance between herself and the silver-haired witchlord. But he smiled and hefted his staff a few inches in greeting, then dropped a blue-eyed wink. Belinda took a step forward, and inside that step the burning after-noon sunlight took him away as thoroughly as it'd swallowed Javier only moments before.

There was nothing left in the air, no hint of power, no whisper that said he'd cloaked himself in magic: he was simply gone, and when her vision cleared again, one of the new guns stood where he'd been.

ROBERT, LORD DRAKE

Of the things that might have gone wrong, Belinda's capture by the Gallic king had not so much as entered Robert's mind. She was too quick, too clever, too bold, and Javier's intimate awareness of her person, both figuratively and literally, too much a danger to her. That they would clash on the battlefield, yes—that much Robert anticipated—but not that she would fall.

Now, sitting on a bored warhorse, Robert wonders if he allowed himself to be blind in this matter. Belinda did, after all, collapse beneath Javier's power in Lutetia a few months ago, but her training beneath Dmitri—and, Robert thinks with a dour kind of humour, no doubt above and before him as well—strengthened her. She shouldn't have fallen, and should now be able to walk free easily. He had watched it all, the distance as nothing to his witchpower. She'd gutted a man and then stood numbed from it, bewildering when he thought of the innumerable deaths she'd brought just that day, nevermind in the course of her young life. Javier'd ridden up to her as she stood unawares, and hit her hard enough that Robert, a mile away, had winced.

So, though there are no doubt a hundred other things he ought to say, when Javier de Castille rides up, what Robert can't help asking is "Who was it she killed, before you captured her?"

"Sacha," Javier says in a flat voice, and says it as though he expects Robert to take meaning from the name.

Indeed, Robert does, and Ana di Meo's whispered warning flashes back to him across the months and across her death: *Belinda is lonely, my lord, and almost nothing else matters.* Belinda was lonely, and Sacha Asselin was a friend to Beatrice Irvine. That, then, explains it all, and gives Robert a measure of horror: Belinda has become soft, if that young lord's death drew her up that badly. "I'm sorry for your loss," he says aloud, and Javier smirks, ugly expression on his thin features.

"As are we all. My lord Drake, we have captured your holy avatar, and we are inclined to keep her as our guest until Aulun surrenders. We are," the young king says, and manages to sound as dry as Lorraine, "willing to accept that surrender now, and save ourselves the trouble of riding back and forth under truce."

"Perhaps your majesty would be willing to consider a ransom instead," Robert says, but his heart isn't in the negotiation. In fact, he has no real idea of what he's just said, because the king's vocal inflections have opened a window in Robert's mind. He stares at Javier de Castille and sees in him the young Aulunian queen, her titian hair long and loose over her shoulders and her thin grey eyes full of pride and wit. Javier hasn't the widow's peak that graces Lorraine's hairline, or Robert might have seen it immediately, but the truth is, Lorraine's features sit better on a man's face than on her own: he's a more handsome boy than she ever was a woman.

If it were within Robert Drake's power, he would retrieve Dmitri Leontyev from the grave so he might take the pleasure of killing him again. Heat stains his face, and Robert doesn't remember the last time he blushed. His hands are cold on the warhorse's reins, and it's only a lifetime's worth of habit that keeps him calm and solid in his seat. He can—*just*—forgive himself for not seeing it, because he's only met Javier once, and that under unfortuitous circumstances. But he should have known. He should have known, and he did not, and that means Robert Drake has been out-played.

Javier has dismissed the idea of a ransom and is waiting for Robert to name an outrageous ransom fee that Javier will take under consideration and ride back to the Ecumenic camp with. Right now, though, Robert can't name a price he wouldn't pay just for the chance to face Belinda and learn how much of this game she was aware of when she came to war. For a rash moment he actually considers surrendering just to achieve that end.

But no, Lorraine would stare incredulously if he did capitulate, and it would in no way serve his queen beyond the stars, and so what he says is ill-considered, but at least it's not a surrender: "I think my Primrose knows, but do you, or has she kept that secret from you, king of Gallin?"

The skin around Javier's eyes tightens, so fine a wrinkling that if Robert had not spent thirty years and more bedding the queen of Aulun he might not have seen or recognised it at all. These mortals learn much from their surroundings, but can do nothing about the form they're given. Though it's stretched across an unknown mind, this face is so familiar it cannot lie: Javier knows that he's Robert's son and Belinda's brother, and if Javier knows, Belinda's the one who's told him.

And that, Robert should think, means they've built an alliance in the shadows, and her capture is not a capture at all, but a deliberate retreat on her part. Only one reason carries enough weight: the child Belinda's carrying, which she has not yet confided in her father about.

Oh, yes, he's been out-played, and to his surprise, he's delighted.

He's known Belinda is clever, but he never imagined she might be a worthy opponent. She was meant to be a tool, not to put pieces on the board herself and set them into action.

Javier has expressed some sort of polite incomprehension, but Robert's no longer listening. Lorraine gave Belinda a cryptic order before sending the girl away, to take care of the matter they discussed. The Titian queen—the Red Bitch, Robert thinks both ruefully and lovingly—would have meant the pregnancy, would not have accepted a daughter with an illegitimate child. This, then, is Belinda's way of protecting the babe, and moreover, she intends on giving it over to Javier de Castille and his new bride, whom Robert would now wager is not pregnant and indeed can never be so.

It's a brilliantly insidious plan to gain the Gallic throne, and Robert is astonished Javier agreed to it. The child isn't *his:* that much Robert's sure of; Belinda's not round enough to be carrying Javier's child. The king must love her, Robert thinks, and the idea takes him aback. The Gallic king must love the girl he's married, if he's willing to go to this length to get a child with her and keep his throne.

He will have to send Seolfor, Robert decides; will have to put Seolfor into play at the Gallic court, so the witchpower child will be under some vestige of control. His other choice is to snatch Belinda back and keep her hidden from Lorraine until the baby's born, but in truth, Belinda's done a fine job of manipulating events herself. He'd applaud her for it if she were here, but he doubts he'll see his daughter again until the new year, when some kind of truce in the war will be negotiated in exchange for her return. That will do, even if he might personally want to face Belinda down; he needs the war to go on, and personal wishes must be subsumed beneath the greater plan.

His mouth is running without his thoughts behind it; he and Javier are snipping over surrenders and ransom, neither of them with any intention of giving in to the other. Robert raises his hand suddenly, cutting off the discussion. "Our beloved daughter remains safe in Alunaer," he says coldly. "Keep this avatar if you wish. All of Aulun has faith that the queen of Heaven rides with us, and if one girl is captured by the damnable Cordulan forces, then when Be-

432 · C. E. MURPHY

linda is called to host the holy spirit again, another woman shall become her avatar here in Brittany."

He wheels his horse, leaving a gaping Javier behind, and gallops back to the Aulunian camp grinning with delight.

Tomas del'Abbate

Javier has gone to make treatise over a prisoner of war, and Tomas has turned to God for guidance. War has undone him in every way: the sound, the death, the rushing sand of time, all of it hissing forward with no chance to sleep, no chance to think. Hours and hours ago Javier sent him away with an order to never again think or speak on Eliza Beaulieu's unworthiness as a king's bride, and in all that time he's thought of nothing else. Rodrigo spent half the night rattling the camp with his new guns, and instead of studying them and exulting in their coming victory, Tomas's thoughts have strayed again to Eliza and Javier. Indeed, even now he should be praying for Sacha Asselin's soul, and instead he's on his knees begging God to let him be happy for Javier, to let him be happy that the young king has gotten himself an heir, a confidante, a wife, in the midst of war. God, it seems, isn't listening, because all Tomas is left with are heartbeats of envy mixed with pulses of sorrow.

He's the newcomer to their group, the one who has replaced one of their own; the one who has lived in that one's place, through a grace Tomas believes, sacrilegiously, is wholly Marius's, and none of God's. He cannot quite make himself believe that it was the Lord's will that Marius die in his place; he can't make himself believe at all that it was God's plan that Eliza should live. That was the witchpower at work, and not just Javier's, but the Aulunian woman's as well. She and Javier cannot both be blessed with God's gift, and so if Eliza lives, it's at the devil's bidding.

Which means Javier has bound himself to Hell in wedding Eliza Beaulieu, and that Tomas has failed in every way.

He feels that madness has come on him, a grief that tears up from the bottom of his soul with the intent to strangle him. His body is by turns cold and hot, his hands shaking even as they're pressed together in prayer. He has failed Javier and failed God, and he's no longer certain which distresses him more.

There is a way out, a terrible way out, and Tomas both shies from thinking on it and pursues it with all vigour. One more death, a death where God intended no life anyway, might turn Javier back to him, and save the king's soul besides. It's a sin, specifically against one of God's great commandments, but for Javier's sake Tomas must consider it. For Echon's sake, he must consider it: Eliza is an inappropriate bride, and the Parnan Caesar has daughters a-plenty to choose from.

Dread certainty fills his heart. Tomas lowers his gaze, whispers a thanks to God for showing him a clear path, and looks up once more to gather strength from the crucifix and the image of God's only son, whom He sacrificed out of love for Man.

A shaft of light spills through the tent, quick brilliance that says another has entered. It turns the jewel-encrusted cross to fire, and the ivory Son to blinding white, and there's an instant where an unusual and clear thought stands out in Tomas's mind: he ought not have knelt with his back to the door.

Then pain sets in, pain so astonishing it might be God's own touch, reached down from the heavens to grace His beautiful son. To burn him where he kneels, immolation in a moment of piety, but instead of God's face, instead of an angel lifting him to Heaven, Tomas feels a brush of lips against his ear, and hears a woman's voice whisper, "Sacha Asselin is dead, priest, and I have no other recourse to hold Javier's ear but to force him to turn to family. A pity. You were so lovely."

He twists, spurring agony through his back, but he can't lift a hand to pull the knife away, nor to mark his murderer in any way. The earth's pull takes him, and he's falling clumsily, toppling backward as soothing blackness begins to overcome the pain, and the last thing in this world that Tomas del'Abbate sees is Akilina Pankejeff's razor smile fading into darkness.

27

BELINDA WALTER
4 July 1588 † *Brittany; the Gallic camp*

Raging witchpower woke her half a breath before Javier's hand in her hair pulled her from the cot and flung her to the floor. Her own power lashed back and she tamped it, training far older than the magic making her small and vulnerable beneath a man's wrath. Instinct made her breathless, wide-eyed, lips parted with fear and excitement as she cowered as prettily as she knew how.

It was the wrong reaction: the wiser part of her knew that, knew she was better fighting than making herself pluckable, most especially in this place, with this man. But this was a game she'd been trained in since she was a child, and for a few seconds all she could do was gaze up at Javier de Castille in half-real terror and utter supplication.

He kicked her, which was unusual for a man superior to her. Even through a red burst of pain in her ribs Belinda was grateful: it helped shake her from her instincts. She rolled back, hiding under the cot, and dug her fingers into the ground, trying to drag her thoughts into a semblance of order. Trying, most especially, to neither make herself an object of desire nor to hit back with magic: there would be a reason for Javier's attack, and fighting back would only convince him he was right in whatever matter had infuriated him. Neither seductress nor witch—that left Belinda with nothing but the woman, and the role was a strange one to her.

Javier flipped the cot away and kicked her again, and this time Belinda screamed, shock as potent as pain. "What? What have I *done*?" That, at least, was born of honesty, not seduction, and helped bring her further from that place which, should Javier's mind clear enough to see it, would very likely end in Belinda's death. She would have no forgiveness for her wiles in his position, not even under the most serene of circumstances.

She scrambled back from another kick, and finally saw that tears streaked the king's face, marks as wild as the fury he indulged in. Belinda lurched to her feet and stumbled to the thrown cot's far side, trying to put something, regardless of how insubstantial, between herself and Javier. He'd been dry-eyed over Sacha, that wound too deep to bleed; this was something else. His magic felt shattered, streaked with black despair, and below his rage, despair boiled over. Impossible loss, so bleak it left a chasm in him; Belinda's heart spasmed in sympathy above her fear and confusion. "What's happened?"

A bolt of thunderous power slammed into her, barely deflected by golden witchpower that seemed to know better than she did that an attack was coming. A gasp knocked free of Belinda's lungs, the charge of shared magic with Javier as strong as it had ever been. She clenched her teeth against desire, refuting it; the magic wasn't stronger than she was, and base needs were things to be put away. There would be other men to satisfy herself with: this man would condemn her soul to Hell.

The next blow she caught more easily, and the next more easily still, until Javier lobbed magic at her with all the finesse of a screaming child, and she only stood deflecting his power as it gradually lost strength. She would not fight; would *not,* no matter the cost. In time Javier slumped, then fell to his knees and bent forward against the earth to scream out rage and frustration. Only then did Belinda gather her nerve and approach him, crouching to hover her hands above his back, not knowing if a touch would earn her another beating. "Is it Eliza?" Genuine fear broke her voice: she was certain her own life would be forfeit if Eliza Beaulieu was dead.

Javier shoved her away, but without the heart of his earlier blows. "As if you don't know."

"I swear on my mother's name that I don't. I can't lie to you, Javier, not anymore. I don't know what's happened."

"It's Tomas," Javier whispered. "Murdered, and with him any hope of salvation for my soul."

"Tomas?" Belinda frowned, then dropped her chin to her chest, eyes closed. "The priest." She had no more words after that, protestations of her innocence seeming gauche, and expressions of sorrow alien to her.

"Why would anyone kill him?" Javier's voice cracked. Belinda put a hand out again, then let it fall, more uncomfortable with offering solace than with his pain.

"To remove your inner circle," she answered, though she doubted he wanted a response at all. "To make you vulnerable, king of Gallin. There are very few who've been so close to you, and most of them are dead now. If I intended on weakening you, it's how I would do it. Marius and Sacha, now Tomas. The only one left is Eliza. Protect her, Javier. Give up your quest for the Aulunian throne, if you must. Don't let her die, too."

Javier lifted eyes gone black with hate to meet Belinda's gaze. "If you intended on weakening me. You would know. Is this what you planned, when you were Beatrice?"

"I thought it would make you too fragile," she said coolly. That was necessary, the icy exterior, for below it she felt Javier's loss, tearing at him until it tore at her as well. Better by far to be the untouchable bitch he thought her than to break beneath the weight of his sorrow. "I considered it, yes, and if it had become necessary I might have taken one of them from you. Not two, not three. Taking one would have made you cling harder to those who were left, and I numbered among them then. This many dead is a waste."

"Who stands to gain from my weakness?" Desperation filled the question, as though the young king of Gallin truly had no answers. Belinda stared at him, then got to her feet and went to ruck through the ramshackled tent in search of wine.

"Aulun, most obviously. Could Robert Drake have done this?" She found wine, poured it, and returned to Javier, standing over him as he drained the cup.

"No," he said less hoarsely when the drink was gone. "I left him and rode straight to Tomas, to seek his advice on what to do with you. Your father's unwilling to bargain for you," he added shortly. "His heir's in Alunaer and her avatar can be replaced."

Worry seized Belinda's gut and forced her to sit, still reserve too distant to support her. Threads of plots came unravelled before her eyes, replaced by grim certainty. "Then he knows what I'm doing."

"What?" Javier turned his own hollow gaze on her and Belinda took his cup away, pouring more wine and drinking it herself. "How can he know?"

"I don't know." Belinda flattened her fingers over her belly, staring beyond Javier. "Lorraine knew, too. About the child. Perhaps she told him, perhaps . . ." She closed her eyes, drawing a slow breath to calm her heartbeat. Too many emotions, twisting in and out of being too quickly. Perhaps that was what war did, tore every possible reaction from deep in the soul and gave exhausted men and women too little time to deal with even one feeling before another rose up to drown it. "We're witchbreed, all three of us," she finally said. "He would want the child born. He'd see it as a tool to be used in the future, a new generation to shape this world. So perhaps he saw what I did: that the only kind of safety I can find is here."

"And the rest of it?" Javier's voice cracked again. Belinda brought her attention back to him, seeing pale skin and grey eyes and ginger hair all working together to make him look sallow. Grief etched lines in his face, aging him and offering no hint that he'd been distracted from his losses by the change in topic. He'd only set them aside, and not far, at that: they scratched just under the surface, until looking at him was painful. She had not, she thought, ever suffered a loss that scored her so deeply; indeed, the closest she'd ever come was in Beatrice Irvine losing Javier de Castille to Belinda Primrose's duties. She looked away sharply, suddenly feeling as though she'd given away too much.

"One problem at a time," she whispered. "This game is hard enough to second-guess. Until we have other proof, let's assume he's looking only as far as the child's birth. I think he wouldn't expect me to look farther." She hesitated a moment, thoughts running ahead of her words, then murmured, "Go to Eliza. Bury Sacha

438 · C. E. MURPHY

and your priest. I don't belong in the midst of your sorrow, and will not keep you from what needs doing."

That he accepted the dismissal, got to his feet and left the tent, might have been amusing, had Belinda not thought of someone else who might profit from his solitude.

It was not done for the queen's daughter to slip from one enemy tent to another in the middle of the night, no more than it might have been done for that same daughter, unacknowledged, to demand an audience with her mother. Still, Belinda did the one as readily as she'd done the other, and did it exquisitely aware that not so long ago, she might have been acting on official orders to enact what she planned. No more. The Aulunian heir would never be sent to assassinate anyone. That part of her life had passed in Lorraine's courtroom, as final as any death.

She'd called stillness, and, wrapping herself, entered Akilina Pankejeff's tent with no one the wiser. She had no proof at all that the Khazarian duchess was responsible for Tomas's death, only a sense of rightness about it. Javier was almost entirely bereft of friends now, and had no one beyond family to turn to. Rodrigo had never in all his years as Essandia's monarch proved himself so cold, but Belinda well knew Akilina's ambition and skill in the game of politics. Even if the priest hadn't died, there was still a matter of Belinda's own vengeance to be answered. Akilina had stripped her bare in Lutetia; she would repay the dvoryanin by stripping her of her life.

In more than ten years of doing murder, Belinda Primrose had never moved with such focus. Death was a duty, not a passion: not until tonight, and she succumbed to the desire to forget all else while she pursued her retaliation. Once inside Akilina's tent she released the stillness to stand and watch a dead woman breathe a while. It was a dangerous indulgence: Akilina might open her eyes, might have time to draw breath and scream. Even so, she'd have no more time than that, and she would die with Belinda Walter's image burned into her mind.

"She's pregnant."

With a silent howl at her own lack of caution, Belinda snapped the stillness back into place, wrapping it tight so that all eyes might slip away from her, but when she turned toward the voice, Rodrigo of Essandia seemed to stare at her still.

She had not seen him. She *ought* to have seen him, ought not to have allowed herself to concentrate so compleatly on her own revenge. Her life was a trinket now, one dangling from the Essandian prince's long and well-shaped fingers. Those fingers were steepled in front of his mouth, and he sat relaxed in a scoop-shaped chair, one leg cocked at the knee and the other loose and straight before him. He was nearly as hidden by shadow as Belinda herself could be, but she ought to have seen him.

"My nephew cannot do what you're doing," he murmured, more curious than afraid. "More's the shame for him, perhaps, though I can imagine why you might have developed that skill where he did not. He was brought up in sunlight, and you, in shadow. I wonder why you dropped this cloak of obscurity at all. Is it so she would see your face and know whose vengeance was exacted in the moments of her death? Let me see you, Belinda Walter. Let me see our beloved Aulunian queen's bastard. Please," he added after a moment, almost droll, when she remained where she was, draped in dark safe shadow. "You and I both know that I'm no match for you, if you want me dead."

Because that was true, and because he knew it, and, in the end, because her curiosity was as great as his, Belinda released the witchpower again. Stillness faded away, exposing her to moonlight and vision once more. She felt beacon-bright, unmasked. A glance at Akilina betrayed her intentions, and she turned her attention to Rodrigo, suddenly aware of the sound of his voice in the air. Robert had once muffled noise around himself: Belinda drew on that feeling of rag-stuffed ears, and built a circle of silence around herself and the Essandian prince. Only then did she dare to speak. "We know why I'm here. Why are you, my lord?"

Amusement creased Rodrigo's eyes. "My lord? How formal. You're well-trained."

Belinda said, "I am," without regret, and looked toward the sleeping woman on the cot. "Will you try to stop me?"

"The child isn't mine."

Surprise snapped Belinda's gaze back to Rodrigo. He spread his fingertips, thumbs still touching, making a wave of indifference with his body that his emotional presence echoed. The temptation to cross to him, touch him and steal his thoughts, raised hairs on Belinda's arms, though she quelled the impulse and instead said, "You're certain?"

"I paid her washer-woman very well for certainty of when her courses came. Even if she'd had the wit to lie to me with her words, her face told me what I needed to know. She should have been bleeding the day we married. She was not, nor has she since. The child is not mine." Rodrigo smiled thinly. "I sit here in the nights, trying to decide which page from your grandfather's book I might follow."

Belinda, suddenly as droll as he'd been a moment before, said, "Let me encourage you to divorce her, my lord prince. Join Aulun in its Reformation, and set Cordula on its ear."

A broader smile flashed over Rodrigo's face. He was handsome, better-looking by far than Javier, though Belinda's insides twisted at that thought. His looks would have left no mark on Javier, of course, but it was easier not to dwell on that, and to try to ignore the taste of ashes in her mouth.

"I think not," Rodrigo said, thankfully not privy to Belinda's thoughts. "I might have the marriage annulled; the Pappas would grant me that willingly enough, knowing the child wasn't mine. He'd grant it anyway," he added shrewdly. "He wants me wedded to one of his own faithful women, the better to control me." His gaze slipped from Belinda to Akilina. "Or I might have her beheaded. No one would blame me."

"Irina might."

Rodrigo's smile changed again, became something smaller and more approving. "You think quickly. Lorraine may have chosen well. But then what am I to do," he said, and his hands spread again, making mockery of the question. "Do I close my eyes and pretend I don't know? Do I raise another man's child as heir to the Essandian throne?"

"Whose?" It hardly mattered, but curiosity had her in its grip, and Rodrigo de Costa seemed inclined to offer answers.

"Sacha Asselin's, I should think," he said. "It was he whom I paid to liberate Akilina from prison. You may have done me a favour today, in cutting down my nephew's oldest friend."

Belinda's heart beat once with the speaking of Sacha's name and hung endlessly in her chest, a pain that struck her breath and did not cease for long seconds after Rodrigo had finished speaking. Witchpower, bright and gold, flooded her mind, her body, and squeezed her heart, setting it to beating again. Then she was across the room, not kneeling at Rodrigo's feet; she, or the witchpower, had too much pride for that. Too much ambition, as well: those things were what drove her hand to touch Rodrigo's hair, drove desire coupled strongly with revenge, and drove a wicked delight that brought many paths in Belinda's life to a full circle. "One throne," she murmured, "might see fit to do another a second boon, my lord prince."

He caught her wrist and moved her hand from his hair, opening a shock of thought that ran counter to anything she'd stolen from a man since her gifts had developed. Oh, she was pretty enough, in his eyes, all bright with moonlight and intense with golden power that was in every way Javier's opposite. He might desire her in an abstract way, in the same fashion a painting or a landscape might be desired, but lying with the wife he'd chosen had not awakened in Rodrigo a particular enthusiasm for earthly vices. He would take Belinda from a sense of duty, but only if he were certain of getting a child, and thereby Aulun, for his troubles.

For a heady and amusing instant, he was easily the most desirable man Belinda had ever known. Habit kept laughter from breaking out loud, but it danced on her lips, and witchpower swirled through her, more than ready to break a prince's will. She shut it away, more pleased with his ruthless pragmaticism than she could ever be with bedding him. She was trained to turn practicality into need, so she might seduce when and where she must. She'd never imagined finding the same remorseless lack of romanticism in a man.

"What," he said aloud, "favours might we exchange, Belinda Walter?"

"Do not marry again. Permit Javier to be your heir. He and

Eliza will have a child within the year; your succession, and Gallin's, will be assured." Belinda's heartbeat ran rabbit-quick with the excitement of setting plots in motion. These were not the plans Robert had, nor even the ones she'd shared with Javier. These were her own, and not even the witchpower struggled against her ambitions.

"Do not marry again," Rodrigo said, with just enough emphasis on the final word, and a glint of interest in his eyes. "My faith only permits me one marriage at a time, till death do us part, Lady Belinda, and my wife is young and healthy. How ever do you imagine I might marry *again?*"

"Get what sleep you may, prince of Essandia," Belinda suggested. "The next days will be difficult, and you'll need all your wits about you in your time of sorrow." She stepped back, and he rose, pausing to study her with a curious expression.

Whatever he found in her gaze seemed to satisfy him; after a moment he went to the tent's door and there stopped to look back and murmur, "Belinda."

And Belinda, who rarely permitted herself the intimacy of a name, said, "Rodrigo," in return, and watched him go.

RODRIGO, PRINCE OF ESSANDIA

What is most violently clear in Rodrigo's mind is that he has just walked away from the woman who murdered his sister. There's room in his thoughts to wonder if it's worse that he has turned that same woman on the perfidious creature who is his wife, or if allowing Sandalia's murderer to walk free is the greater crime. Either way, she's Javier's prisoner of war and his nephew is wise to keep her alive, so whatever ends Rodrigo might pursue in revenge would be ill-advised, and yet . . .

She ought not be allowed free rein of these camps, much less tacit permission to murder his wife, but Rodrigo watched her appear and disappear from his sight, which tells him there's likely no way to prevent her from doing precisely as she wishes. And the worst of it is she would indeed be doing him a favour, and that's a topic he doesn't dare broach with Javier or even breathe to the new priest who will have to take his confession. He can't go to God burdened with this particular plot, but there's time a-plenty to repent, and perhaps in later years he'll be able to face a confessor.

He's unpleasantly surprised, come morning, when Akilina joins him for breakfast. A flush creeps up his face, making him feel the fool, and when the Khazarian dvoryanin enquires after his health, he is forced to leave the fire, claiming a sickness of the belly that is entirely true. Akilina, astonished, drinks the watered wine that's been all she can stomach in the mornings, and lets him go.

It's that afternoon that she complains of cramps, and she is bleeding by evening. The worried doctor feeds her more wine to keep her blood up, and Rodrigo, watching now, begins to feel a slow horror that is worse even than having allowed Belinda to survive. He can't be certain that this isn't nature rejecting a faulty child, and that, he's sure, is the brilliance of the Aulunian queen's bastard daughter at work.

It takes three days, in the end. The child is lost by the morning, but the bleeding will not stop. Not until the second evening is Akilina weak enough to slip into unconsciousness, and Rodrigo keeps vigil during the night, from duty and an uncomfortable conscience. It would have been one thing to awaken to a murdered wife. It is another entirely to stand by and watch her die by pieces, and to know that he didn't stop it happening. That he commanded it happen, in any way that matters.

It's during that long night that he wonders why Belinda Walter is so cruel, though the answer comes to him easily enough. Her father was captured, tortured, and thrown at Sandalia's feet all on Akilina's word; Belinda herself was stripped bare of both possessions and the lies that had insinuated her in Sandalia's court, all at Akilina's bidding. It is a precise vengeance, this death, a repayment for humiliation, and it is deeply telling. It is also profoundly natural, for women die of childbirth and difficult pregnancies all the time. The man in Rodrigo loathes Belinda and the prince admires her; she is a honed weapon, and will be a dangerous, worthy opponent when she sits on the Aulunian throne.

He opens the tent flaps at dawn, wanting, oddly enough, for Akilina to die in the light. Her faith is not his own, but last rites were given in the last minutes of her consciousness, and it seems better, somehow, to take the final journey with the first rays of sunshine touching her skin.

When the flaps are pulled open, he looks at his dying wife, and a glitter of gold catches his eye. There's an amber rose on her breast, a beautifully carved thing that wasn't there when he left her side.

Rodrigo snatches it up and races the few steps to the door, looking frantically through the camp with no clear idea of what he searches for. No, no real belief that he'll see it, though he knows well enough what he imagines is there.

And there she is, slipping out of shadows cast by soldiers' tents, illuminated by the same new sun that guides Akilina into death. Belinda Walter stands in the middle of his camp, her hair alight with morning colour and the oval of her face darkened by the light behind her. She nods, once, as he did when he left her three nights ago, and then sunlight and shadows fold around her and she is gone.

So, when he turns back, is Akilina Pankejeff.

JAVIER DE CASTILLE, KING OF GALLIN
7 July 1588 † *Brittany; the Gallic camp*

The past three days ought to have been a triumph, and instead they'd been a particular and new bleak hell. Rodrigo hadn't slept in two nights, sitting watch over Akilina; the only time he'd left her side was to attend first Sacha's, then Tomas's funeral services. The great guns still fought on, holding the Aulunian line; their enemy had lost both heart with Belinda's capture, and an impossible number of lives to the hideous weapons. Javier had overseen the guns' deployment, had stood and watched numbly as men fell before their fire, and had accepted the cheers and accolades of his own troops as they beat down the Red Bitch's army.

They didn't know, and Javier didn't want to tell them, that they had bullets enough for one more day of slaughter, and then the war would return to the footing they had known: man against man, swords gutting one another, blood in the eyes, bile held back between clenched teeth, feet slipping in mud and muck as they all struggled to survive. Rodrigo had men pouring new bullets into moulds as quickly as they could, but it would be days, even weeks, before they had enough of a stockpile to continue the onslaught at its present rate.

The old man's guns had evened the battlefield. Aulun and Khazar still had more men than the combined Ecumenic armies, but not nearly as many more, now. They could no longer count on sheer numbers to defeat Javier's troops, and that, he hoped, would take their heart from them, too. But then, it ought to have lent him confidence, and somehow it hadn't; it seemed he had nothing left to give, not certainty, not grief, not magic: Aulun had not gotten near enough to his men in the past three days to bother with the shielding, and his own witchpower attacks had been half-hearted. Ghosts sat on his shoulders, Tomas on one and Sacha on the other, urging him to different ends.

"You could finish it." Eliza spoke from behind him, an unexpected interruption to his thoughts. The words so closely echoed what he thought Sacha might say that Javier wondered if she, too, heard voices whispering from their past. She sat at his feet, an odd mix of awkwardness and grace born from the false pregnancy she carried. "We only have enough bullets for another day, and you've got the Aulunian heir locked up in a tent on our side of the lines. She can't, or won't, fight you. What makes you hesitate, love?" She put a hand up to catch Javier's fingers and draw him down to sit beside her. "Sacha would've had you act three days ago. Even Tomas wouldn't want it drawn out. What makes you hesitate?" Her voice was worn thin and dried out, and the new dawn's light aged her. No light was unkind to Eliza, but war, war was kind to no one.

Javier folded his fingers in hers and sat, staring silently at the horizon and the fields of men below it before bringing her knuckles to his lips and pressing them there. "What if I told you I'd had a vision of the future?" he asked softly. "If it seemed this war's continuation was necessary to prepare us for what's to come?"

"A witchpower vision?"

Javier closed his eyes against the memory of Belinda's magic invading his own, showing him what she'd learned, and nodded. Eliza took a breath and held it long enough that a slight smile curved his mouth and he glanced her way. Her cheeks were puffed, gaze distant, and she let the air out in a sudden rush. "I wouldn't care, Javier. Marius and Sacha are dead, and Tomas, and now Akilina and her child. War has its price, and I know it must be paid, but they died in a fight that had a purpose. They died in a battle to reclaim Aulun for the Ecumenic church, not as part of some fight for a witchpower future. It's wrong to change the goals without giving us a chance to understand our new purpose. We can accomplish what you stood in Cordula and said you would do, my love. Between the guns and the magic, you have the power to end this war, and I would see it done. A child is coming," she said more softly. "I would like us to live long enough to see its birth, much less its life."

"And the future I've seen? Do I let it come to pass with us un-prepared?"

Eliza turned to sit on one foot, the other knee drawn up against her chest. She'd taken to wearing gowns since their marriage, and her short hair blew in her eyes and fell away again, making her soft in the morning light. Soft, but for her gaze, which might have been chipped of brown marble. "You're witchbreed, blessed by the Pap-pas and by God. If there's a future this war is meant to lead to, or prevent, you have the magic and the vision to lead us where we're meant to go. If you need another war to follow this one, so be it. I'll stand by your side through it all, but give me one war at a time. Give me a victory before you change our direction."

Javier thinned his lips and looked toward the horizon again, a quietness coming on him from within. "How long have you been waiting to tell me this?"

"Three days," Eliza said steadily. "I was waiting to see if you would act on your own before we ran out of bullets. Sacha wasn't wrong, you know. You've always been too shy of exerting power, whether it's the magic or your crown. I understand why," she added swiftly. "I do, Javier. I would have been hesitant, too, but you can no longer afford to be. We need who and what you are, king of Gallin. End this, and after you're crowned king in Aulun we can look to other wars and far-off futures." She twisted her hand in his and brought his knuckles to her lips in turn, then stood and walked away, a dark-haired wraith in the breaking light.

Javier watched her go and wondered at the women in his life, from his mother the queen to the Aulunian heir and back again to a queen, this one the pauper he'd crowned. They were the fairer sex, weaker in physique but more bloody of mind than he'd ever realised. Ambition, wit, wisdom; the men of his court should be so blessed with talents as the women, and he wondered if more history than he knew had been shaped by women such as these; if kings throughout time were pushed and prodded where their queens and lovers would have them go. He would have to ask Rodrigo, whose expertise with women might be limited, but whose studies of the past were extensive.

Javier rubbed his hands on his thighs and stood, gaze bleak on the sunrise-bloody countryside below. He would ask Rodrigo, if they all survived the day.

ROBERT, LORD DRAKE

Javier will have to run out of bullets sooner or later. Sooner is more likely: even aided by witchpower, even given years or decades in which to work, Seolfor could only have made so many without some form of automation. Robert has been blindsided repeatedly these past few months, but he doubts he could have missed a factory in the Alanian mountains. So when the Ecumenic machine guns are rolled forward on the distant hills, Robert feels a surge of satisfaction: Javier is squandering his advantage, and Robert will soon be able to ride men of equal numbers into Javier's front lines.

What's unexpected is that for the first time in days, Javier calls witchpower at a level Robert hasn't felt since Aria Magli. The first volleys of power are so quick and so strong it takes Robert a few seconds to recover, and to throw up the same kind of shields that Belinda and Ivanova both kept in place during some of the war.

Ivanova: there's a distraction, and one Robert doesn't need now. The girl retreated to the heart of the Khazarian camp after Belinda's capture, suddenly afraid for her own life. It's preposterous: if Ivanova Durova is afraid of anything, Robert has yet to put a name to it. He would dearly love to know the truth of what sent her back to her big-bearded generals, and at the same time is boyishly glad he doesn't. He ought not take glee in being played and out-played, manoeuvred, and out-thought, but this isn't an aspect of conquering that's mentioned in his people's history. Certainly other worlds must have brought cleverness to the fore and done battle against their manipulators, but Robert's people care only for the end result, not the details of arriving there. Other races' ingenuity has been lost, as human ingenuity will be, but discovering and facing it makes for a far more interesting mission than Robert expected to participate in.

Even as he pulls his thoughts back in line, the tone of the witchpower volleys changes. Javier gathers himself and turns his magic against Robert himself. Silver smashes down, searching for weaknesses, searching for a way in; searching, in essence, for paths that will let him into Robert's mind, where he can tear his power apart from the inside out. Robert doubts Javier knows quite what he's trying to do; there's no finesse to his attack, no sense of understanding how he might capture and command another witchlord's magic.

Robert, grinning, lets the boy try.

JAVIER DE CASTILLE

Half a year past, Robert Drake threw up a wall of witchpower that stopped Javier's magic dead, and proved beyond question that Beatrice Irvine was in truth Belinda Primrose, and heir to Drake's witchpower. The world has changed since then; changed in so many ways Javier wouldn't know where to begin cataloguing it if he wanted to, and he does not want to. Still, today, now, armed with the things he's learned, he should be able to stand before the witchlord's power. Ought to be able to turn his attack from the Aulunian lines to the Aulunian consort, and devastate Drake with his will.

The one he can do easily enough: witchpower magic turns from troops to a single man, bearing down with a lifetime's expectation of being accommodated; with the expectation that, like any other man, Robert Drake will bow his head and his will to Javier de Castille, and that the day will roll on in the same way it began.

But Robert's power has the strength of the tide, pulling relentlessly, bending and washing over Javier's own, subsuming it rather than being subsumed. Every volley Javier throws out is absorbed, and when Robert lashes back it's as though an ocean crashes down on him, staggering with its weight. Too little sluices away from Robert's own magic, and with the third driving blow Javier drops to his knees, hands buried in the earth as though he could draw strength from it. Robert is the source of the Aulunian alliance's strength; if he can be defeated the serpent's back is broken and Cordula might triumph.

Cordula *must* triumph, for anything less risks not only Javier's neck, but Eliza's, and that's a price too dear to be paid. Too many high costs have been cut from his heart already, and he'll die here on the battlefield before he'll risk losing Eliza Beaulieu as well.

A crack appears in his shields, Robert's power worming its way inside his mind, and Javier thinks he may well do just that, and lose Eliza after all.

BELINDA PRIMROSE

Javier's voice is a clarion call, crisper than Robert's the single time he touched her mind with words. *Help me,* Javier says silently across the distance. *Help me, or I am lost.*

Belinda Primrose comes to the door of her tent and steps through without the guards noticing her; walks a little distance down green grassy hills to look at the front lines, where Javier de Castille is on his knees, silver magic pouring off him so thickly that it can only be a matter of time, and not much at that, before everything that he is burns out in his battle against another witchlord.

Against Robert, Lord Drake, Belinda's father and Javier's own, though at the heart of it there's almost no matter to that second part: he is Sandalia's son in every way that counts, except that one blood sin they've shared. There, in that small detail, it does matter, matters so much her skin still crawls with it, even when she's looking beyond their paternity and at the lines of battle that have been drawn.

Javier's voice is in her head, his magic drawing her to him, the sharing of an integral part of their souls. He screams of need, and a part of her still responds, perhaps will always respond, in a way she should not. With passion and desire rising to meet need and want, with thought uncoupled from body, so action is all that's worth considering.

But a part of her is given over to thought after all, and thus unwinds desire from need and leaves her with a weighty choice on her hands. There's no return from whichever path she takes: whichever man she turns away from will never forgive her, and Belinda's heart aches in her chest with the strength and pain of that knowledge.

Javier is the easier sacrifice to make. She crawled away from him once, bound to duty; that duty now makes a clear and easy road to follow. He has no love for her at all, and a great deal of righteous hate, and there's nothing in this world or any other that might change that. Not now; not with who and what she is. Eliza's life, even the child's, isn't enough to earn forgiveness, and a part of her wonders at even using the word; it's not one she's ever given a care for. In truth, she has little use for absolution, as she has no loathing or uncertainty for what she's been, any more than she might rage against the snow for being cold. So, aye, Javier de Castille is the easier sacrifice to make in all the ways that she is Robert's daughter.

But she stands on the wrong side of the front lines, in the midst of an enemy camp, and the stillness that wrapped her in safety as she grew up has failed her, because she's cold there in the summer sunshine, and her breath comes short and hard, she can't control it. The truth is, Belinda Primrose isn't the same woman she was a year ago. That woman would never be here; that woman would never debate which of the evils she faced should be grasped, because it would never occur to her that she could, much less ought, to turn against Robert, Lord Drake, her beloved papa.

Belinda lifts a hand and throws witchpower, snaking it along Javier's magic and shoring him up. He can bend a man's will, but it's she who learnt to steal Dmitri's power, and it's that same trick she turns against Robert Drake now, lancing her magic along Javier's until it crashes against the waterwheel that's her father's power. Water, though, isn't a solid at all, and she slips lines of gold light through the individual droplets to search out all the lines of weak-

ness that make up a man's strengths. Ana di Meo: the courtesan's
face flashes in her mind's eye, heavy with regret and sorrow. Lorraine Walter: queen of a realm and a heart, whose fading beauty
makes no difference to the man who loves her. A silver beast in the
sky, alien, repulsive, awesome, encompassing: she is everything, that
monster, and yet somehow has become only part of a whole.

Her own self, from birth to childhood to womanhood, and all
the moments in between: herself, dressed in a new gown awaiting a
queen she was forbidden to meet; herself, in a grown-up lady's dress
at age three, solemnly dancing the steps of a Tinternell; herself,
walking through court with Rodney du Roz; herself, using a
weapon of a word, *father,* and never seeing how that blade struck
home; herself, time and again, holding a place in her father's heart
she's only dreamt she might.

Belinda closes her hand and with it takes Robert Drake's witchpower from him, and in the blackness that's left, sobs.

Epilogue

Robert Drake wakes with what feels like a three-day drunk shrieking inside his skull. For a little while he lies in the dark, admiring the ache in his head, and then a splash of light breaks across his vision and makes him wince. "Ah," says a voice so unfamiliar in its familiarity he can't place it. "You're awake. I was beginning to wonder. Tell me, is the magic there?"

It's such a ludicrous question Robert can't answer for a few seconds, not until recollection rises up and drowns him. He dismissed Dmitri's warnings about Belinda's power, her ability to steal magic, but he'd thought that was a knack born in sharing her bed. Of all the various sins against man Robert's committed over the decades, that particular one isn't on his list, and so he reaches for witchpower with confidence.

And finds a wall between himself and it. It shines like gold, a weight in his mind filled with a sense of justice. It's flawless in its construction, making spheres around his magic, so no matter what angle he approaches it from, he only slips off its cool strength.

Rage floods his vision, turning it red, and he slams his will at that wall, searching for a weak point. It dents; gold is soft, but it's also very heavy, and when he bounces off its weight, it flows back to fill the tiny cavity he made. Insulted, angry, a little afraid, he flings himself at it again, scrabbling and clawing into the shining surface.

Outside his mind, Seolfor begins to chuckle, and then to laugh outright. He's grinning when Robert shoves himself into a sit. "She might've left you dead," he says without even the slightest hint of sympathy. "Dead, instead of neutered. It's what you did to her, isn't it? Ah, Robert, it's a shame you lost control. She'd have been wonderful, on our side."

Robert snarls and turns his attention back to the wall in his mind. He has the advantage over the girl Belinda was: he knows his power's there, and it cannot possibly take so long to free it as it took her. It's a matter of determination and time, nothing more. Seolfor might help.

Might, but ah, this is Seolfor, who only continues to chortle, and after a little while gets to his feet and leaves Robert Drake in a tent somewhere in the Gallic countryside, there to try to woo his magic back, and start shaping this world anew.

A dire order comes from Khazar: Chekov is to return to Khazan with not only Irina's ill-behaved daughter in tow, but the bulk of the Khazarian army, as well. Irina has clearly misjudged the ease of expansion, when inside two months both her first allies failed utterly in their naval sweep of the war, and then her new allies fell before Ecumenic weapons as wheat might fall in a field. Oh, it's bad form for an imperatrix to change sides so many times, so quickly, but it is worse, in Irina's opinion, to leave herself vulnerable. Cordula may well look east once Aulun's been taken, and from hurried messages sent by pigeon, it seems very likely Aulun will fall. Rodrigo of Essandia has new weapons, and all Irina has are men: she wants them all at her border, protecting it. In time she may be able to repair her reputation, at least enough so that it doesn't make ruling an empire more difficult for Ivanova, but for now, Irina commands a retreat and regroup, and will let Echon fight amongst itself while she prepares for a coming war.

Javier's army drives the Aulunians back to the channel after the Khazarian desertion: back to the channel, and then to Alunaer, as Rodrigo turns his attention to the production of rapid-fire guns. He begins there on the still-bloody fields, turning soldiers into smiths.

A brilliant young man has come out of the troops to offer his services. He's young, but silver-haired, and his blue eyes are perpetually amused. He calls Rodrigo a visionary, but it's his insight that builds the first *factory,* machinations leaping forward to build moulds and huge forges with which to pour bullets and barrels alike.

It's he, too, who has mad ideas of *engines* powered by steam and combustion; engines that will power their machines from within, and take vulnerable horses from the battlefield, so the war machines can continue forward against the worst onslaughts. Rodrigo stays up long nights with this young man, working out ways in which wind and water can be used to power the factories to build their new monstrosities.

Through it all a wide-eyed gondola boy runs their errands and thinks himself at the centre of things of great importance. He's right, of course, and there are moments during innovation and argument that both prince and inventor stop to watch the boy, and imagine him to be the shape of the world to come.

Then they all put their heads down, two dark and one bright, and go back to building the future.

Alunaer falls in ten days. Lorraine Walter is too proud to leave her city, and so watches it die. It falls under horse-drawn war machines, some bearing cannon mounts, others the repeating-fire guns she heard tell of through spies and couriers. All good sense would have her turn tail and run to safer grounds so she might fight again another day, and instead she stands on parapets and watches smoke and fire rise from the streets, and waits for the messenger who will explain more than she wants to know.

So when Belinda Primrose—for Lorraine will never learn to call the girl by the surname they both share—when Belinda Primrose comes to the palace, Lorraine gives her leave to enter, for all she knows that her daughter is the spearhead signalling her own fall. Belinda comes with an army behind her, but she herself comes not as a warrior, but as a novice. She's escorted by a handful of Javier de Castille's troops, and the grey robes she wears make her look fragile and lost. Everything about her is afraid, as it should be, if she's just been snatched from a convent to give the Red Bitch an ultimatum. Lorraine doubts there are more than five people in the city who know that's not at all what's happened, and turns a brief thought to history, wondering what story it will tell.

It doesn't matter; most history is lies anyway. Belinda climbs the guardsmen's stairs to where Lorraine stands, full skirts of her robes carefully clutched in both hands so she might not trip on them. Aside from making her look penitent, they also hide the signs of pregnancy. It's possible, even probable, that that's where Lorraine made her mistake. She bore an illegitimate child, but forbade Belinda that same luxurious risk. Had she done otherwise, perhaps it would now be Lorraine walking unafraid into the Lutetian palace to take its crown.

Because Belinda's no more afraid than the wind might be afraid. She looks the part, but for all the ways Lorraine doesn't know the girl, there are others in which she knows her intimately, and her talent for playacting is among those. She stops at Lorraine's side and doesn't so much bother to curtsey, which Lorraine would mind less if it weren't very likely the last time anyone might have cause to curtsey to her.

"This is where it began, for me," Belinda says to the wind and the scent of smoke. "This is where du Roz died."

"I believe down there is where he died," Lorraine says with a droll look toward the flagstones below. She's surprised at herself: her sense of humour is not what she's best known for, and to find even the driest hint of it within herself now is unexpected. Perhaps that's the price of war: it takes everything, and leaves odd dredges behind. "Does it please you, to come full circle and end where you began?"

"None of this pleases me." Belinda lifts her chin as if inviting a hit, and Lorraine, surprised again, studies her.

Belinda will never be beautiful, she thinks, not even the brief and unique beauty of Lorraine's youth, but there's a strength to her prettiness. There's less of Lorraine, and more of Robert, in her, but with her head held high and a regal set to her jaw, Lorraine can see traces of herself in the girl. Stubborn, independent, clever: they're traits Lorraine wanted in her heir, and now rues. But curiosity's stronger than even that, and she's lost the war already, so she may as well ask: "Then why have you done it? You've lost your throne, lost your power."

Belinda turns a hand up and in the afternoon brightness, a flare of gold becomes visible in her palm before fading again. "No one can take my power, and I never wanted a throne. Do you believe in fate, Mother?"

Lorraine's heart goes still and aching in her chest, and for a long time she doesn't breathe. *Mother:* the word's a weapon and a gift, though the way Belinda said it suggests she meant it as neither. She's not one given to casual connections, is Belinda Primrose, and so Lorraine thinks she's building what bridges she can with such a poor tool as language at her disposal. Good sense says those bridges should already be afire, burning between them, but in the end, perhaps blood runs deeper than sense, after all. When she has her breath back Lorraine says "No," and wonders if she should tell all the reasons why.

But it's not necessary: Belinda knows the Walter family history, and it's either fate directing that story or sheer caprice. For all that Lorraine rules by divine right, she has very little faith in God or paths set in stone.

And then, quite clearly, she understands everything Belinda has done, and whispers "Ah" before her daughter has time to speak. "So you're only rebellious."

A corner of Belinda's mouth quirks. "Not that either. I think a fate was being written for us. I meant to rewrite it, and have utterly failed in what I intended. I don't know what happens next, but that may be enough. Perhaps now no one knows."

"I know." Lorraine smiles when Belinda looks askance at her, and lifts her chin in much the same way Belinda did a moment earlier. "Javier de Castille will be crowned king of Aulun. If you and I are fortunate, we'll be given the rest of our days to live in the Tower. But Sandalia is dead, and the pretender to our crown may be disinclined to generosity. We are uncertain if Robert will appear to rescue us," she finishes in a whisper, and knows herself to be weak for allowing the hope.

"Robert fell in Brittany." Belinda says carefully. "No one has seen him since."

"No," Lorraine agrees. "No one's seen him, not dead and not alive. I choose to have hope, Primrose. Grant me that, at least. A queen might have a final wish, after all."

Belinda turns to her, and once again surprises Lorraine by studying her a long moment, then dipping a generous curtsey, her gaze lowered and her voice soft as she whispers, "Of course, your majesty."

It is the last such honour ever accorded to Lorraine Walter, and she will savour it for the rest of her days.

No one, least of all Javier de Castille, can argue that Belinda Walter is the best person to crown him. She's the acknowledged Aulunian heir, and Lorraine, who is deposed and locked in the tower she spent a decade in as a girl, would die before she put a crown on Javier's head. Belinda's the next best choice; she may be able to sway the hearts of her people, and can encourage them not to rise against their new king. Perhaps she can even help lead them back to the Ecumenic fold. History weighs heavily there: Lorraine's sister Constance made a bloody mark across this country by trying to return it to Cordula's faith, and Javier has no illusions that it will be an easy or quick task. Rodrigo counsels leading by example rather than by burning, and Javier, who has a bone-deep horror of the cleansing fires, is inclined to agree. So it must be Belinda, for those reasons and more.

Good sense or not, as she approaches—still wearing novice robes, shapeless and hiding six months of pregnancy—Javier cannot help but remember his mother, and the poison cup she drank from. Cannot help but think how easy it would be to paint the inside of the heavy Aulunian crown with a deadly toxin that will burn away his skin and leave him a monster in the days it takes him to die.

She would not live to gloat, should she do such a thing, but Javier's heart is in his mouth and his chest feels hollow and sick as Belinda lifts the crown over his head.

Her voice is clear and crisp, carrying over the courtroom as though she's accustomed to making speeches. There's no worry or nerves hiding in her tone, and Javier, sourly, thinks it's good one of them isn't concerned. "With this crown I declare Javier de Castille, son of Sandalia de Philip de Costa and Louis de Castille as the true king of Aulun. It is my divine right to offer him this crown: I am Lorraine Walter's daughter, once the Aulunian heir, and I renounce any claim to this throne; it is not a burden I wish to bear."

The crown is very heavy, and Belinda settles it on his head as a priest—not Tomas, as it should be—begins the sonorous and extensive listing of Javier's qualifications, all of which come down to God's will, and God's will alone. He hears very little of it: he's staring at Belinda, and trying not to see the faces who are missing from around him. Sacha should be there; Marius should be there. Sandalia, too, though at least Rodrigo has come, and Eliza will be made queen of this wretched wet island in another ceremony later in the week. She sits at his side, resplendently pregnant with soft round rags, and watches Belinda with untrusting eyes. But there's no poison burning his face, and witchpower confidence begins to imbue him as he reaches toward Belinda with it, and finds no hint of resentment.

Then the priest is naming Javier something more than king of Aulun or king of Gallin: he's naming him emperor of the western lands, and Rodrigo is pursing his lips in a smile while Javier tries not to goggle in shock. He's had no ambition for such titles, and thinking that reminds him again of Sacha, who would be pleased, and so somehow Javier manages a smile. Marius would be proud, and Sacha satisfied, and Eliza will be queen to an empire. That, perhaps, is something; maybe it will salve wounds over the next months and years.

But beneath that proclamation, softly, so no one but Javier will hear it, Belinda whispers, "Javier de Castille, queen's bastard, wearing a pretender's crown though he's the rightful king of Aulun. Rule wisely, brother, for my blade's yet unblooded, and I'll not have my country ruined by your revenge."

She waits a long moment, gaze fixed on his, as though to make certain her words have come home to him, and then she steps back from the throne and lifts her voice to call out "Long live the king!," and all the court takes up her cry. As it gains strength, she nods once to Javier, a mark of respect less showy but no less potent than a bow.

Then witchpower whispers, and that's the last any of them ever see of Belinda Walter, heir to the Aulunian throne.

BELINDA, CALLED ROSA
8 January 1589 † *Brittany*

Rosa, who has no last name and no husband to explain away her swollen belly, is grateful to have been taken on as a serving girl at an estate in Brittany. She and her new masters, the king and queen of Gallin, know that this estate was once her grandfather's; that she herself was born here nearly a quarter-century ago. None of this gives her airs: at times even her lord and lady seem to forget she's other than a favoured servant.

They remember very clearly who she is when the first birthing pangs come on her. They remember who she is, and what, but Rosa has made a promise to them, and though she has in some ways broken all ties of loyalty, she is still a creature of her word. Not long after Rosa realises what the cramps mean, the queen of Gallin is tucked into a warm room with her husband and her favourite servant, the latter of whom will in truth do all the yelling for the next few hours.

No one else attends the birth: these three have enough secrets without adding to them, and the woman called Rosa will not let another game like the one Dmitri began come into play.

To her dismay, a lifetime of willing pain and emotion away is of no use at all against childbirth. A part of her is convinced it once would have been, but she's fallen too far, changed too much. Bellowing her way through the delivery is some sort of punishment for losing her way. That most women do the same makes no difference. The king is useless through all of it, and the queen's beautiful eyes are enormous with hope and dreams.

It seems an eternity later that pain fades into a child's squalling presence. Rosa, breathless, weary to the bone, sits up to see what manner of babe she's given birth to.

Eliza Beaulieu, once a guttersnipe and now the queen of all Gallin lifts the child—a girl; of course it would be a girl—in bloody hands. Javier de Castille, witch king of Gallin, comes to look at the child in some astonishment. A slow smile blooms over both their faces, and the woman who was once the Aulunian heir reaches a fingertip to the protesting baby and chuckles when the girl seizes it. Then she closes her eyes and for a moment lets herself become Belinda Primrose again as she sinks back into the blankets to whisper the words that have defined them, defined them all, for every day of their lives:

"It cannot be found out."

Acknowledgments

A hat-tip to Yei-Mei "Denyse" Chng, who came up with the title for *The Pretender's Crown*. I can't write a book until I've got the title, so that was a rather critically helpful bit. Thank you!

Similarly, thanks are due not only to my faithful beta reader Trent, but also to Rob, Deborah, Lisa, and especially my husband Ted, who all put up with my frustration when I broke two fingers during the writing of this book and was delayed for weeks in continuing. Further thanks to Judith Tarr, Anna Mazzoldi, and Kari Sperring for help with languages I don't speak, and, as usual, both my editor Betsy Mitchell and my agent Jennifer Jackson were full of insightful comments that improved the manuscript enormously.

I'd also like to pass on my thanks to the Del Rey art and production departments, who have given me books of genuine physical beauty. I'm a little bit of a font and layout geek myself, and I cannot tell you how happy I am with the way these books look.

Finally, I've always been a little dubious when writers thank their readers: do they really mean that? I can tell you now that they do, and I would like to particularly thank everybody who's left comments on my LiveJournal or taken a moment to email me and say they loved *The Queen's Bastard* and wanted to know when this book was coming out. Writing this series is a great adventure for me and I'm profoundly grateful that readers have embraced it.

C. E. MURPHY is the author of two urban fantasy series (The Walker Papers and The Negotiator Trilogy) as well as The Inheritors' Cycle and a monthly comic book titled *Take a Chance*. Her other hobbies include photography and travel, though she rarely pursues enough of either. She was born and raised in Alaska, and now lives in her ancestral home of Ireland with her husband and cats. More about C.E. and her work can be found at cemurphy.net.